ALSO BY GIGI LEVANGIE GRAZER

Rescue Me

Maneater

The Starter Wife

QUEEN TAKES KING

GIGI LEVANGIE GRAZER

SIMON & SCHUSTER

New York   London   Toronto   Sydney

SIMON & SCHUSTER
1230 Avenue of the Americas
New York, NY 10020

First Simon & Schuster hardcover edition June 2009

SIMON & SCHUSTER and colophon are registered trademarks
of Simon & Schuster, Inc.

For information about special discounts for bulk purchases,
please contact Simon & Schuster Special Sales at
1-866-506-1949 or business@simonandschuster.com

The Simon & Schuster Speakers Bureau can bring authors to
your live event. For more information or to book an event contact
the Simon & Schuster Speakers Bureau at
1-866-248-3049 or visit our website at www.simonspeakers.com.

Designed by Dana Sloan

Manufactured in the United States of America

10   9   8   7   6   5   4   3   2   1

Library of Congress Cataloging-in-Publication Data
Grazer, Gigi Levangie.
Queen takes king : a novel / Gigi Levangie Grazer. —
1st Simon & Schuster hardcover ed.
p.   cm.
1. Rich people—New York (State)—New York—
Fiction.   2. Socialites—New York (State)—New York—
Fiction.   3. Adultery—Fiction.   4. New York
(N.Y.)—Fiction.   I. Title.
PS3557.R2913Q84   2009
813'.54—dc22   2009002295

ISBN 978-0-7432-9199-6
ISBN 978-0-7432-9876-6 (ebook)

To my children, Thomas and Patrick

PART ONE

◆

SEPTEMBER 2007

1

THE QUEEN

CYNTHIA HUNSAKER Power stood shivering in her kitchen, a silk robe wrapped around her sylphlike body, and wondered whom she'd have to fuck or fire to get a diet Red Bull. Her doe eyes, accentuated by last night's false eyelashes, blinked at the challenge. She flicked her straight black ponytail faded only slightly by age, and smirked. Cynthia's delicate mouth was stained, her beloved Chanel Red No. 5 intensifying her pale skin. *Reality check, Cynthia,* she thought, *when was the last time you did either?*

The chef wouldn't arrive until daybreak, the French butler was still asleep, and the housekeepers and drivers and trainers hadn't even tasted their first sip of coffee before hopping the train into Manhattan. Cynthia was alone in the kitchen, something she hadn't been since Vivienne was a baby. *Had it really been almost twenty-five years?*

She'd been jostled awake by a recurring dream.

"Snakes," Cynthia said out loud. "Even my nightmares are clichés." She imagined her therapist Dr. Gold's reaction: *"Don't waste my time, bubule. I'm a very busy man. I've got a full day of undersexed neurotics."*

Now. Find that Red Bull. The industrial-size refrigerator revealed nothing. There were no other clues. Her designer had prohibited appliances, declaring them aesthetically offensive. The kitchen looked like a morgue.

Open, close, open, open, slam, drawers upon drawers upon cabinets. No luck. Cynthia was sweating in her Hanros when she finally discovered a black machine with sleek lines; could this be a coffeemaker? It bore no resemblance to the dented aluminum percolator her mother had used back in Aurora, Missouri. She squinted, trying to make sense of the buttons and the timers and the vents. Cynthia refused to acknowledge the slow submerging of the printed word into a gray blur. Reading glasses? Forget it. Next, people would be whispering: *"She was a real beauty in her twenties."*

Even if Cynthia could bring Darth Vader to life, where was the coffee? She set the machine down.

And where were her Gitanes?

Caffeine and cigarettes, the breakfast of champions for ballerinas, even long-retired ones. What started out decades ago as a six-pack-a-day Diet Coke habit had morphed into almost a case a day of high-octane diet Red Bull as her metabolism slowed. Cynthia was Sleeping Beauty without her fix. And to make matters worse, Esme, her personal maid, had hidden the cigs from her, instructed to ration five a day—7:30, 10:30, 2:30, 6:30, 10:30—unless otherwise notified in times of crisis. Cynthia knew better than to bother anyone about her blessed unfiltereds at this hour.

Cynthia looked past the custom Bonnet stove she'd never used to the white Carrara marble countertop she'd used once, for a photo spread. The *Town & Country* layout had been featured several bright springs ago—Cynthia sitting sideways on the cold marble, her black mane freshly blown out by John Barrett, her red mouth open in silent laughter (behold the bliss of the wealthy Upper East Side wife, the inside joke of the Park Avenue Princess). She could see her dancer's torso curved backward, one long leg emerging from the slit in her Armani, ending days later in the arch of her bare foot. The caption: "Cynthia Power, patroness of the New York Ballet Theater, feels as at home in her Baron Waxfield–designed kitchen as onstage in a pas de deux."

Cynthia the Perfectionist was known for being meticulous in her performances, onstage and off. Case in point: last night's pas de deux at the Waldorf. Two years to plan her twenty-fifth wedding anniversary party and it was over in four hours. But what a four hours: five hundred of their closest and dearest, including the mayor, the governor, Barbara, Julian, Peter, Anna, Donald, the De Niros, Marc, Harvey, Rupert, Charlie, Woody, Diane, Liz, Nieporent, and the Schwarzmans, feigned obliviousness to the paparazzi penned in on the north side of Fifty-first Street. Once inside, they were ushered into a ballroom, completely overhauled in homage to Versailles's Hall of Mirrors. Gargantuan reflective panes had been installed on one side; faux "windows" had been painted on the facing wall to replicate the intricate gardens. There were twinkling chandeliers and a ceiling painstakingly repainted as per the Sun King's original specifications. There was consensus among the people who mattered: New York hadn't seen a party like this since the Steinberg-Tisch wedding/merger at the Met back in the eighties.

If only her husband, Jackson Xavier Power, had seen fit to show up on time.

"Now what?" she asked herself. She had a full two hours before her Pilates instructor rang, but without a schedule and without her Red Bull, she wasn't sure exactly what to do. She could boot up her social calendar for the upcoming fall season or go through last season's closet and decide which dresses to donate to charity.

On a whim, she decided to go out and get the newspapers. Excited about getting the papers—this was her life. Cynthia didn't fear running into anyone in the elevators at 740—they were perpetually empty. Still, she decided to take the stairs. The eighteen-room apartment (six bedrooms, eight baths) commanded the penthouse of the seventeen-story limestone building, a trek, but Cynthia needed to get her blood moving. She cinched the robe tightly around her waist and walked out the service door into the darkened hallway.

Five minutes later, Cynthia was back in the kitchen, the *Post* spread open on the Pedini island. Her reflection hovered at its edges—forehead pinched, cheeks flushed, mouth agape. She played a game with herself, shutting her eyes, then forcing them open again. The photo remained unchanged.

Screw the Red Bull. Sleeping Beauty was wide awake.

2

THE KING

JACKSON POWER grunted as he rolled over in his Pratesi sheets. "Cynthia?" Jacks reached his long arm out for her. Nothing. His wife was already gone. *What the hell time was it?* Two things Jacks didn't like—waking up alone, and going to bed alone. He sat up, his barrel chest bare over his pajama bottoms, and ran his blunt, manicured fingertips through his famously full, deep brown mane. He glanced at his pillow, checking for hair loss—*not a man left behind*. Jacks Power versus Father Time? Another TKO. But enough. Where was Cynthia? Pacing in the living room? The gallery? The library? (Not the kitchen— never the kitchen.) Fussing over lunch plans? Shopping expeditions? The season's big society event? How would his wife top last night's extravaganza? He couldn't imagine—but knowing Cynthia, she'd figure it out. He glanced at the Louis XV giltwood stool, beneath last night's tux and Cynthia's beaded ivory gown, all of it crumpled and spent. Valentino, Cynthia told him, not that he gave a shit. The dress was expensive and Cynthia looked expensive wearing it. That was all that mattered. Would Cynthia ever wear it again? Probably not. But imagine his triumph when the dress found an eventual home—tax deductible of course—in the Met's costume exhibit.

Life was good.

Jackson Power was the top developer in New York—translated, The World (not according to his critics).

Jackson Power was the biggest single developer of multifamily housing in the United States (a lie so complete it seemed almost true).

Jackson Power was worth six billion (according to the Forbes 500 list—notoriously full of lies).

Jackson Power didn't give a rat's ass, like some of his colleagues, about affordable housing. Manhattan, in his view, was not supposed to be affordable. Let New Jersey be affordable; let Queens be affordable. Manhattan was the Powers' province (inarguably).

Jackson Power was the only developer in New York who was a recognizable face (inarguably).

Jackson Power, in a stroke of genius, had given himself (inarguable, this) his own moniker—The People's Billionaire.

Jackson Power stood for luxury, stood for style, and if you didn't agree with him, well, what did you know? You were obviously a poor person of little consequence utterly lacking in style, "and that's a fact"—Jacks's oft-quoted period at the end of every sentence.

Last night's party was for the charmed inner circle, joining in Jackson's favorite kind of celebration: a celebration of himself. The center table alone held six of the world's most powerful Gargoyles— "Gargoyle," his secret moniker for other Captains of Industry, billionaires whose lifelong trench warfare had carved their faces to resemble stone goblins straight off the spires of Notre Dame. (So far, Jacks's rugged good looks had escaped unscathed.)

The orchestra played Sinatra as Jackson Power and his raven-haired wife of twenty-five years danced, spinning graceful circles on the gleaming parquet floor, but his arm felt stiff and foreign around her waist.

Their reflection bounced off the giant mirrors, Cynthia the very picture of beauty steeped long enough in money to become elegant, and Jackson the perfect leading man, all height and shoulders and hair and that famous "I've Got the Power" grin. *Screw George Clooney and that shrimpy James Bond actor. Next to Jacks Power in a tux, they look like Girl Scouts.*

The teeming, glittering well-wishers, draped in their best Ungaros and Valentinos, their shiniest Harrys and Van Cleefs dangerously circling their necks—mellowed by Krug Clos du Mesnil, watched and smiled and sighed and swayed where they stood, buoying the handsome couple along.

Jackson and Cynthia had moved as one, spinning past the giant floral arrangement in the center of the room. Yellow roses. *Cynthia's favorite.*

"Happy anniversary, sweetheart," he'd murmured into her ear.

Cynthia's smile tightened imperceptibly at the corners. "You are such an ass. Darling."

"Now, now," he cautioned, as he led her past the Gargoyle table, winking as he sped away, "your fans are watching."

"How could you be late to our anniversary party, Jackson?" she'd hissed.

"You throw eight parties a week," Jackson replied, his voice the same temperature as the swan ice sculpture holding court near the stage. "Not including charity luncheons, teas, those very, very important ladies' breakfasts—"

"You were supposed to be throwing this party for *me,*" Cynthia said, "remember? I told you starting a year ago. Damn it, Jackson, I faxed you memo after memo—"

"When do you eat, darling?" Jackson had asked. "Surely, they serve food at all your events." He could feel each of her ribs beneath her gown, hand-stitched onto her body by the doll-like fingers of the ancient Italian designer; he remembered when she hadn't felt like bone. He recalled the lush contours of his girlfriend, who regarded exercise as an acceptable alternative only when one ran out of options. Like fucking. Or something straight up with a twist.

Cynthia's head jerked back, but the sudden twitch in her neck remained imperceptible to their audience; her body appeared as controlled as when she'd danced onstage so long ago. The song was almost over: "The Best Is Yet to Come." Jacks tried to remember her favorite things, even more so now that he was no longer interested; he considered it mental gymnastics, like the Sunday *Times* crossword.

10 Down, Cynthia Power's favorite perfume.

12 Across, Cynthia Power's favorite couturier.

23 Down, Cynthia Power's favorite sexual position . . .
    (Ha. Can't remember. Is there one?)

25 Down, Cynthia's favorite song.
    Wait till your charms are right for these arms to surround
    You think you've flown before, but baby, you ain't left the ground

The song had been played at their wedding, their first dance. Jackson held Cynthia tight as a flash flood of guilt washed over him.

"Do you like the roses?" he'd asked, hearing the softness in his voice as though it belonged to someone else. Yellow ones were her favorite (24 Down). From the first day. From the first apartment. From the first baby.

"I knew you'd get them for me, Jacks," Cynthia said, her jaw clenched. She had an angular bone structure that would prevent her face from falling but aged her with its aggressive geography.

The happy couple's eyes met for the briefest moment. *What did she see?* Jackson wondered. *Did she see everything? Did she see how he kissed his girlfriend? Did she see how he stared into the gray-green eyes of another woman?*

He ran a single finger softly down her spine, knowing he could still make her tremble.

As the orchestra hit the final note, Jackson spun his wife around once more, then curved her body back. Her pale arm reached high over her head; her still-lithe body flowed like a river.

She'd stolen the breath of every person standing in that room. The Gargoyles and their wives clapped.

"And do you love the song?" he'd asked.

"Yes," she'd said, looking past his shoulder. "I knew you would," he'd said, gazing at her beauty as though she were a painting he'd bought years ago and forgotten why on earth he'd purchased it.

NORMALLY, Jacks would have been up at 5:30, working out for the requisite thirty-five minutes of diminishing returns in his personal gym with Petre, his trainer. He'd be on that elliptical thing for twenty minutes, watching MSNBC and monitoring his BlackBerry, his pulse, and his blood pressure before moving on to quads, trunk, delts, and whatever else the unabashedly Aryan Petre had on his cursed mind.

But today he'd given Petre the morning off, and slept in until 6:00. Now he smelled like Irish Spring, the scent a childhood memory of his father; like the leprechaun on the wrapper, he had a lift in his step. Jackson would have Gordo, his personal chef, mix his protein shake. He'd down twenty-four of the forty-eight pills and vitamins he'd taken every day for a decade: five resorcinol pills, vitamins B_6, B_{12}, C, D, E, and K, ginkgo biloba, saw palmetto, and salmon oil. The combination had been formulated by his Park Avenue physician and nutritionist to render him immortal.

He'd scan the papers that were waiting for him on the kitchen table, the business sections always first in line, awaiting his approving eye like well-behaved children. Then he'd be off.

"You stay on top by staying on top," is what his father told him.

Jacks had to stay on top. He'd be in his office by 7:00 A.M. today, like every day, unless he had a breakfast at the Four Seasons, of course.

His unholy mess of an office: framed photos of Jackson with the rich and famous, the best of the best, were carelessly placed on this pile of pictures to be autographed, that pile of proposals to be considered. *Power Vodka? Why not? Power Walking Canes? That's a maybe . . . but we do want the retirees, the ones holding 85 percent of the nation's wealth . . . Oh, hey, why not Power Cereal?*

No other developer he knew of had copies of his press clippings in piles on the floor beneath his desk. He liked to keep them accessible to impress the stream of visitors to his office. A first baseman for the Yankees? Here's five lines about Jackson playing golf with Steinbrenner. A magazine writer with a book proposal? Check out the copy of *USA Today*'s bestseller list. Look who's at the top—well, not at the top, but close to the top ("Actually, I sold more books than that Tony Robbins guy, I did—*that's a fact*"). The new city councilman to whom he'd donated thousands of dollars, who just happened to be considering the questionable tax abatement on his proposed mixed-development glass-and-brass-encased monster? Check out the front page of the *Florida Standard*'s business section. "I'm going to change the face of Miami, it says it right here. South Beach, they want my buildings. Maybe I'll move to Miami. Yeah, I like the sun, I like pastels, I like that *CSI,* maybe I'll move the whole fucking company down to Miami."

Of course, Jackson wasn't moving anywhere near Miami. Jackson didn't even like to vacation, vacations bored him, a waste of time and money. How could he manage his company on vacation? How could he check wiring, metal roofing, and the ambient scent in spec apartments while on vacation? How could he whittle down the plumbing contractor? For Jackson Power, the contractor would take the dive— Jacks knew the thinking: *Get in good with Power, work steady the rest of your days.* Jackson didn't leave negotiating to anyone else; he'd learned this from his father, he didn't care if it was a million-dollar contract or two-fifty for the flowers in the reception area of a new apartment complex.

The mess in his office didn't bother him; Jacks Power knew where everything was. Besides, he thought about the office he was moving into, the one twice as big, the one that could eat the view he had right now of Fifth and spit it out, a view that encompassed the entire avenue all the way into the park and beyond into Harlem. There would be plenty more space for his clutter in the new office.

Formerly his father's office.

Now was time to make the move. It had been almost a year since Artemus Power had turned the reins over to his son. His father, after a lifetime of work, had retired on a clear-skied September afternoon. Aside from the birth of his firstborn, his daughter, Vivienne, this had been the happiest day of Jacks's life.

Who was he kidding? Including Vivienne's birth.

He could see his father's office down the hall from his own, through the door that was never closed, not even for personal calls. Caprice, his longtime secretary, wedged herself between the office door and the hallway to buffer the loud pronouncements that barreled out of Jacks's mouth. Six feet of deep brown sinew with a glare that kept her boys in line at home—she'd never had to raise her voice to Jackson, either.

Jacks checked the schedule Caprice had BlackBerried him. The usual: rant and rave until lunchtime. You deal with unhappy tenants who paid millions for a toilet that doesn't flush, you deal with shoddy workmanship, price-gouging contractors, rent-stabilized bloodsuckers, corrupt politicians, people who weren't quality people—people who weren't like Jackson Power. People who didn't understand that a BRAND-NEW LUXURY CONDOMINIUM HOTEL PROJECT was the only way to salvage a shithole like the Lower East Side. People who didn't comprehend the majesty of blue marble. There had to be blue marble somewhere. Find it. Fuck Italy, think Guatemala, Bangladesh—find the marble and use it up, use up all of it. The Bowery needed a grand and ornate and big, really fucking big Power Tower.

POWER. Holy fuck, what a name. What could be better than to live in a POWER Tower in Manhattan in the twenty-first century? Nothing. That hack who wrote the paint-by-numbers POS biography, *Ultimate Power,* said the original surname had been "de Paor."

Gaelic translation: the Poor Man.

Poor? You mean like a second-rate biographer?

Lunch would be at Jean-Christophe downstairs. If the meal sucked, he fired everyone, hired the next chef himself. People, meetings came to Jacks, unless they happened to be a mayor on the fence about a development, a tax abatement, who was maybe new, seeing himself as an elected official instead of a bought one. He'd learn. Even Clinton, when he was the president, had come to him. Jacks had the photos to prove it. They were somewhere in the pile.

Of course, he couldn't take the mistresses downstairs; once they started begging and pleading to be brought there, they were out. Usually, they went quietly. Sometimes they didn't; sometimes there was a payment required, a personal lawyer called in, a particularly quiet doctor on the Upper East Side contacted to fix a "problem."

Back to the schedule: in the last month alone, he'd spent twenty-eight of thirty nights on the town with people he considered phony and dull and boring. Still, he went out. Still, he smiled at the flashbulbs. Jackson Power was his own masterpiece—he was the canvas; his buildings were merely the frame.

And tonight he'd be looking into the gray-green eyes of his latest mistress. His last mistress. Lara, who sighed softly after each orgasm and burrowed into his chest as though she'd let him be her protector, and not the other way around.

Jackson walked past the gallery and library, down the hallway (where the hell was Cynthia, anyway?) and into the kitchen. He mumbled "good morning" or something that sounded like it to Gordo, and the chef coughed and looked away.

What was the *Post* doing on his plate? Gordo knew Jackson wanted to see the business sections of the *Journal* and the *Times* at breakfast. The *Post* he checked in the car driven by his personal chauffeur, Harry the Russian. Jackson looked at Gordo before taking a swig of the protein shake that tasted like liquid straw.

Then he saw it.

At first glance, he couldn't help but be rather pleased with himself. Jackson Power was no Gargoyle—he was still damned good-looking. The years had been a friend; so had his barber, trainer, and the massage therapist with the great rack.

And that's a fact, he told himself.

Second, it occurred to him that Lara must be ready to kill this morning. He hadn't checked his BlackBerry since the shower. He put his hand on his hip in anticipation of the inevitable vibration.

The photograph captured them in a near embrace outside her apartment yesterday afternoon, bodies touching, heads tipped toward each other conspiratorially. He relived the moment in his mind, the quick flyby before the gala. Where had the photographer been hiding?

The headline read: JACKS ENGAGES IN POWER LUNCH.

The caption: "Jackson Power (always known as a loyal friend of the Fourth Estate) leaves Upper West Side apartment of morning news anchor Lara Sizemore."

"Clever," Cynthia murmured from behind his shoulder. Jacks jumped, dropping the paper on the floor. His Ninja Wife; she could move silent as a nun's prayer.

"I always wondered how they come up with these witticisms," she said, as she proceeded to pick the paper up with her foot and deposit it back in front of him. *Fucking monkey feet,* he thought.

"You made the paper twice today, my dear. Once for your latest acquisition and again for our anniversary." Cynthia flipped the *Post* to another page, to a stunning photo of the two of them dancing, with Cindy Adams cooing, "New York's Favorite Power Couple Snags the Silver!" Her tone remained even, mild. "I'd say that's a first."

Jackson knew better than to say a word. What lies could he tell again? He noticed that Gordo had left his station, leaving not a breath behind. In fact, all the help had suddenly vanished. He imagined them hiding behind doors, trilling in the pantry, having mastered the art of listening without appearing to hear.

"Cynthia."

"I want a divorce," she said.

3

THE KING'S MISTRESS

Lara sizemore had been in a twilight sleep brought on by last night's cocktail of iced vodka and multiple orgasms. She was sprawled like an accident victim in the makeup chair, eyes closed, while Kevan, the makeup artist/diva who resembled Patti LaBelle, wearily worked his magic. Her assistant dropped a copy of the *Post* onto her lap. She arched one artificially extended eyebrow and tried to focus on the front page. It would take her a second to recognize the dress.

This was the worst part of the job for her—sitting still for the endless minutes while Kevan slapped a new face on the one she'd been born with. Why did on-air journalists need to be so frikkin' pretty? Even Stone (too bad about the *Dateline* gig) and Anderson could double as Calvin Klein models. And the surgeries! Chins, lips, noses, hairlines—everyone on set knew what it meant when one of the anchors needed to take "personal time." It meant time enough for the post-op bruises to subside. Edward R. Murrow himself would have his potato head reshaped and plugged in no time . . . narrow that nose, Botox those furrows, slap on some sugar-cube veneers.

A journalist. Lara couldn't even call herself that. C'mon. Cut the crap. She knew she was just a reader; all the skills her job required she'd learned by the time she was in third grade. The girl born with the insatiable "need to know" turned out, much to her own dismay, to be a natural in front of the camera. Blessed with blond hair thick as a thoroughbred's tail and able to withstand hot lights, and a face that looked even better on camera than off, Lara the Telegenic's virtues were quickly recognized by her journalism professor, Moe Greene, at USC.

"You have 'It,'" Professor Greene told her. He'd been a producer for CBS until the marketing execs decided that the Edward R. Murrow/Fred Friendly School of Journalism was, well, annoying. Moe was in his sixties and shook his head a lot.

Lara was flattered. "You liked the writing on that last story? It didn't seem too subjective? I tend to get carried away, but I like to think of myself as passionate; some people have a problem with passion, but passion is what fuels the work—" When Lara got excited, she would talk very, very fast; she was excited all the time.

"I saw your piece," Professor Greene said. "You can take your show on the road. I know people. I can help you."

"New York?" Lara could barely say the words without her eyes going half-lit.

"Phoenix," Professor Greene replied.

"Phoenix?" she repeated. "Phoenix, Arizona?"

"Weather."

"You want me to write the weather? In Phoenix?" Lara's dreams had shredded into confetti.

Professor Greene sighed. "You read the weather. On camera."

"Oh," Lara said, finally understanding. *Thanks but no thanks.* "But I don't want to be on camera," she said. "*They* want to be on camera." Lara looked over at the California Barbies preparing for their "segments"—applying makeup, brushing their hair, running lines as though they would forget their own names once the blinking red light flashed. Lara wanted to write, produce, drink too much coffee, down too much alcohol, smoke too many cigarettes, stay up all hours, never get married, have affairs with Doctors Without Borders. And die before she got bored. *Or worse, boring.*

"Look, the news lies in the writing. The Kens, the Barbies, they just repeat words—if dogs could read, we'd have Chihuahuas doing the top story," Lara said. "Me, I want to write the words."

"Okay, okay, I get it," Professor Greene said, weary but resolute. "Do you know what Diane Sawyer did before she was on camera?"

"She was a speechwriter," she said, "for Nixon."

"She was a beauty queen," he said. "She got her start doing the weather."

Lara shook her head. "Not interested."

The professor put his hands on her shoulders, his eyes bearing down on her.

"Listen to me, young Lara," he said, "I have seen a thousand talking heads in my lifetime—and do you know how many I've said the word 'It' to?"

Lara stared back, alarmed by the weight of his bear paws on her shoulders.

"Two. And both made it on the nightly news."

"I want to write," Lara repeated. "It's all I ever wanted—"

"Shut up," Professor Greene growled, "you're going to Phoenix."

THREE weeks later, she was the weather girl on KGUN, the ABC 9 network affiliate, in Tucson. The girl she'd replaced had been a former stripper whose crystal meth habit coincided with her boyfriend's speeding Porsche. Kabloom.

The station wanted someone young and pretty and able to read numbers. A nice rack wouldn't hurt, either. They'd scooped up Lara after viewing the tape the professor had surreptitiously sent.

The producers bleached her hair glow-in-the-dark platinum, accosted her with fake eyelashes and frosted pink lipstick. She kissed circus elephants, performed a cartwheel wearing a miniskirt, laughed at the sexist anchor's dumb jokes, and slithered out of his damp hands the moment they were off the air. But she stayed in. And awakened eight years later from the nightmare sitting in the third chair at *Sunrise America* in New York.

Did she say "awakened"? Her working life was a Bataan Death March of Interviews: right this way, post-op conjoined twins; here comes the runaway bride; next up, the literate-adjacent lottery winner.

She'd watched from the dugout as the top anchors teed up the decent gets—Hillary Clinton, the Human Rights Watch advocate with the secret Darfur footage, the firebrand senator advocating same-sex marriage—and peppered them with softball questions. Rarely, an anchor was on vacation or location and she'd be sitting in the chair opposite the mayor of a flooded city, or a fallen religious leader.

The taste of these interviews lingered in her mind. She wanted more. She wanted the brass ring: high-stakes reporting from the field. The field being Iraq, Darfur, Louisiana, name your hot spot.

Lara blinked and looked down at the paper. The photograph was coming into focus. *Oh shit.* Last night emerged piece by piece: Jackson leaving her apartment, their farewell in the doorway. She peered at Georgia, the lead anchor for *Sunrise America,* who was getting worked over in the next makeup chair.

"Oh God. I'm dead, right?" Lara asked.

Georgia patted her knee. "Relax, honey, this'll blow over in a few hours. They'll move on to the next tragedy."

Georgia mothered everyone—her three towheaded children, her stay-at-home husband, the cameramen, technicians, producers, makeup artists, hairstylists, guests, the security guy. *Everyone.* And she'd never cracked, never had that bad moment that was rumored about other famous anchors—the popular pixie who went through an assistant every other week; the beautiful Latina whose hairbrush leapt out of her hand and caught her makeup artist on his cheek;

the affable anchor who couldn't keep his pampered hands off the interns.

Georgia had taken Lara to lunch the first week she'd landed at the network. "Maintain a life," Georgia had said. "This is not life; this is work."

She'd shown Lara pictures of her husband, her children, their dogs, the cat. The home on the lake in Bedford.

"This is how I remain sane. This is how I can let it roll off my back. This job is a circus. This," she pointed at her photographs, "is how to survive."

"You'll survive," Georgia was telling her now.

"LAAAAARAAAAAAAA!" Her producer Sarah Kate's Southern accent, all the more unmistakable when she hollered. "I need to talk to you! Now!"

Lara closed her eyes and tilted her head back. Kevan barked at her; once again, she'd ruined her lip line.

4

GATHER THE PAWNS

JACKS HURRIED into the purring black limo waiting curbside. As he slid into the backseat, into the welcome, serene darkness, he realized that he hadn't said hello to the doorman, the man who'd been opening his door for as many years as he'd lived at Seventy-first and Park. He couldn't even recall the doorman's name. Cynthia took care of names and niceties ("How are you this morning, Mr. So-and-So, how's that leg doing? How's your daughter's new baby?") and stuffed Christmas bonus envelopes. (Tipping at 740 was a competitive sport—Jacks had informed his driver to stay abreast of the Tipping Olympics—he'd doubled whatever the next guy offered, until some dickhead gave a trip to Jamaica on his jet to the head doorman, plus full-body lipo for the wife. The entire building was in a furor.) Suddenly, Jacks felt that he should act nice to everyone. Once the separation hit the papers, he needed foot soldiers who would back him up in the ensuing dogfight. "I know Mr. Power," he needed to "hear" the doorman saying to his wife in Astoria. "He's a good guy. I don't care what them papers yak about."

The black boat slid off into traffic. Jacks took a sidelong glance at the papers folded up on the seat next to him. The *Post* was there, but he wouldn't allow himself to open it, even though, for a second, he wanted to stare at that picture, to see the two of them together. They really did make a great-looking couple, he and Lara.

Jacks hadn't called Lara yet, even though she'd called and Black-Berried him. He wanted to reassure her, but he needed to strategize, to think, to fucking breathe.

Calls to make before addressing his irate girlfriend:

He'd have to call his lawyer.

He'd have to call his business manager.

He'd have to call his publicist. That ninny.

He'd have to call his father.

Jacks did not want to call his father.

Jackson Power wasn't afraid of anyone—except for Dear Old Dad, who was anything but Dear. And had barely been a Dad. Old, old he was.

Jackson knew what his father would say. "Whatever you do, hang on to the apartment. A Power never sells."

Jacks wouldn't lose the apartment. He wouldn't lose 740. He couldn't lose 740. Seven-forty, the most important residential address in all of Manhattan. Seven-forty, harder to get into than a virgin bride, had been home to Bouviers, Rockefellers, Chryslers, and of course, Powers.

Here, in Manhattan, the building made the man. And Jacks Power wasn't about to be unmade.

"Harry," Jacks said to his driver as they idled at the red light.

"Hunh." Harry's black eyes barely flickered.

"You read the paper?" Jacks said casually.

"No," Harry said.

"The *Post*?"

"No. No."

"You don't have to sound so annoyed."

"But I am annoyed," Harry huffed. He squeezed the steering wheel, then scratched at the skull tattoo on his middle finger. Harry the Russian lived in an irony-free zone, without any sense of boss-employee etiquette. When you're packing 295 on a six-foot-three frame, etiquette becomes seasonal—the season being whenever you damn well feel like being polite to your boss.

"Just . . . take a look."

Jacks unfolded the *Post* and slid it through the Plexiglas partition. Harry took it without bothering to look at him; he glanced at the paper, then slid it back.

"Well?" Jacks asked.

"Well what?"

"Did you see the picture well what?"

"I see no picture," Harry said. "What picture?"

"The one of me!"

"Yeah. That one. Okay, I see it."

Beat.

"So?!"

"*So,* I see you every day, so?!"

Jacks simmered in the backseat. "Well. I think I look pretty damned good, so!"

"Oh yeah, you real beauty queen, boss!" Harry the Russian started laughing.

"Fuck you!" Jacks kicked at the front seat, then slipped, his ass landing on the floor of the limo.

Harry erupted. "Where you want me to take you, Mr. Sharon Stone?" Irony might not have been his strong suit; comedy, he knew.

"My father's house," Jacks said softly, acknowledging defeat as he climbed back onto the seat.

Harry almost spit a tooth as he turned the corner, he was laughing so hard. His whole life, he'd never known anyone as funny as Jacks Power.

5

IT'S WAR. WHAT SHOULD I WEAR?

TALK TO me, padded cell," Cynthia Power said, as she stood in third position in her giant wardrobe closet. She leaned back on one foot with the other arched forward, anticipating the next twenty-four hours like a general on the verge of a great war. Jackson would fight hard and dirty and win the first battle. But the Hundred Years' War? Welcome to Cynthia's domain. What were Jacks's basic necessities of life? Immediate gratification, instant recognition, and constant reassurance (she'd learned this from her twenty-five-year marriage and parenting-your-toddler books). Cynthia had the discipline for the long haul, to beat him in the trenches. After all, she had squeezed her once-chubby body into a tutu at four. Cynthia could endure years of pain; she'd danced on a torn Achilles, ruptured cartilage, and shattered toes. Growing up, it was her habit to be in bed before dusk, a hollow ache in her stomach infiltrating her sleep. She'd sacrificed any semblance of normality—no first kiss in middle school, no Friday night boys in leather jackets. While other girls were playing spin the bottle, she was camouflaging her bruises with makeup.

And sex? Cynthia had been a virgin until nineteen. She'd had only one lover, an Argentinean soloist, before she'd met Jackson.

Could Jacks have waited that long? Could he have postponed desire, sublimated his urges for art? For beauty? Hell no, he couldn't have done it even for money.

Cynthia flashed on her wedding ring, the size of a marble, reading it like a crystal ball. She could see Jacks, *feel* him. He would already be on the phone, gathering the troops. Would he call his publicist first? His lawyer? His girlfriend? (*Would she be his future wife,* Cynthia wondered, *or just a fling?*)

No, no, and no. Jacks's first call, she knew too well, would be to his father. "Daddy, what do I do?"

Unfortunately, as Cynthia's father was out of the picture, she'd have to make her own calls. First, find a lawyer. Second (maybe first?), call the accountant to prevent Jacks from freezing accounts, and figure out which assets she could mobilize to her side of the chessboard.

For all this, she'd need the right outfit.

Cynthia sighed. *Valentino, Armani, Jil Sander, or Prada? What would be her suit of armor today?* Her closet was a source of pride and guilt; its mere size—larger than the main dining room at '21'—rendered her speechless the first time she'd sat there, on the floor. No one had even noticed that she'd gone off by herself—not her husband, his father, the obsequious real estate agent, the family interior decorator. She was ill, she couldn't eat or laugh. She could barely speak. What was the reason she and her new husband were here in this monstrous apartment? Why was he paying attention to fourteen-foot ceilings, hundred-year-old moldings, names like Roosevelt and Rothschild, nicknames like Muffy and Bax, ancient scandals, tragedies, and triumphs?

A baby.

Not yet even a baby. The ultrasound images resembled a guppy, swimming in a vat of embryonic fluid. The guppy was calling the shots. Even before Vivienne was born ("Vivienne" the name of Jacks's dead mother), Cynthia knew she had been "the boss of me."

How long had it been since the former Cynthia Hunsaker had

been her own boss? She'd left Aurora, Missouri, for St. Louis immediately after graduation from Hoover High. She hardly knew a soul in Missouri anymore. The first half of her life had become a dreamscape, a series of charming and mutable stories to be doled out at dinner parties. "Missourah," she liked to say, knowing it sounded quaint. Being from "Missourah" meant she knew how to sew a dress, hang a line of clothes, ride without a saddle, skin the deer she and her father had hunted with a bow and arrow. What Missouri also meant: watching her mother dive into a tallboy after her father left her for a cocktail waitress he'd fallen for on his trucking route.

It meant standing out in a place where no one and nothing was supposed to. Cynthia had left St. Louis for New York at nineteen, a hundred dollars in her pocket, the name of a famous choreographer on her lips. She debuted with the New York Ballet Theater the following summer. The stage became the boss of her. She'd gone with lightning speed from the corps de ballet to dancing the lead in *Giselle* and *Carmen*. She'd met Jackson Power on the morning of her twenty-first birthday, cutting through Washington Square Park. This young guy, cigarette dangling from his mouth, covered in paint, was playing chess against a regular, Charles, a wiry black man with matted hair. Cynthia waved at Charles, and stopped to watch. The morning air was damp. She pulled her sweater tighter around her body.

The painter made his final move on the board.

"Damn!" Charles exclaimed, as he watched. "Damn!"

"Queen takes king," the painter said. "Can't believe it."

"She good luck, boy," Charles replied, nodding toward Cynthia.

The painter eyed her. "My good luck charm wears leg warmers." He turned back to Charles. "May I?" he asked, his hand hovering over the game.

"G'head," Charles said, "ruined it for me, anyway."

The painter grabbed the ivory queen and handed it to Cynthia. "Queen for a queen," he said. Cynthia smiled and tucked the piece into her sweater pocket.

"Take a walk?" he asked. His voice felt like hot, smooth stones rolling up and down her back. Cynthia fell in love. From that moment, her heart was the boss of her.

A few weeks later, Jackson Power moved into her tiny apartment; he told Cynthia he was getting evicted from his loft. Jacks didn't talk about his childhood. They talked about ideas, they talked about their future, when they weren't fucking—every moment and everywhere: her Murphy bed; her kitchen bathtub; the restroom at Caffe Reggio; a back row seat in the old movie theater on Houston; a graffitied wall; backstage at the Academy School; a random folding chair. Jacks didn't tell her he was one of "those Powers." Wouldn't have mattered anyway. Ballerinas were too busy to read the business page.

Cynthia Hunsaker was pregnant before her twenty-second birthday.

Cynthia became Mrs. Jackson Power.

Vivienne showed up.

Chase showed up. Cynthia's career as a ballerina ended not with injury, but with maternity. Her husband. Her children. This apartment. This frikkin' closet. They'd all been the boss of her.

SUDDENLY, Cynthia's hand went to her mouth. *Oh my God, Vivienne. She had to call Vivienne. What was Cynthia thinking? Her poor daughter— had she seen the photographs?*

"Ma'am?"

A maid was standing in the doorway, dressed in a uniform straight out of a Joan Crawford movie: starched white apron, white cap, nurse's shoes. "What is it, Esme?"

"Telephone call for you, Ma'am. Mr. Stegler."

Cynthia winced. The ghoulish Morris Stegler—finance impresario/vivisectionist known for cutting up the dying bodies of companies and feeding them to the sharks on the Street, the all-around dullard whose one blazing streak of personality was his fevered taste for Chinese food and Korean hookers—was the last person she wanted to talk to. Cynthia sighed and picked up the extension.

"Morris, sweetie? How are you?"

"Fabulous party last night, Cynthia. Incredible turnout. Gave the board a great idea." *Click.* Morris made a clicking sound from the back of his throat when excited, as though recording his words for posterity.

"Can we do this later?" Cynthia asked. She didn't want to hear about ballet board matters. She could read all about it in the *Times*—commingling of funds, sponsorship losses, sexual harassment. What next? Murder? Only preschool admissions were more savage than getting on the board of the New York Ballet Theater: a bunch of rich men rubbing up to the arts—and the dancers.

"We ran it through the nominating committee." *Click.* "Howard's on board, David's with us." *Click.* "Harriet Feingold is in *total* agreement." *Click.* "The Finance Committee's a go." Morris was head of the Finance Committee.

"Morris, could we please—"

"—the Audit Committee, I don't even have to *tell* you where they stand. And Marketing's ecstatic, coming in their fucking leotards." *Click.* Morris sounded like a Gatling gun.

"Morris, what are you talking about?" Cynthia said.

"We want you to be chairman of the Executive Board." *Click.*

"Fred Plotzicki is the chairman," Cynthia said. "And will be for time immemorial."

"Fred's made fools of us, Cynthia," Morris said. *Click.* "We've given him a year. That endowment he promised? Where is it? And the fat fuck, excuse me, fat sweaty *bald* fuck is shtupping that past-her-prime ballerina."

"Suzenka," said Cynthia.

"Screwzenka, you mean . . ." *Click.*

Cynthia flashed on a photo in the Sunday Style section: Fred and the aging Belorussian ballerina. The woman looked like a ninety-pound amuse bouche next to Fred, the slippery Wall Street icon and political kingmaker who had all the physical heft and social graces of a manatee.

"Yes, well, I don't know and I don't give a fuck," Morris said. "But come on. It's embarrassing."

She heard the announcer's voice: "In this corner: Cynthia Hunsaker Power, weighing 110 pounds, our very own Upper East Side Audrey Hepburn in *Breakfast at Tiffany's*. In the opposing corner, he's big, he's bad, he's the billionaire T. Rex."

The billionaire T. Rex, Cynthia thought, *who squeezed nursing home operators, oil company chairmen, and hedge fund CEOs to subsidize the ballet, but neglected to open his own personal bank account. As promised.*

Fred wouldn't give up without a fight. He liked the coating of culture that being chairman of the Executive Board gave him. And he liked the dancers . . .

"We've given Fred more than enough time to deliver. We've got a sixty-year-old company teetering on the brink of bankruptcy. We can't wait any longer. We want you to be the new chairman," Morris repeated. *Click.*

"I'm not qualified," Cynthia said.

"Bullshit. You're beautiful and elegant, you have a wonderful reputation," Morris said, "*and* you pay your endowments. You're exactly what we need."

How many times, Cynthia thought, *can one hear the words "beautiful and elegant" before it gets tired?*

Try never.

What am I afraid of? Cynthia thought about the piece of advice her father gave her when she'd had crippling stage fright. "What's the worst that can happen?" Tommy Hunsaker said in his Missouri drawl. "To hell with 'em. They can't kill ya."

That was just before he'd left. *He was right—that didn't kill her, either.*

Cynthia *had* spent eleven years on the board; she'd sponsored favorite ballerinas and underwrote the ballet academy that fed sleek new bodies to the NYBT. She knew the members of the Executive Board intimately, and she was the only one who had a background in dance. Most important, Cynthia needed an identity—pronto. Now that her "Mrs. Jackson Power" ID was about to be confiscated—

Why *not* her?

Cynthia held on a moment longer. Oh God. The monster would eat her alive. But maybe he'd end up with a mouthful of beautiful and elegant gristle.

To hell with 'em, she thought. *They can't kill me.*

"Morris, for God's sake stop clicking, you sound like you're about to go off," Cynthia told him. "I'm in."

She hung up. *Click.*

She returned to the war room, her closet. The day was only hours old and already Cynthia was locked in mortal combat with two of the most powerful men in New York.

She hesitated, then grabbed a bulletproof Chanel.

6

CONNECTED PAWNS

Now we're pleased to welcome to *Sunrise America* the author of an exciting new book on longevity, *100 Is the New Middle Age!*" Lara trilled at the camera. Before her was an emaciated woman with rutted cheeks, arguing that human beings could live to be 120 years old if they consumed no more than nine hundred calories a day.

The problem, Lara thought, is that you look like you're 120 when a speeding cab flattens you at thirty-eight. *Jackson*. Untimely death made her think of Jackson. She was going to kill him.

"Do you ever get . . . hungry?" *Genius!* Lara gave a forced smile, thinking, *There goes my Daytime Emmy.*

The cadaver mumbled an answer.

Beat his head into a wall . . .

"Uh-huh," Lara said. She was concerned the interviewee would need an IV once they went to commercial.

Mercury in his tennis shoes?

"Okay, when was the last time you ate a Snickers?" Lara asked. *Maybe she would just maim him.*

"A Snickers? I wouldn't eat a—"The woman's eyes darted about the studio. Lara wanted to pin the woman to the ground, burrow her knees into her bony chest, and shove the craft services table into her gaping maw.

"Tell me," Lara said, "this starvation diet—"

"I'm not starving," the cadaver retorted.

"So. This incredibly restrictive diet," Lara said. "What does it do to one's sex life?"

Lara could hear Sarah Kate, the producer she'd taken with her from Tucson, screaming into her earpiece. She was pretty sure half of America could hear as well.

"Well," the cadaver replied. "It does cut down on certain needs."

"You don't have energy for an orgasm?" Lara asked.

Sarah Kate began to speak in tongues. *SEVENAYEMTHISISNOTTHETIMEFORTHISKINDOF TALKESPECIALLYFROMYOU!*

"I happen to think orgasms are overrated," the cadaver said.

"Preaching to the choir." Lara winked, then smiled to the camera. "Next up, winter fashions for your dog—what the posh pooch will be wearing when the weather turns chilly!"

ONCE again, Lara had been called into the principal's office. "The hay-ell did you just do?" Sarah Kate demanded as she stared a hole through Lara's force field of blasé from behind her desk, which was covered with teetering piles of videotapes, DVDs, books, lipstick-stained coffee cups from towns across the United States (Warrens, Wisconsin! The Cranberry Capital!), and far too many pictures of her three cats.

"Sarah Kate," Lara said.

"Door!" Sarah Kate barked.

Production assistants and interns were lingering outside—overhearing on behalf of their bosses. Lara reached over and flipped the door shut.

"First you're on the front page of the *Post,* then you're caught asking an anorexic nutbag about orgasms on camera. Are you fixing to get me fired?" When Sarah Kate Baxter, Ole Miss '88, Kappa Kappa Delta, was angry, her Southern came out fierce. "Yew fixin' t' git me fahred?"

The principal's office. How many times had Lara felt this splash of anxiety in her stomach? Sarah Kate hadn't offered Lara a seat, but one glance at the guest chairs stacked with self-help, political, and summer reads would tell anyone the offer would have been empty.

"You're angry."

"Y'think?" Sarah Kate said, shaking the copy of the *Post* at her. "The whole building's up in arms. America's Sweetheart is not allowed to be a Jezebel Hoo-er."

"They haven't slept together in a year. They don't talk. They're married in name only," Lara said. "And yes, I am a cliché. Worse than that. I'm a shit. I've got to end it."

"So help me, I've about wiped my hands of you, Chicken," Sarah Kate said.

"Lie," Lara whispered. Sarah Kate was softening; "Chicken" was her pet name for Lara—something to do with running around like a chicken with her head cut off during her first months of employ. Lara rocked back and forth in those fuck-me heels the network brass made her wear despite the considerable inches she wielded over the coanchor, a man whose grave demeanor counterbalanced his stint as a game show host. She sorely wanted to check her BlackBerry. *Why did she have to be in love with Jacks Power?*

Sarah Kate continued to stare her down. Her eyebrow had crawled up her dollishly smooth forehead. Sarah Kate possessed much that was beautiful about the feminine form—pouty lips, voluptuous breasts, a high, firm ass—in a body that hovered at two hundred pounds. She looked like Marilyn Monroe, if Marilyn had been soaked in water for a long time.

Sarah Kate didn't care about her attractiveness. She thought men were useless, except to move things.

Lara envied her. *I should break up with Jacks,* she thought, *the guilt is killing me.*

"Let's go, Chicken," said Sarah Kate. Lara marveled at how fast those legs could power the rest of the grand machine. "I got things to say, and you got things to listen to."

WAY TOO EARLY in the day, Lara sat on a high black bar stool, her knees wedged between the bar and Sarah Kate's thigh. *One sound was like no other,* Lara thought: *the last of a drink through a straw.*

"Where are you?" Sarah Kate demanded.

"Sorry," Lara said. "I'll have another." She raised her hand toward the bartender; he was new, Latino, though paled by city life. The first Bloody Mary was good, not as good as her usual—maybe he'd get the next one right. *Hope springs eternal,* Lara thought. *As does vodka.*

"You're not listening to me," Sarah Kate said. "I said, we're gonna polish up this shitpile for you. Jackson Power was in your lobby last night because you're pursuing him for that big story about the Bowery hotel fight, okay? You will deny any extramarital relationship. You will make sure *he* denies any extramarital relationship. We will get this gone. I don't care if you eventually marry and pop out two papooses. No one likes a home wrecker, even if that home was wrecked long before you sashayed in."

"I hate that I'm a part of this."

Sarah Kate waved her off. "If you hated it so much, you'd stop. But, I'm not here to lecture you on morals. You know how valuable you are to the network. And to me. Georgia's contract is up in less than a year. They'll be after her to coanchor the nighttime news. Her kids are almost all in college, her husband is the missus of that familial organization. She'll go for it. That leaves you and a couple other girls who've been dancing around that spot. But no one else has your TVQ. You act like you'd rather have Ebola, but you are a star, sugar.

People watch you, they want to be your friend, your husband, your mother, your sister—"

"I can be everybody's crazy relative!" Lara kissed the smooth glass and sucked another third of the drink into her mouth.

"You know what you're looking at? Fifth Avenue penthouse, full-time driver, seven mil a year." Sarah Kate leaned back on her stool. "Yes, okay, interviewing pop stars gone awry with small children. But ... also the heads of state you've been dying to interview. Iraq. Iran. Afghanistan. Darfur. Real news. The real shit. Everything you and I have been working toward for almost a decade. All because you were born with something only three, four other people in the world possess."

Lara was still staring into the mottled red, picking out the specks of pepper clinging desperately to ice cubes.

"Jim wants you to have it. He wants this more than he wants his wife to have her tits done. Jane Pauley, Katie Couric, Lara Sizemore. That's how he sees it. So keep it together. For both of us."

"My dream is to die in New York City," Lara said, "on a bar stool."

"You don't want to die ugly, honey," Sarah Kate replied. "You're thirty years old. You make a very, very nice salary. You're running around with a married billionaire. And blowing off your interviews. The hell do you think you're doing? I know what you think you want, Lara Sizemore. You think you'll die if you have to do jumping jacks on national television with one more Mrs. America Aerobic Fitness winner. Do you really want to blow it all sky-high when you're so close to calling your own shots?"

"I hate jumping jacks," Lara said. "They make my boobs sore."

"Well, then, do you really want to take away my mother's only source of bragging rights? She's not getting a doctor son-in-law; she's not getting grandkids. Why are you aching to walk away so badly? What is it you want?"

Lara licked at the sudden tears running down her cheeks.

"If you're so bent on destroying this opportunity, you'd better know why," Sarah Kate said. Her cheeks were equally splotchy; a teardrop had rounded the slope of her nose and had nestled just under one delicate nostril, somehow accentuating Sarah Kate's beauty—the saline equivalent of Cindy Crawford's mole.

"You're crying like a big ol' baby," Lara said.

"Look what's talkin'," Sarah Kate said. Their sudden embrace was interrupted by the buzz-bark of a BlackBerry.

"If it's the People's Billionaire, tell him this people wants him dead," Sarah Kate said.

Lara read Jacks's new message, marked urgent, and rubbed the ribbed patch of skin between her eyebrows. This situation was going to turn her into a Shar-Pei.

"Jacks said he's sorry," Lara said. "He'll do anything to make it up to me." She showed Sarah Kate the screen.

"Fine. Tell him to buy me an island," Sarah Kate said. "This isn't fun and games and romance, Chicken. This isn't even his life. This is your life."

7

THE KING MAKER

CIRCLE THE block!" Jacks yelled. "I need more time to think!"

Harry the Russian glared at Jacks in the rearview mirror. "No reason to shout!" Harry shouted back.

"I need a second to think." Jacks's voice sounded defeated and flat. Not even eight in the morning, and already he was exhausted. "Busy day," he coughed out. Jacks often used the phrase "busy day" instead of an apology with his wife, his driver, his flotilla of scurrying assistants. "I've got a lot of things on my plate this morning, Harry. That's a fact."

"So I read, boss," Harry pouted, as he pulled out into traffic. He wasn't one to let go of a grudge, even one so freshly born.

Harry pushed out into heavy rush-hour traffic. They'd been circling past a five-story town house on Sixty-fifth and Madison for the past eight and a half minutes; Jacks had monitored the time on his black-face Patek chronograph, a birthday gift from Cynthia fifteen years ago. Happier times. Cynthia had summoned him home early. They'd enjoyed a candlelight dinner on the terrace. After eating the apple pie she'd made for him, Cynthia had presented him with the watch and a blow job. He remembered how lucky he felt that night, to be with this woman. He remembered peace.

Now even happy scenes, Jacks feared, would take on the sheer coating of tragedy. With a front-page photograph, Jacks had changed not only his future (*Christ, how much would the lawyers alone cost?*), but his history. When he thought of it, he felt the earth bob and weave beneath his feet. He was afraid he would faint if he stood.

Jacks hoped the outside security cameras hadn't picked him up sitting in front of his father's home. There were six cameras, covering corners, doorways, windows, gilded façade. Since becoming super-wealthy, his father had developed two big fears: robbery and kidnapping. (Jacks felt certain his father's potential kidnappers would send him back, pronto.) Inside, there'd be the Israelis. Young, tightly muscled, cartoonishly handsome, eager for a silent, choreographed skirmish to show off their Krav Maga skills.

Who needed the Israelis when you had Harry the Russian? *Krav Maga this, motherfucker.*

Jacks caught the morning sun dashing off the tarnished copper slats on the town-house rooftop. His father had lived here forty years. There were bigger places, grander places in New York—740 Park, naturally—there were none more beautiful.

One-hundred-year-old spiral wrought-iron awnings topped by iron pineapples (a sign of hospitality!) graced the walkway. Tennessee marble columns laced with silver streaks countered the dark, heavy oak doorway carved with fleur-de-lis. The nine-foot doors had been imported from the Belgian Congo on a nineteenth-century slave ship; they'd been treated better than the human cargo. "And for good reason," his father had boasted to his young son. "They were worth more." The exposed brick that pulled the eye skyward until it huddled under sheets of copper roofing conveyed warmth, wealth, and stateliness. The building managed to be imposing and welcoming at once.

Jackson had grown into his admiration of his father's home, as he had grown into his begrudging—extremely begrudging—admiration of his father.

A bout with scarlet fever as a child had left Artemus Power the runt of five brothers. The unusual boy with the unusual name—his mother, Blanche, originally of County Cork, had been free to choose after her husband failed to show up at the hospital to greet his next "mouth to feed"; Artemus Power was fated to stand out.

Blanche attended church every morning, even as her Lord and Savior was failing to save her from consumption. Dead at thirty-six after raising her boys and working three jobs—factory work, seamstress, bookkeeper for the local numbers runner. She'd died to get some rest, is what Jacks's father said.

The father, the original Power, tried to beat ambition into his kids, the runt most of all. The other children eventually scattered across the country. The runt stayed, and became the conduit for his father's ambition. (There were buildings in Manhattan that bore the fingerprints of the first Power to cross the Atlantic on a steamer.) Jackson's father didn't talk about his dad, who'd build things by day and tear down his own life by night. Jackson's grandfather spent his time and earnings on whiskey, on working girls lining Broadway, at gaming tables. He'd finally made some money in real estate, then lost it all on Black Tuesday, and disappeared for good.

But not before leaving his young son with the love of building. Artemus Power did everything quickly, darting rather than walking, snapping rather than talking. When he was barely in his twenties, he scraped together enough capital to build one garage next to a house in a modest Queens neighborhood, then built a house, then bought one run-down apartment building and fixed it up, then another, then dozens. All in Queens. By twenty-five, he owned several buildings in Harlem, convinced there was money to be made there, then gave them up cheap when the heroin trade took a toll on tenants—when he literally could be killed on the third of every month just for the statement: "Rent's due."

It was the last and only time he had lost money. And don't think he didn't remember the blow. Jackson's father would never trust Manhattan again.

By contrast, Queens was dependable: blue-collar, proud, reliable, the equivalent of the man who rolls up his sleeves and gets to work, come hell or hangover.

Shortly after he built the sprawling Queens Parkway Projects, Artemus Power consummated his marriage to Vivienne Langford of the Park Avenue Langfords. She was everything he wasn't: educated, sophisticated, refined. Vivienne was a Vassar graduate, a world traveler, a strong-willed woman with a tongue that made Swiss cheese of steel, flesh, ego. The Original Vivienne was the only person Jacks's father had ever been afraid of. In short order, Artemus Power acquired the wife, then the address. He had arrived, would stay arrived. God help anyone who got in his way.

Jacks's relationship with his father bore all the signs of the Four Horsemen of the Apocalypse of Parenting: Abandonment, Fearmongering, Manipulation, and, when neglect wore thin, Belittlement.

"Why must you get into trouble all the time?" his mother would ask. After Andover, after Choate, Dalton (moving in alphabetical order)—

"Why must you get caught?" his father would demand.

Because I want to, Jackson thought. He wasn't afraid of jumping off a second-floor balcony on a drunken dare, or diving into icy water wearing nothing but white socks, just because some kid hinted that it couldn't be done. But he had no courage in his soul. He was afraid to speak the truth: he didn't want to go into the family business. Jacks didn't give a shit about "holdings." In college, his father drove him around blocks and blocks of soulless utilitarian housing and said, "Look around, son. All of this will be yours someday." Jacks felt doomed.

"I want to paint," he'd blurted out. It helped that he'd thrown a few back. "I don't care about buildings. I care about canvases." Jacks charged on. "My professors say I've got talent."

"They're bullshitting you, boy," Artemus Power said.

"That's not true," Jacks said.

His father smiled, a cold look in his eye. "They just want me to write a check for a goddamned wing. Don't be a fool."

They were standing outside this very town house.

"That's not true," Jacks protested, waving his father's words away.

"The provost called, we had a nice chat," his father said. "We're having lunch at La Côte Basque on Tuesday. I can tell you, that's going to be one goddamned expensive vichyssoise."

"You're a fucking asshole," Jacks said, pointing at his father.

"I am an asshole," his father agreed, "shelling out my hard-earned money to turn you into some candy-ass artiste—"

"If you just looked at my work," Jacks said wearily, "just once."

His father laughed. "Your work, your work. You don't know the first thing about work—"

Maybe it was the vodka running through his veins, or the look on his father's face as he mocked him, but Jacks found himself holding his fist back.

"Go ahead, boy," his father said, with his arms flung out, "take a swipe at your old man. It'll be your last."

His father's driver had dashed around the car, and was putting a hand on Jacks's shoulder. "Calm down, son," he said. "Just calm down."

Jacks shrugged him off, still staring at his father. Finally, he turned and walked away.

"I didn't think so," Artemus Power yelled, lobbing a final insult at his son.

"YOU HAVE family?" Cynthia had asked him. "Here? In the city?"

He could see her young face, held in his hands as though she would break if he let go. Her large eyes were untouched by cynicism, by the hard reality that was his family.

"C'mon," he'd said to Cynthia, "you had to have known. Are you telling me you've never heard of the Powers?"

She'd looked at him, puzzled. He loved that expression; Cynthia was still in the process of discovery. He, like many children of fortune, had already discovered and found much to be lacking.

"Well, doesn't matter," he'd said. "We have to do Thanksgiving with my father."

"Great," she'd said. He felt her waver.

"You don't want to?"

"Why wouldn't I want to?" she'd said, none too convincingly. "What about your mother?"

"My mother's dead."

"Oh, Jackson," she'd said. "Why didn't you tell me?"

He couldn't answer. He didn't even know why himself.

Jacks loved the sound of his name rolling from her mouth. He loved the whiteness of her teeth, the way her pink tongue darted in and out between her lips as she spoke. The way she'd pronounce every consonant of every syllable of every word with a sharp, precise clip at the end. He'd found comfort in her calm, steady Midwestern nature. With Cynthia, he could be himself—bellow, dance naked, forget to eat, paint through the morning, live as an artist without obligation except to the canvas; she was his moon, exerting a gravitational pull that kept him from spinning out into the void. In those last months, with Cynthia Hunsaker, Jackson didn't need to drink until he blacked out, or coke himself up to feel as important as his name. He didn't even need to fuck the way he used to—many women, most days, all hours.

Whenever Cynthia had asked about his family, he'd laugh, kiss her warm mouth, change topics, ignore her questions, twirl her around by her waist—until finally she stopped asking. Jackson didn't want their love tainted. What if her ardor shifted from Jackson the Painter to Jackson the Power?

Their first Thanksgiving at the Power manse. Cynthia had

scrimped for a dress. Crushed red velvet. A bow at the back, riding her small hips. Her hair pulled into a loose chignon. She made Holly Golightly look like a Meat Market tranny.

Cynthia brushed a strand of hair from her face, a simple, breathtaking gesture that could bring a tear to his eye. She insisted Jackson wear dress slacks. They compromised on a clean pair of jeans and the only white shirt that bore no colorful evidence of his painting.

She baked an apple pie.

He remembered the aroma, apples and cinnamon and sugar and butter. Cynthia hadn't used a recipe; cooking was part of her genetic memory. Jackson had dated so many girls who survived on a diet of cigarettes and coke and double espresso. He couldn't remember his own mother putting a home-cooked meal in front of him. Cynthia making scrambled eggs in the morning had been a revelation.

They'd taken the subway to the Upper East Side and emerged on a different planet.

They stood in front of the monstrous entrance to the family town house. "I love you," he whispered, because he felt his throat tightening. It was his first confession, although he'd felt love at first sight of Cynthia dashing through Washington Square Park, her scarf whipping behind her.

"I know," she said.

Jackson's father hadn't greeted them at the door. There was a butler to perform that duty. Actually, there were three men, including a pair of sentries, standing like priceless urns on either side of the entryway. Jackson watched Cynthia carefully as he led her past the Cézanne, Picasso, Cy Twombly, Warhol . . . so many beautiful works that they canceled one another out.

Jacks held Cynthia's hand; she didn't gawk or chatter nervously or any of the things he'd seen or imagined other women doing.

He loved her even more; his heart stretched with each reassuring squeeze of the hand she gave him.

Artemus Power presided at the head of the table. His hair, once red as the brick of his home, was platinum but still dense. He'd barely uttered a word to either his son or his son's date. The chef had spent days preparing the meal for three; a twenty-three-pound turkey, platters of sweet-potato mousseline, haricots verts, and hazelnut stuffing that languished, barely touched, in the middle of the table. Artemus greeted Cynthia's attempts at conversation by mumbling. Somewhere between the final spoonful of stuffing and the pie, Jackson summoned his courage.

"Dad, I can take you being rude to me. In fact, I'm not sure I would recognize any other form of communication coming from you, but I won't stand for you being rude to Cynthia."

His father's gray eyes turned the color of a frozen lake. "Is that so?" he replied coolly.

Torturing others, especially his son, was as much pleasure as it was sport.

"I'm too old to take this shit," Jackson said.

"You're old enough to make a stupidity out of your life," his father snorted. He nodded to the De Kooning hanging over the mantle. His mother had bought this painting, the painting that made Jackson want to be an artist.

"Finger paint," Artemus sneered. Then, "Do you think I'm being rude, Cindy?"

"It's *Cynthia*." Jackson rapped the table. China rattled. The servant holding out the pie started to blink uncontrollably.

"Jackson, it's fine, please," Cynthia said.

"I meant no harm," his father said. He turned to Cynthia. "Did my boy tell you why he was kicked out of his last prep school or how many strings I had to pull to keep him at Harvard? I'd be careful with him, if I were you."

"Jackson is very kind," Cynthia replied. "I've had no trouble."

"I'm sure you haven't. You've probably handled a lot of his ilk, haven't you, Cindy? I imagine it's hard for you to keep track."

"You are way out of line." Jackson's fists clenched.

"Mr. Power." Cynthia stood. "Jackson and I must be going back to our shanty. Thank you so much for a lovely evening. Happy Thanksgiving. Go to hell."

Jackson knew right then and there. He was going to marry Cynthia Hunsaker.

Artemus Power shook his head in amusement. "She's got more guts than you do, son, I'll say that for her."

Then he smiled into his drink, held steady as a mantra.

"You'll be back," he declared.

"KNEW this would happen." Artemus Power pursed his large, clumsy lips together. At eighty-three, he still had most of his hair, but had taken to dyeing it a disturbing tangerine-covered-with-early-frost color. Jackson couldn't look at it without thinking of a bad year for citrus growers.

"Your mother and I were married until the day she died."

"She died early. I was there, remember?" Jackson said, "Twenty-five years beats your record by a long shot."

His father had been steadily fucking the Betty Grable–monkfish nurse while she'd been taking care of his mother for the last months of her life. She'd lived on in the house after his mother's death, drinking his father's good Scotch and wearing his mother's jewelry when his father wasn't looking, until one day she'd been escorted from the premises by security while his father hid in this very study. From inside his bedroom, Jackson had heard the skirmish, her heels kicking at the floor, the swearing.

"I still wear my wedding ring." His father rolled the heavy gold band over with his thumb. Artemus Power's hands had been trained for physical labor. While Jackson wanted to use a size four flat brush, his father knew how to handle brick and mortar and rills and saws and cement and jackhammers. Artemus could still point out his signature on the lone block of stone at the bottom of buildings he had built with those rough-hewn hands. Before he bought them, of course.

"I'm sure your mistresses appreciate the sentimentality," Jackson replied.

His father sat behind a massive oak desk in the formal study. The curtains, silk velvet the color of spilled claret, poured from woven gold cords onto the rich mahogany floors. Fourteen-foot ceilings inlaid with brass, ivory, ebony, and walnut were painstakingly reconstructed from a German opera house. The chair his father was sitting on was made for Louis XVI; the chair Jackson was sitting on was made for a member of his court. The rug, an antique tapestry, was threadbare on the unhappy path from the double doors. It featured a hunting party in their finest silks and furs, astride red-coated horses, accompanied by white Afghan hounds; they carried a boar's body, arched back in surrender, blood seeping from its jaws and from patches of fur where arrows pierced its flesh.

The room was his father's absolute favorite.

"You've called Penn," his father said. Penn was the lead family attorney.

"I have not," Jackson replied, and now wished he had.

"You haven't moved out, obviously," his father growled.

"Well, actually, I do have a penthouse available at the Tower—"

"What kind of idiot have I raised," coughed Artemus.

"I was about to say, no, I haven't moved out," Jackson said. "I left, but haven't moved out."

"See that you don't," his father said. "If you had listened to me twenty-five years ago, you wouldn't have been in this position."

"What position?"

"Marriage. Do not lose that apartment. The Powers do not relinquish their holdings. Not even when they're cold and buried in the ground."

Can we test that hypothesis? Jacks thought. "You care a lot about an apartment you've rarely set foot in," he said. The Elder waved the accusation away. "I've never been disappointed by a building the way I've been disappointed by family."

Jackson imagined the rococo ceiling crumbling in on his father. "Fine. I won't move. I'll stay in the guest wing."

Jackson would still be living at 740 with his starter wife. The starter wife who had legal rights—he imagined her changing locks, selling off his art.

He imagined Lara's colorful response to Jacks's still living with Cynthia.

And then, for distraction, he imagined Lara's breasts.

"...the publicity!" his father was saying. "Are you listening to me?"

"Mmmm."

"You've taken my good name and made a mockery of it. Now it's associated with all kinds of unseemliness."

Jackson was amazed at how quickly he became a twelve-year-old boy in his father's presence. He scratched his chin and was almost surprised to find stubble. He straightened his tie and patted his hair. He was well on his way to becoming a playground of tics.

"Thanks for your time," Jackson said, getting up from the ass-breaking French chair.

"I'm coming back," Artemus said.

"Coming back where?" Jackson looked back at him, puzzled.

"To my office."

He held those last three words until he was sure he had Jackson's attention. Artemus Power didn't like shooting people in the back when he could do it face-to-face.

Jacks felt the familiar, carbonated gurgling of resignation in his stomach. His father was through basting in retirement; he wanted the Power power back.

"We could use a good man," Jackson said finally. "When do you think—"

"Today."

"Today," Jackson repeated numbly.

"I need to steer my company through this mess. Your emotional state is not conducive for business." His father pulled those blubbery lips up into something resembling a smile. "I'll be using my old office, assuming you haven't annexed it yet. And I'll be needing a secretary. Good legs, nice tits."

Jackson knew this wasn't a whim based on his emotional state. Since when had his old man ever cared?

"We can't afford to let that idiot screw up the Bowery deal."

"That idiot" was the mayor. The liberal Samuel Krach (pronounced "crack") was a native son who was proving to be a major pain in Jackson's own native ass. Jackson had spent over a decade prying his way into downtown Manhattan. Now there was an opportunity to turn an entire block of eyesore—a zesty stew of broken brick, vermin, and pigeon shit—into a gold, phallic high-rise, a veritable monument to the power of Power. High-end shops with names that end in vowels! One hundred and twenty-five first-class condos! Rooftop pool! Indoor squash! Eight-table micro-eateries serving fifty-dollar crepes! Construction at cost! Not to mention tax abatements! The last mayor had been closer than a short hair to signing off before being unseated. But this Krach wanted to be a hero to a cadre of working-class tenants who should've had the good sense to move. Jackson was offering them more money than they'd ever seen in their sorry little lives. Team Power was back to square one on the Bowery.

Artemus pushed back from his desk and stood. "I'm the one with the balls to stand up to him and finish this project. You're too distracted by your personal life. You should have been a starlet, not a businessman. All looks, no brains." Then his father grinned, and re-marked, "And that's a fact!"

That hurt, Jacks thought. *That really fucking hurt.*

JACKSON could feel the craving eyes of the Israelis upon him in the anteroom. Seconds later, in the backseat of the limo, a sheen of per-spiration appeared on his forehead. Jackson Power felt as though he were drowning in a clear pool in the middle of his city. He wished he could be sure that the woman he loved would save him.

8

QUEEN'S COUNSEL

IT'S YOUR mom," said the girl with the bored expression standing in the doorway of Vivienne's student apartment overlooking Washington Square Park.

"Hello," Cynthia said, stretching her neck and tilting her chin toward the ceiling, a turtle reaching for food. It was unconscious, as she always fell back on her training when she was nervous. Cynthia could see the tops of trees from the bay windows as she stood straighter, pulled everything in, shoulders back—she exerted more energy standing still than most women did running a marathon.

Cynthia's perfect Upper East Side armor—the two-piece Chanel, salmon and eggshell plaid, pearls, hair yanked back into a chignon—seemed a little off below Fourteenth Street.

Especially since the girl at the door was naked. She turned as though wending her body through a wall of water. She had skin the color of burnt butter. Not a trace of sinew. Small breasts with nipples that looked like brown stars. Black hair chopped close to her scalp on a child-size head. A tattoo at the small of her back. And not one hair on her vagina. ("Oh, Cynthia!" she could hear Vivienne say, "it's not your mother's vagina anymore—the word is 'pussy'!" Vivienne had addressed Cynthia by her first name since the day she turned twelve. What's more annoying than a precocious twelve-year-old? Nothing.) Cynthia thought briefly of the Brave New World about to greet her—hairless vaginas and tramp stamps being just part of the sexual potpourri. She had a lot of catching up to do.

The girl moved noiselessly on small, elegant feet down the hall. Cynthia was an expert on all things feet; her own were gnarled after years of punishment.

She felt a jolt of jealousy.

Cynthia had thought this space too dark when they were apartment hunting, but Vivienne had hopped from the Town Car and dashed inside. It reminded Cynthia of how many times she'd seen her daughter hop out of her car, away from her arms.

"Vivienne never cries for me when I leave her at preschool," she'd said to Jackson, when Vivienne was three.

"That's a good thing," he'd said, with pride. "She's Little Miss Independent."

"Other children cry," Cynthia said insistently. She was a young mother, Vivienne was her first baby, she was worried. Why didn't Vivienne need her? Now Cynthia perched uncertainly on the Chesterfield couch she'd bought for Vivienne, who hadn't wanted it. Her daughter had the quaint idea that she could live on bare floors with nothing but a sleeping bag, an iPod, and a cappuccino machine. Vivienne, the professional student, was starting on her third degree. She'd begun in film at Tisch, then shifted to Gallatin and backed into a music degree. She'd formed an all-girl rock band, playing bass. They named themselves Ain't We a Bitch.

Yes, well.

Now, Vivienne was going for her master's in creative writing at the New School and playing chess in the evening against the hustlers in the chess park beneath her window—with moves handed down by Jacks to his daughter when she was still in elementary school.

Cynthia's smart, capable, strong-willed twenty-five-year-old daughter had yet to actually hold down a job.

She heard muffled voices, Vivienne's rising.

"You are not the boss of me." Cynthia could still hear her toddler. Full baby lips grimacing. Blue eyes sharp and defiant. Vivienne's strawberry-blond curls a fortress against a mother's reproach; try disciplining a child who resembles a cherub from *The Birth of Venus*. Cynthia smiled at the memory.

"This is a nice surprise, Cynthia," Vivienne said, as she bounded into the room and leapt into a chair. All six feet of her clothed, thankfully. She wore an antique silk wedding kimono Cynthia had bought on a trip to Tokyo, number 5,832 in a series of not-so-subtle attempts to feminize Vivienne's taste. *Not only Vivienne's taste,* Cynthia revised, *but Vivienne herself,* whose curls were now worn in a wild halo.

Cynthia stood up, clutching her alligator Birkin to her chest, and announced, "Your father and I are getting a divorce." And then she sat down again. Vivienne finished lighting a cigarette and tossed the match into a coffee shop ashtray. *Not* a Cynthia purchase.

"About fucking time," her daughter muttered. "I've been waiting for this since before my boobs hit double-D."

"Breasts," Cynthia corrected automatically, then snatched the cigarette from her daughter's hand and set it on her own lips. She inhaled, calling urgently upon her second-favorite vice. Which reminded her—*how was she surviving this crisis without her silver/blue cans of diet Red Bull?* Cynthia drew the smoke into her lungs, then cocked her head toward the bedroom door. "You picked a fine day to be a lesbian, Vivi," she said. Not that she hadn't been "aware"—just not so naked-hottie-in-your-face aware.

Her daughter snorted. "Our timing has never been very good, Cynthia."

"I was going to ask you to coffee," Cynthia said. "I didn't want you to hear about the news from someone else, or read about it . . ." The *Post* photo popped into her head. She wondered if rage could keep her skinny. The Rage Diet.

"I'll have Aiko make breakfast," Vivienne said.

"I've already eaten," Cynthia lied.

"Cynthia," Vivienne said pointedly, "did you read the *Times* piece on middle-aged anorexics the other day?"

"Must have missed it. Sounds fascinating."

"You need Red Bull rehab," Vivienne said, as she jumped up from her chair. "And make an appointment with your attorney!"

"I will, I will."

Cynthia's phone started ringing. She looked at the number. A name flashed—one of the board members.

"When? Don't be your usual trusting, naive self, Cynthia. You have to put yourself first. Use muscles you haven't used in a long time. Like your brain?"

Cynthia let that one go. "Have you talked to your father?"

Vivienne laughed. "Oh yeah—it went something like this: 'Hi, Vivienne, how am I?'"

"I meant this morning."

"No, of course not. I'm on the emergency contact list somewhere below Liz Smith."

"Your father cares for you very much, Vivi."

"Mom, it's me, Vivienne, your wayward daughter. This isn't family therapy hour. You are getting divorced from one of the most powerful pricks in the country—"

"Vivi. Stop. He is your father."

Cynthia's phone rang again. Another board member.

"Which is why I know," Vivi said. "I have firsthand experience. Get a killer lawyer. Raoul Felder, or his wife—she's the brawn in that operation. You should be meeting lawyers *today*. I guarantee Dad is. And you're going to need a forensic accountant. Before he starts hiding his crap. You could wake up next week, and all of a sudden he owns nothing. 'What buildings?' " she asked, impersonating her father's voice.

"Jackson wouldn't do that," Cynthia said. Unconvincingly.

"If you can't do it for you, Cynthia, do it for me. I'm into the pretense of poverty, not the actuality," Vivienne said. "Did he move out?"

"Well, no—but he left."

"Change the locks."

"I can't do that."

"You want the new Mrs. Power moving in?"

Cynthia winced. Vivi had guessed she'd been replaced.

"It's not personal, Cynthia," Vivienne said softly. "He just can't be alone."

Had Vivi known about all the other affairs?

"Of course I don't want the other woman moving in."

"Well, if you're not going to change the locks, at least make it very, very uncomfortable for him to stay," said Vivienne, as she swung her legs onto the floor and headed for the bedroom, "Aiko! Can you make that omelet you made yesterday morning—Mom, I swear to God, it was like biting into the inside of my lover's thigh."

"Vivienne!"

"What?" asked Vivienne innocently.

Cynthia's phone rang again.

"One step at a time!" her mother commanded.

9

THE KING'S OPENING MOVE

As harry the Russian steered the Town Car back into traffic, Jackson's BlackBerry awakened. He knew without looking at the number that Lara was calling him back.

"Honey—"

Lara was off and running. "You've ruined my life. No, no, you haven't ruined my life. I've ruined my life. And your life. And your wife's life. And your daughter's life."

"Lara, slow down—"

"Sarah Kate and the network have been putting out fires all morning. I could lose my job over this, but that's the least of it—"

"Lara, I—"

"This whole thing is beneath me. I feel dirty. I don't like being the other woman. I'm not this person. I can't do this anymore, Jackson."

"What do you mean?" he asked, a lump in his throat.

"Sneaking around, meeting up at event after event and shaking hands like strangers after we've spent the last hour in bed. What we're doing is wrong. I have to figure my life out. Being with you is a distraction."

"Wait a minute, what?" Jackson had never been called a "distraction." He'd been called worse, but never a *distraction!* Was he being dumped twice in the same morning? Was this covered by the romantic bylaws of the Geneva Convention?

"I'll send your stuff over to your apartment. No, not your apartment, your office, right? I have that blue blazer and you left a pair of cuff links." She faltered.

"Where are you? I need to see you—"

"Are you crazy? I don't want to see you! I can't see you! I hate you and I miss you!"

"Marry me, Lara," Jackson blurted. He seldom blurted. It hurt.

There was a pause.

"Fuck you," Lara replied.

"I'm serious," Jacks said. "Cynthia wants a divorce. And I love you. I truly love you. Let's get married."

Beat.

"Oh . . . fuck you . . ." Lara said, almost tenderly. "I'll get back to you." She hung up.

Jacks glanced up, saw the look in Harry's eye.

"What?" Jacks asked. *"What?"*

"Can I be ring bearer, boss?" The big man started giggling.

"Shut up and drive," Jacks replied.

10

THE GOOD BISHOP: ZORBA THE THERAPIST

Yᴏᴜ ʟᴏᴏᴋ like someone stuck a hose up your ass and sucked out all of your kishkes," said Dr. Gold.

Cynthia sighed, her major means of communication this morning. The Cynthia Sigh; she should brand it.

"I feel paralyzed," she said. "You saw the paper?"

"I don't read the paper. Who wants to know? Same thing, different date, yadayada." He took a sip of the tea she'd brought him. "I'll read my obituary."

"I'll just make the complete demise of my marriage short and sweet," Cynthia said. "Jackson's been seeing that girl from Channel 3. She's blond. She's vivacious. She has big teeth. She is everything, in short, that I am not."

"She sounds like something you keep on a leash."

"You wouldn't say that if you saw the picture. Front page, the *Post*. Jackson was late to our twenty-fifth anniversary party. He was busy celebrating between her legs."

"The gift that keeps giving. Until you get married." Goldie laughed at his joke.

"I asked him. No, I didn't ask. I told him I want a divorce."

"And?"

"And now I'm so scared. I'm almost scared enough to go back."

"Wouldn't it be strange if you weren't?" Dr. Gold sat back in his easy chair, clutching two speckled hands round the roundest of bellies. *My Jewish Santa,* Cynthia thought. Cynthia and Goldie had a somewhat unprofessional relationship. If Goldie so requested, Cynthia would bring him pastrami on rye. If she canceled on him, she'd have to field his indignant calls during a dinner party. If he complained about money woes, Cynthia wrote him a check doubling the fee for their session. They were poster children for codependency, but he'd been her anchor through Jackson's affairs and tribulations with Vivi; her grief over Chase. And he was generous with the hugs.

"Are you there, Sunshine?" Goldie was asking. "Did I just lose my patient? That's the third one this week—"

"Goldie, the ballet board asked me to be the new chairman." Cynthia wanted to light a cigarette. She still hadn't had her caffeine fix, and the day was heading into lunchtime. A headache was coming on. *How would she survive?*

"You must be pleased," he said.

"No," Cynthia replied. "I'm terrified. The erstwhile chairman, this monster—"

"A monster."

"Fred Plotzicki. He looks like he eats puppies. And it's not because he's abnormally large."

"And I'm just normally large? You got something against big men? Go on."

"Well, he's out. The board wants me in. Already he's fighting, stirring it up. I've been fielding calls all morning from board members. Divide and conquer is his sport, his Saturday tennis match, if you will," she said. "He's setting up dinners and invited them all to his fiftieth birthday party in St. Bart's, on one of those three-ring-circus yachts. I'm guessing my invitation isn't in the mail."

"He should invite you, if he's smart. Keep your enemies closer . . ."

"Why would I even accept this position, Goldie?" Cynthia asked. "There's no winning."

Goldie smiled serenely. "Because you have to. This Fred, he makes waves, get a bigger surfboard. These guys care about one thing: winning. No, two things: winning and power. I've heard the stories, not just from you. But not everyone's the monster you think they are. Some can even be rehabilitated. Kind of like Betty Ford for Billionaires."

Cynthia was thinking about water. About drowning.

"I had two dreams last night," she said. "The first one, I'm skiing downhill. I'm going fast, out of control. I felt cold, so cold that I woke up and checked the windows."

Goldie bent forward in his seated position as far as his belly would allow. He placed his hands on his knees. "Your marriage went downhill. Snow is white, the absence of color. You are drained . . . the cold represents your lack of sexuality."

"Oh really?" Cynthia asked, startled. "I'm not sexually attractive?"

"When was the last time you had sex?" Goldie asked.

"You're not allowed to ask me that," Cynthia said, busy calculating. Her eye caught porcelain rabbit salt-and-pepper shakers humping each other. Goldie collected humorous sexual artifacts from all over the world. His clients, society matrons and pro bono patients alike, had purchased each iconic figure or cartoon for Goldie. Not one of his patients traveled without Goldie in the back of her mind.

"Honey, I already know the answer," Goldie said. "Bubule, go ahead and have your midlife crisis, already. Before your term is up?"

"What do you want me to do? I can't screw the first guy who

walks up to me on the street," Cynthia said. "I haven't been on a date with another man in decades. I don't even know what *not* to order!"

"Look at me," Goldie said. "Yeah, I'm gorgeous," he patted his stomach. "I got it all. But I can't even get a hard-on anymore without meds and a forklift—"

"Goldie! I'm already having nightmares!"

"You need to get out there, sweetie," Goldie said. "You're drying up! You don't want to be the Park Avenue equivalent of the Dead Sea."

Cynthia opened her mouth to speak, but her words had abandoned her like ungrateful children.

"Think of Zorba," Goldie said. "Take control of your life by letting go. Look at him. He's happy!"

Anthony Quinn was dancing on a poster on the wall.

"Goldie, if Zorba were a woman, he'd be ostracized. I don't know *how* to have a midlife crisis! I know how men do it. Come get the diamonds! Come get the Caribbean vacation! Good girl!"

Goldie waited.

"Those two have completely ruined the whole morning news show thing for me," Cynthia continued. "But who could blame him? If I were a guy, I'd screw Lara Sizemore, too."

"My opinion?" Goldie said. "Because I'm the joker with the plaque on the wall. You don't sound jealous of him. You sound jealous of *her*." Goldie reached forward and touched Cynthia's knee. "Honey, it's so easy. Miss Morning News represents something missing from your life. What is it?"

"Mystic tan?" she asked. "Hair spray?"

"Adventure," Goldie said. "The Battle of the Board can be your Everest. Hell, it can be your twenty-two-year-old yoga instructor." She smirked as he peered at her over his glasses. "Okay, you know what? Forget about the midlife crisis. Maybe you are past your prime. Let's hold a retirement party for your libido."

"That's it," Cynthia said, "I'm leaving." She pulled herself up, clutching her Birkin to her groin, protecting her private parts from further indictment.

"Wait a minute!" Goldie said. "Give me the second dream."

Cynthia hesitated. "Snakes."

Goldie laughed.

"Not funny!"

"Right," Goldie said, choking. "I'm a genius! Why did God give me such gifts? So, the usual? Friday at eleven?"

"Fine," Cynthia said, as she walked out and slammed the door behind her. Goldie's laugh followed her down the hallway and into the elevator.

11

THE KING'S COUNSEL

So THE father returns." Caprice, Jackson's secretary, arched an eyebrow as he strode past her into his office. "Mr. Artemus, he want me to call HR, get him a secretary. Pleasant phone manner, WordPerfect proficient, good steno, legs up to the chin. His words." Caprice pursed her full lips in full disapproval.

"Yes, Caprice, Artemus Power will be gracing us with his presence once again," Jackson managed to reply without swallowing his tongue.

"He say he want his old office back. Does this mean you'll be wanting me to cancel the contractors?"

Jackson's shoulder went into a spasm. He suppressed a grimace. After a blissful twelve months of his father's retirement, Jackson finally had an architect draw up plans for a remodel. Tear down the wall between the two offices, install a conference table, a media area, automatic blinds. *Why had he waited so long? Why?*

Love is the time-efficient man's enemy.

"Yes, Caprice, cancel the contractor."

"And the interior decorator? She'll want to be paid. All the furniture is ordered."

"Cancel." He thought about the conference table, special-ordered from Luxembourg. He felt like weeping.

"And the architect?"

"Cancel. Cancel. Cancel." He would get out of paying the full contractor and designer fees. After all, he was Jackson Power. *To everyone except Daddy.*

Caprice simply nodded. Jacks glanced at the carryall she kept by her desk. The *Post* was peeking out, but Caprice was too smart to ask questions.

"Let's roll calls," Jacks said, as he walked into his office. On his desk was a blue sliver of paper, with a daily proverb courtesy of Caprice, who calibrated biblical injunctions to her boss's perceived infractions:

"He will die for lack of discipline, led astray by his own great folly."

Okay, fine. But did he deserve to have his new conference table taken away? *Did he?*

"Mr. Power, Mr. Garrison regarding the Bowery project, line one."

From her desk, Caprice could lean forward and their eyes would meet. She preferred not to shout out names, but Jackson didn't have time to care who knew his business.

Jacks picked up. "Those tenants didn't have a problem with me when I offered them a cash deal," he bellowed. "Who got to them? This is bullshit! And that's a fact! I'm calling a press conference!"

"Mr. Power, Mr. Howard on line two."

"Ron, Ron, you're a genius, loved your last movie, what was it . . . Listen, I'm wondering, how'd you get such good press all the time? What? . . . 'Don't cheat on your wife.' Thanks, thanks a lot—"

"Mr. Power, Mr. Steinberg on line three."

"Don't hand this to the lawyers. I don't want some idiot lawyer sending a missile before I make a decision. I'm the guy with the golden gut. And that's a fact! . . . By the way, you see my picture in the *Post*? I look good, right?"

The radio host with a face that looked like it had been attacked by a cheese grater called, asking for help ($$) with his pet charity. The former business rival who recently decided he wanted to be the next mayor called, asking for help ($$). And then, the calls from his father, each one ending with Jacks's face in a silent opus of twitches. Artemus was asking a lot of questions about his new project in the Bowery. *Not even in the building yet,* Jacks thought, *and already trying to pry the business from his son's hands.*

Jacks's only respite were his calls to Lara; the phone would ring straight to the exquisite torture of her voice mail. But at least he could listen to her voice.

At lunchtime, Jackson decided to forgo his usual visit to the ground-floor restaurant. Too risky. He decided to take a walk around the block.

Five minutes later, he was standing in front of his greatest promise to himself, the old Brooks and Baer Building on Fifth Avenue. Made of fine limestone, with stairs and columns of rare black marble shot through with gold vein. He'd sworn that he'd own it before his thirty-fifth birthday. Oh, he loved that building. As a young boy holding his mother's hand, he'd linger before the scenes the window dressers had devised, entire love affairs with beautiful people in exquisite finery acted out.

A piece of art, the Brooks and Baer building. A testament to the history of New York. More than that, a testament to the power of memory.

A week before his thirty-fifth birthday, Jacks bought it.

And proceeded to tear it down.

Well, sure, he'd tried to preserve it. What was he, an animal? He'd said that very thing in his first press conference, held in front of the Brooks-Baer to celebrate his victory over this historical society, that preservation society, the city planning commission. He wore them all down, with lies he wasn't fully aware he was telling, with promises he couldn't keep and with good-old-fashioned bullying that felt like a stifling embrace.

Look, there were times when you had to throw in the towel. Move on. Admit that you couldn't save something, not even a grand old building built to last centuries. Developers destroyed in order to create. Sometimes the destruction was achieved with a wrecking ball. Sometimes with a carefully orchestrated fire.

And another Power Tower would rise from the ashes.

(The *Post* photo, Jackson thought, was just the inferno to set ablaze the rickety structure known as The Power Marriage.)

"Let's face it," he'd told the four or five bored reporters shivering outside on one of the coldest winter days on record, "I love this old building, but it's like a woman of a certain age who's had a lot of surgery. Sure, the outside looks fair, but the inside is a stinking bag of tricks. If I don't take it down, it'll fall down on its own in a couple years. And that's a fact."

The press conferences had caused one of the first shouting matches between him and his father. Artemus Power would have to have a gun to his head to talk to reporters. His son Jackson had a different approach. *Go ahead,* he practically taunted the reporters, *I dare you not to write about me.*

After his treacherous foray into the art world, Jacks no longer cared that the press loved him—he cared only that they noticed him; his new persona would be his finest work.

Jacks remembered Cynthia standing in the kitchen this morning, her petite frame, the bones in her face hardened, like sand into glass. He had heard the rustle of her silk robe, and felt how it wrapped around her almost twice. *When did she start disappearing?* he wondered.

"I want a divorce." Funny, before Cynthia uttered the words, the thought had never occurred to Jackson. He wondered if he would

ever have found the courage to shovel the coal that would fire the engine of this new business known as The Power Divorce. How many people would be making money off of their breakup? Journalists (charitable term for bloodsuckers), photographers, media owners, lawyers, fucking lawyers. Jacks thought he should at least get a cut.

And why now? The affairs were nothing new. But somehow Cynthia knew that the games had stopped, that he'd fallen in love this time. *"I want a divorce."*

He replayed the scene again and again, and each time he saw the anger scribbled all over her features. She'd looked different to him, as though someone had moved her nose just a little to the side, had pushed her eyes closer together. *This is what anger does to a face.*

Now this marriage would have to be rendered nonexistent. Mistakes were to be denied, swept under the rug. Get rid of the old life, start the new one.

He dialed Lara. Voice mail. He walked back to his office.

Caprice met him in the hallway. "Line one, Mr. Power. Penn Stewart. He say your father say to call you. He say it's urgent." Jackson walked over, punched the line, and jammed the receiver to his ear.

"Your father says you're filing for divorce. True?" One could hold a lit cigarette to the palm of Penn's hand and the tenor of his voice would not alter.

"True," Jacks said.

"Start making a list of assets," Penn said. "At the top of the list, put the number 740. At the bottom of the list, put the number 740. Your father will never forgive you if you lose that apartment. More importantly, he will never forgive *me* if you lose it. We're meeting today."

"I'm busy," Jackson said. He sat straighter, like a dog who hears the report of the shotgun behind him, eagerly checking the sky for falling birds.

Falling birds. Like his marriage.

"Two o'clock," Penn said.

"I have a two o'clock," Jackson said.

"So do I," Penn said. "So does everyone in the city. So, I'm guessing, does your wife. With her attorney."

"I'll see you at two," Jackson said.

"Good man," Penn replied.

12

PLAYING THE BOARD

CYNTHIA DASHED up the stairs to Brooke Astor Hall. She'd missed a full day of meetings, meetings that COULD NOT TAKE PLACE WITHOUT HER PRESENCE. Her first official day running the board, and she'd blown it off. She hadn't answered her phone, had ignored it with vigor, until it had finally, pathetically, issued its last mechanical cry before the battery drained.

Margot Ashford, premiere ballet mistress of the NYBT, greeted her in the rehearsal hall like the old friend she was. "Well, Princess Grace, nice of you to show up. Where the hell have you been?"

And then she coughed. Margot's voice sounded like one part Dame Judi Dench, two parts Harvey Fierstein.

"Are you feeling okay?" Cynthia asked. She watched as the dancers were put through their steps.

"Am I okay? Why wouldn't I be okay?" *Cough.* "Are *you* okay? That's what the board wanted to know," Margot said. "You could have saved me from the truffle pigs. Once again, they know nothing."

Cynthia checked her watch.

"I'm sorry. I've been busy getting divorced."

"Yes. I saw the photograph. Photographs, I should say. *Très* French, *oui?*" More coughing. Margot and Cynthia had roomed and danced together when they arrived in New York—both from small towns, though Margot's was north of London. As baby ballerinas, they'd sized each other up and hated each other immediately. Margot was muscular and dark, her black hair cropped short (shocking for a ballerina) with thick bangs. She was the Patti Smith of classical ballet. Cynthia, with her perfect dancer's profile, her signature mane, her unparalleled extension, was Snow White to her Evil Queen. Margot's self-destructiveness was her calling card, smoking cocaine and screwing everything, including the married, bisexual head of the NYBT. She was, by far, the most promising ballerina in the company; there was no more exciting dancer than Margot, no one with more explosive raw talent.

And no one who would waste more of that talent.

When Margot's latest "beau" beat the hell out of her and left her face a purple, swollen mess, Cynthia covered for her and nursed Margot back to health. There'd never been two stronger rivals or two closer friends.

"Was it the big topic of conversation?" Cynthia asked.

"Of course. I told them to shut the fuck up."

"In the most polite way possible."

"Bruce's got his nut hairs in a knot over the idea of you taking over. I told him to go wax his sphincter." Bruce Harold Raymond was the artistic director of the NYBT.

"So he's Team Fred."

"He's snug as a homo bug in the big man's pocket, Princess, of course he's Team Fred." Margot did not fuck around with niceties.

"Where is he?" Cynthia looked around nervously.

"Upstairs. In his office. Relax. I'm sure he's busy staring in a mirror."

"The rest of the board?" Cynthia inquired, bracing herself.

"You're good. You've got Bartlet, Reynolds, Kitty, Morris, of course, Margaret Lord Foster . . . who else? Jasper. You have a clear majority." She paused. "It's exciting."

"Then why do I feel like throwing up? And I don't mean like the fun throwing up. Two things I've avoided for years: running the board and getting a divorce. Now I have to do both? I'm going to resign before I have a nervous breakdown."

Margot waited.

"And to this, you reply . . . ?" Cynthia asked.

"Cynthia. Princess. If you don't embrace this position, you are a gutless cipher."

"Thank you," Cynthia said.

"You've been kept under glass long enough. When are you going to take Cynthia seriously? When are you going to grow up?"

"What's my timetable?" Cynthia asked.

"That's all I'll say on the matter. I don't like being nice. It doesn't agree with my stomach."

"That was *nice*?"

As they spoke, the line was put through their paces onstage. Margot grimaced at them, then turned to Cynthia.

"I'll bring over some Chinese tonight. I'm famished. Along with the bronchitis, I had the flu. Haven't eaten in three days. I've never looked better. Look at these hip bones. You could cut paper with them."

"I need some alone time tonight," Cynthia said.

"Alone time? Fine. I'm calling Rafael. Someone's got to bear witness to my wasting away."

"Rafael?" Cynthia gestured toward the stage. "He's nineteen!"

"He's on a steep learning curve." Margot smiled. "Can I just say one more thing about divorce?"

"Can I stop you?"

"Divorce is the new Retirement Plan."

"Love you," Cynthia said, shaking her head.

"Beyond," Margot replied.

13

THE KING'S PAWN

That drink is not going to mix itself," the man in the suit said. They all wore suits, of course. This was Midtown.

Adrian West was supposed to be simply mixing a drink. Supposed to be, but what he was actually doing was far more interesting than measuring the exact one-third/two-thirds ratio of amber liquid to clear. Any monkey could mix a drink. But could a monkey scrutinize the process? Could a monkey watch himself mix the drink, examine how his hands moved, how the mind directed the mouth to form words: "I'll add it to the tab, you like some nuts, can I get you anything else, think you've had enough, sir?"

Could a monkey ponder the history of that liquor? Where did the corn that made up 51 percent of the bourbon grow? The Blue Mountains of Kentucky? A lord's bog in Scotland? How many hands did the bottle pass through on the way to its home behind this antique bar? How much pain, sorrow, happiness, tragedy had that bottle touched?

Welcome to Method Bartending.

"Can I see the bottle?"

Adrian shrugged, handed it over. Let the guy play the Big Man.

"That's not the year."

Adrian looked up, his six-foot-two ex-track-star physique cutting a silhouette on tricky Old King Cole himself in the bar's mural.

Like hell it's not the year. Adrian smiled. A smile, happy. A smile, a celebration. A smile, warmth. This smile—steel and granite and diamonds and titanium.

The man tried the drink. "It's good," he said.

Adrian dropped the smile. Fuckin' amateurs. Think they're experts in all things because they're king of one—money. Big deal. Money. Great men did not care about money; great men cared about ideas. Adrian West, ex–juvenile delinquent and South Jersey boy, was about to have his shot at greatness. His first play, *Jersey Hearts,* was about to debut. Off-Off-Off-Broadway, sure, but still, Adrian would prove he was no monkey. And his girlfriend, the luscious Miss Tracy Bing, was playing the lead. Adrian's long days and nights of mixing drinks and debating years on bottles, they were fucking numbered.

"If it isn't the starving artist," the voice said. Unmistakable. *And that's a fact.*

The crowd drew back and watched with furtive eyes as he slid onto his stool. The man pretended not to notice the attention. The familiar crooked smile gave him away.

"If it isn't Mr. Famous," Adrian said.

"Fuck you and get my bottle," Jackson said, as he always had since Adrian had made the mistake of pouring the house Scotch for him once, during his first week on the job.

Adrian reached down for the special bottle they kept far away from sharp eyes and questions. The 1937 Glenfiddich, property of Mr. Jackson Power.

Adrian set the bottle up on the bar in front of Power, who always managed to clear an area on the right-hand side, second stool in.

From that stool, one could see, reflected in the mirror hanging behind the bar, the faces of every customer; the round tables in the darkened corners; everything and everyone in the bar.

And more important, everyone could see you.

"How goes the raping and pillaging?" Adrian asked. Same question, every time. Jackson came to the bar at least once a week, always with an eye toward Adrian. Although twenty years apart, they had an understanding. If either of them had been gay, they probably would have fucked already.

"How goes the fag business?" Jacks countered.

"I believe it's called 'theater,'" Adrian said. "You know, like one of those quaint turn-of-the-century halls you keep tearing down and turning into stacks of shiny boxes."

"You'll always be poor, kid," Jacks said.

"Nothing wrong with being poor," Adrian said. "Poor but honest."

Jackson snorted. "A regular Abe Lincoln, that's what you are."

"Let's hope I don't get shot during my first production."

Jackson pushed that drink back fast, Adrian noticed. His hand tightened on the bottle to pour another. But then he stopped himself. *Give it a beat, don't want Jacks to think his alcohol intake is being monitored.*

Adrian closed his eyes. Twelve hours on his feet, wearing the shoes his girlfriend had bought him as a good-luck gift. Black leather lace-ups that radiated a rich man's gleam even in the dark of the hotel bar. He'd kept wearing the Italian instruments of torture because Miss Tracy Bing had chosen them for him. And he wanted nothing more in the world but to keep Miss Tracy Bing happy.

Another customer walked in. She was in her forties, alone, diamond ring now on the right hand, skittish eyes. She would order a cosmopolitan because somehow it made her feel younger. Lighter. Adrian sorely wanted to mix her a Manhattan.

"Cosmopolitan, please," she said. She unwound the scarf from her neck and ventured to look around. She was meeting someone she didn't know.

Adrian could feel Jackson's eyes on him. He made his way back to him.

"When's the play open?" Jackson asked.

"Next week," Adrian said. "I've got three more nights here, then I'm done. You'll have to pick on some other sucker."

"Least I won't have to tip him like a high-priced hooker," Jackson said.

Adrian laughed. Like Jackson Power would ever need to be attended to by a hooker. "You'll be the first person I thank at the Tonys," Adrian said.

"You picked a tough road, pal," Jackson said. "Haven't you heard? Art died in 1983. Nobody cares about artists, not even the artists themselves."

It was their favorite subject: Art vs. Commerce.

"But commerce lives on, in all its soul-sucking glory," Adrian said.

"Commerce is necessity, kid," Jackson said. "Commerce is food, clothes, shelter. Commerce is life itself. Commerce, barkeep, is noble."

Adrian's laugh barreled out, then stopped short when he saw the expression on Jackson's face.

"When are you getting married?" Jackson suddenly asked.

"Soon, I hope," Adrian said, surprising even himself. "If she'll have me."

He'd never said those words out loud. But there they were, true as the night, as the murmuring crowd, as the bottle in his hand. Was there a vision more delicious than Miss Tracy Bing? Skin like white chocolate. Black licorice hair. The perfectly formed triangle of soft pinks and cream. He would lay his head between her legs for hours, he would sleep there, he would awaken in her softness in the morning. And her smell . . . roses were too strong, vanilla too sweet. Her scent was simply a reason to live.

"Women. Are. A fucking mystery," Jackson groused. "I'm not telling you anything 'new.' " He scraped the air with his blunt fingertips. "What I'm saying, it's not profound. Men are stupid. And women, unknowable." He winked at his reflection, behind Adrian. "Face it," Jacks lumbered on, "you marry a stranger in white lace." His thick yet usually nimble fingers, smooth and manicured, were betraying him as the Scotch tumbler trembled in his grip.

"And that's a fact."

Adrian detected something in Jackson he hadn't seen before—defeat? Weariness? He'd never pried into Jackson's personal life; why would he need to when his every move was all over the papers? The guy couldn't take a shit without alarms going off. Adrian poured him another drink.

"It's going to be all right, my man," Adrian said.

"Fuck it," Jackson said. "To your opening." He raised his glass and nodded toward Adrian to grab one for himself. Adrian poured himself two fingers of Scotch that cost more than a used Lexus and met Jackson's glass with his own.

"To Art," Adrian said. They drank their Scotches silently.

"Damn," Adrian said. He was bitch-slapped by how good the Glenfiddich felt. Like being seduced by a beautiful woman throwing bundles of hundred-dollar bills at his feet.

"Commerce bought that, my friend," Jackson said. He was smiling again.

14

CRITICAL POSITION

Twenty minutes later Jackson and Lara were at the room at the Plaza, fucking. The Plaza, that was novelty. The fucking part; this wasn't unusual. She was on top. This wasn't unusual, either. She'd entered him—no, no, that's not right, he thought, *what is wrong with you?*

He'd entered her.

She was going to kill him.

Sound. Panting. Short staccato breaths, an aggressive aria, free of cumbersome notes. *We never play music,* he thought. *Maybe we should play a little music. Did she know Chet Baker? Billie Holiday? Or would he have to play Aerosmith?*

Lara's legs were bent at the knee; her thighs clutched his sides, squeezing out his breath. His hands held on to those thighs, slick with her moisture, smooth and strong. She gripped his shoulders, hurling herself forward and back, and then she screamed, her head whipping side to side, her hair flying, fanning the room, and there was no time to think about all the chest hairs she was pulling out, the nails that were burrowing into his skin, but the pain made this moment even more exciting.

He held her, his hands assisting her. *Can I get you anything? Will you be requiring anything else this evening?* How many orgasms could a woman have? This must be her third, her fourth—he would hold on. It was his pride, of course it was his pride. He wanted her to come again. He wanted her to need him as much as he needed her. Who can make you come the most? That soap actor you used to date? The hockey player? The huge black sports reporter? Who?

Me, I make you come the most, don't I, honey?

Don't I?

She screamed, the final one. Raging and wild, the note of it ribboned through the air and flew around the room. He thought of Chinese acrobats doing floor exercises, strips of red satin streaking the room with color.

Then her laughter. He felt her fold into him, her cheek, her chin, breasts, torso. He could feel her shuddering, as though her body had been suffocating, suppressing this laugh just for this moment when it could roll out from way deep inside until it was freed, dancing in a room that was once silent and waiting.

Lara rolled off him at last and Jackson leaned forward, his elbows on his knees. His dick hung to the side, limp, a little wary, dark brown in this light, a baby wallaby tucked into his mother's pouch, blind and hairless.

He thought of that Viagra commercial, idiots playing banjos and singing about hard-ons. *Viva Viagra. Cheers, Cialis!*

He knew his cock's days were numbered. Look at it. It had been grabbed, pulled, squeezed, pinched, licked, sucked, mounted, bent, drained, drained again, curled, singed, peeled, gorged, kissed, tickled, and detonated.

Don't you see, his dick said to him. *She's going to kill you. I'm the weapon she'll use against you. You and I could be happy with lesser things. We don't need so much. We could retire with our memories, you and I. Remember, Jacks, remember that Bulgarian model, halfway through dinner at Babbo she opened your zipper with her foot? Her foot! She had to finish us off in the bathroom, just as Charlie Rose was walking in. Did she care? No!*

Jacks wasn't listening to his guilty appendage. You can't ask a man in love to listen to Reason, even if Reason is coming from a foremost part of your body. Lara had stopped him cold. He didn't even know he loved her until it was too late. It had been so long since he'd been in love that he hadn't recognized the signs.

Jacks met Lara at a major function for Alzheimer's. Tuxes and feathers, smiles and bullshit (bread and circuses!). They were seated at the same table, across from each other. He'd tried to catch Lara's eye—he knew who she was—and even if he hadn't known, she would have stood out in this or any crowd. Jackson had watched her walk to the table, shoulders flung back, long strides. Like she was walking onto Centre Court at Wimbledon. He'd been in the midst of an affair with a thing wispy and boring and teeth-gnashingly beautiful. He was trying to get out of it after a month. Jacks's affairs were getting shorter and shorter; his attention span for limp, shiny objects was diminishing.

Lara wouldn't look at him. She seemed to find the mousy magazine publisher and his hausfrau wife more fascinating than a live sex show.

Jackson stopped her as she was leaving. Stood and introduced himself, essentially blocking her exit. (*Stomach in, check, palms dry, check, bedroom eyes, the promise of a great fuck in the Power grin, check and check.*)

"Jacks Power."

"Yes. I know."

"If you know, why didn't you acknowledge me? I've been staring at you all night."

Pause. Lara tilted her head, the hint of a smile.

"Because I know," she said, then left.

He called her at work the next day. The model with a terminal case of ennui a mere memory now.

She would not go out with him.

"You're married."

"Ish. Married-ish. Not happily. She's not happy, either—you'd be doing both of us a favor."

"Let's call your wife and see how she feels," Lara said.

That was the end of the first phone call. Jacks was hooked. He arranged to "run into" her again. On the street (difficult to manage; he'd had to wait forever at the curb), at the gym; he'd never gone to a gym outside his home. Jacks Power had become a stalker.

Finally, Jacks waited at a neighborhood watering hole near her Upper West Side apartment. He stood at the bar facing the entrance. She walked in with a heavyset girl, arm in arm, the thick scarf around her neck reminding him of a younger Cynthia. She saw him immediately, and broke off from her girlfriend to address him.

"You're trouble," she'd said. "I don't need any more."

"Have another," he'd said, signaling the bartender for one more watered-down waste of liquid. "Tell me all about your life. I want to hear everything. Start at the beginning."

She looked into his eyes; he didn't waver. There was an opening there, right there, in her gaze; Jacks was wearing her down. He lowered his voice.

"Lara, I want to hear what your mother ate when she was pregnant with you. I want to hear what you wore on the first day of kindergarten. I want to hear about your first kiss. The boy who broke your heart in junior high."

She looked away.

He had her.

Oh, Jacks had a rap. He was good when he wanted to be. But this time, he really did want to know. And that's how he knew he loved her. Even before the illicit first kiss. And even before he vowed to beat the shit out of the boy who broke her heart in junior high.

Back in the dimmed light of the hotel bedroom, Jackson noticed his gut, caught in the triangle of his arms. He could stick his forefinger into his belly button and lose half of it. When had this happened?

Note to self: suck in the gut when you're on top.

Lara reached over and turned his face toward hers.

"It'll never last," she said.

"Why do you say that?" He was suddenly so hurt that he found himself blinking back tears he had no right to spill. Jesus, second time tonight. What was going on? He was the Cheater, after all, the Black Hat.

"I'm not a settler," she said. "You know I've never been with one man for longer than a year."

"A settler," he repeated. Jacks stroked her hair, soothing the Beast. He flattened his breath, counting in, one-two-three-four, out, four-three-two-one. He would be everything that was calming. Soft rain, light breeze, the scent of baby powder. He would be her prescription Xanax.

Lara waved her arm to indicate the anonymous room. "And how much longer do we have to sneak into hotel rooms?"

"What choice do we have right now, if we want to be together? We can't exactly show up at Le Cirque at eight o'clock on a Friday night. The press would be a nightmare. And they already have my spare apartments staked out, you know that."

"You don't seem to understand what I'm risking."

"Then tell me," Jacks Xanax replied.

"My job, for one. My reputation. That's two."

"You don't like your job."

"Jackson, I have to keep it in order to move on to the next phase of my life—"

"I can take care of you."

"I can take care of myself."

Oh, thought Jacks, *this is where the conversation bogs down. Of course*

Lara could take care of herself. She had all of her life. But why should she, when Jacks could provide everything any woman could ever want? But he wouldn't ask her that. He wanted to live through the night.

"I don't even understand how you talked me into this affair," she sighed. "I don't want to be this person."

"Blame my pure animal magnetism. You couldn't help yourself."

"Jackson. This isn't going to work."

Heartbeat rapid: pulse 124.

"I'm scared of marriage."

Blood pressure: 130/110. "Uh-huh."

"I'm selfish."

Pupils dilated.

"I will hurt you," she whispered. This was no purred threat. This had a sound like the sharp report of a piece of silverware dropped in a fancy French restaurant. The sound of arrows finding their target deep in his heart. He thought of the tapestry in his father's office. The wild boar, hanging upside down.

His fingers curled around the nape of her neck, fingertips circling her taut muscles, searching for clues to unwind her thoughts . . .

"I'm a big boy," he finally said.

Lara turned to face him. Their noses touching, breathing in each other's breath.

"I have to go," she said softly. "I have to get some sleep."

"Sleep here, I won't bother you. I won't even look at you. I'll sit in the chair while you sleep."

She touched his cheek.

"Am I the only one who knows how sweet you are?" she said. She turned and rolled out of bed. He watched as she got dressed, smoothed her hair back, and threw him a kiss as she walked out the door.

"I'm a big boy," he repeated to himself.

15

A RARE ENGAGEMENT

A FLOWER CAME for you, ma'am."

"A flower?" Cynthia asked, as she followed the maid into the sitting room. There on the maple side table was an orchid with snow-white tails, covered with tiny pink dots. Cynthia stared, as though a magically beautiful woman had just floated in.

"There's a card," said the maid, gingerly handing Cynthia the tiny white envelope. (Cynthia surmised that word was out among the servants; the master and mistress of the house were splitting up.)

Perhaps Jacks was having second thoughts. What a lovely and surprising way to express it—with a single, rare orchid.

Cynthia ripped open the envelope.

"To a worthy and beguiling opponent," the card read. "Fred."

Cynthia shook her head. *How stupid am I?* she thought.

Cynthia's gaze swept across the room, buffeted by chintz and English antiques (the space would have fit nicely in the Cotswolds) to one of the most celebrated views in the city. Gray was descending over the steeples of St. James Church, embracing the treetops of Central Park; God had gently tossed a cashmere blanket over Manhattan.

The vision wasn't enough to distract Cynthia from the sadness that was creeping over her, the bloom of unease coursing through her body. Cynthia felt like a crystal glass, slowly being filled with grief. She backed her way onto her sofa, the shiny silk fabric so tight across the cushion that there was no give, no way to settle in. Every piece of furniture had been selected for the same reason—for show. There was no comfort to be found here. But oh my, the couch was beautiful. Expensive and beautiful and hard. *Not unlike its owner,* Cynthia thought; *no wonder Vivienne had insisted on moving out the moment she turned eighteen.*

No wonder Cynthia was getting divorced.

The other morning with her daughter had been a revelation. Vivi urged her girlfriend to a quick departure—"I think I'll just hang out with my mom," Vivi had said, then had planted a bold kiss on the girlfriend, who cast a feral eye toward Cynthia as she strode out the door.

Where had these young women birthed the self-confidence to open a door naked? Or to kiss your female lover in front of your mother? Cynthia didn't trust confidence in women. Vivienne was born with it; Cynthia had only tasted it—but that was long ago. *Had she ever opened a door naked?* A smile snuck onto Cynthia's face before she could reach up and snuff it out like a cigarette beneath her cruel alligator pumps. There was that one time, she thought. She'd been dating Jackson for a few weeks. Her roommates were gone for the entire weekend. She'd buzzed Jackson in, slipped off her tights and T-shirt, and waited for him at the door with only her leg warmers on.

Vivienne had worked to resuscitate Cynthia from the utter deflation that she had worn like a shroud since seeing the *Post* photograph. Goldie had given her a second transfusion. But when alone, truly alone, the reality of her life hit her with full force.

Cynthia bent forward, her arms forming a shield around her body, and cried and wondered when her tears would dry up. Every night she would cry. *How long before she would have relief?*

Still, there was a small, shimmering part of her that felt a brush of satisfaction: *She, Cynthia, was still capable of feeling loss.*

She thought she'd stopped being a feeling person when the unthinkable happened. She'd thought she'd gathered up every drop of the Feeling Cynthia like some unlovely fluid that had spilled and not yet soaked into the carpet.

Chase had been five months old. Weeks after his first smile. Days after he'd laughed and been surprised and delighted at the sound of his laughter and so he laughed more. He was sleeping through the night. Cynthia was still breast-feeding, but starting to feel like a human being again, not just a flesh-covered pump.

Imagine: Cynthia hadn't wanted Chase. She hadn't wanted another child. She'd held out hope that she would dance again. Her body had snapped back, more taut than before Vivienne was born. Was it possible? Was her body not ready to give up the dream? Cynthia felt human only when she danced.

She lived for the feeling of space under her body, of lift, her legs impossibly scissoring the air; she didn't even understand how she arrived there, and when she tried to understand, the power left. It's an addictive relationship, bordering on toxic. Cynthia secretly liked the feeling of a sprained ankle, of bloodied toes. Injury is a friend, injury meant that Cynthia had performed, had known what it is to feel alive, had done that one thing she was put on this earth for. This is love, and need, and desire, this is the very meaning of life. Cynthia had no control over it.

Vivi was barely a year old when Cynthia returned to the academy. Every spare thought, every drop of energy, every moment not with the baby was spent on the notion that had started out shapeless and unfocused and became sharper and sharper until it appeared, bold, like words on a marquee: Cynthia would dance again.

Her period stopped. Big deal. Dancers lose their periods all the time. No body fat, no period. Besides, she was getting over a pregnancy, she had just stopped breast-feeding. Hormones were in flux. All normal stuff.

Dizziness. Lack of nutrition will do that. Having a young baby will do that. Cynthia would eat a little more at breakfast. Cut down on the Gitanes she'd started sneaking again.

Nausea. Cynthia's stomach had never been very strong. Perhaps cut the caffeine (*yeah, right*).

Weeks went by; weeks filled with denial.

One afternoon, Cynthia found herself in a room filled with bright light, like an interrogation. White walls, white ceiling, white blinds, white blanketing her shoulders as though she were caught in a snowstorm wearing only a paper robe. Cynthia's feet swinging back and forth under the cold, padded fake leather examination table. That lilac-like color that doesn't touch nature. *How,* she thought, *is it possible to make lilac an ugly color?* Cynthia's bottom sticking to the thin paper. She could feel her sit bones, the slick of sweat and lubricant between her legs from the doctor's exam. Cynthia was both shocked and not in the least surprised at the news. She would cling to her dignity as though her world were an ocean and she were clutching driftwood.

"I'm sorry, doctor, but you'll have to fix this," Cynthia said.

"What?" the doctor asked. But it wasn't a question. It was a judgment. Cynthia wasn't surprised. She knew how awful the words sounded to anyone who didn't live in her body, this finely calibrated instrument set aside to rust. Her final leap. Her last entrechat.

"Nine, ten weeks. You can still do it," she said.

"If I'm to understand you—"

"I think you understand me, doctor," she said. Even she was surprised at the tone of her voice. Cold, atonal. *Atone,* she thought. *Atone for your sins.*

"Perhaps we should call your husband." The doctor, a white-haired veteran, used his best soothing voice of reason, to be hauled out in case of emergency. Cynthia imagined she couldn't be the only crisis that afternoon in this Upper East Side sanctuary. More spa than medical office, the space had recently been featured in *Vogue*. The nurses and doctors there could cater to venereal warts, herpes, whatever your dear husband brought home to you that didn't come wrapped in Hermès orange or Tiffany blue, but they wouldn't take care of something as ugly as a rich, spoiled woman's desire to abort her fetus.

"I'm not aware that I'd have to get permission from my husband," Cynthia said, "and furthermore, you are n-*not* allowed to share this information with him—" She could hear her heart punctuating her words; she hated that she'd stuttered. Did the doctor know how scared she was? How much she needed a kind gesture right now? A hug? A hand on her quaking shoulder?

Tell me, she thought. *Tell me how the pills you gave me didn't work. This is your fault, doctor,* Cynthia was thinking. *You keep the baby.*

"I won't do it," the doctor said simply. He walked out. Rustling coat, the snap of the pen, righteous steps muffled by expensive carpeting.

How dare you, she thought. *How dare I.*

Cynthia had sat there, still. A trickle of sweat lingered then wandered down her spine. Her foot had ceased its swinging. She could see her knee, pink and bony, a thin crooked line on the outside, as though drawn by a child that morning. Her fingertips barely touching, hands cupped to the sky. The back of her simple wedding ring. The sound of white noise, of water rushing. Her blood being pumped through this body, through two bodies. And she knew, this was the last of her dream. It died here, in this room. She would not dance again.

Cynthia didn't remember getting dressed, or walking past the reception desk, or the faces in the waiting room.

She'd been in bed when her husband got home.

"You're not killing our baby," he said. Then he shut the door behind him.

• • •

CYNTHIA snapped back to the present. She walked over to the orchid and picked it up.

"Esme!" she called. "Esme!"

The maid came scurrying.

"Yes, ma'am?"

"Throw this out," Cynthia said, holding the orchid away from her body, as though it smelled like week-old Chinese leftovers.

"Throw out the flower, ma'am?" Esme asked, as she took it. "It's very beautiful, ma'am."

Cynthia put her hands on her hips and assessed the orchid, clutched to Esme's ample chest.

The damn thing was breathtaking.

"Yes, it is, but it's also a threat. Maybe I should send it back. With a note: *I don't negotiate with terrorists.*"

"If you send it back, ma'am," Esme said, "then it shows you care. If I may say so."

"Fine," Cynthia said, "I think you're right. I'll keep it. But—I won't send a thank you note."

"That'll show him, ma'am," Esme said. She placed the orchid back on the side table.

ONE BOTTLE of '82 Château Margaux later, Cynthia held on to the wall as she made her way to the master bedroom. She balanced herself in the doorway and looked around the room, focusing on artworks Jackson had collected during their marriage. Famous names and familiar subjects, all. *Just like Papa.*

Cynthia flashed on her long-forgotten wish list of artists and photographers. Kahlo, Lempicka, perhaps an iconic shot by Lee Miller. Jackson had overruled her suggestions. He'd had his reasons; she couldn't for the life of her remember why she'd acquiesced.

Is it possible for a woman to sleepwalk through decades?

Still fully dressed, she slid between the sheets on the colonial bed and put her hand over the spot that was empty and would remain so, for now. *Or forever?* How long? She imagined Jackson, sleeping in the guest wing. *Or was he at his girlfriend's apartment?*

Sometimes Cynthia swore she could hear him, his snoring, the way he cleared his throat in the morning, the particular way he paced the bathroom floor, grumbling, when he was agitated. Various bumps in the night she hadn't noticed when he was in bed with her. (*Was it the same with all new divorcées? With all recent widows?*) Sometimes, she thought she smelled Jackson—his soapy scent left behind in the parlor; his cologne adrift in the elevator.

It was as though she and Jackson were playing Chutes and Ladders, 740 Park Edition.

Cynthia wondered if Jackson ever thought about the baby. Did he ever wonder what would have happened to them if Chase had lived? If he hadn't fallen asleep and stayed, forever, asleep? They'd managed to stay together, they'd managed that much, even while the fabric of their relationship unraveled. Jacks filled the void left by Chase with other women. Cynthia filled the void by leaving it empty. The void became her.

She stared up at the ceiling and conjured up the image of Chase's smiling face. Chase, who had taken her with him.

The baby had been her favorite.

You lived, Cynthia suddenly thought. *You survived. You can survive anything.*

Her tears stopped, her eyes drying almost instantly.

"Come get me, Fred," Cynthia heard herself say, in the darkness. "Come get me, Jackson. I can take it. I'm ready for you."

16

HEAVY HANGS THE HEAD . . .

THE GUEST wing. Well. Jacks put down his briefcase, sat on the bed, and closed his eyes. How long had it been since he'd even seen the guest wing—and here he was, living in it. He opened his eyes. The décor was just as expensive, if not as personal as the main part of the house. There were fewer happy silver-framed photographs of family Christmases in Gstaad, Easters in Jamaica, a decade-ago summer spent in the South of France.

Not that he'd been to any of those vacation spots for more than three, four days. Hadn't he always left early? There'd been a business emergency. And another. And another.

On the far wall was a large painting, a specter of something that once lived. The piece was one of his, set in a room rarely used. His focus narrowed.

Well. For obvious reasons; it wasn't very good.

He lay back, fully clothed, his body spent.

And fell asleep.

There was the baby. But Chase was walking, which he'd never had a chance to in his short life. There he was, unsure of his baby steps but moving, moving forward and sideways at the same time.

Jackson urging him on. *Come to Daddy. But don't fall. Don't hurt yourself. Careful. ¡Cuídate!,* he heard the Dominican nanny say. The baby's arms outstretched, little sausage arms, like balloons with rubber bands at the elbow, at the wrist, around each tiny joint of each tiny finger, the baby reaching for him.

Jackson woke up, his face slick. His cool sheet wet with nerves. He wiped his hand across his forehead. His sweat smelled like anxiety and alcohol. And Lara. His tongue felt like it was coated with fine sand. *Where was he?*

He pushed himself up to a sitting position, pulled his legs over the side of the bed, and planted his feet. He felt grounded again. But for how long? What was coming?

He turned on the lamp. He was still fully dressed. Were his shoes still on? Yes. Unbelievable.

His painting, his past, looming over him, half lit.

The baby. His baby boy. The boy who flew away before he ever took a step. Why this dream and why now? The last hours were finding their way back to his consciousness, clawing over the dark expanse of short-term memory. He could remember things from years ago so well, exact colors, measurements, sounds, pixelated, high-definition memories—but an hour ago, two hours—those were murky and torpid, like swimming underwater in a canal.

He pictured Cynthia at the opposite end of the apartment, lying alone in their bed. The vision made him sad, imbued his guilt with shape, a physical presence—a cube lodged in his throat.

Two hours earlier he'd lain in bed next to the girl who said yes but maybe no, and now he was thinking of the girl who said yes but maybe no all those years ago . . .

The mid-eighties, Jacks remembered. When the East Village resembled postwar Berlin; he'd loved it.

There was a gallery owner, dressed in the uniform of the trade: black boots, severely tailored sheath, dark tresses draped over the shoulders like a cape. Like all galleristas, she was nocturnal. They were like bats, hanging in artists' caves, sniffing blood, life force, enticing these boys, these comers, a third of whom would be dead by the end of the decade. The galleristas were very thin, but not frail; they dined on espresso and smoke was oxygen to them, and they could supply you with heroin and were only too happy to suck your dick while you shot up, if that's what would get you through your next painting, next showing, get them on the cover of *Artforum,* get you to hand over 80 percent of the sale price. They supplied you with anything you needed: rent money, drug money, diaper money, young pussy, young boys.

Jacks wanted to please the vampire as much as he wanted his next breath. He was in his mid-twenties and feeling the weight of his age, already. He was like a model who was watching the new Cindys, the Christies, the Naomis take to the runway; one bold step and they took flight.

There were rumblings. Names wiggled under doorways from rooms where people were too high to be coherent, yet these names formed clear and were suddenly everywhere. Jackson yearned to be one of them.

There was something called Graffiti Art. An entire brick wall, a burned-out building. Jacks had stared in wonder, unnerved. He stared as though a beautiful woman had just walked up to him on the street, slapped him, and moved on. Slashes of black, of white, of red. Words and skulls. Demons and Angels. It was political exposé. It was art. It was not art at all.

Jacks had been at this game for a few years; he'd been to art school. He was smart and had some talent and something to prove, but so did they all. So did they all.

Cynthia was pregnant. He hadn't yet proposed.

Jacks's first thought: get rid of it. There was too much pressure. He hadn't sold anything. He couldn't go back and he couldn't move forward.

Then he became determined. The baby would be a good omen. They would keep the baby, and his art would sell.

Cynthia hadn't come to a decision yet. She was, after all, a ballerina, ethereal, as though she should be flying around their loft, flitting over the paint cans, canvases, torn white sheets, stacks of toe shoes ragged with wear.

A ballerina couldn't have a baby.

Jacks had completed a new series. He'd pushed himself, taken risks. For the baby. What was the thing no one else was doing? Rockwell twisted. Americana—and what was America? Baseball. He'd begged a few of the Great Ones to sit for him. The young, handsome Dominican. The retired, surly black hero. The manager, his feuding owner. He felt the series was good, good and different. But the talent of the other artists attacked him at night, in the dark, when Cynthia was sleeping next to him. He would wake up feeling dead from a hundred gorgeous cuts, each from a different hand.

In his head, he screamed at the competition when he saw the flashes of their brilliance. Why this color here? Why this subject matter? Broken dishes. Warhol revisited. Elementary figures. Child's play. Words on canvas. Revolutionary! Stagnant! Sometimes, he screamed because he didn't understand, and in his heart he felt he never would.

"You're brilliant," the gallery owner told him, stationed on her knees, looking up at him. Her eyes were dark behind her black-rimmed glasses. He could see the faint gray stripe down the middle of the part of her dark, glossy hair. *Skunk,* came the unbidden thought.

He hoped to God he could finish. What would she do if she had to suck him off much longer? He wished he were gay, like her other charges, her favorites. He doubted that they would have to endure this humiliation. A grown woman wearing the colors of her profession, black and more black, on her knees, her one hand manically teasing his balls, her violent red mouth full of him. He heard her choking noises and this gave him satisfaction. Let her choke on it.

And then, comforting epiphany: he was doing this for Cynthia, he thought. For the baby, the baby he was sure would be a boy. He was doing this for his family's future. He had nothing else but this showing. Nothing else but these paintings. The gallerista wanted to celebrate her "discovery," though there'd already been an article in the *Times,* mentioning his art and his bohemian lifestyle, the way he'd "turned his back" on the family fortune, on his father. The anxiety of his life in black and white; he didn't want to be the trust fund baby who becomes a dilettante artist. He wanted only to be an artist.

He needed to sell something. There was no money. They were living on a ballerina's salary. Enough for food and his canvases. He'd have to find work soon, but he was trained to do nothing.

He came.

"Lick my pussy," the gallery owner said, her voice hoarse with desire, but also something else, something more intoxicating: power. She slipped off her fishnet stockings and wiped the sides of her mouth, tattered red with her signature lipstick. He would forever try to forbid Cynthia to wear red lipstick, unable to give a reason that made any sense.

He hiked up his pants and knelt before her, as if he were praying.

Jackson was so nervous before his art opening, he threw up over and over until he and the porcelain ring were old friends. Cynthia held his hair back from his face. She was succumbing to morning sickness. Soon they were taking turns—*you go first, no please, you*— until they were vomiting and laughing at the same time.

"We're going to be late," Cynthia said.

"You go," he said, "I'll stay here."

She talked him off the floor of the bathroom and into clean clothes; she pushed her fingers through his hair. She was a vision.

And so wan, she looked like something he could dip his finger into. The pregnancy was making her more beautiful.

The thought brought on a flash of anger.

They walked to the opening; it was three blocks away. The cold pushed them closer together.

The street was lit up from the gallery; noise made the light more intense. Chatter and bass. Jacks could feel the circus. "No journalists," he'd warned the gallery owner. "Let's slide into town, under cover of night. I only need to sell a few."

A few will tide me over. A few will save me, he thought. *Us.*

Suddenly, he dropped to his knee. Cynthia started to pull him up. "What's wrong? Are you still sick?" she asked.

"Marry me."

"What?" she asked.

"Marry me." He pulled on her. "Please marry me."

Even as he said it, even as he was begging her to marry him, he felt it was the last thing he should do. Somewhere inside he knew he would drag her down with him.

"You don't have to," she said.

"I won't go in there unless you say yes," he told her.

Cynthia's hand brushed his face; he kissed her cold fingers. She looked straight into his eyes, and it seemed like hours before she said yes.

The next day, there were headlines in a newspaper that his father's friend published. Jacks didn't read the article; he didn't need to. He knew what they'd said.

Not one painting sold. Not one.

The millionaire's son couldn't buy talent.

Jacks knew it wasn't true. He knew he had talent, but he also knew it didn't matter. Truth is not a solid, he thought. Truth is as malleable as clay. The lesson would stick with him, and serve him.

Two weeks later, Cynthia started bleeding. Her insurance premium had run out. There was no money for the doctor.

Jacks went to his father.

"I knew you'd be back," his father said. He didn't even bother looking up from his soup.

"If there were any other way—"

"You're in good company, Jackson," his father said, drowning him out. "Hitler was a failed artist, too."

Jacks didn't know it then, but he would never lift a paintbrush again.

The painting hanging before him reached out over the decades and the victories and the disappointments. The sorrowful, rheumy eyes, the tilted Yankees cap, the flaccid flesh of the old base runner. *Who would want this hanging in their dining room? What had he been thinking?* And the lines—oh, they were technically sound—deliberate and anxious, but the lack of sensuality hurt him. He'd never let go. The rule was: know technique cold, then let go.

First, Jacks thought, first his dream died, then his baby, then came the long, drawn-out death of his marriage. Oh, he and Cynthia had lived together as man and wife long after Chase was gone, but it had been over. He thought back to his first affair, the comely secretary. Such a cliché. Three months after the funeral. Lush body and wanting to please, and, oh, she had dark, hungry eyes—and he felt terrible, terrible—but the terribleness died down with each affair, until the girls became just another petty obligation—brush your teeth, run three miles on the treadmill, fuck that girl you met in the elevator.

Suddenly Jacks felt famished. What was the quickest route to the kitchen from the guest bedroom? Jacks tried to picture the blueprint of the triplex, flipped it around in his mind.

He'd have to bear left.

AFTER winding turns and dead ends and irritating discoveries of powder rooms and maids' rooms and side closets he didn't know existed, Jacks was finally facing the blank inside of the industrial-size refrigerator. The room was quiet as a stone, except for a symphony of beeps. The machines were awake, but hidden. He could hear them, muffled robots mocking him.

There were no leftovers, of course. No eating in the house? No leftovers. However, there was bread. And butter. Perhaps, God willing, he could find the toaster.

He opened a cabinet. The coffeemaker was on, dripping, beeping. What was it doing on at this hour?

Jacks suddenly sensed that he was not alone. He turned and saw Cynthia the Ninja watching him.

Neither spoke as they continued to be serenaded by electronic katydids.

"Are you hungry?" Cynthia finally asked.

"Yes," he said.

"What happened to room service at the Plaza?" she asked.

First strike. "Can we keep this civil?" Jacks asked.

"Absolutely," said Cynthia, "if you move out by morning, I'll even pack for you."

"So much for civil," Jacks said. "You're the one who should be moving out. I own 740. The family owns 740."

"And you're welcome to own it for as long as I live," Cynthia said. "And I prefer to live here. And my lawyers prefer that I live here. And so does the state of New York."

Poker face, Cynthia thought, *steady . . .*

"I don't want to get ugly right now," Jacks said plaintively, "I just want toast."

Jacks turned and opened another cabinet. No toaster.

Cynthia opened a cabinet. There was the toaster. She put two slices of bread in, pressed the lever down.

"Thanks," Jacks said, "I never could have found it."

Cynthia nodded. It had taken her twenty minutes to find the toaster a couple of sleepless nights ago. Now the thing was locked in her memory.

"So," he said, "what were you looking for?"

"A cigarette."

"You're smoking again," Jacks said.

Something flickered in Cynthia's eyes—*Shame? Epiphany? Disgust?*

Disgust.

"I never stopped," she said. She opened a drawer, grabbed a pack of Gitanes, and left.

"Smoking's bad for you," Jacks said as he watched her leave. From behind, Cynthia looked about sixteen. He wondered how old she would be before her ass dropped. Then he reminded himself that they were getting divorced and he hated her.

"Have another one!" he called out.

The toaster beeped.

17

MIDDLE GAME: WEEK ONE

LATE TUESDAY night: Cynthia and Jacks run into each other again in the kitchen. They exchange words. Jacks flips her off; Cynthia throws a cigarette pack at his back. They retreat to their wings.

Wednesday Morning: After calling her lawyer, Ricardo, Cynthia has a locksmith change the locks to the master suite.

Wednesday Afternoon: After calling his lawyer, Penn, Jacks changes the lock on the guest wing door.

Thursday Morning: Cynthia leaves a typewritten note for Jacks: Ten Rules for Houseguests. Number One Rule? *Stay out of host's way.*

Thursday Evening: Cynthia finds a small, wrapped gift at her bedside. She opens it. Inside the lovely package is a lovely vibrator. Cynthia throws it at the wall and screams.

Friday Morning: Cynthia hands Gordo a prescription for Viagra in Jacks's name. Jacks tries to bribe Esme to leave Cynthia and work for him.

Friday Night: Jacks blasts *The Ultimate Barry Manilow* in the guest wing, puts it on endless repeat, locks the door, and leaves for the night.

Saturday Night: Cynthia retaliates with REO Speedwagon's *Hi Infidelity* album. She spends a very comfortable night at the Carlyle.

18

MIDDLE GAME: WEEK TWO

MONDAY MORNING: Cynthia buys a Yorkshire terrier. Jacks is allergic to dogs and dog shit (which he promptly steps in).

Tuesday: Cynthia can't find her dog. Anywhere.

Wednesday Morning: Harry innocently thanks Cynthia for the dog. His wife loves it.

Wednesday Afternoon: Cynthia buys another dog. A Chihuahua.

Thursday: Jacks tries to get a restraining order against the dog. Cynthia tries to get a restraining order in the name of her dog against Jacks.

Friday Evening: Jacks hosts a cigar party with his Gargoyle pals. Cynthia calls the fire department.

Saturday Evening: Penn and Ricardo meet at their monthly book club and shake their heads.

PART TWO

TWO WEEKS LATER

19

THE PAWN IS ROOKED

ADRIAN HAD returned to bartending at the St. Regis and he was happy about it, so kindly fuck off.

"Nothing wrong with being a bartender. It's honest work," he'd said to Miss Tracy Bing.

Off-Off-Off-Broadway. A mile and a half and light years from the Great White Way to the cramped cobblestone street where the non-Equity theater sat next to the Venus Flytrap sex shop. Theaters were closing down. It was getting harder to find a venue, a sponsor, an option that will end your days of "What can I get f'you?"

Adrian thought he'd hit the fucking Lotto.

Adrian had been working on this play since he was sixteen. There was an English teacher, a grad student. Mr. C, they called him. Adrian couldn't remember his full name, a fucking shame, because he planned to thank Mr. C when he climbed up onstage to receive his first Tony.

Adrian remembered the day Mr. C entered the classroom. *Classroom?* More like a cage. Adrian and, like, thirty gang members, a low-level stew of Latin Kings, Bloods.

Adrian and his parents lived in a neighborhood that never knew "nice." They could have run out long ago, like everyone else, but his father refused. His dad, a mailman, wore steel-toed boots and carried mace to ward off drug dealers' slavering pit bulls. Dad would crawl home and put on a jazz album, not just Miles Davis or Chet Baker or the Bird, but the guy who played backup bass on an album produced in a tiny studio in Le Havre.

Dad was caught in some sort of time warp where the feeling was mellow, the sounds cool, the music a uniting force.

You been outside lately? Adrian would wonder.

Mr. C tried to teach the kids about metaphors: crack is a snake; the needle is Mommy's boyfriend; your eight-year-old self, a baby crawling through a minefield; melody is a pillow; rap an AK-47.

Adrian approached his teacher after class. "Jersey City is a giant mouth, with sharp teeth. A shark of a city . . ."

He stopped, embarrassed. What if Mr. C thought he was a fag or something? What if Mr. C tried to touch him? Adrian grabbed his backpack, he was outta there.

"You're very visual, Adrian," Mr. C called out. Adrian stopped; he wasn't going anywhere after that compliment had been lobbed over the firewall. Mr. C's simple words wrapped themselves around Adrian's shoulders and held him there.

"I like what I've read of your work. You've got an ear, you can tell a story. So tell me," his teacher said, "what are you going to write next, Adrian?"

Did this man see Adrian?

Adrian skipped track practice and started writing and didn't stop: on paper bags, napkins, forearm, his palm, gum wrappers. Sometimes even a piece of paper. Mr. C gave him stuff to read. Mamet, Shepard, McDonagh, and Parks.

Adrian got it in his mind that he had a play in him.

Ten years later, Adrian proved it. He had his play. He needed investors. There was a guy who came into the bar, Wall Street, so slick you could throw a glass of water on him and he'd be dry as toast in two seconds. The guy tipped big, talked bigger. Soon Wall Street was offering ten grand to set up Adrian's play. Adrian found the theater in the West Village. Ten grand would cover actors, props, lighting, promotion, rent—for one week.

Wall Street insisted they celebrate the deal over dinner at the Waverly with their significant others—Tracy Bing and Wall Street's debutante fiancée, a girl born with a crest on her ass. Ass Crest eyed Miss Tracy Bing like something you wouldn't get out of the car for if you ran it over in the street. Where Miss Tracy Bing was soft, Ass Crest was hard; where his girl had curves, Wall Street's chick was all sharp corners.

Adrian left the dinner grateful for his small (but soon to be expanding) life.

Jersey Hearts closed after forty-two minutes. Miss Tracy Bing was last seen turning on her dainty heel, arm in arm with Wall Street. Adrian remembered the moment as though he had taken a bath in it.

Adrian thought he'd heard his heart break. Not like an explosion, more like a kid tinkering with the high notes on a piano. Cracks appeared with a flurry of high Cs, spreading with the staccato stab of an A-sharp.

Fuck it. Forget it. Adrian picked up another glass, gave it a clean sweep, then whisked the rag over his shoulder. He checked the well, the guns, the bev naps, turned the top-shelf liquors so the labels were facing forward. *Dead Man Bartending,* he thought.

Nothing wrong with being a bartender.

He thought of Tracy Bing's ankles.

This week he would kill himself.

'Course it would take a while to write a note, since he swore he'd never put pen to paper again.

What was it that pale-faced blogger wrote? *"Stop him before he writes again."*

Why *the fuck* did everything have to be so complicated?

Adrian mixed a Gordon's with a twist for a 007 look-alike, then started in on polishing glasses. He tried not to think of Tracy's ankles.

"Hey, champ, you still here?" The voice rolled over his memories. "You turning that glass back into sand?" Jackson's baritone sauntered into Adrian's brain, pulled up a chair, and settled in. Adrian put down his rag.

"What happened to art?" Jacks asked.

Despite himself, despite the fact that Mr. Famous was talking to a Dead Man, Adrian smiled. This time the smile was genuine. He could tell because the fucking thing hurt his face; it'd been so long.

"Fuck you," said Adrian. "And where you been? Haven't seen you in weeks." His hand went round the Glenfiddich and the memory of the taste of its velvet contents warmed him. Adrian thought about stealing it, draining the whole fucking thing, lingering between its thighs, as it were, before he took a gun to his head. If Adrian had the balls to pinch the whiskey, he would have to blow his brains out before Mr. Famous and his Russian henchman with the skull tat on his knuckle hunted him down. He'd be nothing but a spleen; nobody fucked with the man's bottle.

Adrian poured a perfect inch and a half into a perfect glass and watched the Man drink.

"Hey, Petunia," Mr. Famous said. "Another. Then you're going to tell me why you look like shit if shit looked that bad."

Adrian's sigh reached down into the pinched, torturous heels of the Italian shoes that were prolonging the misery that was his life, the shoes that mocked him by existing where *she* did not anymore.

"Tell me something." Adrian leaned close to Jacks. "Tell me the fastest you've ever heard of a play closing."

Jacks couldn't tell if Adrian were holding himself up or aching for a fight. Shooting stars shot through Adrian's eyes. Adrian had made a visit to Crazy Town and hadn't returned.

"You doing blow?" Jacks inquired.

"Minutes. Give me minutes," Adrian said.

Jacks tilted back. He felt as if Adrian had fallen where there was no net.

"Two hours?" Jacks said.

"Forty-two minutes," Adrian replied.

"No. Impossible."

"I've timed it a hundred times. End of the first act—forty-two minutes. Everyone walked out. Not two or three people, Big Man, not some old lady offended by language or the obscured sex act. Nah. Forty people got up and left. Where'd they go, huh? *Where'd they go?* Did they head to the john and forget to come back? Did they think it had ended? They vanished! Like the fucking Bermuda Fucking Triangle in the middle of fucking downtown!"

"Easy, buddy." Jacks noticed that Lionel, the old bartender, had raised an eyebrow toward Adrian. There was a couple waiting. He sensed their urgency; they wanted a drink, they wanted to fuck. The drink was the conduit. *No drinkie, no fuckie.*

"She left me."

"Tracy Bing left you?" Jacks said. His eyes skipped to Lionel, engaged, exchanged pertinent information, then skipped back to Adrian.

The old bartender whispered in Adrian's ear. He put a hand on Adrian's back. Adrian's head was resting on his chest, his eyes closed, listening. Jacks threw back the rest of his drink. He motioned to Lionel to grab the Glenfiddich. Then he poured one more for himself, and one for Adrian. He imagined he'd be there all night, nursing the wounded puppy back to life with a bottle of the best Scotch money could buy.

Commerce saves, Jacks thought. *Art kills.*

20

PASSED PAWN

4:30 A.M. The sedan picked Lara up outside her apartment. She paused before stepping into the Town Car; was this the same outfit she'd worn the day before? She pulled at her sweater's neckline, pressed it to her nose; there was the faint, noxious mixture of body odor and musk and she knew she was doomed.

"Fuck!" Lara said. The driver didn't flinch, but Lara was instantly ashamed.

"Let's stop for some coffee," she told him.

"We don't have time," he said.

"I need coffee," she said. Same conversation as yesterday. She hadn't looked in the mirror that morning; she was afraid she'd find the puffier, older version of herself, the version that wasn't quite so puffy and old yesterday.

And she realized that she didn't really need a coffee; she needed alcohol, a shot of something. She lifted her hand and watched, horrified and fascinated, as it trembled.

Last night, she and Jacks had used the back entrance of the Plaza. She was familiar with every back entrance of every hotel from Midtown to the Upper East Side, from the Four Seasons to the Lowell to the Waldorf. Back-door gal, that was Lara. Instead of ducking SCUD missiles, she was ducking the sidelong glances of hotel maids and room service waiters. Her life was one big adventure.

Yes, she'd put up another fight about the hotel room scenario, but there didn't seem to be a way around it, not yet. Not until Jacks's divorce was final.

"I've spent most of our relationship looking at ceilings," she'd said. While looking up at yet another one.

"Then I'm doing something right," he joked.

People didn't know Jacks was funny. Or sweet. Or soft. Or insecure. Or kind, incredibly, inconceivably kind and generous. If there was anything Lara needed, before she knew she needed it—work advice, roses, the latest Philip Roth, a plumber for her sink, a drink, no more drinks, a hug, a latte, Christian Louboutins, a foot massage—Jacks would give it to her.

He was the only one left for her; she wanted no one else.

Lara placed one hand on top of the other, trembling one and held it down.

"I need coffee," she said again, meekly.

Lara thought of the blonde she'd seen on tape years ago. One of the first female news anchors. A legend, for better, for worse. Both she and Lara were flaxen-haired, throaty stars; both their names held comic-book appeal. The star had died in the eighties, a freak car accident many years in creation. Coke, alcohol, pills, men, the nightly news recorded in a river of slurred words. Her body had been discovered in a ditch, arms spread like angel's wings.

Lara pressed her body into the leather seat, her hand held firm.

"ROUGH night, little girl." More accusation than question. Standing with arms folded in front of his arrays of tubes and glosses and powders, Kevan assessed his uneven canvas and found it not to his liking. He didn't need this shit. Diane didn't drink; Katie didn't do drugs. Why was he saddled with this troublemaking white girl?

"Do your magic, K," Lara said. She slid her hands between her legs to quell the tremors.

"I always do," said Kevan, who could be sweet-talked easier than a fifteen-year-old virgin whose parents are out of town. "I always do," he repeated, then dug in and found what he could beneath the troubled surface—the full upper lip, the smooth forehead, that jaw-line. What he could not bring back was the gleam in her eye. He would work hard to manufacture the quality she was slowly, willfully destroying. This girl was a star; this was the reason he'd been brought in, stolen, in fact, from ABC with an offer of double salary, travel, expenses, publicity. Her face, her future (and his) were in his hands and every night she would take that face apart, have a great fall, and every morning he would put that face back together again.

"Humpty Dumpty," he murmured, coaxing a cheekbone out with a flash of shimmer.

Her eyes rolled slightly back in her head; he felt the dull vibration of a snore.

Fine, Kevan thought, *I can work with a dead woman.*

Lara's mind turned back to the impromptu office party three days ago. Noisy congratulations, people jostling her, Scotch and champagne in plastic cups. She caught Sarah Kate by the arm and squeezed; her arm felt like a ripe peach. Lara would sneak in those squeezes like a lover's stolen kisses.

"I need you," Lara whispered, holding on to the arm.

Sarah Kate's face was flushed and billowy, her top unbuttoned to show ample cleavage; her inhibitions were loosened like a necktie after hours. She might have had as much to drink as Lara.

"You got me," Sarah Kate said. "Even though I'm this close to getting laid."

"By the intern?" Lara said, looking at the fresh-faced Brown grad.

"I'm not carding."

"I'm afraid," Lara said suddenly. "I wanted the promotion so badly, and now I'm just so afraid."

"Of course you are," Sarah Kate said, "I am, too."

"You are?" Lara asked. Sarah Kate wasn't even afraid of Mike Wallace—she'd beaten The Legend to a "get"—a high school girl from her hometown who'd been kidnapped by a white supremacist. "The fat girl beat me!" Mike was heard screaming at his producing team. Fear found no harbor in "the fat girl."

"Second anchor," Sarah Kate said. "Who knew the People's Billionaire was going to make you an even bigger ratings darling? It's a big responsibility. A big step up for you. But don't worry, Chicken, I got your back."

They both glanced over as Jim Kramer, the low-key senior executive producer, appeared at Sarah Kate's side, looking flustered. He rarely looked flustered.

"A word in private, Sarah Kate," he said. It wasn't a question. "Excuse us, Lara," he said, looking back.

Sarah Kate widened her eyes and winked at Lara, then walked off.

Ten minutes later, an ashen Sarah Kate slipped the drink out of Lara's hand and gulped it down. "I've been shitcanned, Chicken," she said. "They just strapped on the platinum parachute and shoved me off the cliff. They didn't feel I was 'moving in the same direction' as the show."

"What?!" Lara asked. "How could Jim do this?"

"Jim's a wreck," Sarah Kate said. "It came down from Mount Olympus. That new goof Scott's your new executive producer."

"They can't break us up!" Lara said. "They can't do this—"

"Sweetie, they wanted to break up the team. That way they have more power over you. It's control, Lara—it's all about control. That's what the power guys want."

"Fuck that, I'm not doing this without you!" Lara wailed. "Scott can fuck himself if he thinks I'm going to work with him—Where is he? I'm telling them all right now!"

Sarah Kate grabbed Lara's wrist. "No, Chicken. We both worked too hard to let you crash and burn. You can't do this to yourself. And you can't do this to me, and all the work, all the years I put into building you."

"If they want me, they get you, too, period. This is unfucking-acceptable!" Tears started rolling down Lara's cheeks; she could hear murmurs and feel all eyes on her. She didn't care.

"Don't you worry about me. Tomorrow morning, I'm lawyerin' up and I'm gonna turn my platinum parachute into a Lear," Sarah Kate said. "They're going to pay for this."

"Please don't go. Please. I'll pay you to stay," Lara said, holding on to her. "I'm begging you. I can't do this without you. I can't do anything without you."

"I can't stay, under the circumstances, you know that." Sarah Kate tilted Lara's head so their eyes met. "But if you need me, I'm a phone call away. Besides, Chicken, I got plans. I've had 'em for as long as I've been here. Always keep an alternate life handy, sweetie."

"Like what plans?" she asked softly, feeling a little like a betrayed lover. *Since when did Sarah Kate not tell her everything?*

"An intern or two, for starters," Sarah Kate said. "It ain't sexual harassment if I've been fired. 'Sides, Chicken, I've got my eye on a piece of land far, far away. And this time, it's not chickens I'm gonna be raising."

Lara awakened, her eyelashes fluttering like butterflies against Kevan's palm.

"Ah, you messed it up," Kevan said.

21

KINGS FIGHT FOR EMPIRES, MADMEN FOR APPLAUSE

FOR WEEKS, it seemed there was no story other than the Power Divorce. *The Scandal,* that's how the tabs played it. Forget the "official denials," the headlines stayed the same: THE PEOPLE'S BILLIONAIRE VS. THE BALLERINA—PAS DE DUEL, REAL ESTATE TYCOON AND WIFE: HEADED FOR SPLITSVILLE: THAT'S A FACT, POWER DIVORCE TRUMPS THE TRUMPS. Of course, Cynthia got the time-honored role of victim: *Can you believe he left his wife? His pristine, charitable wife, as perfectly formed as the china ballerina atop a music box?* And of course, Lara was cast as the Home Wrecker, the Ambitious Career Woman, the Bloodsucking Blonde. But every sobriquet boosted her Q Factor and ratings points. There had even been a photograph doctored to look as if Lara and Cynthia were boxing each other in the ring. Jacks had canceled his subscription to the *Post,* even closed his eyes as he passed newsstands. But that didn't stop Artemus, now firmly reensconced in his office, from waving the photographs in front of his son as he passed. Nor from painstakingly reading every snide remark aloud. The man made an ellipsis sound like an indictment.

Jackson had slipped security an extra hundred to alert him if his father was in the vicinity, e.g., their now-shared private elevator. On his office floor, Jacks moved silently along the hallway, nodded to Caprice, cracked open his office door and slipped inside, where he'd find another Bible quotation resting on his phone sheet.

Today's was "*A fool shows his annoyance at once, but a prudent man overlooks an insult.*"

Ignore the press, Jacks thought. *Got it. Check.*

Since his father's arrival, Jackson found himself buzzing Caprice on the intercom instead of yelling out, hiding his phone sheet, his date book, and his putter, and trying to conduct his business in secret. It didn't suit him. His personality was too big for secrets. He felt like Tom Cruise without the special effects.

He was a grown man who worked for Daddy. In a few short weeks, his old man had wrested a commercial skyscraper deal from his hands, canceled a press conference, invited himself to private lunches and meetings, and pissed off the head of the city planning commission, several tenants groups, and Local 731.

Relationships that Jacks had been grooming for years, Artemus had ground to dust in one phone call. No more deals from the plumbers' union; that florist on Third Avenue cut off his supply; and the head Realtor for the Power Tower was threatening a sexual harassment suit.

Artemus Power was a stealth bomb without the stealth.

And now he was trying to take over Jacks's baby: the Bowery project.

Light curved around Jacks's face as he looked out onto the street. He recalled looking out from this space when he first arrived at this office, after he'd let go of his paintbrush. Jackson had tried to combine the two, commerce and art, but soon enough he realized the effort was doomed. So he gave himself over completely to commerce, leaving the art world behind and moving toward baby sounds and wife sounds and smells and meetings and conference calls and late nights and office affairs. Up to that point, he'd never made any big decisions—and then the decision had been made for him. *How, he'd thought then, will I not hate my baby daughter? My wife? Myself?*

Twenty-five years later, he realized his father had made the decision for him once again.

Every day, and it didn't matter what time he arrived, within five minutes, Jacks would hear the *thump, thump, thumping* of his father's hooves along the eighteenth-century Aubusson carpet lining the hallway.

His heart rate would leap at the sound. *Pound, thump, pound, thump, pound, thump*; Jacks's hysterical heartbeat and his father's footsteps—like a garage band's amateur rhythms.

Jacks's breathing would become shallow, raspy. His throat would dry up. He would reach for his water glass, and his hand would shake.

Artemus would enter Jackson's office, the wretched paper, thick with un-news, in his hand. He would have to unfold it first; unfolding was part of the game.

His father would fumble with his reading glasses, and then his earpiece would catch on his suit, lengthening the torture by long seconds. Meanwhile, Jackson would fill his mind with pleasant thoughts:

Lara's pussy. (Blond curly twisted hairs!)

Her lower lip.

Money.

Larry King was his friend.

Then: *snap* went the paper.

"You read this one, this morning, boy? You're not going to believe this one," crowed his father.

Jackson summoned the image of Lara unwrapping herself from slick hotel sheets and walking into the bathroom while he pretended to be asleep. A smile weaved its way into his mind without disturbing his poker face. He'd found his image.

"The self-proclaimed People's Billionaire, developer Jackson Power—"

Lara was shy about the ass he loved. She didn't like the bubble molded by hours spent performing gymnastics.

"Blah blahblahblah," his father continued.

The bubble never fit right in designer skirts made for Popsicle-stick figures. And forget designer jeans.

"When I was coming up, you avoided this hooey like the plague, I'll tell you—you never saw the Roses in the papers, the Zeckendorfs, the Speyers. Never!"

Lara got too tall, shoulders too broad, too big for a sport for little people. He pictured her as a teenager. *Did she have braces?* Jackson couldn't believe he didn't know.

"Jackson? Are you hearing me?" His father's voice reached around. "You are losing it, my boy. Losing it!"

Meanwhile, in the warmly lit hotel suite snugly situated in his mind, Jackson waited patiently for Lara to come back out of the bathroom. Jacks felt tiny pricks of desperation. He sensed Lara slipping away, her muscle and bones becoming loose in his hands, turning to water, flowing through his grasp even as he gripped tighter.

Was this love or insanity? Was there a difference? The only distractions from obsessive love were work, drink, and new pussy. But the thought of new pussy was a turnoff to him, though he would admit this to no one.

"You're ruining the name I created!" his father growled. "You keep this up, I'm taking over the entire operation!"

Thump, thump, thump, slam.

22

KEEP YOUR GAME FACE ON

THE HUMILIATIONS continued to pour in.

"Darling, I knew he was cheating with her, everyone knew of course."

Cynthia's service had reported over twenty calls a day—friends, relatives, reporters, people she hardly knew, asking her to a "casual" lunch at Serafina or La Goulue.

"That tart. I can't even watch the show anymore. Did you see who she interviewed today?"

Cynthia avoided answering most. The calls she did return were claws wrapped in silk.

"The hair. Is it Ukrainian extensions? That's not found in nature, is it? It's so fabulous!"

In her "padded cell," Cynthia sucked down a diet Red Bull and assessed herself in a full-length mirror. "You look like a boy dressed up in Mother's tea suit," Cynthia murmured. Turning to profile, she wondered about her once-stylish ballerina breasts. *Was everything about her outmoded?* Suddenly, it seemed to her, the Upper East Side had become the Las Vegas strip. Seventy-year-old matrons were getting boob jobs! Was it only a matter of time before she succumbed to Silicone Fever? And if she did, would she fall over on her face?

Cynthia held out her hand, unadorned by a wedding ring for the first time in twenty-five years. Over the past two weeks, she'd scanned every left hand on the street for the telltale ghostly white band of skin on the ring finger. She felt like the Colombo of Dumped Wives.

Cynthia's eyes lighted on the Monet print she'd hung above the nightstand. She'd been to that garden, that bridge, seen the drooping trees, their branches forming lace curtains; she'd heard the gurgling water, felt the sun's fingers on her face. Artemus Power owned the original. He bought beautiful things because other people said they were beautiful. He was circled like carrion, by vultures in pearls and sleek suits, executives from Sotheby's and Christie's, hoping for a shot at the collection upon his passing. They didn't know what Cynthia felt from the first time she'd met him; here was the first man who would cheat Death.

She shuddered to think that her husband would one day inherit the responsibility for such beauty.

Husband? *Was-band*.

Mental List of Things Not to Do: Do not cry in public. Do not sit in a dark room at five o'clock, when the light is dim and the air in the room feels like something you can sink your hand into. When you run into Wasband at 740, do not give him ammunition: no splotchy skin, no watery eyes, no tics, no frowning, no evidence of momentary weakness.

Do not smile incessantly. Smiling is plaster on a million lies. *Do not* forget the decisive moment. The photograph, the black-and-white sucker punch of the lovers' near-embrace. *Keep in mind, Cynthia, how you stared at that photograph until finally it had dissolved into pinpricks.*

Do not ask him back. Ever. (*Remember when the publisher's wife asked him back? He never stopped talking about it!*)

Mental List of Things to Do: Sleep. Eat. Exercise. Still your mind. Pop a Xanax. When you run into Wasband, look effortlessly stunning and acquire Zen-like, Dalai Lama/Richard Gere state. Repeat in your mind: *I am a pond. I am a still pond. I am a still pond sprinkled with water lilies. I am a Monet.* Also, call your lawyer.

Ah! Cynthia dialed.

"Ricardo Bloomenfeld, please," Cynthia said.

The secretary patched her through in a nanosecond, a sure sign of the money Ricardo stood to make on the settlement.

"Cynthia, darling, how are you?" The voice wrapped her in clouds. A talking head on CNBC whose pithy quotes crept their way into *People* magazine, Ricardo Bloomenfeld held the hands of many an aging Manhattan divorcee during acrimonious legal proceedings. Every time a billionaire's marriage hurtled toward rancorous oblivion, you could count on hearing Ricardo's observations.

"Ricardo, the situation is unlivable," Cynthia said. "Jackson's in the guest wing. For weeks, we've been running into each other. He's doing it on purpose. He obviously wants me to move out. Last week he threw a tantrum and smashed an antique cassolette. He hurt his hand, by the way. I just ignored him. Like what you do with a three-year-old. I could stay at the Four Seasons or the Plaza—Vivi says I could move in with her." She stopped to take a breath.

"Absolutely not," Ricardo said. "Stay right where you are. This is about justice. Dignity and justice. Do not move a nail file until that cheating bastard of a husband pisses out a ton of dough. He insists on staying, you insist on staying. Share meals, share the bedroom, share the fucking bidet if you must. 740 is our leverage. Got it?"

Cynthia figured. Jackson Power had been too weak to stand up to the pressure from his father, who'd threatened to block him from his will if Cynthia didn't sign a prenup. *Could Ricardo crush it?* Cynthia signed. Money wasn't an issue then. *Then.*

"Got it," said Cynthia, and hung up. She checked her tasteful diamond-encrusted watch.

"Showtime," she said.

. . .

TO PARAPHRASE Benjamin Franklin—nothing in Cynthia's life was certain except for death, taxes, and Fashion Week. Cynthia Power could find her seat blindfolded in Oscar's front row—two seats down from Barbara, directly across from Anna. She loved the parade of hats, tweed half-coats, the sparkle of third-generation diamonds. The society ladies who filled the room wore white gloves on dotted hands, their spindly legs crossed at the ankles; their hair was "set," lips painted on, for their own ceased to exist. Here was civility, sophistication, a return to the old ways.

Cynthia found her seat next to Buffy Mortimer and felt the warm glow of relief. She'd chosen the pale cast of her chenille suit carefully, and had slipped off one of her gold chains. At her age, Cynthia utilized the ultimate fashion accessory: moderation. After sixty, one could pile on loads of rings, gold chains, wear long, heavy earrings that accentuated the great monuments to gravity—earlobes. The widows were the boldest fashion plates of the ladies whose hunting grounds ran from Ninety-second to Sixty-second and east from Madison: widowdom (kids grown and sex drive dimmed to the glow of a pin light) conferred the ultimate social standing.

"Darling," Buffy said. She smiled with stained teeth, her red lipstick making stick figures above her lip line. She wore a hat of green-and-white houndstooth. In her lap sat a Yorkshire terrier with a diamond-and-emerald collar, customized to match her owner's outfit. Buffy put a curled, speckled hand over Cynthia's, her rings weighing more than Cynthia's leg. Cynthia felt a thrill. Buffy's clear acknowledgment of her was a watershed. As the grand doyenne of the crumbling estate of old-money Manhattan, every move the woman made was analyzed under the subatomic microscope of the New York Social Diary.

Cynthia had survived!

. . .

THE MUSIC started. Cynthia recognized the ribbon of sound—the hypnotic Pachelbel Canon. She had danced to this enchantment. Clearly the planets had aligned.

Suddenly, light flashes and scurrying. A ball of people rolled toward Cynthia and cracked open. In its center was a tiny teenage creature with a ratty mane and pouty lips, eyes rimmed by lack of sleep and a kohl pencil. Those eyes were on Cynthia.

"Um, that's my seat," the Creature whined.

A harried woman with a black ponytail and severe cat's-eye glasses, her face floating above a stark black ensemble, started to pull Cynthia from the seat she'd inhabited for years. The seat she'd grown up in, in which she'd been pregnant, twice. The seat that she had made, the seat that had made her.

"Get up," the woman in nervous breakdown mode said. "Nicki's sitting here. Get up."

Cynthia's mouth opened. "This is my seat—"

"A-14," the woman said. "Get up or we will have you escorted out."

Escorted out? Cynthia's hand grasped at her ticket. "But this has always been my seat," she said. The Creature was wearing an Oscar; Cynthia wanted to rip the dress off of her. *Oscar, who had dressed Audrey, Jackie, had created Sophia—how could he let this happen?*

Cynthia's ticket was torn from her hand.

"Second row," the spider in black sneered.

Cynthia's catapulted from her seat and fled down the aisle. She didn't even look back as the flamingos took to the runway.

23

THE QUEEN AS WING-MOM

CYNTHIA WAS hyperventilating when she hit the sidewalk. She signaled her confused driver, then jumped into the car, panting and mortified. *Where to go? Margot's apartment?* Margot would tell her to bomb the place. The only thing she hated more than a fashion show was a fashion show plus an after-party.

Dr. Gold?

Vivienne!

"Vivi," Cynthia said into her cell phone.

"Cynthia?"

"Can I come by?" Cynthia asked, repressing her hysteria.

"I'm on my way out," Vivi said.

"I'll come with you," Cynthia said.

"But, Cynthia—I'm going to a bar."

"Perfect!" Cynthia exclaimed. "I could use a drink."

"Cynthia—it's—"

Cynthia cut her off. "Where? Just tell me. I'm heading there."

"Okayyy . . . ," Vivienne said, "it's on Vestry and Greenwich. The Cat's Meow."

"Cat's Meow. Got it." Cynthia hung up.

Vivienne met her outside, smoking a cigarette. Cynthia grabbed it and took a puff.

"Disgusting habit," Cynthia said. "Unless it's a French brand."

She tossed the cigarette to the curb, then walked inside, arm in arm with Vivienne.

Wall-to-wall patrons. Cynthia and Vivienne squeezed their way to the front of the bar.

"I'll have a Lone Star," Vivienne said to the bartender, a platinum blond rocker, nose piercings, tattooed shoulders, tight leather vest.

"Do you have white Burgundy?" Cynthia asked. The Pink doppelganger looked at Vivienne—

"And a Lone Star for my mother," Vivienne said.

Cynthia's eyes focused in the dark; she looked closely at the clientele and turned back to Vivienne.

"A lesbian bar," she whispered. "You didn't warn me."

"And you didn't even think to ask," Vivienne replied.

Point, Vivienne.

FIRST BEER

"So," Cynthia asked, sneaking glances at the customers, "how come no one's looking at me?"

"Because you remind them of their mothers," Vivienne replied.

SECOND BEER

"Wait a minute," Cynthia asked, attempting the merest shimmy just along the edge of the dance floor as Mariah Carey wailed, pointing at three girls huddled at the bar—"how come those girls arc looking at me?"

"Because you remind them of their mothers."

"Ewww!" Cynthia cried and stopped bouncing. She looked at her daughter—"So . . . Keiko!"

"It's Aiko!"

"She's a dancer, right?"

A bull dyke, short hair slicked back, plaid shirt, interrupted them. "Want to dance?" she asked Cynthia.

"No, oh, no, thank you," Cynthia replied. "But thank you for asking!"

The dyke shrugged, and walked away.

"Aiko's a Japanese folk dancer," Vivienne said. "I know, a little weird. I have a Mommy Complex—I'm dealing with it!"

"So . . . where is she? Is she joining you?"

"We're having a thing. It's nothing. I'm too bossy. It'll blow over. She's just being overly sensitive."

"That's what your father used to say about me—'Cynthia's overly sensitive!' Until I wasn't anymore."

THIRD BEER

Cynthia and Vivienne were slow dancing, like a father and daughter at a wedding—Vivienne's head on her mother's shoulder.

"I wanted to be like you, Mom, but I'm built like a softball player."

"No, you're not. You're just . . . big-boned," Cynthia said, and then, "You're stepping on my toes." *Mom,* Cynthia thought. *She called me Mom.*

"It's true, Mom, come on—" Vivienne said. "Would you let me lead, please?"

"You've been leading the whole time!" Cynthia pouted. "You're just showing off."

"Can I cut in?" A woman appeared at their side.

"No," Vivienne and Cynthia said at once.

"Anyway, I always felt ashamed," Vivienne continued. "You're a dancer, you're perfect. But here"—Vivienne swept her arm around the room—"I saw other girls who look like softball players. And I haven't been leading—"

"Vivienne . . ."

"It's not that I love you any less, but I have to be who I am. Can you just follow me, here?"

"You know something? You know something?" Cynthia asked.

"May I?" A younger girl, a grad student type, tapped Cynthia on the shoulder.

"Go away!" Cynthia said, without taking her eyes off her daughter. "Vivienne, you're a hell of a lot braver than your mother."

"Don't sound so serious, Cynthia. Just have fun."

"Fun? I have a vague memory of fun," Cynthia said. "Between the ballet board and the divorce, there's not a lot of room for laughs. That horrible Fred Plotzicki just got Gislaine's grandchild into Spence. How do I compete?"

"Play a different game," said Vivi. "C'mon. Aren't you Cynthia 'I'm in Control Here' Power? I've spent most of my life intimidated by you."

"Really?" Cynthia felt herself blush.

"Mom," Vivienne said, "the board struggle, the divorce—it's like chess. Think three moves ahead."

Cynthia thought about Jacks's teaching Vivienne chess—she'd caught on so quickly that Cynthia had actually felt jealous. Cynthia had never mastered the game—until now.

Manhattan: the Ultimate Chessboard.

"I could throw an amazing dinner party."

"Um. I was thinking along more aggressive lines. But I guess the right dinner party could be menacing."

"Finger bowls, ivory-handled fish knives, formal attire, Marcus Samuelson!" Cynthia exclaimed, then, "You're really intimidated by me?"

"Of course," Vivienne said.

"Then can I give you some advice?" Cynthia asked.

"No," said Vivienne. "And for a dancer, Mom, you really don't know how to stay on beat."

24

QUEEN'S GAMBIT

At precisely 2:56 p.m. the girl with the bold teeth and bridge-and-tunnel accent led Jackson Power and his lawyer, Penn Stewart, to the conference room in the mediation office on the forty-third floor of a skyscraper owned by the Tishmans. Neutral territory.

"It'll be just a few moments," promised the girl. She had a tiny roll around her midriff at the top of her hip; it looked delicious. A lifetime ago, Jackson would have called her on a phony pretense as the first step on the smooth road to getting what he wanted: Fresh Pussy.

The girl offered a bland smile. "May I get you two anything to drink?"

Jackson nodded. "Can I have—"

"Mrrrrmmmmrrr." Penn shook his head balefully.

"If I could just have some—" Jackson tried to say.

WRAGHUM. The noise shot out of Penn's throat. "We're fine, thanks. Perfectly fine," Penn said.

"You don't need anything?" the girl asked.

"Nothing at all."

Jackson looked at Penn after the girl had left. "No water?" he asked.

"Thirst is a sign of anxiety." Penn placed his slim briefcase on the table, opened it, and took out three sharpened pencils and a yellow legal pad. He straightened the corner of the legal pad, then placed the pencils on top in a tight row. "We have no reason to be anxious."

Jackson had known Penn for almost thirty years, but would be hard-pressed to say what shade his eyes were, what color his hair. Penn was devoid of all traits of character except one: he went to Princeton, and this colored everything he did—from his bathroom habits to the restaurants he frequented to the woman he chose to be his wife to the names of his children to the type of dog he owned. But even though Penn radiated a gentlemanly, Princetonian manner, he still had cartilaginous gills underneath that suit and he would swallow you whole before you even knew a limb was missing.

"Too close," he said to Jacks, who pulled his chair a few more inches from Penn.

Penn had schooled Jacks in the minutiae of the Conventions of Seating before they'd arrived; he'd even drawn a seating chart. "You and I will sit here," he'd said, poking his smooth hands at two seats. "We'll get there ten minutes early. We've got clear weather this afternoon, I had Delia check, the sun will be about a ninety-degree angle from the east at that time, which means we want to sit with our backs to the windows." Penn indicated the chairs facing them, his monogrammed cuff peeking under his blue pinstripe.

"Which means?" Jacks ventured to ask.

"Which means that the sun will be in their eyes. Advantage Power/Stewart," Penn said, satisfied.

"I didn't realize I'm sitting with the Federer of marital law."

"If you'd rather have the pro from Central Park, I'm sure he'd be happy to oblige," Penn replied.

Jackson gave him the appropriately doleful look.

"Good. We will remain seated when they arrive. I do all the talking. And remember," Penn said, wiping his palms on his handkerchief, "we have nothing to be anxious about."

"I'm not anxious," Jackson said, his voice rising. "I just need to move on with my life. Jacks Power doesn't wait for the dust to settle. And that's a fact."

"You know what you need to do? Nothing," Penn said. "Do the math: you're vulnerable. Vulnerable men make stupid mistakes. Stupid mistakes cost stupid amounts of money. I'm paid to make sure you don't make them on my watch."

Was Lara a stupid mistake? Jackson wondered. *Was that what Penn was implying?* How I wish, Jackson thought, that Lara needed me more than I needed her. She barely called and e-mailed only when she felt like it. He knew she loved him only when she was naked and spent, curled up in his arms, when the muscles in her neck stopped twitching, her breath slowed, and she drifted off to sleep. Then he knew he had her.

"You never say it," Jacks told her.

"Say what?" Lara asked.

"You know," he said, so close he could kiss the tip of her nose.

"You know I love you," she said.

"Tell me more," he said, sounding like a teenage girl and hating himself for it. Was he asking her to paint it in bold letters on the side of the building, or would a simple note do? (*Had she ever written him a note?*)

"Forget it," he said, ashamed. "Let's just fuck, forget the whole thing."

"No," Lara said, her eyes steady and serious and on him, "we will never forget."

Jacks was afraid he would cry. Love must always be unequal. Jacks knew that he, who had everything, who could buy the world, could not purchase for Lara the one thing she needed.

Freedom.

There was nothing to stop her from becoming the next Couric, the next Sawyer, the next Big Blonde, with all the freedom that position allowed. Sure, Jacks was prepared to knock Freedom out with all the tools at his disposal. Could Freedom buy a fourteen-carat canary diamond? Did Freedom fly private to Aruba? Could Freedom park next to Diddy's yacht in St. Bart's over Christmas? Could Freedom get a corner booth at the Waverly at eight o'clock on a Friday night at the last minute? Look out the floor-to-ceiling windows in this conference room—could Freedom claim ownership of five of the most magnificent buildings in your eyeline?

"I do the talking," Penn repeated.

"You do the talking," Jackson parroted, determined to be the good student.

Bridge and Tunnel reappeared. "Mrs. Power and Mr. Bloomenfeld are going to be a few minutes late," she said, flinching slightly in anticipation.

"Damn it all," Penn said as the girl hurriedly exited. "They call the meeting, now they're late. It's a classic gambit."

"Can I have some water then?"

"No," Penn said.

Fifteen minutes later, Cynthia and her lawyer, Ricardo Bloomenfeld, walked in. Bloomenfeld held the door open like a grand courtier. He sported a tan, looking like a man who's just stepped off his G5 from Jamaica, veneers flashing like after-dinner mints, wrinkles ironed into plains, paunch disappearing under his $11,000 William Fioravanti suit. Bloomenfeld, Jacks observed, cosseted himself with the same perquisites of the Upper East Side society wife: chin lift, brow lift, hair transplant. Jacks's eyes fell to the handcrafted Silvano Lattanzis peeking out from the pinstriped legs. Ten thousand euros a pair. *I paid for those shoes,* Jackson thought. *Those are my fucking shoes.*

Ricardo put his hand on Cynthia's waist, guiding her to a chair, a move both protective and predatory. Jackson wondered if he were already sleeping with Cynthia.

Jackson shot up, allowing himself to tower over Ricardo, forcing Penn to stand as well. Ricardo eyed Jackson as if he were a six-foot-tall flashing neon dollar sign.

"Ricardo," Penn said, aware that the two dogs in the fight were sizing each other up. "Cynthia," Penn said, settling back into his chair and motioning Jackson to do the same. "You're looking well."

"Well?!" Ricardo exclaimed. "She looks incredible!"

Jackson's face became a wall of ice; anything thrown at it would have shattered on impact.

"I want to get this divorce moving," Jackson said. "Here's what we're going to do—"

"What my client is suggesting," Penn interrupted, "is how best we might move forward with this action. I'm sure your client, as well as mine, would like to move on with their respective lives."

"My client"—and with these words, Ricardo looked at Cynthia before covering her chilled body with a blanket of soothing words. "On the contrary, Cynthia isn't sure she even wants a divorce. She sees hope of reconciliation."

Jackson looked at Cynthia. Her face was impenetrable. No, wait. Was there a tight smile behind that façade? He checked out her dress; the brown color didn't suit her. Her hair, in a tight chignon, made her look even more severe. She didn't look like a woman who wanted to hold hands, much less fuck, unless you liked fucking a pair of scissors. Jackson's legs slapped together.

Penn looked at Jackson, his eyes asking: *Is there a sliver of a fraction of a token of a crumb of something that was once called love left? Anything? Anything at all?*

Jackson knew better. Cynthia would have worn something alluring had she wanted him back. And anything but brown. Brown was his least favorite color. Didn't he yell at the interior designers whose trembling hands presented sample after sample of textiles—*"No brown!"*

He hated the dress, and she knew he would hate it.

Why would Cynthia put her lawyer up to this scheme? What could she want? Was it a stalling tactic? For what? More money?

Suddenly Jackson realized. Cynthia would hold up the divorce for as long as she could, and Jacks would lose Lara, who waited for no man. Not even Jacks Power.

"No fucking way!" Jackson said. It was as though he'd released a pack of wild dogs in the room.

Penn cleared his throat. "My client begs to differ."

"So we heard," Bloomenfeld said. "My client is prepared to wait out the full term of the separation agreement in order to give her marriage to your client every chance a twenty-five-year union deserves."

"Oh, come on!" Jacks yelled.

"In fact," Ricardo continued, "as my client does not wish to remarry, she sees no reason that this marriage can't go on indefinitely."

Penn laid a firm hand on Jack's forearm. *Down, boy.*

"My client feels that he and Cynthia," Penn said, "should move on with their lives in happy, productive ways. The term of the separation agreement is egregiously long—"

"New York is a fault state," Bloomenfeld said, almost bored by now. Perhaps, Jackson thought, he was daydreaming about another cosmetic procedure.

"Exactly!" Jackson suddenly yelled. "It's clearly my fault!"

Cynthia recoiled. Ricardo widened his surgically enhanced eyes.

"Allow me," Penn interrupted, rubbing his temple. "Cynthia, I don't want this to get ugly for you. My client is in fact willing to offer a legal basis with which to facilitate a quick divorce."

"Such as?" Ricardo said, this little morsel awakening his senses.

"I'm a dog, a rat, a beast!" Jackson said, hysteria putting a gleam on his words. "If there was a week where I was faithful to this beautiful woman in the last ten years it was only because of back surgery!" Jackson knew instinctively that no one is above flattery, not even the woman radiating her disdain for him in the form of an unflattering brown wrap dress.

"My client has no reason to believe that your client has been unfaithful," Ricardo replied, the bland tenor of his statement suffocating a laugh.

"I have proof," Jacks said. "I'll depose half of Manhattan! We'll go to court if we have to!"

"That will be all," Penn said, snapping his briefcase shut.

"So be it," Ricardo said. "But my client's hope springs, like the flame, eternal."

Cynthia sat, still as a corpse. She and Jacks exchanged a look. Suddenly her mouth curled up at the edges. *Was that a smile? A sneer? A sneer! Bitch!*

"We'll see you . . . in a year, or so," Ricardo said, as he escorted Cynthia out the glass doors.

Jacks sat down, hard, then turned and looked out the windows. *Cynthia had won,* he thought. *A year? Lara's life would move on.*

"Enjoy 740 while you can," Penn said, his voice made sour and petulant by a) Jackson's behavior and b) the fact that he had not had a chance to fit Princeton into the conversation at any time.

CYNTHIA fixed her eyes on Bloomenfeld's back as they boarded the elevator. *Was he a pawn? A knight? A bishop?* Whatever. On Cynthia's chessboard, he had utilized his move properly. "Thank you," Cynthia said as the doors closed.

"Don't thank me yet," Bloomenfeld said. "You know I think this was a mistake. We should settle on a number, go in, and get it."

"We will," she said. "But until then—"

"I'll have to trust you," he said unhappily as they walked the marble floor to the revolving doors.

"Yes, you will," she replied, taking a deep breath before being swallowed up by the crowd.

25

NICE PIECE OF . . .
THE NAKED AND THE DAMP

Lara's bold smile drilled the lens, the silver light of the fall morning sliding off her Viking features. "Here I am, on the street, with the lady responsible for the hottest new line of bath oils."

Fine bubbles clung to Lara's chest. She felt like a human parfait. *I will kill Scott whatever-his-last-name,* Lara thought. *Sarah Kate would never have put me through this!*

"Welcome, Tamra," she said, as the camera pulled back for a two-shot with the cool brunette on the other end of the tub. Cocking her brow, the brunette lifted her leg out of the water and extended it, nearly revealing her recent laser work to families across America.

"This isn't pay-per-view, Tamra." Lara feigned an amused tone. "Siberian Tiger, Mongoose, Polar Bear, California Grizzly. Tell us. How did you come up with such a unique line of bath products? You call it 'Endangered.'"

"Tam-AR-a," the brunette said, with an indeterminate accent. Her leg disappeared into the bubbles, though her kneecap made promises above the waterline.

Snap. Lara hated being corrected, especially on air. *Why would she spell her name "Tam-ra" if it was pronounced "Tam-AR-a"? Fucking Princess Di Wannabitch.*

"Can you explain the curious genesis of your products? The names, for example?"

"Lara," TamARa said, "I'm an active environmentalist. I love the Earth and all its creatures. Did you know extinction threatens millions of species within the next fifty years?"

"Very distressing," Lara said. *Can we add one more to the endangered species list?*

"I decided to combine two of my fiercest passions—beauty, of course." TamARa smiled. Her pursuit and capture of Beauty were only too obvious. Lara surmised that it had been a long, hard, bloody, expensive battle.

"And?" Lara pushed on.

"Animals." TamARa sighed.

"And right now, we're soaking in . . . ? " Lara asked.

"Wild Boar," TamARa said. "Isn't it fabulous?"

"It has a certain . . . malaroma," Lara said. "And you say a percentage of your profits goes to helping these animals."

TamARa's features twisted, assessing Lara's comment. Lara loved making up words during annoying interviews; the brass hadn't picked up on the trick yet. Only Sarah Kate knew what she'd been up to. "Almost a full half percent," TamARa said.

"A great cause, and an interesting product," Lara said. "Congratulations on your success, Tamra. By the way, our research shows that the wild boar isn't endangered. Although we wish they were when we go to dinner parties!" TamARa smiled and blinked in confusion.

Lara turned to the camera. "Next up, Matt's exclusive interview with the latest victim of the recent alligator attacks in Florida. Why alligators are biting back."

The cameraman signaled a commercial break, and Lara clambered out of the tub. "It does have a nice malaroma, doesn't it?" said

TamARa, flirting with the cameraman. Lara grabbed her assistant's elbow as she strode off. "Where's my robe?" she asked.

"Scott told me to put it in your office," the girl replied, shaking slightly.

"Are you fucking kidding me?" Lara asked. "Why would you listen to that asshole? He probably told the snaparazzi to shoot me—"

"I'm so sorry," the girl said as Lara charged for the elevators, her arms covering her breasts, dripping pig-scented bubbles. She slid in sideways as the doors closed, bumping the gloating curve of her glutes. Lara nodded at the men in the elevator, who found much to contemplate, as her nipples telegraphed the drop in temperature. Everyone was dressed in wool suits, overcoats, hats—bulwarks against the fall chill.

The elevator doors slid open suddenly, and three more people squeezed in. Two men, one woman, their foreheads almost touching as they murmured in Arabic. The men were that rarest form found in Urbania: the anti-metrosexual. They still sported original noses and facial hair. The woman was dark, with a masculine profile. The men's attention was fixed entirely on her.

"Yasmeen!" The name ejected itself from Lara's mouth, exhilaration trumping despair over her unseasonable attire. The two men parted, leaving the short, dark-eyed woman open for appraisal.

"Yes?" Yasmeen asked, the word stretched out like Marilyn Monroe on a chaise longue, belying midnight bottles of Arak, hand-rolled cigarettes, nights that bled into mornings, weeks without seasons.

Here, inches from Lara, was The Dream. "I thought it was you!" Lara said, her hand extended, though they were close as matches in a book. Yasmeen smiled, and the two men mimicked her easy response.

"You thought it was me," she said, "and it is."

Lara was suddenly, horribly aware that she was wearing a bikini while meeting her idol, Yasmeen Ali, she of the rumpled shirt, unbrushed hair, ability to speak five languages, passport a palimpsest of

stamps. Lara wondered what the sex *out there* must be like (incredible!). What did food taste like to this woman? Did men taste different, too? Did women? Was color more bold? What was it like to be so fucking *alive*?

"God, I'm so sorry." Lara winced, indicating her seminakedness. "My new EP's idea of a story. I'm a big fan," she said, grasping Yasmeen's hand and holding on until they stepped out onto the main news floor.

"Can we talk," Lara asked, "please?"

"I have very little time," Yasmeen replied. "I have to be on a plane—"

"It's a matter of life and death," Lara said as tears sprang to her eyes. *What is wrong with you, Lara?*

Yasmeen arched her brow, then nodded to the two men, who filed down the hallway. "Five minutes," Yasmeen said as she lit up a cigarette, brown and slightly misshapen, tobacco wrapped in paper by thick, worn fingers a world away. Every ten feet a sign in the building said THANK YOU FOR NOT SMOKING.

Lara moved toward her office under the battering glare of fluorescent lighting. Yasmeen followed, a spark of bemusement gilding the steady gaze she had trained on world leaders, on terrorists, and now, on this big blonde in bare feet and a soaking wet bikini.

After sneaking a furtive glance down the hallway, which was alive with ears, Lara shut her office door. Lara knew phone calls were made daily to media outlets, calls that became screaming headlines: LARA SIZEMORE LOSING HER SIZZLE?, LARA SIZEMORE COURTING A NEW LOVE: JACK DANIELS, et cetera. *Who in this building was a friend? Who was a foe? Who was jealous of her ratings?* To be a celebrity; it was like learning to live without skin.

Lara donned the robe hanging on the back of her door. "Well?" Yasmeen said, leaning against the desk, cigarette smoke filling the room with the smell of an intoxicating future. Lara could lick the air.

Lara found herself blinking back tears again. She thought of Sarah Kate. "I can't do this anymore," she said. Her words were soft, as to a lover with whom she had shared much but could no longer share herself. "Look what they made me wear."

"It's your job," Yasmeen replied.

"My job," Lara said. "I talk to the pregnant wife of a dead miner, and the next second I'm discussing vaginal rejuvenation with a surgeon who looks like Beetlejuice. Then I have to watch you with your baggy pants and frizzy hair and teeth that wouldn't know a cosmetic dentist if they bit one. So fucking *authentic*. You challenge the world, and I'm spoon-feeding bullshit."

"It's not all that glamorous." Yasmeen put her hand on Lara's shoulder. "I think you might have the wrong idea."

"Don't patronize me," Lara said. "*My* job is glamorous. You're not getting a two-page spread in *Us* magazine."

Yasmeen peered at her. "Ahem," she said.

"I don't want glamour," Lara said. "Glamour is poisonous. I want a life. Tell me how to get it."

Yasmeen pulled one long drag off her cigarette, then put it out on Lara's desk. She then grabbed a pen and a piece of paper and wrote down a name and a phone number.

"My first producer," Yasmeen said. "He's in London. He might be able to help you. They won't listen to you here. They have you in a box, a pretty, padded box. You'll have to quit or force them to fire you. You'll get a reputation for being crazy. But there is a chance." Beat. "A very small chance," she sighed, as if already anticipating Lara's demise. "The benefit of being ordinary is you can't be traced as you make your moves. No one sees you, even as you're standing before them, even as you're taking their job."

Yasmeen placed her hand against Lara's cheek, sticky with makeup and tears. She brushed away a long strand of hair and put it back behind Lara's ear.

Then she kissed her on the mouth. And lingered.

"Be careful," she whispered. "Even thoughts leave tracks." Then she let go, and walked out.

Lara put the soft pads of her fingers to her mouth and was surprised to find a smile there.

26

KING'S GAMBIT

I F ESTELLA gets any bigger, we're going to have to hire NFL line-backers to lift her—"

"Call the Tisches! Maybe the Giants can lend us one of theirs!"

"Remember the good old days, when she was bulimic?"

"She lost half her molars, but her grand battement was incomparable!"

The arena: formal dining room, penthouse, 740 Park.

The players: puppet masters; board members, NYBT.

The sport: gossip.

Welcome to Cynthia Hunsaker Power's coming-out party.

"And the Ukrainian—"

Collective groan.

"She needs two dressing rooms? Why?"

"One for her ego!"

"Who is she, Jennifer Lopez? I mean, is she even that good anymore? Has anyone else noticed the turnout?"

"Maybe she's got turnout burnout?" Cue laughter.

Strategy, Cynthia, strategy, she counseled herself, even as she smiled at the joke. Cynthia was not about to let the gossip derail her. She knew the true meaning behind this dinner, and so did the board. Cynthia had to set the course for the NYBT in the coming year. She had to show them that they had not made a mistake in handing her the reins.

Cynthia had worked on a speech.

"I swear I thought I heard the floor shake during the last allegros of the grand pas."

"Well, if you were married to Roan, you'd have trouble concentrating—"

"Is he really that bad?"

"That bad? Half the line has had pregnancy scares!"

"... and that's just the women ..."

Finger bowls had arrived. Cynthia took the fish knife and tapped the side of her crystal goblet. She stood, waiting for all eyes to be on her. *C'mon, Zorba,* she thought, *be a mensch, help me out.*

"I want to thank our illustrious board members for coming tonight," Cynthia said, having cleared her throat as the first line of her speech made it to the surface. How perfectly dull, she thought. "We have an exciting year ahead of us, and we have so much to be proud of." The members smiled and nodded. "I am honored and humbled that I was chosen to lead our company into a bold new era. My only fear is that I will disappoint you."

"Well. I'm a little disappointed," a familiar voice said.

Cynthia turned and grabbed her chest. Jacks was standing in the entryway, his head cocked, smiling. "That I wasn't invited," he continued.

Cynthia narrowed her eyes at him, took a deep breath, then turned back to the group. "There are some changes I would like to suggest," Cynthia continued.

"Changes?" someone asked.

"What changes? I'd love to hear them," Jackson said, as he crossed to the table. "I'm all for change."

"I love our company," Cynthia said, willing her eyes not to move to the human distraction now standing mere feet away, "and I have for many years. But I think there comes a time when we have to try new things or risk becoming redundant."

"Oh, I agree with that," Jackson said. "What's that you're eating?" His eyes peered over at Cynthia's plate.

What to Do/What Not to Do, Cynthia thought. *Do not: scream, slap, stick Jacks with a knife. No felonies. Do: have Jacks escorted out, or, retain Zen-like calm and stay on my game.* The first wave, Jacks walking in the door, had knocked her over, but she hadn't drowned. Cynthia knew there would be more waves, and more paddling. *Suck it up,* she told herself.

"I'm starving," Jacks said. He jerked his head at a servant, who brought him a chair. Jacks squeezed in between Margaret Lord Foster and a bloodless fellow wearing granny glasses on the top of his head.

Jackson leaned into the servant's ear. "What's the entrée?"

"Roasted cod, sir."

"Cod. Sounds good. I'll have two."

The servant scurried away. *Probably rushing to tell the rest of the help about the reality show unfolding in the dining room,* Jacks surmised.

"You won't believe the day I had, hon," Jackson said to Margaret Something Something, whom he'd met many times, but whose name he could never remember. And why should he? He was Jackson Power. She was lucky to know him, the old blue hair.

"Will you be staying for dessert?" Cynthia asked, acknowledging Jacks at last.

"Good to see you, Joseph, I didn't see you there," Jackson said to a guest seated down the row. "How's your wife's rehab going this time?"

"As I was saying," Cynthia said, "we have priorities for the NYBT. Getting out of debt is number one. Raising funds and advertising revenue is, of course, of the utmost urgency. But I have been asking myself an even more important question. What is our vision? Do we have one? The NYBT is reliable. Our regular subscribers depend on us to bring them the performances they recognize from their child-hoods. But we need to be more than that. We need to become a little more dangerous."

The servant placed Jackson's meal before him. The plate had barely touched the ivory tablecloth when he started cutting in.

"Dangerous? I'm not sure what you mean by 'dangerous,' " Margaret Lord Foster said.

"We could perform *The Nutcracker* in thongs," someone suggested.

"Cynthia," Jackson said, his mouth full, "I'm sorry, what's for dessert?"

Cynthia rolled her fingertip around the top of her wineglass, thus preventing herself from throwing it at him.

"Jackson, how long are you planning on staying?"

"Good question," Jackson said, chewing loudly. He started to choke. He grabbed Margaret's wineglass and sucked down its contents. "That's very nice—what is that, a '62? From my cellar?"

"May we talk, Jackson?" Cynthia said through gritted teeth. She gestured toward the hallway. Suddenly, a clamoring was heard. Muffled voices, one a bassoon, the other tremulous and high-pitched. A mini-concerto of antagonistic notes.

Harry the Russian, wearing a shearling coat that made him look like a truck trying to stay warm, and a beaver hat (*Twelve dollar! Canal Street! Real beaver!*), materialized like a furry natural disaster, carrying a briefcase that Cynthia recognized as a Christmas present she'd given Jackson after she'd ceased using her imagination.

"Where you want this?" Harry the Russian swung the briefcase, gruffly addressing Jackson. He hated being up here, in this fanciness; his place was curbside. He felt like he was part of a conspiracy to humiliate this very nice lady, Cynthia, who was like mosquito, so skinny, and that made him sad, which made him angry, and he swore when he got home he was going to throw that lousy nephew out on his ass, because Harry could not afford to go to prison right now if he did what he felt like, which was kill him, yes.

"Take it to the master, Harry," Jackson said.

Harry the Russian stood there like a wall built thousands of years ago with strong hands.

Jackson sighed. "Please," he said.

Harry gave a curt nod, and turned.

"Wait," Cynthia said. "Jackson. You are not invited back into my bedroom."

"Our bedroom."

"It *was* our bedroom," Cynthia told him calmly. "It is no longer our bedroom."

"Ah, but it is," Jackson said. "Good news, everybody," he said, as he turned toward the table, "Cynthia and I have decided to get back together."

Confusion spread through the faces of the dining companions. Jackson turned back to his former mate. Panic flashed in her eyes, like a beacon to him.

"Jackson. Outside." Cynthia stood up.

"That *is* what you wanted, right, Cynthia?" Jackson asked, trying to sound innocent and failing. "You said, through Bloomenfeld's veneers, that you wanted to get back together. I've thought about it, and I agree. What we have is too important, too good to give up.

"Toast!" Jackson turned to the table. "To my bride of twenty-five years! Two of them very good ones!" Beat. "It's a joke, people, come on!" Was he being too cruel? A flash of memory: the birth of Vivienne, their daughter. Cynthia's forehead glowing with sweat; he'd kissed her and tasted her struggle. Jackson set down his wineglass.

Suddenly Cynthia lifted her glass. "Why not?" She smiled. "A toast, to my loving husband, partner, and friend." Jacks looked at her.

Why is Cynthia beaming like a new bride? Something awful has happened. He had dropped the ball for one second and she was dribbling down the court. After prolonged hesitation, their dining companions lifted their wineglasses and joined the toast.

Cynthia held her glass out for Jacks to clink. *Clever bitch,* he thought, as their wineglasses touched.

As the table settled, Cynthia started conversing with the man on her right. "Arnold, where should we seat the big donors at the gala?" she asked. "Always such a nuisance, making sure each one gets enough attention. Remember when Ivan's wife swapped place cards? And the meal requests! How many are on the new chili pepper diet?"

Others at the table had picked up where they'd left off before Jackson had entered the room; his presence was no longer news. This was more than Jackson could stand.

"Jesus, it's hot in here, isn't it?" Jackson said as he started loosening his tie. His hands whirled, pulling at Hong Kong silk, yanking at fine-woven cotton, tugging at the thick leather band around his waist.

Within seconds, he was naked.

"My God," Cynthia said when she turned.

A silver ladle tumbled onto a china plate, shattering it. The Irish girl who was nervous when serving soup from the left gasped, stifled a cry with her fist, and ran back into the kitchen.

"That's better," Jackson said, and began to cut into a stalk of white asparagus. He smiled at Margaret. He thought he caught the glimpse of a smile back.

"Harry!" Cynthia screamed. Harry came running down the hall. All ears awakened to the *thud, thud, thud* of his boots, his body weighed down by that shearling coat.

"Oh, for Got's sake." Harry stopped short, taking in the full spectacle of his boss's back end, mercilessly turned toward him.

"Escort Mr. Power out, please, Harry, or I will call the authorities," Cynthia said, reclaiming her dignity.

"I have a right to be naked in my own house!" Jackson said. "And the fish needs more sauce."

"You're making a fool of yourself, Jackson," Cynthia said, "a complete fool."

"Divorce me, then," Jackson said. "You don't love me. You can't stand the sight of me. What do you have in your veins, Cynthia? Paint thinner?" Jackson pounded the table. "Divorce me!" The silverware jumped, but not as high as Margaret Lord Foster.

"Harry!" Cynthia said. "Help Mr. Power out. Now."

Jacks leapt up. "Grab that," he said, pointing at the Jackson Pollock above the mantelpiece. Harry stood there, shaking his head.

"You can't take the art!" Cynthia said. "You're insane!"

"It's probably alarmed," someone suggested.

Jackson leaned against the mantel and lifted the painting from where it hung from tiny hooks. He was lucky it had never been bolted.

"It's mine, I'm taking it with me," he said. "Just like everything else in this apartment!" At which point, Harry, who'd grabbed his clothes, lifted Jacks under his arms, painting and all, and walked out.

"Except for me," Cynthia said. "I don't belong to you."

Someone at the table clapped.

"YOU'RE FIRED!" Jackson yelled at Harry, on their way down to the guest wing. "Put me down!"

"Idiot," Harry grumbled, as he walked Jackson into his bedroom, and stood over him. "Put your clothes on." Like a five-year-old getting dressed for school, Jacks started with his socks.

"King Cole," Jacks said. "I need a drink."

"You need more than drink," Harry said. "You need ass whop."

Moments later, they were driving west.

"I just thought I'd try a civil dinner with my wife—she's still my wife," Jackson said, from the back of the limo.

"You think I am fool? I have fool for boss," Harry said. "You are in Russian winter of your life." He turned onto Fifth. Jacks shook his head. He'd been shaking his head a lot, befuddled, as though he had nothing to do with the direction his life had taken. As though he were hanging on to the back of a runaway horse, except the horse wasn't a runaway at all. The horse was him.

"What's the big deal about Russian winters?" Jackson asked.

Harry couldn't believe that even his boss was this obtuse. *Come on. Where to start? Peter the Great? Napoleon's retreat? Okay, World War II. Germans sent to the Russian front. Thousands die, their corpses frozen stiff, human Popsicles. A natural ending to the unnatural force of war. And what was his boss heading toward, if not the unnatural force of war?*

"How's your health insurance?" Harry asked.

"Always with the smart comments," Jacks said. "And still I don't fire you. Why don't I fire you?"

Harry knew the answer to Jackson's question. What they had here, inside the confines of this expensive hulk of metal, was a marriage. Jacks couldn't let two marriages fall apart. Harry represented stability. Harry was his ugly wife, but one he loved as well.

"What's more stupid than young men in new love?" Harry asked.

"I think you're going to tell me," Jacks said.

"Old men in new love," Harry said.

"Thanks," Jacks said as Harry struck the steering wheel with the butt of his hand and exploded in laughter.

"WHAT DO you mean, doesn't he work here anymore?" Jacks asked Lionel, the old bartender.

Lionel shrugged.

"Give me his address," Jacks said impulsively. Adrian hadn't shown up at work. The St. Regis crew hadn't heard from him in a week. *If I'm the good guy I think I am,* Jacks thought, *I should track the kid down.*

Lionel wrote down an address, handed it to Jacks.

"My bottle," Jacks said. "We're going to need it." Lionel grabbed the Glenfiddich, handed it over.

Minutes later, Jacks found himself knocking on the door marked 4C of a fourth-floor walk-up in the East Village, around the corner from the Bowery project. He'd kept his elbows at his sides, trying not to touch the walls with his cashmere coat. *How could people live this way?* Jacks thought as he looked at the bare lightbulb above his head, failing in its bid to light the darkened hallway. If the building were demolished, it'd be an improvement.

"Adrian!" Jacks yelled. "Come on, open up! It's Jacks Power, here!"

Jacks had downed a couple of shots on the way, to bolster his newfound sense of heroism. He would have pressed his ear to the door, but he didn't want to catch anything.

He thought he heard shuffling. *What if I have the wrong address?* Jacks thought. He wished he'd brought Harry and his scary tattooed knuckles up.

The door opened. Adrian, half-naked, pale and gaunt, was staring out at him.

"What the hell are you doing here?" Adrian asked.

"You look like crap," Jacks said. "Come on. I'm taking you out."

Adrian stumbled back in his tighty whiteys. "Welcome," he gestured. "Maybe you can suggest something for the décor. I'm thinking marble columns and a Persian rug. Like the Shah's last palace. Or is that too much?"

"Funny," Jacks said.

"Oh wait," Adrian said. "Who needs to decorate? I'm going to be dead. Thank God! I hate dealing with swatches!"

"Get your clothes on," Jacks said. "We could both use a good meal. I found my dinner rather unsatisfying tonight."

Jacks picked up a pair of pants that were on the tattered sofa, threw them at Adrian, then wiped his hands.

"Don't worry," said Adrian. "You can't catch poor."

27

THOUGHTS FROM A KNIGHT
ON THE TOWN

MEN ARE *fools,* Harry thought, *and two of the biggest ones in this city are in the back of my car.* He turned the radio down two notches. *Elvis Satellite.* If the conversation got interesting, he'd turn it down another two. He looked in the rearview mirror at the man Jacks had maneuvered into the back before Harry had a chance to open the door.

The guy was over six feet but he looked like something you could break in two just by giving him the stink eye. His hair was unkempt and too long for Harry's liking, but he was young, maybe that was his excuse. He wore a wrinkled white shirt with cuffs turned up on his forearms, which were crossed in front of his face, as though warding off a demon.

Harry could feel unhappiness coming off his body like an odor. *This guy,* Harry thought, *he's* heyaya—*bad luck.*

Harry wasted no time sliding into traffic; he wanted to be rid of him as soon as possible.

"Cipriani," Jacks said.

"It's late," Harry grunted.

"Now," Jacks said.

Harry turned the car around the corner as though he were pushing it himself.

"Adrian needs something to eat," Jacks said, explaining. "And Harry, if there are any photographers . . ." Jacks caught Harry's eye in the rearview mirror.

"No worry," Harry said, cheered. Jacks had given him license to do damage. He cracked his knuckles against the side of his face and sped toward Cipriani.

Jacks and Adrian slipped in through the private entrance and were whisked to a covert side table by the host, though Adrian had to be tugged gently, like a puppy on a leash.

"C'mon, Adrian," Jacks said. "It's okay, just sit, sit down. C'mon." He patted the seat next to him, and held out his hand, as though coaxing a resistant lover into bed.

Cipriani was quiet, unusual even at this late hour. The chandeliers, at home for over half a century, provided a crystal serenade.

"Those fucking chandeliers will be here long after we're gone, kid," Jacks said. Adrian tilted his face up, and diamonds of light danced across his face. Jackson was struck by the effect; fuckin' guy looked like a modern Adonis, a rock star without the guitar.

Jacks signaled and glasses appeared, the waiter silent and expressionless. Jacks ordered linguini with clams; the choice would provide Adrian with the right amount of warmth and comfort. He waved the waiter off while he poured the Glenfiddich, then placed the glass in Adrian's hand and molded his fingers around it. Jacks wondered if he'd have to swallow the drink for him as well.

"Salud," he said, with false cheer.

Adrian tipped the glass back as Jackson knocked his own back and set up another, the thought of a meeting with his father in the morning flashing in his head like a red light.

"Fuck it," he said. The second one went in.

"Tell me how I get this boulder off of me," Adrian told Jackson, pouring his heart out as though all the receptacles in the world—thimbles, cups, bowls, pitchers, empty swimming pools, reservoirs, entire canyons—couldn't hold his sorrow. "I'd rather die than live like this."

"You know what you need?" Jackson asked. "Distraction. That means new pussy, a new job, travel—"

"I can't even look at another woman," Adrian said.

"Maybe you can work for me," Jackson said. *Why did I just say that? Does this kid remind me of myself?*

"Doing what?" Adrian asked. "I'm an artist. What can I possibly do for you?"

Jackson suddenly figured it out, how to help Adrian and at the same time, of course, help himself. He was a businessman, after all. Commerce would be everyone's friend in this exchange. *And that's a fact!*

"Ever act?"

"Act?" Adrian muttered, making a face.

"In high school, college?" Jackson asked. He measured his words.

"Nah. I'm no fucking actor, I'm barely a writer," Adrian said. He could feel the words roll over one another and out of his mouth. *When did I get drunk?*

"I think you're missing a bet."

"Fuck that," Adrian said. "I'm a playwright. I mean, I was a playwright."

"You want to hear a sad story?" Jackson said "I got one for you. You ready for it?"

"Sure," Adrian said. He looked at Jackson.

"I'm almost fifty years old, and finally, I've met the love of my life. It's like I've been in training all my life to get ready for this girl, to love this girl, and this is my one shot at true happiness," Jackson said. "And she's going to leave me."

"Why?"

"She's restless," Jackson said. *Don't let that thought land,* he telegraphed. "It's not another guy," Jacks added.

"So what's the problem? You love her. Get divorced, and get married. Easy."

"You don't understand. My wife won't give me a divorce. It could take two, three years, if she wants to hold me up."

"That sucks, my friend," Adrian said.

"And that's a fact," Jackson sighed.

"Who can stand in the way of true love?" Adrian asked the empty restaurant.

"I'm glad you feel that way," Jacks said, "because I want to make you a deal."

"A deal." Adrian knew better than to be excited. *A deal to a rich man meant squeezing the little guy. Hadn't he just learned his lesson? He'd traded his girlfriend, the love of his futile, ridiculous life for a lousy ten grand. Adrian started hating Jackson, but still he poured himself another inch of that amber seduction. Why not.*

"Don't you want to know what it is?" Jackson's voice rattled.

The only card Adrian could play was nonchalance.

"Maybe," he said.

"I'll pay you a hundred grand to seduce my ex-wife."

"Are you fucking crazy?" Adrian asked. "Do I look like a whore?"

"Who called you a whore?" Jacks said. "I'm trying to give you a purpose in life."

"I'm not fucking some dried-up ex-wife. Isn't that how you describe her? Her pussy's lined with sandpaper, right?"

"Look, barkeep," Jacks said, pissed, "or should I say ex-barkeep—I'm offering you a hundred thousand dollars to seduce a woman. And not a bad-looking woman at that."

"Why don't I just stick my head in your car window and offer you a blow job?"

"Oh for Christ's sake!" Jackson bellowed. "Who are you, the fucking Pope? What are we talking about here?"

"I'm an artist," Adrian said, his voice weakened. The explosion of self-righteousness had depleted his body of whatever mojo he had left.

"You're an idiot."

"I'm an idiot with standards. The People's Billionaire," Adrian scoffed. "You think you can buy anybody or anything, even love." He stopped himself. *Isn't that what Wall Street did? Wall Street, who walked off with Miss Tracy Bing, his everything, in soft skin and a dress—*

Oh God, Adrian thought. *My baby's a whore.*

Jacks was determined to close. He decided to do what good businessmen do under the circumstances: up the ante. "If you get her to fall in love with you, that's another hundred thou coming your way," Jacks said.

"I'm going home," Adrian slurred as he shot forward, almost knocking over the table.

Jackson shook his head, touched and amazed by the cojones of this kid. *Turning down a deal from Jacks Power!*

"Lemme drive you, at least," he said.

"I got legs. I can walk."

"You couldn't walk out of a fucking hat, you drunk bastard," Jacks said.

"Fine," Adrian said. "Take me home, but that doesn't mean I'm your bitch."

"What do you think," Jacks said, "I'm going to take you home and fuck you?"

The two men lurched onto the sidewalk and stumbled over each other into the waiting limo. Harry pulled the car from the curb as though he was carrying the entire mess on his shoulders, alone.

28

ISOLATED PAWN

O*H GOD,* Adrian thought as he lay across his bed and watched the ceiling pitch and yaw. His bed. *Their bed. Here it comes, the relentless, cruel train of memory.* Figures formed. Late afternoon, the light round and full. Tracy Bing wearing pink cotton panties. She had never worn a thong; she didn't find them dignified. Everything she did was from another era, like a character from a Raymond Chandler novel. She was the girl who walked into your office and ruined your life, dismantling it in one fell swoop, one turn of the ankle.

In his memory, Adrian rubbed the softness between the tiny pool of her belly button and the satin bow on her underwear. The bow, as though his girl were a gift. Which she was. *Was she?*

Then Adrian started crying. Happiness, he'd read, can't be found in contemplating the past or the future. It's found in being fully in the present. The Now. *Well,* Adrian thought, *this is idiocy. If he were to be merely of the Now, and he had a gun, he'd shoot himself.*

Adrian realized two things, as he settled in the Now:

1. He didn't have the guts to kill himself.
2. He was going to take Jackson up on his offer.

• • •

"SO. YOU haven't died." Goldie was peering at Cynthia, his eyes dancing above the black-framed glasses sliding down his nose.

"I haven't died," Cynthia agreed.

"You don't even appear overly traumatized," Goldie said. "Although still too thin. But then, I always did like a full-figured gal. You should have seen my first wife——"

"You were saying," Cynthia prompted.

Goldie leaned forward, not easy to do with the belly. "You are in the heat of battle, my dear, and you appear to be enjoying it."

"Ah. I'm not enjoying it, but it hasn't killed me."

"Not even a flesh wound."

"There've been a lot of dirty tricks." Cynthia counted on her fingers. "Fred got a donor's kid into the Ninety-second Street Y, impossible without letters of recommendation from Nobel Prize winners and a million cash. He got Bill Clinton to speak at another donor's company retreat, and, this is the worst, he got a third one's daughter-in-law's parents into Chez L'Ami Louis during Fashion Week in Paris."

"Oh." Goldie pondered this. "He's good."

"Yes, he's good," she agreed. "He's good at being bad."

"So, what's the damage? I don't see you backing into a corner and curling up in the fetal position."

"Well, I appear to be in control of the board."

"And how can that be?" Goldie sat back, waiting for the answer. *His* answer.

Cynthia paused. "I'm being honest, straightforward. I have a good reputation. I have good ideas. I'm not making promises I can't keep. And I have finely tuned hosting abilities under the most dire of circumstances——"

"So . . . you don't have to buy anyone off. Because people actually . . ."

"*Like* me?"

"And?" Goldie asked. "Come on. Think. This shouldn't be too hard."

"Trust me? . . . Respect me!"

Goldie stood and clapped. Then sat down again. "This therapy thing is exhausting, saving lives left and right!"

"You know what?" Cynthia said. "These skirmishes with Fred and the board, this *is* saving my life. I'm distracted. Let's face it, Goldie, I was left, publicly, for a younger woman. I shouldn't even be able to get out of—"

Beat. *Oh boy.*

"Cynthia." Goldie leaned forward.

Cynthia started to cry. *Damn it.*

"It's okay. It's okay. Let it out." He held a box of tissues out to her.

Cynthia took one and dabbed at her eyes, then worried the damp ball of tissue. "How could he like her?" she asked, in a little girl voice, "when he liked me? We're so different."

"I'm sorry." Goldie reached over and touched her hand. Traffic sounds from outside played backup to her muffled sobs. "It will get better," he said softly.

"Goldie, I think he loves her," she said.

Goldie leaned back. "When everything goes wrong," he said, "what a joy to test your soul and see if it has endurance and courage."

"Zorba, I presume," Cynthia said.

"The greatest philosopher of all," Goldie said. He stood. Their fifty minutes was up.

"JUST WHEN do I pass this 'test'?" Cynthia asked.

"There's no passing," Goldie said as he walked her out, his hand gently touching her side. "There's only experience. The more fully you live the experience, the more healthy you will be. I promise. And maybe you'll gain a little weight in the tuches."

Cynthia stood in the hallway after their session and gave her nonexistent rump a squeeze. "Have a frikkin' milkshake, Cynthia," she told herself.

Minutes later, she was sitting at the dusty bar at J.G. Melon. The bartender sized her up. "Chicken salad?" he guessed.

"Cheeseburger," Cynthia replied. "And fries. Fast as you can make 'em."

"Hungry much?" he asked, amused.

"Starving," Cynthia said. "I've gone hungry long enough."

Zorba!

29

YOU-BOOB: PATZER MOVE

Y OU KNOW how you like being famous?" a man's voice asked.

"Who is this? Penn?" Jacks followed the glow of the digital clock. 5:20 A.M.

"Yes, it's me," Penn continued. Toneless as ever. "You know how much you enjoy people recognizing you on the street?"

"Penn, what's going on?" Jacks swung his feet onto the floor. He could have used those extra ten minutes of sleep.

"You're about to be more famous than ever," Penn said.

Jacks's ears perked up. "What do you mean? What'd I get? Charlie Rose? Bastard has never asked me on his show, you believe that—"

"No. Not Charlie Rose. Your publicist called me this morning. She was too afraid to make the call herself," Penn said. "Ever hear of something called YouTube?"

Jackson rubbed his eyes, looked around for his robe.

"Yeah. It's the Internet, right?"

Penn cleared his throat, his equivalent of manic hysteria. "You might want to get to a computer."

"Okay, YouTube?"

"Y-O-U-T-U-B-E. Dot com. Type in your name. I'm at my home number."

A minute later, Jackson was in his home office, looking at a computer screen, wearing his reading glasses. He tapped his name into the YouTube website.

"JACKSON POWER LOSING HIS SHIRT... AND SHORTS," submitted by InServitude, was the latest video on Jackson, sent in earlier in the morning. Jackson noted, with satisfaction, that there were more than fifty others: press conferences, TV interviews, news clips. He clicked on the tiny video screen and it whirred to life.

The picture was a little blurry, but it appeared to be Jackson, seated next to Margaret Lord Foster.

Cynthia's dinner party.

Jackson's mind flipped to cell phone technology—they all had video capability—

Jacks hated this new world. *Was nothing sacred?*

"Does it feel hot in here?" he heard Video Jackson ask.

"No," bleary-eyed Jacks replied, "no!"

Seconds later, Video Jackson was naked.

Jacks grabbed the phone and punched at numbers.

"Penn!" he yelled. "Start firing! Start suing! Start now!"

30

PROMOTED POISONED PAWN

To GET ready for her lunch with Scott, the unknown, unqualified quantity who decided her fate, Lara dressed in a Gucci pin skirt and silk wrap blouse (with requisite cleavage) from the blessed Ford era and had Kevan reapply her makeup and futz with her hair until it relinquished its wave and settled into an anchor-worthy helmet. She assessed her "look." Too much gray? Would the spike heels survive the walk to the restaurant? Her wish was to look professional yet alluring when she asked for a demotion. She'd called Yasmeen's producer immediately; the smell of Yasmeen's cigarette smoke was still lingering in the air when she'd dialed. But he hadn't called back. She'd called again, two days later.

Nothing. And then again. No response. Lara had no choice but to plead her case with Scott (first name or last?).

She and Scott the Producer were having lunch at a place on East Fiftieth, a favorite retro spot. The waiters—career waiters, not waiter/actor/whatevers—wore white aprons and served ice-cold martinis at lunchtime. The menu included lobster thermidor, creamed spinach, and baked Alaska. You could imagine Ava Gardner and Frank Sinatra "canoodling" in a corner booth, the spectators relishing the view, knowing that something so beautiful could never last.

Lara and Scott sat in one of those padded booths. She studied him as he perused the menu, and noted the faint thinning of hair at his crown, the intense, deep-set eyes. *Tennis was probably his game as a kid,* she thought. She imagined his boyhood room, untouched, like a mausoleum, a testament to his success and his mother's.

Scott was still in his early thirties. He jogged, a lot, except he didn't call it "jogging," he called it "running" and he had "run" marathons. He had a girlfriend whose job, it seemed, was to "run" with him. She was a small thing with large, waxy calves that looked like apples, her hair always in a ponytail, ready to sprint off with her Scott at a moment's notice.

Scott had come over from sports, no surprise there. Was he a "phenom," as the press crowed?

Scott looked up, caught her eye, and smiled.

"You eat here a lot?" he asked.

Before Lara could answer, a waiter appeared, Lara's favorite. Angel was Puerto Rican, his wavy black hair with its thick white streak combed back and gleaming from pomade. His smile was like a welcome-home banner.

"Ah, Miss Sizemore," he asked, "the usual?"

Lara nodded and closed the large menu and set it aside, not sure why she'd opened it in the first place. The waiter turned toward Scott.

"I'll have the Cobb, but can I have the blue cheese dressing on the side, no, not blue cheese, could it just be balsamic, yes, great, and only chicken breast, no bacon, if you could just use spray, do you have spray? A side of spinach, but no butter on it, I'll have it steamed, okay, a little olive oil. And a Diet Coke. No ice."

Angel nodded.

"And all at once."

Angel nodded.

"No ice, but ice on the side. A large glass of ice."

Again, Angel nodded.

"And all at once, please. Can you take the bread basket away? Thanks."

Could you hate someone, Lara wondered, *after just one food order?*

She glanced at a nearby table, where two businessmen, older than Jacks (but not by as much as their countenances insisted) sat. Probably on their third martinis. Their faces were bloated and flushed. One was hunched over, balanced on his elbows, describing something, maybe telling a dirty joke. Lara could taste the liquor in their mouths. She thought about the way a good martini wrapped itself around her tongue.

"Straight up, twist?" Angel was asking.

"Olives," she responded. "I need my vegetables."

Later, she'd ordered another and had barely sampled her creamy, buttery appetizer. Meanwhile, Scott had finished his abstemious lunch and two more Diet Cokes, ice on the side. He had done all the talking, but Lara was content to listen for now, to wait on her courage. She knew it was in there somewhere; all it needed was a little time. And one more drink. Always one more drink.

"I know I'm a rookie at this game," Scott said. He'd pushed away his plate, leaving three good-size bites.

"I figure there's a couple plays I've got to make," he continued. "Number one, we've got to take down the top team. Number two, that means I've got to get my best players on the field."

She looked at him. *What the fuck was he talking about?*

"So here's my pitch," he said.

She waited. *Should she duck?*

"I'm pulling Georgia out of the game. I'm benching her and putting you in."

Oh, shit. Oh shit, shit, shit. SHIT.

"Georgia's old," he said. Georgia was maybe forty-four, a crone, a wizened grandmotherly type.

"She has six months left on her contract," Lara stammered. "If you fire her, you'll screw up her negotiations for the nightly."

Georgia was heading to the lead anchor seat, nightly news. Better hours, more prestige. Scott leaned back, tilted his head. His bemused expression made her want to slap him.

"1989. Kareem Abdul-Jabbar. He could have played one more year. He had knee problems, a bad disc. But people loved watching him play, they couldn't get enough of the skyhook. You seen the skyhook? Money in the fucking bank. And those big glasses. He was the first one with the goggles. Plus, he had class."

He paused. Lara found herself staring at her drink, look at the shape of the glass, like a tit on a stick. Calling her with smooth, sexy, soulful, hypnotic notes: *Edith Piaf, straight up.*

"And along comes Earvin 'Magic' Johnson. There was no one bigger than Kareem. Until there was Magic." Beat. "I don't need two stars. Not when I got a young, hot one who can do it all, pass, shoot, score—and look fucking awesome in a bikini."

Sing to me, martini, Lara prayed to her drink. *Sing your silvery song.*

"That bathtub segment was one of our top-five all-time pieces, by the way, the network fucking flipped for it," he said. "We're going to stick you in a bikini so often, the audience is going to think we're the Playboy Channel. It's good that you're not eating."

Lara's eyes led her back to where the businessmen were on their next round of drinks.

"I quit," she heard herself say.

"Pregame jitters," he said. "It's natural. I'm handing you the ball, and you're going to run with that fucker. This is a slam-fucking-dunk."

"Please," Lara said. "I want to go overseas. I want to be in the story. I want to be in khakis, not a thong. You could help me, make me Yasmeen Ali, Christiane Amanpour, Anderson Cooper. I'll do great, I promise." *Anderson doesn't have to wear trunks and oil up his chest before an on-air.*

"Anderson Cooper?" Scott snorted. "He's like the Ryan Seacrest of anchors."

"Look, I want a demotion," Lara said. "No more bathtubs and carb-free diets. I want to be where the action is."

"Fuck you," he said.

"What?" Lara's hand went to her cheek, as though she'd been slapped.

"I'll tell you when you can have that job. In ten years, when the drinking has finally caught up with you. Then you can go to whatever fucking desert mountain secret towelhead hideout cave you want. But right now I'm using up your last good years in a studio with fucking lighting and fucking hair and makeup and wardrobe, and you're fucking going to love it."

"I'll tear up the contract," Lara said. "I am a human being—"

Scott snorted. "You're not a human being, you're a tool, and you work for me. You think I didn't see this coming? The walls have ears, sweetheart, they have ears and pie holes. You try to get out of your contract, we'll sue you. Nah. We will literally kill you, because you won't be able to handle the pressure. If you don't do what I tell you, if you don't drive when I say go for the fucking basket, you're a fucking corpse."

Scott stood up and brushed away imaginary bread crumbs from the imaginary piece of bread he hadn't eaten.

"Oh," he continued, "and don't bother crying to your boyfriend or fiancé or whatever the fuck you call him, I could give a shit. No matter what the tabs say about your drinking and that asshole, you and your bikini are a ratings darling. That's all I care about. Do I look like Don Hewitt to you? It's called entertainment programming, and no stupid bitch is going to fuck this up for me."

Scott suddenly smiled. "Have a great rest of the day," he said. "If you want to go on a run sometime, let me know. We'll have to do this again soon."

He turned and walked out the double doors.

Lara sat there. She waited as Angel came by to tell her the bill had been paid by the gentleman, and to offer her another drink. She waited as plates were scooped up and the tablecloth cleared. She waited as her BlackBerry vibrated, and she waited until all of the other customers had left, save the two sitting directly in her eyeline. She waited until there was one left.

She stood, cradling her purse, drink in hand, careful not to spill, but spilling all the same. She sat down next to him.

"Shitty lunch?" the businessman asked, sizing her up.

"I've had better," Lara said. "Actually, the company was shitty. But the martinis were delish."

"Cheers," he said. Their glasses touched. She was struck by the color of his eyes, the thickness of his hair, his mustache, his wedding ring. She wondered if he was good at eating pussy.

She watched him over the rim of her glass.

"You're that girl," he said. "My buddy and I, we recognized you."

"Yes," she said. "I'm that girl. That's what I am."

"I gotta tell you," he said, "you look frikkin' hot in a bikini. You could be a Hooters waitress. Seriously."

She stared at him. "Thank you," she said.

"Are your tits real? My buddy and I, we had a bet going," he said. "I said they were." His face veered closer to hers. She could taste his breath. *Can you smell heart disease on a person?*

Can he smell me spiraling out of control?

Maybe Scott was smarter than she'd given him credit for. She'd seen her future in women in their fifties, crossing quickly on the street, buying dry soup at the Korean market, loitering at the old Italian coffee shop; women with their cigarettes and their wrinkles and a ring not on their ring finger but on their thumbs, their hair gray and wiry, because what's the point. More often then not, they were walking their beloved dachshunds. They always knew where you could still sneak a cigarette in a bar. They went after five, after they'd walked their dogs, and they told themselves that at least it was after five, and after five wasn't so bad, and if they weren't picked up by eight o'clock, it wasn't such a huge loss, after all, *Survivor* was on at eight. Maybe they had rich ex-husbands, kids they didn't talk to. Lara stared at them as though she had a crush. The pretty ones killed her, the ones whose falls were steepest. No one looked at them twice now, except Lara. She coveted the curve of a cheekbone swathed in pale, wrinkled flesh, the faded almond eyes hooded by age, by gravity, by the lasting impression, like a thumbprint, made by disappointment. The teenage models who roamed the streets like vacant-eyed antelope didn't interest Lara. Nothing was as fascinating as the specter of what she could become: one bad choice led to this face, to that body, to those hands, that tremor.

Lara excused herself from the table, but not fast enough, and not with enough equilibrium. The table seemed to hurtle toward her as she attempted to stand. The businessman had suddenly multiplied and was screaming at her, his florid-faced clones yelling, too.

Angel grabbed Lara under the arms as she began to retch, and carried her into the bathroom. Lara burrowed her head into his chest. Her stomach felt better; it was time for her mind to feel the worst of it.

"Do you think I got my point across?" she asked Angel as she turned the water on and washed the last of herself into the sink.

31

GAME ON

THUMP THUMP THUMP. Artemus Power's footsteps on the Aubusson echoed the throbbing in Jackson's brain. His office door flew open.

"Idiot!" his father yelled.

"Now wait a minute." Jacks stood to take the blow.

"*YouTube?* You have made a complete mockery of my name. Who did I raise, Paris Hilton? Your mother would roll over in her grave!"

"Dad. Just calm down. I've already had the video taken down and fired the kitchen staff," Jacks said. "I'm suing countless assholes. Everything's under control."

"Everything is out of control. I'm taking over the Bowery," his father spit. "I've gone over our quarterlies. We can't afford to blow this deal because your head's up your ass or up that news reader's ass—I'm meeting with Krach today and telling him I'm the Power to speak to. You're out."

He exited, slamming the door before Jackson could reply.

Jackson massaged his temples. He'd spent countless hours sweet-talking Krach, hoping the mayor would sign off on ordinances and tax incentives so they could break ground. His father had not only muscled his way to the negotiating table, he was shoving Jackson out altogether.

Caprice knocked at the door. "Your one o'clock is here. Should I set up the conference room?"

The conference room was glassed in. *No, thanks.*

"I'll take it in here."

"It's messy," she said. "Chinese. Lots of containers."

"I'll take it in here, Caprice," he repeated. "Just send him in—without the food." He didn't want to say Adrian's name out loud. What if they needed to create another identity? Already his plan was complicated, even before any useful information had been exchanged. And why'd he ask Adrian to come to his office? Jacks, the Lord of Loutishness, the Duke of Deception, was bungling like an innocent. Too late to change his mind; Jacks was pinned to his office with meetings and calls. This would be the first and last time he would invite Adrian up to the tower.

Fuck all. And why'd he offer a hundred thousand? Why not fifty? The guy was unemployed, for crying out loud. He'd have to talk Adrian's price down—

"Okay, Big Man, I've had a few thoughts since we last spoke," Adrian said, materializing in front of him. Was this guy some sort of magician? He'd have to be, to get Cynthia wet.

"Took you long enough," Jacks said.

Adrian had cleaned up. He'd shaved, was wearing a black leather jacket, crisp white shirt. Jeans. Black shoes. A good make, pricey for a bartender.

What kind of game was this kid running?

"You're a prick," Adrian said as he sat down and folded his arms across his chest. "I wanted to get that out on the table. But I'm taking you up on your sleazy offer, which means I'm a prick, too. Given that, I'll do the best job possible. You won't be disappointed."

Jackson stared at him. *The kid's audacity took nothing away from his looks. Annoying.*

Caprice poked her head in. "May I take your drink order?" she asked.

"The gentleman and I will just have water. Flat. No ice. And no interruptions."

Caprice nodded. If she found this particular summit unusual, you couldn't decipher it in her eyes or the tone of her voice. *Thank God I can rely on one person in my life,* Jacks thought.

The water was delivered. Adrian started in. "I've made a list of questions," he said, taking a piece of paper from the leather jacket that still reeked of the cheap cigar preference of its previous owner.

"What is this?" Jackson said. "You don't ask for shit, kid. I ask for shit."

Adrian smiled and handed the sheet to Jackson, who was forced to put on his reading glasses (he hated having to put on his reading glasses).

"The Cynthia List," Adrian said.

"Favorite color?" Jacks read out loud. "Favorite fruit?" *What is this?* "Favorite season? Favorite time of day?" *Makes no sense, no sense at all.* "What side of the bed does she sleep on? Favorite flower?" *Easy one.* "Favorite perfume?" *Another easy one.* "For daytime/nighttime?" *Ridiculous.* "Pet peeves?" *Me, Jacks Power.* "Childhood fears? Secret sexual desires?" *This guy's dead.*

"I need to know everything about your wife," said Adrian. "I need to live inside her brain, to know her intimately without ever having met her."

"Fuck you," Jacks said, "I'm not answering these—"

Adrian had touched a nerve, and found that he liked it. "Why not? You're her husband. You saying you don't know her?"

Jacks suppressed a smile and his blood pressure. It was a good play by the kid, but he didn't want to upset the power balance by showing appreciation.

"This is what I have so far," Adrian continued. "Cynthia Power née Hunsaker, born in Aurora, Missouri. Parents deceased. Father left when she was eight—you know that's a crucial year in a child's growth, eight years old—especially between a daughter and father. Kids never get over that sort of thing. Right in the middle of her Electra complex—" Adrian paused. "That's harsh."

"Cry me a fucking river," Jacks said. "I would've liked to be rid of my dad at eight."

"Nice. I can see why she likes you so much," Adrian said. "Okay, Cynthia danced since the age of four, became professional at eighteen, moved to New York."

"How did you find all this out?" Jackson asked him.

"Google, phone calls. I don't use computers when I write. Bad for the artistic process. Words should be written by hand, pencil to paper. Take that away, you lose the experience of the word, the life of the word." Adrian paused.

Jackson was lost, thinking about Cynthia when he met her. How could he describe her skin? An untouched canvas. No freckled shoulders left by carefree days in the sun, no scars from climbing fences or falling off a bike, no impressions left by earlier lovers. Her skin carried the somber tone of her early years, the adultlike child, no fun, no play, but the sacrifice she'd made gave birth to perfection.

"You want to marry your sweetheart?" Adrian pushed. "You want to get on with your life?"

"Yes," Jackson said. He thought about Lara, every piece of her a testament to living. She was a verb, his girl.

"Good. Answer those questions," Adrian said. "I'll have more tomorrow. And I'm going to need some cash. I need a new wardrobe, and enough money to take your wife to the best places. Oh, I need a BlackBerry. I hate 'em, but if I'm on a date with your wife, or in bed or something, and I need info—"

"Stop," Jackson said, holding up his hand.

"Hey, that's what we're hoping for, right?" Adrian asked. "I need an apartment for six months—that should be enough time—"

"You'll need to work faster than that."

"I will," Adrian said. "But I'll need a quiet place to rest my head afterward."

"Not a problem." He'd had to get rid of the "love nests" scattered throughout his buildings in Manhattan when reporters got too nosy, but he could borrow the show apartment he'd used to lock in sales on the latest Power Tower. "So we have a deal."

"We have a deal," Adrian said, and stood up. "I need a good, personal photograph of your wife, clear and close-up, something that captures her essence. I've seen the Google stuff—like, I want a picture you've taken."

"Her essence. That's rich," Jackson said. He opened his desk drawer and slid a photo in a silver frame across to Adrian. It was one of Cynthia, alone. Staring into the lens. The hint of a smile.

Hello, Mona Lisa.

How long ago had he taken it? And when had it found its way from proud display on his desk to inside a desk drawer? Adrian stared at the photo, slipped it from the frame, and put it inside his jacket.

"Let's meet tomorrow," he said to Jackson. "I'll call you."

"I'll call *you*," Jackson corrected.

ADRIAN walked out of the office. His hand brushed his jacket, feeling for the photograph. Seeing Cynthia's face made him feel dirty. She was attractive and sophisticated, but what struck him was the vulnerability in her eyes.

I'm going straight to hell, he thought. *I'd better give her a good time.*

He tapped the elevator button several times. Office buildings made him nervous; he'd avoided the nine-to-five life as though it were a communicable disease.

"Asshole," Adrian muttered. *Was he angry at Jackson for past transgressions or at himself for future ones?*

"Accurate description," said the old man in the plaid suit with the questionable shade of red hair, though he didn't bother looking over at Adrian as he stood waiting for the elevator.

"Sorry," Adrian said. What do you call the father of the King of the Jungle? He recognized Artemus Power. He stayed beneath the press radar, unlike his son, but there were still a few articles on Google. Why was he riding with the commoners? Here was an animal who didn't need to wait for anything—food, drink, people, elevators. The ground floor could be brought to him, if necessary.

Adrian tapped the elevator button, again.

"Someone once said, the less time you have left, the more patient you get," the old man said.

Adrian turned, his cheeks suddenly hot. *He's right—why am I in such a hurry to commit fraud?*

"They were dead fucking wrong," Artemus Power said.

32

BISHOP'S ADVANCE

CYNTHIA FOUND when she squinted and tilted her head in her closet mirror, her body looked hot—not twenty-year-old ballerina hot, more like forty-five-year-old hopped up on caffeine-water hot.

Why was she so nervous? Why should Cynthia be intimidated? As a potential friend-with-benefits, Ricardo Bloomenfeld was unimpressive. Not because he wasn't good-looking; Ricardo Bloomenfeld was handsome and groomed and yet inelegant. He was too deliberate; his mannerisms, his walk, his tan, his blinding teeth, all bore instructions transcribed from *GQ*.

But Goldie was right. Cynthia had to surf the next Big Wave. Sex.

"I should just pick up a stranger?" Cynthia had asked Goldie.

"No, but people do it," he replied.

"Like people I'm divorcing, for example," Cynthia said.

Goldie chuckled, but then got down to business. "There's someone out there. Someone you're already comfortable with. We're not talking about love here. We're not talking long term. I'm looking for the man, the experience that will launch you into the world. Who will appreciate you, and whom you can then let go."

"A hit and run."

"More like an eat and run." Goldie choked on his line.

When, oh when, Cynthia thought, *will I find a professional thera-pist?*

That's when she thought about Bloomenfeld. But how good were Bloomenfeld's eyes? Would they catch the knrinkles (wrinkles above the knee)? Would he see her elbows? Oh, cruel elbows! Like rings on a tree, they revealed the age of the oak in the sleeveless dress.

Hide the neck! She grabbed a scarf, suddenly a staple in her ward-robe. Was it just last year her neck was a trophy? Cynthia's swan neck had taken a dive.

In the car, she instructed the driver to stop at Bloomenfeld's of-fice on Park, then checked her outfit. Chanel suit. Sheer ribbed stockings. A classic pump.

Once they arrived, the driver held the door open and the city enveloped her, pushing her toward the doorway with the brass marker: BLOOMENFELD AND ASSOCIATES.

Cynthia counted the days since her last period. Her periods were becoming erratic, but pregnancy was not impossible. Lately, when she'd skipped a cycle, she'd think, *Pregnancy or menopause?*

She giggled, and rang the buzzer.

"CYNTHIA POWER for Ricardo Bloomenfeld," she announced herself to the receptionist. The lobby, redecorated every two years, reflected the anxiety of Bloomenfeld's taste. The current incarnation was very dark, very masculine, very foxhunt and cigars.

"Is he expecting you?" There was an edge in the girl's voice. She obviously thought she'd screwed up appointments.

"No." Cynthia felt the smile creep across her face; he certainly wasn't expecting her proposition.

Moments later, she was staring into Ricardo Bloomenfeld's eyes, so blue and so clear that one could see the workings of his devious brain.

Here we are, Cynthia thought, *suspended on the tightrope between double-cheek kiss and doing the nasty.*

Dive in. "I was wondering," Cynthia started, and hated herself immediately. Who would want to fuck a person who began the question with the words "I was wondering"?

Ricardo waited, the handsome lawyer paid handsomely to be patient.

"I was just at my therapist," Cynthia said. *Agh! Who doesn't want to screw a depressive?*

"Never been to one," Ricardo said. "I don't want to know how crazy I am. And frankly, I fear I'd be out of work if I listened." He gave her a conspiratorial grin.

"Yes, well." Cynthia faltered. She'd never asked a man to have sex with her. Should she start with coffee? Would he charge her for a Starbucks run?

No reason to beat around the bush (*note to self: laser?*), Cynthia. She pictured Bloomenfeld's mouth on hers, his tongue writing songs on her neck, his manicured fingers inching up the inside of her thigh. *Not unpleasant.*

"Would you like to have sex with me, Ricardo?" Cynthia asked.

"I'm sorry, I can't," he said, not unkindly. As though he'd been expecting the question.

Time stood still. Cynthia cleared her throat. "When do you anticipate our next meeting with Jackson and his attorneys?" she asked.

"Cynthia, do you want to know why I can't have sex with you?" he asked.

"This is my favorite time of year in New York," Cynthia said, her face burning. She stood to leave.

"You are a stunning woman." Ricardo got up and walked around his desk. "I am flattered beyond belief to be on the receiving end of such a tempting offer."

"Please," Cynthia said, turning from him. "I'm embarrassed enough as it is." The door seemed miles away.

"It's not you." Ricardo lowered his voice. "It's me. I just got back from Brazil. I had this procedure done."

"Procedure?" Cynthia asked.

"A phalloplasty," he said. "I'll be ready to go in two weeks."

"Oh, dear God," Cynthia said. Ricardo's door danced farther from her reach.

"It's all the rage," he continued. "I can't keep up with all these technological advances. I would prefer, of course, that this not get out."

Cynthia nodded, then leapt out into the hall, followed by Ricardo's voice.

"Two weeks, Cynthia!"

Cynthia dashed past the receptionist and onto the street, leaving behind her favorite scent and an anticipatory smile on her phalloplastied attorney's face.

33

STUDYING THE BOARD

JACKS MANAGED to ignore the questions Adrian sent to the office daily. A stone-faced Caprice dropped the faxed pages on his desk and between calls, between meetings, when he would have five seconds to himself when his father wasn't yelling about this or that, Jackson would slip a page from under a pile of today's must-dos and read a question.

A few of them were softballs:

Favorite Flower: Yellow roses.

Favorite Song: "The Best Is Yet to Come."

Favorite Perfume: Coco Chanel (Jacks had bought it for her every year. Until he'd seen the unopened boxes in her bathroom cabinet.)

He'd answered these right away and felt damn good about himself. What man could know his wife better than he?

But most of the questions were like this:

If your wife had to choose between a glass of red wine, say a Bordeaux, or a martini before a meal, what would she choose? If she chose a martini, would she choose gin or vodka? What brand?

Well, Jacks wondered why the fuck this was important—he was hiring Adrian to screw his wife, not analyze her.

What was this? First Wives 101? Okay, so he'd skip through a few more pages.

He'd hear the *thump thump thump*. His father, off to use the restroom. Every five minutes, it seemed. So goddamned embarrassing to have your father at work every day; made Jacks feel like a kindergartner.

What's the longest wait? *Waiting for someone to die.*

How about waiting for someone to divorce you?

More questions:

What is your wife most likely to get into an argument or heated discussion over? Politics, religion, or whether the neighbor's hedge is against code?

What size shoe does she wear? Has it gotten larger with age and pregnancy? (What?)

There were a hundred questions by now. Jackson slipped the list under the pile of papers he actually had to deal with. He'd come back to them after his breakfast meeting with a Gargoyle.

The Four Seasons at breakfast. Anything discussed here, in the morning, would be up on the WSJ website within the hour. Jackson rushed to his usual table, and there he was: the New Zealander who had more money than God, although Jacks never understood that statement. Why would God care about money? What would He spend it on? Would He out-yacht Ellison or Allen or Diddy?

Jackson had called the Kiwi a week ago. Important to stay on top of these relationships, especially when Artemus Power was trying to isolate Jacks. *Soon, he'd have to be air-dropped basic staples.*

Jackson listened to the Kiwi, nodding and grunting affirmatively. He couldn't understand a word coming out of the Kiwi's lopsided mouth.

Jacks liked the Kiwi as well as he could like anybody who had more money than him. Since his heart attack and new wife, he'd been ingesting the balm of the upper-class male, Lipitor, had enlisted a trainer, had stopped drinking ale, and forsworn eating those lyonnaise potatoes he so dearly loved.

At least, that's what Jacks believed the Kiwi was telling him over his steamed asparagus and egg white omelet.

"Facking dite," said the New Zealander. "The weef is effter me." (*When she wasn't out at nightclubs,* Jacks thought.)

"Mm," Jacks said, remembering the real reason he'd called the breakfast. The Kiwi had been married to his first wife for over thirty years before he'd left her for the underwear model trophy wife, who appeared to be *all trophy, no wife*. Could the Kiwi answer the wife questions Jacks was struggling with this morning? Had the Kiwi known the woman who'd been mother to his four grown children? The woman who knew him before the billions became his closest friends?

It occurred to him that the Gargoyles, at a certain point in their lives, do not want Truth. *They want comfort.* They want stroking. "You are a Genius." "The rules don't apply to you." "You are special." It's a rare first wife who can keep up the Big Lie. It's a rare first husband who doesn't want to hear it. Constantly.

Jacks thought about another Gargoyle, who'd made his mint in telecommunications and dumped wife number one, a corporate attorney, for a Cambodian stewardess—only to discover after the honeymoon that the reason she so enjoyed the wonders of anal sex was that "she" was born with a penis.

"She 'as this designuh, bloke wants fifty for an Oriental reg, fifty thousand dollars," he said. "That's a hundred thousand dollars 'fore texas—if I paid texas!"

He laughed, a bit of egg white sticking to the telltale patch of white stubble on his chin. Jacks wondered at the dye jobs of the Gargoyles. The ones with young wives appeared to have become intimate with Clairol. Jacks was surprised the man hadn't purchased the company. Then he realized that Clairol was owned by a conglomerate owned by another Gargoyle.

Gargoyles would not touch one another's conglomerates, just as they would never fuck one another's wives. Feuds among Gargoyles didn't last long; they needed the semblance of human connection, no matter how insincere. Jacks recalled a dinner at the Bel Air in L.A. A theme park Gargoyle casually mentioned firing five thousand people that day, then congratulated himself (over a sublime Sancerre) on the stock price, which, of course, had gone up as a result of the layoffs. Stock price had long replaced cock length as the ultimate measurement.

The New Zealander had recently purchased an Internet bandwidth streaming Wi-Fi digital downloading message board, making instant billionaires out of the two shaggy-haired guys in Birkenstocks who created the site. This new world was traveling at hyperspeed on an invisible highway made of electronic nerve pathways. All Jacks could do was build.

The Gargoyle wrapped up the breakfast after a half hour. A meal with a Gargoyle, no matter how memorable the food, never lasted more than an hour. The sensual side of life—food, drink, sex, wives, and children—was a distraction from what really fed the billionaires: making coin.

The Gargoyle inquired about the penthouse of Jackson's building on Fiftieth. He and the new wife had just purchased a sixty-million-dollar teardown on the Park. "We need a place to stay," the Gargoyle wheezed. "We're practically homeless!"

Jacks watched him as he wheezed and sputtered—*the Kiwi, he's happy, right? He's trim and he's got a young trophy wife and a teardown on the Park—he's rebuilt his whole life from the ground up—that's happiness, right?*

Right?

Jacks was alone on the sidewalk on Fifty-seventh; the Gargoyle had batted his wings and flown off to headquarters at the top of his building on Sixth. Gargoyles preferred their oxygen thin, their perches high above the crowd. Harry was at the curb, flouting the law, ignoring the taxis honking as they veered around the corner.

Jacks consulted his BlackBerry. Caprice's schedule had his next meeting set in an hour. He wasn't sure how to make the best use of this pocket of time. So he began to walk.

Walking alone in the city, at a pace calibrated by himself, was rare. Jacks Power felt as peaceful as if he were atop a mountain range; the skyline of New York stood in for the Rockies.

His mind relaxed. His long-forgotten painter's eyes gathered up the pocked sidewalks, pretzel vendors, office workers shouldering briefcases, their hands softened around warm paper cups; then his gaze crawled up vertical monuments, finding harbor at the top of a church spire, or in the glassy reflection on a new building of vapor trails left by a lone plane.

New York was artwork, an entire city built, literally, to encourage man to see beyond the mundane. To experience possibilities. *Had the thought occurred to anyone else?*

So what were his Power Towers? Testaments to the imagination, or ego running roughshod? Would a true artist destroy a thing of beauty because it had become redundant? How many times had he replaced charm with utility? Expensive, boastful utility, but still. Charm and beauty had bent to his will; the old department store on Madison, the hotel that had housed artists a century ago on Broadway, half a city block of history in Hell's Kitchen.

Jacks reassured himself; *I'm no Robert Moses.*

Commerce vs. Art. As he'd told Adrian, *commerce would always win, in the end.*

Look at my own life, Jackson thought. *Lara, the shiny, new symbol of my name and power and money. Look what I can buy! And Cynthia, all charm and old-world beauty and obsolescence. Look what I can destroy.*

Harry was trailing him and honking his horn, trying to get his attention. *Fucking guy.*

"You have nine-tirty!" Harry shouted, tapping his watch. Jacks looked back at the church, at stone carvings at the roofline; a lion grasping an elk's neck, a nun's serene expression, demons caught midhowl, and the gargoyles, one more intricate and fearsome than the next.

Where had the time gone?

His reprieve was over.

34

OPENING PREPARATION

I'M COMPLETELY unfuckable!" Cynthia sobbed.

"I blame the shoes!" Vivi announced, the guilty parties swinging from her fingers. Cynthia was lying on her bed with an ice pack over her eyes. *Oh, she'd had better days.*

"And nothing says, 'Take me, I'm yours,' like a scarf!" Vivi said.

"Scarves are elegant," her mother protested feebly.

"Mom, these are nurse shoes!" Vivi said of the sensible cream pumps. "Geriatric nurse shoes!"

"They're good for my swayback," Cynthia said.

"Fuck-me heels they're not. But they might be good for changing bedpans. And Mom, your hair was in a chignon. You were dead before you walked in the door," Vivienne concluded. "Who wants to fuck an ice sculpture?"

Cynthia rolled over on her stomach and groaned.

"Do lesbians have it this tough?" she asked.

"You can't be a lesbian, Mom. You've chosen a team, now work on your pitch."

"I'm buying a rake and moving to Vermont, where old ladies go when no one will look at them!"

"Mom, I'm done with you," Vivienne said. "You and I are going shopping."

"What?"

"We'll be Ivana and Ivanka. We'll hit Cavalli, D&G, Gucci," Vivi said. "No more daytime beige, and no more nighttime ruffles and bows. You look like you're going to the prom. With Elvis."

Cynthia did a double take. "Since when do you know anything about fashion?"

"I've always appreciated couture," Vivienne said.

"Hold on—as a child, you hated all those darling Lilly Pulitzers, then you wouldn't even look at the Calvins and Laurens I bought— and remember, in high school, you wore those Frye boots until they stunk—"

"My style works for me," Vivienne said.

"You wore a kaffiyeh and overalls to my ballet gala when you were fifteen!"

"Mom. Teenage boys hide *Playboy* under their beds. I hid Italian *Vogue,*" Vivienne said. "Once I saw Carine Roitfeld on the street and followed her for six blocks. If I could get her to autograph my chest, I would. I would marry that bitch. I know exactly what you'd look fantastic in."

"Vivi." Cynthia sat up. "Are you sure I'm not a lost cause?"

Vivienne sat down next to her and cupped her mother's face.

"Mom, when I'm done with you there's not a person in the city who won't want to ravish your body and make you say their name."

"Promise, Ivanka?" Cynthia managed to smile.

"I'M NOT buying this silly thing," Cynthia said in a strained voice. "I don't even know why we're trying this on." She tugged at the leopard-print bustier Vivi was hooking up in back.

"Do you need help?" asked the Italian shopgirl, standing just outside the plush VIP room. She'd been asking questions incessantly: *Can I get you anything? Tea with your feathered bodice? Peanut butter cookies with your tiger-print mini? Put on these heels, they're uncomfortable and they run small, but they're fabulous. Which designer water do you prefer?*

"We'll yell." Vivi dismissed the helper with a wave, then turned to her mother. "Lean forward, Mom." Cynthia leaned forward and Vivi reached into the bustier and pulled her breasts up.

"What on earth are you doing?" Cynthia demanded, slapping away her hands.

"Look!" Vivienne said, pointing toward the mirror.

Cynthia turned, and gasped. "I have breasts!" she said. The bustier had transformed her from Cynthia Power, Upper East Side doyenne, into Gina Lollobrigida, international screen star.

"All you had to do was find them," Vivi said.

A thought came to Cynthia. *Could a bustier have saved my marriage?*

"More," Cynthia said, breathless.

"What?"

"More!" Cynthia said. "Dammit, Vivi, get me more!"

Cynthia and Vivi hit Cavalli, struck Dolce & Gabbana, swept La Perla, and then they were done. Cynthia handed the bags to the downstairs maid, preparing to drag her body upstairs. If the maid noticed the boss's new Louboutin gladiator boots on which Cynthia teetered across the foyer, she said not a word. If she noticed the slice of Dolce skirt that hugged Cynthia's body like a lost love, she allowed no acknowledgment. "Ma'am," the maid said, averting her eyes from the call of Cynthia's bustier, "there's a gentleman waiting for you in the sitting room."

"Who? I'm not expecting anyone. Why did you let him in?"

"He said it was urgent, ma'am. He said that you would want to see him."

"What's his name?"

"Fred Plot–um . . . sorry, ma'am, that's all I can remember."

Cynthia froze. "I can't see him."

"Of course not, ma'am. Forgive me, ma'am. I'm new here."

Fear had transformed the girl's eyes into spinning plates. *Does she see the same in mine? Screw that.*

"What's your name?" she asked the quaking girl. *And whatever happened to Esme?*

"Sabrina, ma'am."

"Fine, Sabrina. I'll be right in. I just have to change. No, no, I have to freshen up. But I am *not* changing."

"Yes, ma'am. I'll tell him. The madame is freshening up, but not changing," Sabrina said, standing there like a tree shaking delicately in a breeze.

"Go," said Cynthia.

"Thank you, ma'am!" Sabrina scurried off.

THE BEAST of Wall Street had pounced, using the element of surprise to neutralize his prey. *Is there a chapter called "Board Politics" in* The Art of War? Cynthia wondered as she walked into the parlor.

Fred's back was to her, staring out the window. She noticed him check his watch. The big man wasn't here to settle in for a comfortable chat.

"Hello, Fred," Cynthia said. "What a pleasant surprise."

Fred turned, speaking before registering her presence. "Cynthia," he said, "I wanted to talk to you myself." Niceties dispensed with. Point, Plotzicki.

"Fine, thank you." Cynthia answered the unasked question. "How are you, Fred?"

"Oh, ah, good, thanks." He faltered, as though seeing her for the first time. *Did he just blush?* "You look very nice."

"Thank you," Cynthia said, "you're looking well." Truth to tell, Fred's waistline had shrunken. *Perhaps a high-protein low-carb diet of freshly inducted associates?*

"Cynthia," Fred said, clearing his throat, "I'm here because I want to give you a graceful exit. You deserve that much after all that you've given to the NYBT."

"I can do graceful, Fred," Cynthia said, "but 'exit' is not what I had in mind."

"You're in a vulnerable position. I know. I've been there myself. We don't make good decisions when we're in the middle of divorce proceedings. You should see the plastic surgery my first wife had when we separated. Her eyebrows are in her hairline. That kind of thing doesn't go away."

"Do I seem vulnerable to you, Fred?" Cynthia asked. She watched him take in the leopard-print bustier, the gladiator boots . . .

"I don't want to fight you," Fred said.

"Then don't," Cynthia responded. "You have your strengths, I have mine. We can both win."

"Cynthia, I don't often lose. I have an excellent memory, and I can't remember the last time."

"There's a first time for everything," Cynthia said. "Today was the first time, for example, that I've worn these." Why did she want him to look at her boots? Was she willing to garner attention from anyone, even Fred Plotzicki, her archenemy?

Well . . . yes.

He looked down at the boots, then seemed to lose his bearings.

"I'm giving you one last chance to step off the plate, Cynthia," Fred suddenly said. "I don't want this to get ugly for you."

Cynthia smiled. "That's the second time someone's said that to me lately. I wonder why people feel they have the right, as though I can't protect myself without their consent." Beat. "Good evening, Fred. I'll have Sabrina show you the door."

Cynthia turned and strode out like a lioness on the savannah, hoping that she'd bump into Jacks—she'd tear him apart.

(And she was teetering only slightly.)

35

OUTSIDE PASSED PAWN

JACKSON'S EYES opened in the early morning gray of Lara's bare apartment. *Taking a chance, being here. The vultures are probably outside, cameras ready, waiting.* Last night made the risk worthwhile. Lara had fallen into a dead sleep on top of him; Jacks had even moved his hand across her rib cage to confirm her breath. *If only he could have died pinned under her.* Then he'd remembered that his day was very busy, and his life even more so, and that, at not even fifty, he was one of the most powerful men in America, and if America is the most powerful country in the world, then he, Jacks Power, was one of the most powerful men in the universe.

Dying? Dying was out of the question.

He'd watched, hawklike, as Lara bent over to pull on her sweats. Her skin gave off a slight gleam, the matching indentations above her hips like perfect thumbprints left by an unseen hand. Her blond curtain of hair descended over her features. She slipped out the door after grazing the top of his head with a kiss. Jacks was proud of her. He could live with his future wife waking early and leaving their bed. He could live with her fame. He could live with it because the job would make her stay. He and the job would work together to chain her to their city, to that desk, and to that camera, to his embrace.

Jacks Power went back to sleep, smiling.

FOUR-THIRTY *in the morning.* Lara, suddenly sober as a nun, was up and at 'em. The gradual awakening of the Beast gratified her senses; hulking shadows morphing into buildings as lights blinked, rectangular eyes, one there, another here. The *snap-thud* of bundles of newspapers hitting a sidewalk.

Five feet from her apartment, Lara had already lost the scarf around her neck. Today would be bright and sunny. Today, everyone would be reveling in the weather, and she would be the only one, as usual, lamenting the warmth on her face, forced to reveal herself.

"It's gonna be a beautiful one," the driver said as she crawled into the backseat and closed her eyes.

Lara was greeted at the back of the studio by security, then escorted by the perky intern to her makeup chair. Coffee was inserted into her grasping hand, pages placed on her lap. She glanced at them, flipping each page to the floor one by one. Lara was not as studious as her coanchors about the plot of the new Evanovich mystery, or the epidemiology of monkey flu hitting South Asia, or how to organize your purse in three easy steps. But to her great fortune, Lara was in possession of that rare gem, a photographic memory. *Read once, regurgitate later. Repeat, ad infinitum.*

Lara was still in her makeup chair when Georgia attacked her. Georgia, the beloved den mother. Georgia, possessor of the world's greatest brownie recipe. Georgia, who wrote thank-you notes to every single guest she'd interviewed, even the hateful ones spitting sharp knives out of their mouths. Georgia, who'd lent a shoulder and a vacation home to the assistant cameraman who'd recently lost his mother. This Georgia flung herself at Lara and pounded her with those helpful, loving hands, rolled up so tight Lara could see knuckles spinning toward her like drills.

"I'm going to kill you!" Georgia shouted. "You fucking bitch! You cunt!"

"What?!" Lara shouted back. "What?!" But she knew what. *She knew what.*

Suddenly several men were holding Georgia back. "You SNAKE!" Georgia screamed, spitting like one of her crazy guests. "You STOLE MY JOB!" Lara recalled Georgia's interview with a drooling, growling serial murderer; it was like questioning a rabid German shepherd.

But, oh, the ratings! The serial murderer had handpicked Georgia through his agent (his *agent!*). The interview had been promo-ed at the top of every hour for two weeks. The ratings were outrageous. The whole news team celebrated after work. *We poured champagne on the graves of his victims,* Lara thought. *For shame. All our hands are dirty.*

Georgia became Murderer's Choice for interviews.

"YOU'RE FUCKING SCOTT, TOO! YOU FUCKING SLUT!"

The screaming, Jesus Christ, it was endless and yet had been going on less than a minute.

"YOU FUCKING DRUNK!"

Georgia, the woman who'd written a thank-you note to the Drooler, had to be hauled off by the assistant cameraman who'd lost his mother. The last Lara saw of her, Georgia was trying to take a bite out of his arm.

Lara could see Scott (first name or last?) out of the corner of her eye. He was standing, arms crossed loosely in front of his athletic body, bouncing lightly on his runner's toes. His posture was altogether casual, as though watching a game on television. Their eyes met through the whirl of activity.

And he was smiling.

Lara took over anchor duties that morning.

AFTER he awakened, Jacks went through the answers he'd scribbled furiously into the night after Lara had rolled off him. *Fuck. I can't read my fucking writing.* Jacks knew time was running out—Cynthia needed to agree to a divorce, Adrian needed to seduce Cynthia, so Jacks needed to answer Adrian's questions.

Jacks realized there was one person, one trusted soul, who could decipher anything he wrote: Caprice.

"MR. POWER, Caprice don't know what you're up to," Caprice said, so angry she was slipping into pidgin, "but maybe you should find another executive secretary."

Every syllable that came out of that flamboyant mouth sounded like a Jamaican lullaby, even when she was blasting him.

She'd arrived at the office early, as usual, and set her daily Bible quotation on his desk. Today's offering: *"There may be no trumpet sound or loud applause when we make the right decision, just a calm sense of resolution and peace."*

Resolution and peace, Jacks thought. *Sounds good. But lack of applause? Why shouldn't I get attention for doing the right thing?*

Jacks called Caprice in to help him "with a confidential assignment of a personal nature" and handed her his sheaf of scrawls. He watched her lips move as she stumbled through the first three questions:

1. *Is your wife a rose, an orchid, a carnation, or a daisy? And which flower (and which color) does she prefer?*

Which seemed quite innocuous to Jacks, given the next questions:

2. *Which part of your wife's body would she consider most sensual?*

And:

3. *Is your wife a top or a bottom? If she's a bottom, has this changed over the years? Was she ever a top? Why did this change (if applicable)?*

Caprice lowered the stack of papers and pursed her lips in disapproval.

"Please, Caprice," Jacks said, "I'll pay you double to get this done today—"

Now Caprice was glaring at him. Bad call. Caprice could not be bought. (*Dummy, dummy, dummy,* Jacks thought, mentally pounding his big, stupid, photogenic head.) She walked back to her desk and started packing up that canvas tote she carried everywhere. *What is in that thing?* Jacks wondered. Every morning Caprice entered the place looking like an elegant pack mule.

"I will do anything, anything, for you to help me," Jacks said. "I'm begging you, Caprice. Jacks Power does not beg, you know that."

"No, Mr. Power," Caprice said. "I cannot do what you are asking."

So what does a man do under the circumstances?

Jacks closed the door to his office and pretended to cry.

"What you doing there, Mr. Power?" Caprice asked, alarmed. Her Jamaican lilt sounded high notes.

Jacks waved her off. "The pressure," he said, "it's just too much. Just—leave me alone." He stumbled backward into his chair. And counted.

On five, she knocked at the powdered glass door. He turned and saw her sad, opaque figure on the other side.

After waiting the appropriate recovery time for a man who was emotionally destroyed, he opened the door.

"Mr. Power," she said, looking down her chin at him, as she

would her children, "I will be calling the Father on this matter. I will be using his guidance."

Jacks waited, not patiently, through two meetings, always aware of the curve of Caprice's body, bent over her phone and talking in hushed tones to a Bronx minister who would decide Jackson Power's future.

After the cagey congressman from the Fifteenth finally left (Jackson had cut the meeting from his habitual fifteen minutes to ten), Caprice was ready to capitulate. There was only one catch.

"Mr. Power, you must agree to go to church," Caprice said.

"What?" Jacks asked.

"If I do this for you, you must agree to the church," she said. He saw the look in her eyes. Those beautiful black eyes. *Okay, so, big deal,* thought Jacks, *would it kill me to go to church?*

"Fine," he said.

"This Sunday," Caprice said. "We go together."

"This Sunday?" he asked, in the face of her implacable expression. "Sure." Jacks shrugged. Is it possible for a body and its cells and the nuclei of all the cells to be screaming NO at once, but for the word "sure" to come out of one's mouth, smooth and easy as a bead of warm water?

Sure, it is.

"Can't wait," he said, as he ushered her in and watched as she sat down and pressed her knees together, her notebook on her lap, pen at the ready. For now, she would simply transcribe. Jacks wondered how long it would take his father to try to steal her from him. Yet another reason to hate Artemus Power.

36

OVEREXTENDED PAWN

O*H HOLY shit,* Adrian thought, as he used the keys that were sent to him that morning to open the apartment on the fifty-fifth floor of the Midtown luxury building that featured the name you saw everywhere in Manhattan, not just on silver-skinned towers but on golf clubs, ergonomic chairs, garment bags, bottles of water. *Get a grip,* Adrian thought, *get ahold of yourself, rookie, you've been in nice places before. You've served a few bottles of gin at palaces on the Upper East Side, or artists' lofts in Tribeca so pristine that it was hard to believe any art had ever been created there. Snap out of it, junior.*

He set his bag down.

He'd never slept in a place like this before. Normal people in Manhattan did not live like this. Fuck that. *People* did not live like this.

Had he ever seen the Hudson from this angle? He'd only thought of the river as the city's toilet. But look at it, murky and torpid and gloomy . . . and awesome. And over there, the George Washington— wait till you see that bridge at night, the windows sang. Like a photograph framed in diamonds. Oh, dude, you haven't even seen the fucking bedroom yet. The master. You ever sleep in a master? I don't think so. This can be yours. Well, maybe not this exactly, but close to this. Nice, like this. And all because you've agreed to seduce some guy's wife.

Adrian took in the living room. Gray velvet couches faced each other. Two silver leather chairs. Plexiglas coffee table. He touched everything, all of it.

Oh, Life was Good.

He walked into the kitchen. Haven't had a kitchen in how long? Years. Always ate off the bar menu, or a slice on the street. The kitchen was as big as his apartment. The blacktop center island was the size of his bed. And on the Tibetan blue granite countertop stood a gleaming Gaggia Titanium. *Cappuccino, Mrs. Power? Should I call you Cynthia? Okay, Cynthia. I make a mean cappuccino, Cynthia.*

The Sub-Zero refrigerator was filled with Power bottled water and protein shakes. Adrian tasted an allegedly chocolate one. The first disappointment. Until he looked over at the adjacent wine cellar. He pressed his nose to the glass, then opened the door.

On this side were the French wines. Bordeaux, Burgundies, Château this, Maison that. On the other, champagne. Bottles and bottles of champagne. Krug, Cristal, Dom, Perrier-Jouët, Armand de Brignac . . .

He backed out, slowly, taking in every label he could. He grabbed a Mouton Rothschild and hugged it to his chest, then skipped down the hallway on an ivory rug, and into the master bedroom.

Four-poster bed. Check. Silk sheets, cashmere blanket, down pillows. Check, check, and check.

He bounced up and down on the bed. Noted the forty-two-inch flat-screen mounted on the far wall. Thought about what he'd be doing later in this room.

Please, God, don't let Cynthia's pussy feel like tree bark. What if I get splinters in my dick? Adrian took that thought, wrapped it up in his mind like a package, and walked back into the living room, sinking into the couch that had summoned him with its fine velvet, its soothing palette.

What have I done?

The enormous windows seemed to loom over him now, closing in, the receptive sky turning claustrophobic.

How could he . . . ?

A clear, high-pitched ringing punctuated his thoughts.

Adrian swiveled and picked up the phone on the black coffee table.

"Hello?" No one there. The ringing continued.

Adrian followed the shrill tone past the pantry, guest bedroom, powder room, to the fax machine in the small office at the end of the long hallway. A paper peeked through the roller on the top of the machine and then showed itself. The answers were coming.

Adrian picked up the first sheet and began to read. He was impressed; they were more detailed than he had anticipated. He was halfway through when his cell vibrated.

"Hello," he said, then paused. "You want to meet me *where?*"

ADRIAN walked to the corner of Seventieth and West End, where he summoned the nerve to look up at the huge black spider, straight out of a Japanese horror film, but with steel legs and a web of metal and alloy and girders and long plates of smoked glass. The spider was extremely loud, a wall of sound, so that the men crawling up its legs and onto its back could communicate only two ways: shout or gesture. The construction worker who'd handed him the orange hard hat merely waved for Adrian to follow him.

They stepped onto a metal plate and the man semaphored for Adrian to hold on, and the thing jerked and before Adrian could scream he was hoisted up into the belly of the spider, tunneling through until he was sure he was going to faint. The man finally put on his own orange hard hat and gave Adrian a half smile lacking sympathy. Maybe this was the line of demarcation between men: those who could handle heights and those who could not.

"This way," he mouthed to Adrian once the metal plate had stopped. Adrian's legs would not move and he was in agreement with them. Who was he to argue with his appendages?

"Come on!" the man shouted. Adrian unclenched his hands and wiped them on his pants and somehow moved forward until he saw Jackson Power talking to a few workers, gesturing wildly, his arms wheeling away from his body, his face clenched, hair whipping in the wind.

When he spotted Adrian, he put his arms out and strode toward him as though they were in the lobby of the Pierre. *Jesus Christ, what is this,* Adrian thought, *a test?*

"Damn guy's trying to screw me on the glass. I know what he's doing. You see there, you see that?!" Jacks pointed to a building across Seventieth. Adrian didn't shift his eyes.

"Forty-second floor, see, the panels don't match up. That looks cheap to me. Does that look cheap to you?"

Adrian just nodded, pinned by abject fear to the top of the heaving metal spider. *Glass panels? Who cares? We're going to die, don't you see, you crazy rich fuck? One false step, and our intestines will be lacing someone's boots!*

"Okay, so we're good. You got my answers, you're ready to go!" Jacks shouted.

"I'm good!" Adrian shouted back.

"Don't fuck this up!" Jacks shouted.

Adrian looked across a breach where the metal plate had dropped him. Silhouetted by the sun bouncing off the turgid river, he saw an angel, wings outstretched, light dashing around his body. Adrian blinked. The angel's wings folded, and he barked. "Who told these guys to take a break? I don't take a break, they don't take a break! Screw the union!"

The orange-haired lion in winter: Artemus Power. Adrian watched the old man step along a steel beam as though he were walking on the beach at daybreak.

The whole family is fucking crazy, Adrian thought.

"You need an identity!" Jacks was shouting, ignoring the fact that his father was doing a mean imitation of a high-wire act. "A job. You can't just be a bartender, or actor or writer . . . it has to have substance and when I say substance, I mean money."

Adrian deflected the rub. "How about an architect? Artistic, yet has some dough?"

"No," said Jacks, waving away the notion like a virus. "First of all, I hate architects. They all think they're fuckin' Picasso or something. The guy who did the plans for this place—he almost had a seizure when I moved a line. One line, okay, so I erased it—and this brick, you see this brick?" Jacks picked up a mustard-colored piece of brick. "Beautiful, right? It's beautiful, there's no doubting its beauty. Mr. Harvard School of Archishmarcitecture hated it. I fired him."

"It looks like puke," Adrian said.

"Shut the fuck up, you don't know." Jacks tossed the brick to the side. The thing came this close to sliding off the edge and ruining someone's Christmas. "These people, they don't have vision, and on top of that, they think they're geniuses." Jacks took a breath. "You want to know how many geniuses I've fired in my lifetime? You couldn't count that high, my friend." Jacks pointed a finger at Adrian's chest. "You're a hedge fund manager."

"Hedge funds?" Adrian said. "Aren't they passé?"

"Hedge fund manager and trust fund brat. She'll never even question it. No one does, except other bottom-feeders. Get yourself business cards, buy a few suits. And get a haircut. You need a haircut."

"My hair is fine."

"Of course it is. If you're a chick."

"My girlfriend loved my hair. The only chance I have to get her back is that Mr. Wall Street's going bald. Why would she like him?" Adrian willed himself to stop speaking.

Jacks stared at him. "Don't make me answer that. You really want me to answer that?"

"Money. Right. Money." Adrian sighed.

"You go here"—Jackson flipped him a business card—"you talk to this guy, tell him you're my long-lost nephew of the cousin I don't speak to, he'll take care of your mop. I need you up and running by the end of the week.

"Did you watch TV this morning?" Jacks added suddenly. "My fiancée. She's on *Sunrise America*. She's like the fucking lead anchor now. She did it. My girl."

"Good, good for you," Adrian said, sullen.

"Good? You know how many morning anchors there are?"

"No idea. Nine, ten? A hundred?"

"Fuck you. Oh, I got something else for you. You're going to this thing, you'll sit next to Cynthia, it'll be a big fucking surprise."

He pressed an envelope into Adrian's hand.

"And that, barkeep," Jacks said, pointing at the brick, "that's called 'Bloom.' There are few things in this life more beautiful than that brick. And that's a fact."

Jacks turned and stepped away from Adrian, leaving him alone in the fretful sky.

CYNTHIA knew she was about to enter a shit storm without a poncho. How would personalities collide? Who would be left standing once the ego dust settled? She took a last look back and let the cool gray of the early afternoon satiate her. Then she stepped inside the Brooke Astor Hall.

Bruce Harold Raymond, the artistic director of the New York Ballet Theater, greeted Cynthia with his back turned.

Ah, the un-welcoming committee, Cynthia thought.

"You're the first to arrive," he said, not bothering to rotate his perfectly oval bald head. He watched the dancers move as though he longed to be onstage again. He was tall, still admirably slim, and so studiously hygienic that some whispered he hadn't had sex in decades. Cynthia thought about the first time they'd met, when they shared a company—his aloofness even then commensurate with his unremarkable talent. He was an average artistic director—always choosing the safe options, never challenging the audience or the critics. But he was canny. He'd survived several board regimes by making himself just useful enough, and just dangerous enough. He knew where the bodies were buried and he could dig them up: overdoses, affairs, bribes, eating disorders, AIDS, theft, alcoholism, kinky sex, extortion. The behind-the-scenes shenanigans at the NYBT would make the Desperate Housewives blush.

Cynthia smiled, almost appreciating his frank rudeness.

"Lovely," Cynthia said flatly, appraising the *La Bayadère*. She'd come early on purpose; she'd wanted to catch Bruce alone, to get an accurate temperature reading: *Freezing.*

One for Team Fred.

Cynthia wondered what promises had been made to B.H.R. by Fred the Manatee. *A co-op on Gramercy Park? A hundred thousand in an offshore account? A Bermuda vacation?* Cynthia would have to lace up her old toe shoes to maneuver around Bruce Harold Raymond and his questionable judgment.

Margot emerged from the stage, where she'd been squatting on her heels, her spine erect as a two-by-four. "Princess!" Margot, Ballet Mistress and Captainess of Team Cynthia, said, embracing her. "You look thin and drawn. How do I look?"

She twirled, lithe as a butterfly.

"Thin and drawn," Cynthia said.

"Thank you!" Margot exclaimed. "What'd you think?"

"As exquisite as last year. And the year before."

"And the year before that. I do my best," Margot said, glancing at Bruce Harold. "Within my confines."

Bruce Harold Raymond's eyes remained glued to the stage, though Cynthia knew he was listening with his entire undefiled body.

While the conductor murmured quietly to the musicians tuning up in the orchestra, other board members were starting to file in. "Where's my dancer?" asked a stout woman made stouter by a fox fur brought out prematurely. "I don't see my dancer."

"Twenty-five thousand dollars to sponsor, and she thinks she owns the poor girl," Margot muttered.

"There she is!" the woman exclaimed. A tall, athletic redhead was standing off to the side of the stage, watching a principal dancer lift a ballerina above his head.

"Come over here!" the woman demanded as she made her way to the foot of the stage. "I own you, come talk to me!"

"Cruella de Bitch," Margot said. "I could kill her."

Amazing, Cynthia thought, looking at the dancer with the porcelain skin, *that mortification doesn't make a sound.* The redhead had captured Cynthia's imagination when she first signed on with the company several years ago. Her athleticism made her stand out among her peers, perhaps too much, as Bruce Harold Raymond had not seen fit to promote her. Cynthia had tried talking to him about the girl. Wouldn't she be great in the role of Medora in *Le Corsaire*? She could even dance the Sugar Plum Fairy in *The Nutcracker*? Or perhaps Odette in *Swan Lake*? Her suggestions had fallen on deaf ears.

"Let's begin," Cynthia said. "That'll cut her off."

"Avoiding bloodshed?" Margot smiled, then headed up to the stage. The board members took their seats. The orchestra quieted down with a final, plaintive blast of horn. The dancers hit their marks.

Cynthia felt a stir in her chest. But this time, her excitement wasn't about art, it was about business. The business of saving art.

Maybe I can do this, she thought. She'd pursued meetings with potential investors. One or two sounded promising, a young hotshot hedge fund manager in particular. *Younger people would be open to new ideas—to my new ideas. Maybe the NYBT would meet their budget this year.*

Maybe.

"Cynthia Power?" a man called out. "Is there a Cynthia Power here?"

The conductor's chin shot up, the dancers lifted their heads, still beautifully in character. Cynthia caught the moment as though it had weight. She turned in her seat, feeling every eye upon her. A man was charging down the aisle, his khaki overcoat billowing out behind him.

"Are you Cynthia Power?" he said.

"Yes," Cynthia stood, holding the back of her chair.

"You've been served." He slapped a folded paper into her outstretched hand.

Cynthia didn't sit back down until after he'd left, his rapid, heavy footsteps marking each beat of her heart.

"THAT FAT motherfucker!" Margot remarked. She had leapt from the stage to Cynthia's side, and was reading the summons. "Who does he think he is?"

Cynthia was being sued by Fred Plotzicki for libel. *Libel?* The article in the *Times* announcing her appointment hadn't helped, but Cynthia couldn't have been more circumspect in the interview. *"We've had our problems in the past, any board has, but I'm looking forward to a new year of growth for the NYBT"* was much more kind than *"The maniac is not only screwing the talent, he's screwing the company."* The NYBT lawyer had informed her of the possibility of a nuisance lawsuit; Fred Plotzicki would not go quietly.

Cynthia swiveled in her chair. "Nothing terribly dire, I assure you," she told the board members. "Bruce, let's begin." Bruce Harold gave her a basilisk stare, then nodded at the conductor, who raised his baton. The board members settled in. The music started. Soon they were treated to a rendition of the balcony scene from *Romeo and Juliet*. Cynthia's heart quieted and her breath found its meter. A graceful, playful demonstration of innocent first love was the perfect antidote to being served with a subpoena.

Even if she'd seen it a million times before.

"I DON'T like my seat for the opening night," the fox fur woman bellowed from across the conference table. The official agenda of the board meeting was to tie up last-minute plans for the fall opening-night gala. Cynthia's agenda? Exit polling. *Who remained enthusiastic about her ascendancy, and who had jumped ship? Too late to change anything about opening night,* she told herself. *The fall lineup had been chosen by Bruce Harold and the executive board months ago. There would be no disappointments. And no victories. The gala after-party at the Plaza would be filled with bland superlatives.*

"The performances were very nice," Cynthia said to Bruce Harold, seated next to her. He bowed his head.

If you want to take a nap, she thought.

"I need to be seated front and center. I can't have people in front of me. I get sick," the fox fur woman complained.

"I was allergic to the centerpieces last year," Morris Stegler clicked. "Pollen. I had to leave early." *Click.*

Screwzenka, whom Fred had appointed to represent the dancers, waltzed in late, then drew her chair fitfully across the floor, making a screeching sound.

Which was all Cynthia needed to know that Screwzenka was still screwzing Fred Plotzicki. Cynthia eyed the dancer. *Where was Tonya Harding when you needed her?*

Cynthia got down to the budget. "I've touched on this before, but we are treading water. Our audience is, let's be frank, old. The board has to woo the younger crowd who've spent millions on paintings and planes and designer drugs and are looking for a new hobby. The NYBT should be their baby. It's the only way we can stay alive."

She checked. They were listening. Now: Artistic Vision. NYBT was the stolid workhorse of the New York City companies. *Nutcracker, Romeo and Juliet, Coppélia, Cinderella,* and *Don Quixote* year after year, season after season. "We need to utilize our star power," Cynthia told her captive audience. "We need danger and excitement. We need, for lack of a better term, sexuality. This year, I'd like to try new things—new dances, different choreographers. I don't want to say we're tired—but I think we could mix it up a bit."

Cynthia assessed the board at 35 percent Plotzicki, 65 percent Power. The signs were on their faces—and in their nodding heads.

After the board filed out, Cynthia leaned back in her chair, stretched her arms over her head, and exhaled as though she'd been holding her breath for years. Then she stood and levitated an ankle onto the windowsill, a makeshift barre. She stretched over, pushing out her chest; her nose kissed her knee.

She still had it.

"Nice," a voice said, the interruption as unwelcome as the one earlier that day. Cynthia looked up, annoyed. The man in the doorway was young and striking. *Too tall and good-looking for a financier,* Cynthia thought. But his easy, five-hundred-dollar haircut, his suit with its silk pocket square (a bespoke Tom Ford?), and his Italian loafers screamed "Help, I've been kidnapped and forced to work on Wall Street." Was he as self-assured as he appeared? His confidence reminded Cynthia of someone; it became clear a few moments later that that someone was her husband. Her ex-husband. Her soon-to-be-ex-husband. *Wasband. Has-band.*

"May I help you?" Cynthia asked, as devoid of emotion as metal.

Adrian had to bite his tongue to keep from saying "With that extension, I think we could work something out." *Oh, he couldn't believe his luck. No denying it, Cynthia Power was hot. The silver-framed photo of the ice queen hadn't done the flesh-and-blood woman justice.* Cynthia pulled her full form up to standing while he stared. "I said, may I help you?"

"I'm here to help you," he said. "Cynthia Power?"

"For the second time today, yes," she said, making sure he could measure her annoyance in her eyes, the tilt of her chin.

Fine, Adrian thought. *You think I haven't seen bitchy before? I can do bitchy, honey. You try shoveling liquor into people like you.* "Jordan," he said, "Robert Jordan." Oh, Adrian felt guilty even saying the name out loud. Robert Jordan, the doomed romantic hero in Hemingway's *For Whom the Bell Tolls.* One of the few books he'd read in high school—one of the few characters to whose traits he could aspire. "I believe we had a meeting," Adrian said, "but if you're not up for it, I can take my money elsewhere."

Remember, you're a hedge fund guy, Adrian told himself. *This is how they speak. They're assholes. That's why women love them. They love talking about money, about how much they paid for that painting, that car, that driver, that house, that nanny, that school, that landscaping, that illegal rooftop structure, those shoes . . . that wife.*

That girlfriend.

"I'm sorry," Cynthia said. "I've had a rough morning."

"Really?" Adrian said. "I can't say the same. I had a particularly good morning. I made two million in the time it would take to take a leak, pardon me." *Bitchy enough for you, Princess?* "I've got twenty"— *check your Panerai, Adrian, check it*—"and then I'm on the helicopter to the Delaware for fly-fishing."

"Great, well," Cynthia said, wondering why men like this thought talking about money was polite conversation, or conversation at all. Two million? Two million doing what? Trading one object for another? Her hope for the new generation of art lovers was flattened in seconds.

Adrian feigned impatience. "I'm interested in dance; I'm tiring of the art scene—so overpriced, and for what? But I did make a mint off the sale of my Hirst. Didn't go with the couch." *Easy, boy, don't lay it on too thick.*

Cynthia almost swallowed her own face. "Let's get on with it," she said. "I don't want you to be late for your . . . helicopter ride." She made the words "helicopter ride" sound as crass as a trip to a Village porn shop.

"Would you like to take a tour of the auditorium, the stage, see the dancers? They're rehearsing." She could see the young dancers floating across the stage. Without the music, their feet lightly thumped the wood floors. Intoxicating, that sound.

Adrian dearly wanted to see the dancers, but he needed to stay in character. He'd been told specifically by Jacks—Cynthia likes men with money, with power, with confidence to the point of obnoxiousness. Every woman does. (Look at Tracy.) And Jacks thought he should play it cool, reel her in slowly. Not too slowly, Jacks said, he did have to get divorced and remarried in a matter of months.

"I don't think that's necessary," he said to Cynthia now. "I've looked over your portfolio, was dragged to a couple of performances last year by my girlfriend." There, he dropped the "g" bomb; when he made his move, she wouldn't know what hit her.

Cynthia wasn't surprised. The money men usually loved the dancers, but they just saw tits, ass, the small of a back, the smoothness of a thigh. They had no idea and did not care that they were looking at a human canvas, salivating over a moving, flying van Gogh.

"They're quite stunning, our dancers," she said. "I think it's best if I show you a brief performance." If she could clarify the lure of their bodies, perhaps that would seal the deal; toe-shoed sirens is what she called them. "And of course, you'll want to attend our fall gala. I'll make sure you receive an invitation."

"Fine," Adrian said, making a show of looking at his watch. He still couldn't get over the smooth, sharp beauty of the Panerai—it was like walking around with a live rare snake around your wrist. "Let's go."

Cynthia forced a smile. Here was everything she'd grown to hate in one Calvin Klein billboard–ready package! It was almost as though he were trying.

But this Jordan character, he had money, and no doubt had pull with his brethren. Her objective was to attract a younger, moneyed crowd. The "scions," "children of," the "debutards," the boys who worked at art galleries their parents owned, the girls who worked at Christie's and Sotheby's while awaiting their spread in a fashion monthly.

Cynthia smiled and held the door open for him and held in her pity for the poor girl whom he would someday marry.

Adrian smiled at her sweetly as he walked through, and Cynthia could almost see, in his eyes, the child who'd been slowly dismantled by ambition. Despite her instincts, she warmed to him.

"You know, you remind me of my mother," he said. Then he walked down the hall at his hedge fund manager clip. She couldn't see the smile on his face, she couldn't tell he was repressing a laugh. No, Cynthia was busy picturing the handle of a knife sticking between those broad shoulders, lacerating his handsome silk cashmere overcoat.

37

FORCED MOVE

O<small>H, A SATURDAY</small> without plans! No charity event, no library gala, art opening where pretension fills the room like a gas, garden soiree, Gargoyle brunch, no something honoring somebody, no premiere of a film incomprehensible in any language, no photography exhibit of people you could care less about if they jumped out of their frame; no birthday party, book signing, bar mitzvah, or taping.

Like two normal people, Lara and Jacks settled into the French coffee shop across from the park and ordered. Jacks felt brave, making this public appearance together—enough time had passed, enough headlines had screamed—he no longer felt like hiding. He and Lara had discussed it, debated the timing.

And so, he waited for someone to notice. And waited. Meanwhile, Lara's teeth had stopped throbbing from her hangover, calling her out with their presence—*your teeth are here, here we are, Teeth!*

Jacks was starting to get impatient. And not just with not being recognized. *Why hadn't that Adrian punk called?*

"I'm heading to the bathroom," Jacks said. He hated telling her even a minor lie. Did a small violation mark the beginning of the stream of infringements, leading to an ocean of transgressions? Actually, he did have to pee, and in the meantime, he'd call Adrian.

Jesus, had he and Cynthia already slept together? Whore. Who cares. Bitch, she'd closed her legs to him like lobster pincers. *What's wrong with me? I'm great in bed! Fuck it, I'm glad.* How did he feel about this new twist? Adrian and Cynthia, tormenting their naked bodies into pretzel shapes.

Jacks wondered as he held his dick in his hand and waited, waited for his—

He decided he'd feel okay about it. Here Jacks had the best girl in all of New York City, and if it's all of New York City, than that's the world, pal. And her little problem would be solved, easy. He would even stop drinking, too, he thought. Fine. He didn't need to drink. Trump didn't drink, he'd done okay. He'd gotten divorced too, married a young, beautiful thing. Not younger than Lara. Lara was younger, he was pretty sure. At least by a couple of months.

No pee ... no pee. Oh, the pressure was there. Was it in his head? No. Oh, what a thing to be obsessed over. Peeing! How had his life come down to this? Jacks Power, trapped in a bathroom stall in a French café where the service was mediocre and no one had even recognized him this morning? Another reason to hate the French!

This humiliating trifle, this mignardise of mindfuckingness—the fact that he couldn't pee on command—was happening more and more. He calculated that he used up more minutes in the day trying to pee than in the actual act of peeing. Normal for his age, his bearded fuck of a doctor had told him. He hated that guy's hands. Fat and smooth with the big gold ring. What was *he* so happy about? *Hey, I'm happy, I'm the fucking billionaire, I got the young hot successful best-in-the-business girlfriend. I'm the happy one!*

Fuck. He dialed Adrian again, with his thumb. Not easy. No

answer. Again. Who did this punk think he was? This was no way to run a business. Jacks would ream him out first chance he got. As he walked back to the table, no one even looked at him. He hated the French.

Lara was standing at the window, holding her cell phone. The paper had dropped to the floor.

"What's wrong?"

She didn't look at him. "She's dead."

"What? Who?"

"I have to go to the newsroom," she said. "They're going to screw her—they don't want me to go—"

"Lara, who's dead?" Jacks asked again.

"Yasmeen," Lara said. She gripped his arm, her eyes like flashing lights. *Danger. Danger.* "I have to go," she said, though her legs weren't moving. "Scott doesn't care. He'll fuck this all up. He called her Radio Face—"

"What about your latte?" Jacks asked. Now he was the desperate one. *Don't leave me alone in this French restaurant where they don't even have the manners to greet you properly—fucking Gray's Papaya greets you right, but here, NOTHING.*

"I love you," she said, and then she was on the street, her white-blond hair whipping her face, her arm reaching into the sky. She was swallowed into a yellow cab and gone.

He sipped at her latte. Someone had died, what was her name? *Radio Face.* So here he was, alone. Jackson Power was in love with a woman who placed him, in her priorities, below work, below this dead stranger, and, he hated to say it, probably below her next dirty martini.

Cynthia had understood "The Deal." If one is married to a Power, one must forgo the idea of "self" in return for a life filled with social engagements with interesting, clever, successful, dynamic people (when they weren't dull) with private jets, dazzling jewels, and stunning homes. Everything a woman could ever want.

Except this woman. Shit. Jacks was nothing if not a total pro at feeling sorry for himself.

"Would you like to order?" the waiter asked. He was in black, as were the rest of the waitstaff. He spoke with no trace of a French accent. "Mr. Power?" he added.

Jacks smiled. The morning was turning out all right, after all.

ADRIAN ignored the insistent trill of his cell phone. This art show was coming up: he had to think this through, create a backstory worthy of a playwright. Worthy of Cynthia Power.

Your name is Adrian West, newly christened Robert Jordan. You are no longer a bartender hailing from South Jersey; you're Philadelphia "Main Line" all the way. You attended Yale, then Wharton. You're close to your mother. Your father passed away. He was head of a large auto parts conglomerate, factories that started in Pittsburgh, then moved to Puerto Rico, then the Philippines and Asia. You didn't know your father well; he traveled constantly. He occasionally made time for your lacrosse games. You did fine in school. Not a genius, but when your father went to Yale, when your grandfather went to Yale, when there is a small yet architecturally significant administrative building on campus bearing your name—you go to Yale.

You move on to business school—your father thinks you might want to run the company someday. He thinks wrong. You move to New York City. Your father dies shortly thereafter. By that time, you're ensconced in your work. You look up your dad's fraternity brother's cousin's nephew. This trading thing sounds interesting. You hate numbers, but you love money. You start on the lowest rung of the money ladder, but you have a clear view to the top.

Five years later, if you look down from that ladder, you'll see the bodies. You don't bother. You've dressed the part since day one, way before you were anointed: the shoes, the socks, the underwear, the suit, the suit, the suit, the suit, the shirt (the dry cleaner—you fired three before finding the right one), the cuff links, the tie, the haircut. There's not one too many of anything—not a hair, not a thread. From day one, you look ready to win.

Adrian conjured a few stories to "charm" Cynthia: the hotel heir who snapped and threw himself through a plate glass window, the pit boss who'd carried on a long-term affair with an Asian tranny. He'd downloaded articles on hotshot hedge fund managers, and he still for the life of him couldn't understand what it was they did except make money procreate. They didn't make anything, didn't construct anything, didn't write anything, didn't teach anything, didn't fix anything or break anything—there was a lot these guys didn't do. What they did do was figure out a way to have rich people's money fuck other rich people's money and have lots and lots of litters of money.

His ignorance about hedge funds wasn't why he was dodging all those messages on the BlackBerry and cell phone.

The problem was, Adrian *liked* Cynthia.

Cynthia had walked him, silently, to the Astor Hall auditorium. After the "mother" remark, it was clear to Adrian (as though spelled out in broken glass that he'd stepped on barefoot) that Cynthia didn't like Adrian (or "Robert"). On this point, Adrian had succeeded. Look, he'd been up nights watching old romantic comedies.

What he learned at the movies: dialogue, pop, pop, pop, dip, fox-trotting words—the two leads start off *hating* each other. Can't stand the sight of each other. Can't share a cigarette, much less a bed.

Well, Cynthia didn't like him. Could he recover, spin this record by dint of personality? Charm? The ultimate acting job, and there was no script. There was just him, Adrian. *Make that Robert.*

Was he lovable? Maybe. He'd have to make sure. At the very least, he was fuckable. Was there an *Idiots Guide to Cunnilingus*? Cynthia was used to the touch of an older man—a very experienced (too experienced, it would seem) man. What did he, Adrian West, bring to the table? Energy? He could and had fucked five, six times a night.

(Oh no—did she like the word "fuck"? Or would it have to be "make love"—he didn't mind "make love." He rolled the words over in his mouth.)

But he had the key: three-by-five cards that held the answers to the questions Adrian had posed to Jacks. He'd painstakingly transcribed them from the list Jacks had faxed over.

Adrian had to guess at more than a few. Jacks wasn't a detail man when it came to his wife. Perhaps if she were a building, she would have warranted more attention to detail. *The Cynthia Tower.*

Too late for Jacks. Adrian would have to scale this one himself.

The First Floor of the Cynthia Tower was staring up from his hand. Heavy eggshell stock, silver ink. The engraved invitation. An art opening at the Greer/Nockus Gallery honoring *ArtFocus* magazine's latest media darlings. Tomorrow night, at a white linen-covered table, Adrian would be sitting next to, *surprise, surprise,* Cynthia Hunsaker Power.

He would order her favorite, Clos du Mesnil champagne, from the nonplussed waiter who already had too much on his hands, *thank you very much,* what with serving a lamb chop, salmon, or vegetarian (your choice) dinner to several hundred of the best the art world had to offer: the artists, the new and greedy, the old and jaded, the crazy, the deliberate, the moribund-but-still-a-name-so-let's-invite-them.

The collectors: surprisingly old; surprisingly unadorned; surprisingly committed.

The buyers: the movie people taking the same view of Art as they would a Mercedes or a Rolex. If I buy this, will I look smart? (And how much will it be worth in ten years?) How many do I have to buy before I'm called a "collector" in my next *NYT* article? Three? Five? Twelve? When can my six-year-old be called a collector?

Adrian had studied up on the artists represented by the gallery. He would grease Cynthia up with his knowledge of Art, his appreciation of Form, his vast understanding of Content. And like Claudette Colbert, Barbara Stanwyck, and Irene Dunne, she would be surprised, then charmed. Just like the movies. The Hudson view wasn't far from his grasp.

LARA walked quickly, launched by a sense of purpose she hadn't felt in over a decade. Past the large, square glass sculpture outside the studio. Past the chunky tourists in their ill-timed, ill-fitting khakis, their wide white flesh a buttress against this new cold, as they waited for that big, wondrous toy store to open.

Today, she headed straight past the weekend security guard to the service elevator to minimize the chance of running into anyone, then up to her floor. She strode past the cadre of cubicles where the mini-producers sat during the week, coming up with ideas, and feeding them into her daily packet.

She closed the door to her office, so impersonal, not one photo of herself, family, or friends, as though she hadn't planned on staying. Why was that? Who was this woman without sentiment? How did she survive? And how many fatal flaws could such a person possess until it was . . . fatal?

In the quiet, she booted up her computer and the headlines sprang to life on the screen. Car bombing. Baghdad Highway. IED. Improvised Explosive Device. *Improvised.* It sounded almost quaint.

Two cameramen, a driver, a translator, and Yasmeen. All dead.

Lara had an idea. A five-part series on Yasmeen's life, broken down into tasteful, bite-size pieces to feed to the morning viewers. She would do Yasmeen's life justice. But there was one person she'd have to call before she set the idea in motion.

"Yeah?" Sarah Kate answered. Even her annoyed tone was a comfort.

"It's me," Lara said. "Did you see the news?"

"Did I see it?" Sarah Kate asked. "How come you waited so long to call?"

Lara smiled. Someone out there understood her. Still.

"I want to produce a series on her life—five stories, five minutes each."

Beat.

"You got my ear. Now tell me what you want from me."

"Tell me it's the right thing to do."

"Of course it's the right thing. Now, is it the smart thing. That's the question."

"No. Of course not."

"Good. Go with the right thing," Sarah Kate said.

"I'm going to make it irresistible. It'll be the best human-interest series since we followed that teenage girl who'd lived through Hurricane Katrina."

"I hated that series," Sarah Kate asserted.

"You produced that series."

"So I have an expert opinion on it," Sarah Kate said. "They edited it down to a nub. In this climate, they wouldn't even bother shooting it—unless she was wearing a miniskirt."

"Should I even try?" Lara asked.

"You have to do it. If you don't, well, don't bother calling me and the goats again," Sarah Kate said. "Besides, what do you have to lose?"

Lara thought about this. "Everything," she said.

"Exactly," Sarah Kate replied.

"I'd better get started, then," Lara said. "I'm going to come see you. Soon." Lara still couldn't quite picture her former producer in overalls, frolicking among the goats on her farm upstate. Who knew that all these years Sarah Kate had been harboring a Heidi complex?

"I'm here. Not holding my breath. Although I'd like to, with the goats and all."

Lara hung up and started writing. She called two guys, associate producers, who normally didn't work on weekends. They were interested and available and they would help her find footage and piece together the story. Yasmeen did not live quietly, Lara thought, and she would not die quietly. Not if Lara had anything to do with it.

By midnight, Lara had everything she needed. It occurred to her that Yasmeen's death had given her the best story of her life. What she'd created could earn this morning program a small foothold of legitimacy. Even Scott would have to go for it. She'd sell it to him as the smart thing to do.

The right thing to do.

WHAT Harry had been noticing about his boss lately, and don't think he liked it, was that his boss was . . . nicer. Maybe even, shall you say, sweet.

Oh, he didn't like this new Mr. Jacks.

Just the other day, let me tell you, was funny story if it didn't happen to you. Just the other day, Tuesday, yes, Mr. Jacks, he get out of the car, he's home, after dinner, Elio's.

Harry was waiting, yes. He was dropping off Mr. Jacks, get out, get door, as per the usual, you know. And Mr. Jacks, he got out and— give Harry a hug. *A hug.* Harry stood with his arms straight out. Where to put his arms? Very confusing. And when it was clear Mr. Jackson wasn't letting go—well, Harry hugged him back.

Harry was one strong man, but hugging his boss took all his power, like that Superman hugging kryptonite.

"Thanks, Harry," Jacks said. "Great job."

Beat. "You, too, Mr. Jacks," Harry had said. Okay, not good answer. His wife told him later. Not good. Then she spent all night worrying that Harry would lose his job and then what would they do—that's why she needs a job, she says, that's why—starting Number 143 of their ongoing arguments that were now the knots that held the string of their marriage together. She said she was unhappy.

None of this would have happened in the old country. They

would have been unhappy, yes, but they would have been unhappy together. Here, in America, they were unhappy, separate and alone.

Maybe Jacks was onto something with this "nice"?

He would approach her differently tonight.

ADRIAN observed the crowd gathering in front of the huge steel doors, the darkened twelve-foot windows lining the Greer/Nockus Gallery. The men wore slick, lean suits. No ties. Colorful shirts. Outgroomed the women by about a mile.

The ladies—all over the place. A few to-the-floor gowns, shimmering like fish in an aquarium. Others, perhaps artists themselves, on the deliberately unkempt side—*I have no time for appearances,* these women challenged the viewer, *I only have time for my art.*

A few models. Didn't really matter what they wore or even if they showered in the last week. And they knew it.

Finally Adrian flicked the remains of his cigarette to the street and merged with the cool, the crazy, and the overconfident into the pop purple lighting of the gallery.

First off, it was impossible to see. The room was huge and cavernous and barely lit. Adrian's eyes focused and discovered that moving shapes were people, lots of them. Every one with a cocktail in their hands. Tables were set up past a series of murals that were constructed especially for the occasion. On every panel was a couple—one man, one woman, two men, two women—engaged in a sexual position. Even though it was hard to tell with the lighting, Adrian was pretty sure he could see dick.

Adrian hid part of his face and ordered his drink from the bartender he'd recognized as a former coworker. The reverse wasn't true. An added bit of interest, this. A taste of something dangerous. Adrian liked it.

A heavyset man with hair popping out of his open-collared shirt like a party favor leaned into Adrian.

"I know you," he said. "I know your face."

"You can see my face in this light?" Adrian said. "Congratulations."

"I'll place it," the man said, waving a chubby finger at his nose. He was already hammered and the party had started only twenty minutes ago. A woman stepped up behind him, black leotard, pink streaked black beehive. File under "deliberate."

"Stop it," she said to the big guy, then turned to Adrian. "Is he bothering you?" Accusing the both of them simultaneously.

"To the contrary," Adrian said. "We're just trying to figure out how we know each other. Maybe school?"

"You went to Yale?" she asked.

"Calhoun, '99."

Adrian could have hit himself over the head. He hadn't recognized Beehive from his research, but should have. He watched her walk away.

"She used to paint me," the chubby man said. "When I was, you know, in better shape."

Adrian listened. *Unbearable, the shattering of a heart.*

"We met at Yale, like everyone else here." He laughed too loud. "She loved my face, my body, she would have me pose for hours."

Like bones breaking.

"I'm kind of famous, you know, because of her portraits of me. But she's in the stratosphere . . . she's so good . . . I was good, I mean, competent."

Did he just finish another drink?

"Then we—she had a baby."

"Congratulations," Adrian said. He said it small, kept it small. *Is it possible to watch someone die and not want to save him?*

No.

"I offered to pose for her new series. Erotique-A."

Adrian stared at the panels. None of the participants resembled the artist's husband. *Sadness,* he thought, *has a shape and a smell and a sound.* He looked back as the man zigzagged like a drowsy reptile into the deep purple crowd, leaving his receptacle of grief behind. Adrian had a job to do.

Guests walked into the vast dining area as though they were in a tug-of-war with their appointed tables. Adrian checked out the terrain and surreptitiously moved his name card so he would be sitting next to the name scripted in calligraphy: *"Cynthia Hunsaker Power."*

Already seated at the table was the slim, effete editor of *ArtFocus,* a famous designer who smiled dimly from across the table, and a scattered few who seemed famous but for reasons unknown. A countess gallantly feigned interest in his musings as a young, stinking-of-new-money collector. Adrian trotted out his newly acquired knowledge of all things postmodern well into dinner, waiting for Cynthia to take her empty seat. *Where was she?*

Finally, during a movie about the making of the latest issue of *ArtFocus,* he heard a rustling and scraping as a woman took the seat beside him.

Not Cynthia. It was a much younger woman with a Medusa's cap of wild strawberry blond curls and full lips from which no apology for tardiness seemed imminent. *Artist?* Adrian wondered, as he assessed his new tablemate. She was tall, wore cowboy boots, a long skirt, a shawl that covered her large, proud chest. On her left wrist was a row of shiny, delicate bracelets. *Gypsy artist?* Who wears cowboy boots? Someone with cojones.

She attempted to shrug her shawl off her shoulders. He motioned to help her, but she didn't welcome the gesture. Then she breached the bread basket, the first such movement at the table. Maybe the first at the entire dinner.

"I'm starving," she said, reaching over him for the butter dish.

He handed it to her.

Now two fleshy women on the large screen writhed as paint splotches accented their limbs. The painter's voice droned a narration as though reading a medical brochure.

Adrian peered carefully at the woman. She was frozen, staring at the screen. The roll was still in her hand, the butter knife held aloft, contemplating not hunger, but murder. On the screen a head disappeared between blossoming thighs.

"You okay?" he asked.

The woman drove the knife into the roll.

Adrian leaned over. "Thinking of someone specific?"

"It's nothing." She gripped each word.

"I know everything about nothing," he said. There was the slightest movement, a mere fluttering in his peripheral eyeline. If he hadn't leaned in, if he hadn't said those words to this woman, this wounded bird, he wouldn't have received the signal:

Morse Code: *Tracy Bing is seated five tables away from you and she has seen you but you have not yet seen her and she is about to gather her things and her Wall Street boyfriend and leave.*

Their eyes didn't meet across the crowded room, like the song, like the movie; they didn't have to. Adrian saw the pale of her cheek, the arch of her eyebrow, her soft shoulder. Were there still imprints of his lips on that shoulder?

"My lover left me today." The woman looked at him. "At about three A.M., so that's today, right?"

He sized her up quickly. Her eyes were blue, but so intense they might as well have been black. He could draw constellations in the freckles across her nose and the tops of her full cheeks.

Intelligence was here; resentment over there; rebellion rested in her full chest; fear was well hidden.

"Your lover—was he a good kisser?" One eye remained on that shoulder, continents away. He could see a bracelet (shiny, throwing light), a delicate hand tightening on an evening clutch.

"Why would you assume my lover was a he?" They were speaking in low whispers now.

"Ah," he said. "Well, was she a good kisser?"

Her hand found her lips.

"Question answered," he said. "When was the last time you kissed a man?" Nothing good, it seemed, could come of the Greer/Nockus Gallery.

"Are you serious?" she asked.

"You don't have to answer," he said, "I'm just curious as to who's better."

"Women," she said. "In fact, I'd say any woman is better than any man."

"Ouch," he said.

"So, you're going to tell me I haven't met the right man."

"I can kiss you better than any woman. Or any man."

She looked at him. "You're out of your league."

"I think you want to prove it to yourself right now."

"Fuck you."

"You're thinking about it, that's all I'm saying."

He leaned in. Their shoulders met. The gaze of the violet eyes of Miss Tracy Bing was tightening around his neck. His voice became a mantra. "You're thinking. Maybe it wouldn't be so bad." The video continued to barrage the audience with pornographic images, two men going at each other's junk. "I don't really remember, you're telling yourself, forget the first in high school, the one with the heavy tongue, remember the one in college, he was pretty good, he had a way with the tip of his tongue, gentle, soft as he was tall."

The woman focused hard on the screen. But she was listening. He could tell. Adrian leaned in closer.

"Way taller than me, that's different, that's what you thought, and he took his time and sometimes you wonder whatever happened to him."

The woman put her bread down, released the knife.

"Whatever happened to that boy?" Then his hands were on her face, his lips on her mouth, and they held that kiss as the movie ended and lights came on and because his hearing had become acute in the way of a blind man, he could hear the delicate turn of the ankle, the sound of stars falling as Miss Tracy Bing headed out the door.

"What's your name?" she asked as they released each other and returned to the people they were before they had met.

And yet, not quite. Not quite.

"Adrian West," he said, deciding, in that moment, on the truth. He held out his hand. "Bartender." Fuck it, no one else at the table was paying any attention to them anyway.

She shook it, her grip firm and professional, her curls bouncing with the movement of her arm. He liked the way all of her could be in motion at once.

"Who's Robert Jordan?" She was looking at the place card in front of him.

"A real douchebag," he replied. "And you are?"

"Vivienne Power," she told him. "Lesbian." She gave him a sweet smile.

Vivienne Power, Adrian thought. *Motherfuck.*

"The kiss was good," she said.

Get it together, A. "Well, thank you," Adrian managed.

"But not better than a woman." Still with the smile.

Oh, that's a nice smile, Adrian thought.

"Well," he finally replied. "You've given me something to shoot for, Miss Vivienne Power."

PART THREE

38

UNSEALED MOVES

CYNTHIA COULDN'T remember a less auspicious beginning to a ballet season—even ABT's 1990s "Nightmare Years," when the company, beset by financial and legal woes, almost went bankrupt.

Cynthia had taken to listing calamities on her NYBT calendar above her desk.

Calamity Number One: Lead ballerina Martina Blatsoryinka had been hit by a taxi while crossing the street on her way to rehearsal. Her pelvis had been broken. Young Martina would be out for the entire fall and winter seasons.

Calamity Number Two: Fred Plotzicki had maneuvered around the board like the youthful Baryshnikov performing the Prince in *The Nutcracker,* pirouetting around ethics, grand jetéing over common sense. Cynthia was losing ground in the battle of the board. *How the hell was he keeping his day job?*

Calamity Number Three: The NYBT had lost a main sponsor. Margaret Lord Foster had rescinded her support, a move akin to the Detroit automakers pulling advertising from the Super Bowl telecast. The NYBT endowment (one-tenth of the City Ballet's) would take a million-dollar hit; Cynthia might have to cancel the fall gala.

Cynthia should have seen the writing on the padded silk walls when Margaret forwarded the "invitation" to tea in her suite at the Carlyle the morning after the *Times* Arts and Leisure section had devoted a cover story to the series of setbacks and misadventures that had afflicted the NYBT under the leadership of one Cynthia Hunsaker Power. Cynthia was sure the silent hand behind this missive was none other than Fred Plotzicki.

Calamity Number Four: Morris Stegler had left his wife. Why should this have any bearing on Cynthia's role as head of the board? Because—he'd left his beloved Millie, who'd stood by his side through decades of incessant clicking, for none other than . . . Screwzenka.

Calamity Number Five? Cynthia was still going through the most high-profile divorce in the city. Every morning, with only the teeniest guilt for the hex she might be putting on their marriages, she'd pray to see the over-lit faces of another "power couple" under a headline that declared the marriage kaput. MELANIA TO TRUMP: HAIR-RAISING SPLIT, GIULIANI READIES FOR WIFE #4, DIANE TO MIKE: I SAWYER MISTRESS!, KELLY TO MARK: YOU RIPA'D MY HEART APART!

"You're starting to depress *me*," Dr. Gold said as Cynthia relayed her miseries. "*I'm* going to need therapy!"

"The board wants me out there drumming up business, but how can I when I'm putting out fires fifteen hours a day? I can't keep turning down invitations or sending Vivi out like a placeholder. Oh, have I mentioned that my daughter the lesbian has broken up with her girlfriend?" Cynthia whipped out a Gitane. There was a place in this city where one could still smoke: Dr. Gold's office.

"Mercy!" he cried, shaking his hands at the ceiling from his prone position on the floor. He looked like a bearded knoll; spread a checkered tablecloth on his belly, and you could enjoy a picnic lunch.

"And I still haven't, you know, 'gotten laid' yet."

Dr. Gold sprang to his feet.

"First things first," he said. "Number one: you've got to take control of the board. You are letting Fred make decisions for you. I suggest taking him to lunch," Dr. Gold continued. "Which reminds me, you owe me a pastrami."

"I'm trying *not* to kill you."

"You'll go before I will, lady, don't kid yourself."

Then he stood and opened his arms for his traditional borderline-unethical but sweet end-of-session embrace.

"And for God's sake," Goldie said, looking Cynthia in the eye, "the next time you're in here, I want to hear that you slept with somebody, anybody, older, younger, inappropriate, your daughter's ex, your doorman, the dog, anybody! In all of New York, I'm the only psychoanalyst saddled with a patient who's not fucking around!"

Cynthia smiled at him, but Goldie gave her a serious look. "Don't waste it, Cynthia. Think Anthony Quinn—think Zorba. Cut the string!"

"Zorba. Don't the villagers kill the widow? What would they do to a divorcée?" she asked, knowing this would get a reaction. She picked up her purse. "I'll see you next week, Goldie."

"Not next week, I have a thing next week." Goldie glanced away. "I didn't want to use up time in the session. I'm out for two weeks. They found something in my prostate."

Cynthia stared at him.

"It's small, tiny, ridiculous, but the doctors, they want to get it before it kills me in twenty years. Cancer is the new black, I've heard." He offered her a small smile.

"They can't let it go?"

"They're after my cute ass, I'm thinking."

Cynthia paused. "But I'll see you in two weeks?"

"Two weeks," he said. He reached out to her and pinched her cheek. "Go get 'em, tiger," he said.

CYNTHIA was shuffling through the pile of paperwork in her office that she'd ignored or been too busy or too sad to address, when a business card caught her eye, followed quickly by a vision: *Dr. Gold asking if he should make an appointment for her at the nearest convent.*

Cynthia dialed the number on the card before the brain cells in her reasoning center realigned themselves into cease-and-desist formation.

"Jordan," he answered. He sounded different—younger, less secure. Maybe, beneath that Teflon surface, there was the beating of a heart. But Cynthia's mission wasn't about his heart. There were other parts of his anatomy she was more concerned with.

"Robert," Cynthia said, "do you still have a girlfriend?"

A hesitation. "No," he said. "We broke up. It was mutual."

"Good. Are you busy tomorrow night?"

"I have no plans after work," Robert said.

"I'd like to discuss your possible role on the board." *Why not? Isn't this what men did? Make up stories to seduce women? Why couldn't Cynthia have her own casting couch?*

"Sure. Eight o'clock?"

"Eight-thirty," she replied.

"I'll make reservations at Le Bernadin," Adrian said. The notecard said Le Bernadin was Cynthia's favorite French restaurant; its escargot trumped Tour D'Argent's.

"Oh God, no," she said, "how about Raoul's?" Raoul's! She hadn't been to Raoul's in twenty years, wasn't even sure it existed anymore. But her dim memory of dark booths, lurid oil paintings, a crowded bar, red wine in carafes, and piles of French fries on thick white plates sang its siren song.

"Are you sure?" he asked. Adrian knew Raoul's. It was downtown, in Soho, an artist hang. *This was all wrong.*

"I'm sure. Oh, and Robert," Cynthia said, "wear that suit you were wearing the other day, charcoal gray, I can't remember the label, you know which one."

Cynthia hung up on his gasped response, and leapt into the air, clicking her heels together and landing with a thud that reverberated in the downstairs parlor.

The staff looked up from their respective household duties. Then they heard a word, a name screamed at the top of their mistress's lungs. They could not fully understand—*who or what was this Zorba?*

LARA hadn't had anything to drink the night before; the alarm at 4:30 had failed to wake her because she was already awake. And prepared. At this hour, in the gray between night and morning, she knew that today was the day she began to fix what had gone wrong with her life.

Although Lara had found reporting in Tucson mostly trite, there'd been harrowing moments, excitement, pulse-quickening and insistent: a flash flood, a middle-of-the-night house fire, a domestic dispute turned murderous. Lara, the weather girl turned local reporter, would be one of the first called to the scene. Lara and the other local reporters formed a ragtag fraternity. There was the guy who always had a bottle stashed in his hatchback, the ambitious, obnoxious girl they'd all avoid—but mostly there was camaraderie. And a life lived "at the scene."

The higher she climbed, the more successful she became, the more money they waved in front of her, the less her work mattered. Lara had a team of people to write "her" copy. Lara no longer came up with stories; there was a team responsible for tracking the story.

Spending the weekend devoting herself to Yasmeen reminded her of how much she'd sold out. And how far she'd have to go to give her life meaning.

But what kind of an asshole fucks up a cushy dream job as a morning anchor for a shot at getting shot at?

Well, who would miss her if she died, anyway? Very few: Lara's mother, living with her stepfather in Washington (she'd never even seen the house), her father with his many girlfriends and their dramas, her older brother living in Los Angeles. Lara hadn't seen anyone in her family in years. Thanksgivings had come and gone, winter holidays weren't particularly nostalgic for her. (Certainly not the girlfriends who had peeled away one by one, lost to marriages, families, the inability to match her paycheck for paycheck.) *Who would miss her?*

Jackson.

The thought of Jacks's growing old alone, without the woman who'd finally reached him, who'd tunneled through all of his layers—Male Ego, Childhood Issues, Fear, Control—

How had she managed, Lara mused, to find the soft core hidden beneath his blustery package? She'd fallen in love with what she'd found and hadn't even been looking for. The relationship was surviving, thriving, even through the shift from the clandestine to the public; it now touched on the simple sweetness of the normal. She'd lived through public disgrace, her baptism by fire came in headlines. Now, what was left: no more lies. No more gut-churning guilt. Waking up in each other's arms as sunlight tiptoed into the room. Maybe, just maybe, with luck and patience, they, too, could be that old couple, arm in arm, helping each other across the street.

Lara felt a tremor in her gut as she walked past the newsroom cubicles, exchanging short greetings with the associates and production assistants who appeared like a neat row of scalps. She was holding the Yasmeen piece on a DVD she'd created with the help of her Special Forces team. The piece made those jaded examples of what a life in a newsroom can do to the masculine form sniffle and wipe their eyes. She took a deep breath, and knocked on Scott's (first name or last?) door. "Come in," he called out.

"If you don't cry at this," she told him as she stepped inside, "we have a heartless android running the morning show."

Scott (first name or last?) hung up the phone, checked his watch as she slipped the DVD into the player. For the next three minutes,

Lara was mesmerized, though she'd seen it many times; the trepidation in "Radio Face's" well-bred voice as SCUD missiles flew overhead was palpable.

Scott took deep, impatient breaths, tapped his foot, rolled up a piece of paper and shot it into his wastebasket. The segment wasn't even over before he turned to her.

"Great. We'll give it thirty seconds. Nightly is devoting sixty."

"Thirty seconds?" Lara cried out. "But you're giving two minutes to—what is it—'This Spring, make a Statement with your Stockings'—"

"God rest her soul, this story is a downer. The American housewife does not want to deal with downers, unless they're prescribed," he said. "They want to know what to wear under their skirts. Or if they should even be wearing skirts. Or how long or short those skirts should be. Plus, the models are hot. Totally hot."

"Oh, yeah, the American housewife, whatever that is, really cares about hot young models," she said.

"People, especially women people, do not want hard news in the morning. We've done the research." Scott was working his way up onto a soapbox. "Here's a news flash for you, Lara." His voice became grave. "Life is tough enough."

Lara's body hardened into the titanium fused into computer shells and high-end credit cards. *Men in positions of power weren't necessarily the brightest,* she knew. *Time to manipulate.*

"That's true," she said (*breathe in, 1-2-3-4*). "Life is hard. That's why women people need inspiration—women people should know more about Yasmeen Ali than Lindsay Lohan Spears Hilton!"

So much for manipulation.

"Now, hold on—" Scott (first or last?) said.

"When did news become gossip and gossip become news? And when do we become embarrassed?"

"You just talked yourself down to twenty-five seconds, Sunshine."

"Could you even pinpoint Iraq on a map, Scott?"

"Twenty seconds . . ."

"Quick, what is Tangiers?" Lara asked, sweetly. "Hint! It's not an orange liqueur!"

"And," Scott continued, "we just extended your interview with our fashion expert on the spring line, which begs the question: fishnet or opaque?" He tapped a manila envelope against her chest. "Here are your notes and a pair of purple fishnets, size six. I expect this segment to be . . . scintillating."

She walked out and slammed the door, dumping the manila envelope into the trash as she strode past the cubicles.

39

CASTLING KINGSIDE AND QUEENSIDE

21. Grey Goose vodka martini, rocks, twist (she would drink half of it, then move on to half a glass of white Burgundy).

5. Baby greens salad, light dressing. If artichokes are in season (are artichokes in season? Adrian decided "yes"), then steamed artichoke, no butter.

3. Preferred entrée: Fish. White fish, no oil, no butter.

Adrian flipped through his notecards. He would amaze Cynthia with his uncanny knowledge of her food and wine preferences. He would "know" her, "understand" her—isn't that what we want? To be understood? Even if it just comes down to a fish order?

37. Topics of conversation: Well, Adrian had been given an anemic list by Jacks. Something about the dance board. A couple of suggestions about working out and antioxidants. Vivienne, their daughter, had been the last item.

Vivienne. Adrian had found himself saying her name out loud at odd times. In the morning, when he was spreading cream cheese on a bagel; when he'd take a walk down the street, west to the river to watch the gulls swerve and dive and paint the sky. He'd hear her name in their cries. Why? It was a pretty name, Vivienne, the Royal American Lesbian Princess. Who could kiss a man and make him forget the one, even briefly, who had left heavy tracks on his heart.

9. Dessert: Fruit and/or sorbet.

52. Favorite teaser: Tongue in the Ear, a move that had driven Cynthia wild—and paved the way for little Vivienne to be born, Jacks had noted with pride.

And the pièce de résistance:

28. Making Love: Cynthia didn't like to take the lead, so Adrian would have to. At her core, apparently, she was shy; she might even be frigid. Jacks and Cynthia hadn't had sex in the six months prior to his leaving.

Under this topic, Jacks had written two things: "Good Luck" and "Get the Job Done."

Adrian had decided that Raoul's was to his benefit. He knew downtown; knew the late-night bars; the nightclubs with no signs on the doors; he knew the language and could speak "gorgeous young unidentifiable man" with ease. He felt more normal in these climes than in a white-tablecloth restaurant in the East Sixties or Seventies. Cynthia was in his territory now.

The sky was drifting toward evening. Adrian checked himself, blue-black in the growing reflection of the floor-to-ceiling windows. Stenciled onto the diamond-laced bridge, the streets, the river, was the reflection of a man in a white shirt and bullet-gray suit, his hair cut just so, his cuff links winking just beyond his jacket sleeves. The bartender and failed playwright carved a Byronesque figure into the glass. He'd hoped that his prey, this woman, would find him irresistible; that she would wonder about her fingertips finding secrets written on his skin; that her lips would desire his, that his scent would be pleasing to her.

But what about love? Did he hope for that?

No. He didn't want Cynthia to fall in love with him. There was no room in his heart to reciprocate and maybe there never would be. His own pain was all he could handle; to bear another's, to be responsible for someone else's heart, would be impossible. He needed merely interest, intrigue, infatuation—just enough emotion to divest Cynthia of her marriage, to allow Jacks, and her, to move on. For Jacks to make new mistakes (of this, Adrian was certain), for Cynthia to find, maybe, true happiness.

"I DON'T know why I called and I don't know why I picked the place, and I really don't know why I'm going!"

Cynthia was standing in her bra and stockings, refusing to get dressed. Vivienne, almost six feet and packing at least thirty more well-placed pounds than her mother, was standing over her, hands on hips, looking grandly annoyed.

"You *are* getting dressed right this minute, young lady!"

"I don't want to go out! I want to stay home!"

Cynthia reached for the phone.

"What are you doing, Mom?" Vivienne asked.

"What'd you just call me?" Cynthia asked, briefly stopping the freight train of misery.

"Mom."

"Mom! Have you noticed that you've started calling me Mom again?"

"I always call you Mom."

"No, you don't. You call me Cynthia."

"Mom," Vivienne said, "don't distract me. What do you think you're doing?"

"Canceling."

Vivienne pulled the phone away from her.

"Give me back my phone," Cynthia insisted. "You can't make me go out!"

"Oh, yes, I can." Vivienne hugged the phone to her chest. "Watch me!"

"Is that a threat?"

"I'll give you ten—okay, five ... one good reason why I'm not going to give you the phone," Vivienne said. "Sex is the greatest wrinkle eraser! And it uses up calories!"

"He's way way too young. I'm way way too old!"

"So view this as a dry run! Don't take it seriously!"

"Oh my God, I told him what to wear—"

Vivi's eyebrows shot up. "You told him what to wear? Really?"

"I know! What's happened to me? I can't go! I can't go!" Cynthia, Hysteria; Hysteria, Cynthia—we think you've met.

"No! This is good, so now, now you'll recognize him—"

"I don't even think I like him." Cynthia looked up at her daughter, who was waving a Dolce & Gabbana dress at her mom. Another trophy from their shopping expedition. It was sheer, shiny, stretchy, and about the size of a scarf, if the scarf had been shrunk.

"Meaningless sex is better when you don't like the person. And that's a fact," Vivienne said, "as Jacks Power would say."

"How did I let you talk me into getting this?" Cynthia took the hanger reluctantly. "*I* should be dressing *you*. Do you know how many times I've tried to get you to dress up?"

"I don't remember. A few."

"Aunt Julia's wedding, cousin Lucy's first communion, your debutante ball, countless bat mitzvahs, and how many Christmases and anniversaries and birthday parties ..."

"I like this, with these—"Vivienne held up boots, ignoring her mother's litany. Black patent leather, gold buckle. The footwear equivalent of a flashing neon sign: "Let's skip dinner and fuck!"

"I can't wear those boots," Cynthia pouted. "I'll feel like a tramp. You made me buy those—"

"Exactly what I used to say," Vivienne said.

Cynthia grabbed the boots. "Fine."

"Tell me more about him," Vivienne asked.

"Oh God, he's young. I said that."

"He's not like fifteen, Mom, is he? He *is* of drinking age."

"And so handsome. And such a . . ."

"Prize?"

"No."

"Sweetheart?"

"No, not quite that, either."

"Mom—"

"He's . . . an asshole," Cynthia said. "Just like your father, I'm sorry to say. He's in finance, of course, how fascinating, hedge fund manager of some sort—"

"Sounds horrible," Vivienne said. "And convenient for the short term. Like a revenge fuck on Daddy—"

"Vivienne, please, that's disgusting."

"Truth is Beauty, Mother, and you're going to look beautiful tonight. Besides," Vivienne said, waving the boots over her head, twirling them like batons, "there's another good reason for you to go, a very good reason."

"You have my attention, daughter." Cynthia needed another reason to go; anything would do.

"It would make Jacks Power so very mad." Vivienne rocked the boots back and forth.

"Hand me those things," Cynthia said. She slipped into them. And stood, arms out, for her daughter to help her on with her dress. Oh, the comfort of the smallest gesture—her daughter helping her fit into a sleeve.

"So at that art opening, the other night . . ." Vivienne said.

"Yes?"

"Did you know any of the people at the table? It was your ticket, I thought you might—there was someone . . . cute . . ."

Cynthia looked at her. She wanted her daughter to be happy.

"Who was she?" she asked. "An artist?" Cynthia sat down at her mirrored makeup table. Sarah Bernhardt had used it sometime during the twelve years she'd lived in New York. The mirrors made any light in the room dance, which in turn made putting on makeup well-nigh impossible—a fact she'd learned only after falling in love with its romantic history.

"Mom, the she's a he. It's weird, I know. I'm such a traitor for even mentioning it," Vivienne stammered. Vivienne never stammered.

Cynthia raised an eyebrow, and kept her mouth shut.

"I know, it's horrible. I'm the Kim Philby of Sappho-world."

Cynthia waited, a supreme effort.

"It was the strangest thing . . . Aiko left me that day, for the last time—and here, he, this . . . boy, sitting next to me, you were supposed to be in my seat, remember, and then, for no reason—"

Any false move, any reaction from a mother in a moment like this could swing the pendulum from a June wedding to a greaser chick named Paul, short for Paula.

"We . . . kissed," Vivienne said.

Cynthia was careful not even to catch her daughter's eye in the mirror. Concentrate, Cynthia cautioned herself; keep your face poker smooth, your eyes on that dreaded falling eyelid. Grunt, delicately. Maybe.

"And it was . . . ? " she offered at last.

Cynthia looked up. Fah! She couldn't help it. Her eyes met Vivienne's and in that moment her daughter could see everything, she knew it, as she knew her own mind—she saw the embossed wedding invitations, the bouquet, the bridal train, the fluttering around the guest tables at the house in the Hamptons, the fretting over a latent June squall—

Vivienne put her hands on her mother's shoulders and peered into the mirror behind her. Could any mother and daughter look less alike? But then, Cynthia saw something—

"Meaningless," Vivienne was saying, "a freak thing . . . vapor . . ."

Defeat snatched from the Jaws of Victory by one unblinking eyeball. Cynthia would have to live with her mistake—but still, still, if a boy, somewhere, had brought about this . . . adjustment? Could "adjustment" be the word? With Vivienne, well, anything was possible.

"I called Aiko," Vivienne said. "She hasn't called me back, but I know she will. I know she will. She can't . . . she can't just not love me anymore. Right?"

Looking into her daughter's eyes, Cynthia saw a piece of herself, a single brushstroke of sturdy Midwestern stock. "Impossible," Cynthia said, to both of the faces caught in the net of lights dancing off the mirrored table.

IT WASN'T as though Jacks didn't have enough problems. Pick any five minutes out of his day, hell, thirty seconds! What was he dealing with? Solutions? NO! Problems!

Only now, most of the problems were generated by Artemus. Thanks to Dad, Jacks Power was in danger of losing the Bowery project altogether. Artemus Power had stormed into his principle architect's ("Mr. Fancypants") office, demanding shortcuts he'd routinely gotten forty years ago with housing projects he'd built over landfills—galvanized steel pipes instead of copper, cheap wiring, unlicensed workers, Chinese drywall. This for the newest, most sensational, not to be denied Power Tower. "Value engineering," Artemus called it. But Jacks, who'd had his own issues with architects, saw it for what it was: crap.

Then the lead contractor mutinied, taking his crew with him. Something about "never fucking been fucking talked to like that since fucking graduating fucking PS fucking Thirty-fucking-three."

At the 7:00 A.M. meeting with the lawyers (bunch of idiots, he thought, bending to the whims of his father), Artemus railed against the tenant association and the preservationists in the East Village. Jacks knew how to handle tenants; he'd listen and talk and listen and answer questions and listen. Then he'd do exactly what he wanted.

Worked every time.

Even those who hated everything he was and stood for could be won over with a few choice words, a few thousand bucks if necessary.

Except here now was his father, determined to steamroll over the Bowery tenants.

Artemus's thinking was old school, before frivolous lawsuits and Murdoch's media octopus—"You don't want to move? Fine, I got someone here to have a nice talk with your kneecaps." Or, simple, pay someone to burn the building down. Then, send the insurance inspector away on a Caribbean vacation. He'd set his son back years in tenant relations. There would be a lot more pockets to line come Christmas.

Jacks's meeting with the tenant/preservationist association was a free-for-all. They were carrying picket signs with bloodred commands: DOWN WITH POWER and POWER'S OUT! and TAX THE POWER, HOUSE THE POWERLESS! They were angrier and uglier than usual. Thanks to Artemus.

An old woman—Jacks made out her name to be Ellie Mae or Mae Ellen—started hollering: "I will not be moved, scum lord!"

Jacks tried for humble. "Well, actually, Mrs. Mae—I own that corner, I bought it fair and square—"

More screaming and hooting from the peanut gallery. The usual: "Tax breaks!" "Cronyism!" "Bribery . . . !"

Yawn. He'd been here before.

"And I've made Mrs. Mae a very nice deal, tell them, Mrs. Mae. You remember the deal my lawyers offered just last week? And you and I, we had that very nice chat—" (And all he was thinking was *Please shut your lice-ridden mouth, you disgusting riffraff, where is the decency?*)

Through it all, his father just sat back in the chair next to him. Jacks could hear his breathing, clear through the maelstrom. He could feel the old leopard smiling lazily, as though he were toying with his prey—and the prey didn't even know it yet. He couldn't tell—was he, Jacks, the prey? Was his father just hoping, willing, that his son should fail?

The press was there, with the usual questions.

"What do you say to your detractors who claim that you're breaking the law by making this a condominium/hotel project?" one of them shouted from the back.

"Well, Larry, it's not their fault. They don't understand the letter of the law, here. It's all about percentages. Sure, if I were making every unit into a condo, we'd have an issue. We aren't and we don't. Nice tie, by the way."

Jacks had called them in just like he'd done for the past twenty-five years. Just a few good members of the fourth estate in their cheap sports coats, the morning sun bright on their bloodshot eyes; Jacks noticed . . . a few more. Odd. He pointed at the next out-stretched hand signaling his attention. "Hector, you had a question?"

"Is it true you're planning on using blue glass on this forty-six-story monster? Is that in keeping with the historic flavor of the Bowery district?"

Monster? thought Jacks. Fuckin' *Village Voice.* "Historic flavor? It's called the friggin' Bowery for a reason, Hector, you know that. Come on. I'm an agent for change. I'm a master improver. I improve, by great leaps and bounds, on the dilapidated, the old, the tired. I guarantee you, Hector, this Power Tower will be by far the most beautiful piece of architecture to hit the Lower East Side in a hundred years. And that's a fact!"

More reporters filtered into the room. Several had camera crews. Strange; Power hadn't requested local news camera crews. He didn't mind, though. Why not?

"Who's next?" Jacks asked.

Then, an energy shift in the room. He felt it, everyone felt it. Hands sprung out from the sea of faces. A hundred arrows in the form of questions shot through the air; their target, Jacks.

". . . any comment on her complete meltdown on national television this morning?"

"People are saying she's had a nervous breakdown—"

". . . alcoholic . . ."

"How do you feel about what happened this morning?"

". . . pill-popper . . .".

"The press is calling this the biggest disaster on a morning news show in an age—"

"Is your girlfriend on hallucinogens?"

Jacks saw big cameras, with big guys grunting beneath their weight. Forget the *Daily News,* the *Post*—these were national television cameras, the kind that captured and molded public opinion.

Jacks smoothed his jacket. Ran a hand through his hair. Sucked in his gut. No matter; he'd get through this. He smiled.

The tenants were quieting down. All eyes were still on him but instead of anger, he saw something else—confusion. Well, he wasn't going to look confused. Confusion was for pussies. He offered another confident smile. "Gentlemen, you'll have to bring me up to—"

More arrows fired, quickly slicing the air.

"Lara Sizemore's meltdown on national TV. Do you think she'll be fired? Do you think she'll be sued?"

"Is it true you've asked her to marry you?"

"Just how unstable is she?"

"What about her going into an Arizona rehab this afternoon?"

"Will she ever work in network television again?"

"Have you talked to her since the incident?"

Jacks smiled the practiced, benevolent smile of the People's Billionaire. "It's all going to work out," he said. "Everyone's going to be happy. I promise. People, this is a win-win situation." He could feel the eyes of the lawyers on him—why were they just staring at him? Why wasn't anyone talking? Then he could feel their eyes shift and latch on to their BlackBerries. What didn't he know? What the hell had Lara done?

Jacks's smile remained on his face, severing itself from the rest of his features. "And that's a fact!" he said.

"Are you still picking up your award tonight?" someone shouted.

Get your hands off of me, Jacks wanted to shout, although no one was touching him; no one had come close to touching him. The blows still felt physical.

"Of course," Jacks said, his smile speaking for him, "why wouldn't I go on?"

"Jacks, is Lara Sizemore another Jessica Savitch?"

"Do you regret leaving your longtime wife, Cynthia?"

A woman's voice.

Finally, a lawyer jumped up. "That's all Mr. Power has to say on the subject. This meeting will adjourn and we will continue our talks at a later date . . ."

Jacks was already in the elevator, punching numbers and praying for the doors to close before the next assault.

But not before he caught a glimpse of Artemus, smirking as his prey fled the premises.

JACKS wasn't supposed to be out for another half hour. If Harry was surprised to see him, or anxious that he'd been "caught" smoking a cigarette, his ass up against the car door, nothing showed. He merely flicked the cigarette to the street and opened the door for Jacks as though he'd been expecting him, then and there.

"Lara's place," Jacks said, watching his BlackBerry for clues . . . Nothing. She hadn't written.

Was this another sign of the Apocalypse of their relationship?

What the hell had happened? Jacks stared out the window at the people scurrying to appointments: businessmen and women, secretaries, security, food service workers, nurses, kings of finance. How could they not know his world was coming apart at the seams? That all the gold thread in the world couldn't keep it together? Didn't they care?

Tonight. Another awards dinner, this one at the Waldorf for the Big Brothers and Sisters of America. Krach himself was giving him the award. Any other day, he'd be excited. He loved trophies—he had an entire case, specially built and lit to highlight all the ones he'd received—there was this forgotten charity and that, the police academy, the New York State Builder's Association. All told there were forty of them. He could say he didn't care, could walk right past the trophy case when people gathered in his sumptuous home with the fourteen-foot ceilings and the art collection that rivaled his father's. But the trophy case would be properly lighted for the occasion. (He winced at the memory of yelling at Cynthia once for not turning on the light before their annual Christmas party.) And everyone, of course, would notice the gold and silver and marble constructs winking at them from behind glass . . .

The car wove lazily in and out of traffic, and Jacks's mind wandered with gravitational force toward the mayor's speech: What would he say about Jacks? Jacks had sent over his bio, the youngest this, the most successful that, the billions won (and lost, never mind) over the years . . . he'd sent the list of awards, the proud father stuff. (Oh God, got to call Vivienne, was she coming to-night?)

He e-mailed his daughter.

He wondered . . . if she showed up, what would she be wearing? It hurt him that his daughter didn't seem to care more about appearance. It hurt him because he could see judgment in other people. When she was small and chubby, and loved horses and looked like a kielbasa wrapped in white breeches when the other girls were petite, upright, dancing sticks, he'd wanted to shout, *But her IQ is phenomenal! She read my press releases at three and a half! She's funny! She can beat her father at chess—and I've beaten a master! She's got one-liners! Stop sneering at her pudgy thighs! And don't look at me; I don't know where she got them!* Of course, she hadn't ridden for long. What's meaner than a snarling pack of real estate developers? Prepubescent girls in white breeches.

Vivienne was supposed to be his trophy daughter; she and those goddamn cowboy boots had turned out to be only too human. And what about Chase, he thought, *Who would he have been?*

The car pulled up to Lara's apartment. Jacks was feeling better now. He could count on the mayor to come up with the proper superlatives, elide over whatever unpleasantness hovered over Lara. And if not, he could talk to him before the speech just to make sure. In fact, he would give him a call this afternoon. And this Lara thing, how bad could it be? Lara was a smart girl—she'd know how to pull an ace from a bad hand. Whatever it was she'd done, it'd probably blow over by tonight.

THERE were already two news vans outside Lara's apartment. The doorman was trying to wave them off. Jacks took a deep breath, as though he were diving underwater, and walked past quickly, his head partially hidden by his collar, ignoring the shouted questions hurled at him, the lights popping—

Lara's apartment was in a postwar building on the Upper West Side. Jacks hated it because it wasn't one of his, and no matter how much he'd cajoled, bribed, begged, he couldn't get Lara to move.

He had just finished his crown jewel, Power Pavilion, a mixed-use tower on Fifth and Fifty-sixth. Breccia Pernice marble and brass made the interior look like a sultan's palace. Lara wasn't having any of it.

"I'm not a big fan of marble everything," she'd said.

"Then you're in a very small minority, young lady," he'd said to her.

Maybe that's why he'd liked her best. Maybe that's why he'd fallen in love. After Chase died, he'd kept his heart wrapped in aluminum foil and put it in a special drawer in a hidden compartment in a lockbox in a safe in a vault in a fortress made of steel on an island in the middle of the ocean accessible only by air and even then you'd need a special code—

And here, this girl had turned his offer into a bit of dust that settled on her jacket that she'd brushed off with a hand that could use a manicure. Would his heart fit into that hand? His eyes reached hers and he was embarrassed because within minutes of meeting her, his eyes were already translating for his heart, imploring . . .

Be gentle, because I've just handed you something that I haven't given in so long I wasn't even sure it existed anymore . . .

Jacks was thinking about that moment, which made him forget who he was and what he'd done to get here and then he was standing in front of Lara's apartment, ringing the doorbell. He didn't hear any sound. He opened the door with his key.

"Lara," he called. The apartment depressed him. She'd been here since she first came to the city and never upgraded. The apartment didn't reflect her standing in the world. There was nothing on the walls, no photos of loved ones displayed, no sign of a human being residing here. His love lived like a spy. Was there anything of him in this apartment? Anything besides a change of underwear, a few ties?

"Lara?" he called out. Trying to keep panic over here and his voice over there. *What if she'd hurt herself,* he thought suddenly, sharply, the words frozen in his head.

He ran into her bedroom. Oh God. Water running. Water running in a bathtub after a bad morning: never a good sign. He threw open the bathroom door.

Lara's eyes were closed, her head leaning back against the tub. An arm draped over the side. She looked as though she was sleeping. The prescription bottle tipped on its side on the bath mat, open.

"Oh God, oh God!" he cried out. Jacks cradled her head in his hands. His heart burst and flooded his eyes. "Why?" he sobbed.

"Why what?" Lara said, lazily opening her eyes. "Jacks, what are you doing?" Her eyes all gray and hazely and what color were they anyway, they were lit and shooting signals all awry, what was she saying? Was she talking?

"Honey?"

He wiped his nose. On his sleeve! On his sleeve!

"Are you okay?" Lara asked. Her eyes were level now, the lights had faded and were merely glowing warm. Oh what he saw there—shock and annoyance had flamed out and all that was left was concern.

"I thought you were—I thought you had—" Jacks said.

"Taken a hot bath?" Lara asked.

"How many of these did you swallow?" He grabbed the prescription bottle.

She reached up and snatched it from his hand, not bothering to cover herself. "None of your business," she said. "I needed to calm down."

"What the hell *happened* to you! I heard you completely self-destructed. On air."

"You can see it for yourself on YouTube," she said. Shame made no impression on her voice.

"What did you do?"

"I interrupted a previously scheduled segment for a retrospective of an internationally renowned news figure." She sounded as though she were rehearsing. "I was fired."

"In the middle of the show?"

"During the commercial break, so yes, in the middle of the show."

"You don't seem . . . upset." Upset? She didn't seem . . . alive.

"I was shaking when I got here. That's why I took one of those things . . ." The pills.

Jacks took the bottle, shook one into his hand, and swallowed.

"I actually feel relieved," she said, smiling now. Then tears started spilling from her eyes, landing on her cheekbones. Line up the most beautiful women in the world, show me the girl in those Bollywood movies and every *Playboy* model from the seventies when they were really hot and that crazy movie star with the crazy eyes with all the children and her husband, also beautiful like a girl, line them all up, and maybe those tropical fish you see when you're scuba diving in Aruba, and then, maybe you'll come close to the beauty of this crying, smiling woman. *Who is driving him mad.*

"I'm so happy," she said.

He hugged her wet head to his chest; he didn't hesitate even though he was wearing one of his favorite suits. *That's love,* he thought.

"I'm happy you're so happy," he lied.

"I'm just so proud of myself," she said, and then, "You want to fuck?"

"Only if you dry off first," he said. Maybe he couldn't get rid of this insane happiness right away. Maybe he could fuck it out of her. If he couldn't get rid of her happiness, he could at least enjoy the ancillary benefits.

He thought of Adrian. And the Deal. And how that little bastard had better be holding up his end, or at least his soon-to-be-ex-wife's end.

"Let's set a date," he said. "I want to get married. Soon." *Soon, even though I don't know you at all.*

40

DRAWING LINE

MY GOD, she looked luminous. Is that the word? Like when you've stared at a lightbulb a moment too long and all you see is the ghost of its filament when you close your eyes. That's what Adrian was thinking about Cynthia Hunsaker Power.

She was standing outside Raoul's. Looked like she was smoking a cigarette but when he came up he saw she had ditched it. He liked seeing a part of her that was ashamed, as though she'd flashed him her underwear by accident or revealed the name she was called in eighth grade when everyone thought she was a freak. (With those legs, he guessed "Stork.")

Adrian went in like he was kissing her cheek but instead passed her and opened the door for her to enter—*let her wait a little longer, he thought. I'm still in control of this situation; she just doesn't know it.* He fingered the note cards in his pocket. Just in case he forgot anything. Just in case he drank too much. Just in case.

They were seated at a banquette, he'd called ahead, then tipped the host, they squeezed past the crowded bar, slid onto the weathered leather cushions, and he watched as her eyes ate at the walls, at the art (if you could call it that), at the clientele—here was a young girl dining with her grandparents, here was a couple choking each other with their tongues, here were models with eerie faces and their sponsors, practically peeing on their legs to mark territory. Her eyes ate and ate and then turned back to Adrian.

"I love it here," she declared over the din rising to the tin ceiling.

"Would you like a drink?" he asked. He turned to the waiter, who had appeared and now stood still, hands clasped behind his back, no need for pencil and pad.

"The lady will have a . . ." *Vodka martini.* Adrian looked at Cynthia. "The lady would like a Grey Goose martini, very cold, straight up, with . . ." He eyed Cynthia.

"A twist," he concluded.

"The nerve," she said, smiling.

"I'll have the same, but with olives," Adrian told the waiter. "Lots of olives."

He suddenly wondered—should he be ordering what Jacks ordered? His brand of Scotch? No, no. Be yourself, be yourself, only someone who's pretending to be someone else. Charming.

"Can we get French fries right away?" she asked the waiter before he slid away.

"You eat French fries?" he asked her.

"I love them," she said. "And let's order their table wine—I remember it being delicious."

"Table wine?" *What happened to the white Burgundy?*

Would he have to scrap the cards altogether? They felt like they were on fire, burning a hole through his pocket.

"Do you know of any nightclubs around here?"

"Nightclubs." *Nightclubs?*

"You must go out a lot," she said.

"I didn't really plan—"

"I'd love to go dancing, I haven't been dancing in a club in forever."

"Dancing," he said. *Dancing.*

Their drinks came. In his mind, the cards had melted and dripped down the side of his pants onto the sticky floor. *Fuck them. Useless. Who knows the mind of a woman? Not her husband!*

"Cheers," she said, holding up her glass. Adrian's eyes caught the faint crow's-feet as she smiled. They were like a frame built to accentuate her beauty.

"Cheers," he said, revising his entire game plan. He was the football coach entering the stadium to discover he wasn't playing the Bears after all, but the Patriots. Completely different animals.

She sipped at the drink. "Perfect," she said, and then, "I have something to celebrate. You'll think it's stupid."

"Not at all," he said, grateful for the glimmer of an honest moment. "Please . . . tell me."

"You know I'm much older than you," she said.

"Age doesn't mat—"

She waved her arms, "No no no, that's not why I'm telling you. Of course, age matters. If age didn't matter, I wouldn't be in this booth. Anyway, I have a daughter, she's a little younger than you . . ."

"Really?" Adrian asked, hoping he looked surprised.

"She met a boy," Cynthia said.

"A boy? Really?" Adrian wondered if she noticed that he'd already sucked down half his martini.

"At an art show," Cynthia said. "He was sitting next to her. I was supposed to go, but I've had so much work with the ballet—"

So much work, but she looked happy about it, Adrian thought, Jacks hadn't mentioned that she had a passion. Kind of hard to miss, living with someone who has passion. But then, if you're Jackson Power . . .

You miss a lot.

"Anyway, it's kismet," Cynthia said. "See, Vivienne, my daughter"—she was sipping at her drink like it was a delicious secret—

"she's a lesbian, but not a complete lesbian, a proto-lesbo, if you will. She's had boyfriends. She's . . . she's rangy, tall, it was tough on her at Spence. Anyway, she'd just broken up with her girlfriend, who let me tell you was head-to-toe beautiful."

Cynthia, he realized, was talking as though no one had listened for a long time. Would this be all he had to do? Listen? Listen himself right up under her skirt?

"I've seen that girl naked, there's nothing God did wrong on that body. But the personality, not so great." Cynthia scrunched up her nose.

Adrian was trying to get past the picture in his mind of Vivienne and her girlfriend locked in some sort of limb, limb, lip, tongue, hair, waxed, pierced, wrestling thing.

"Robert?" She was peering at him.

"Yes, so proto-lesbian," Adrian said.

"Vivienne kissed a random boy at the art show."

Vivienne. There was that name again. Vivienne. He looked at her mother for signs of the daughter. *Here and there, here and there.*

"I think she likes him," Cynthia said.

"After just one kiss?" he asked. *He had to ask.*

"A kiss is everything," Cynthia said. "Would you like to order another?"

He was back at that round table, next to Vivienne. "Yes," he said, "I would like another."

"I would like that table wine now." Cynthia giggled. "I would like the last quarter of a century back."

SO JACKS had asked Lara if she still wanted to go to that thing with him tonight. His head was between her legs at the time, his face covered in her sheen. He could hear her. The neighbors could hear her. Half the island of Manhattan could hear her. She wasn't going anywhere. She'd be asleep within twenty minutes.

Of course, he didn't really want her to go. Yes, it would have been their perfect official debut as a couple. The dark corners of no-name restaurants, the aborted brunch at that French place—didn't count. Those appearances were fodder for the gossip columns and snark-infested websites. *And who were all those spies, anyway?* Jacks had begun to assess people he'd never paid attention to—the particularly attentive waiter, the coat check girl, the doorman, the maître d' he thought he could trust. Manhattan had become a National Geographic special populated with parasites, with Jacks as the official "host." Tonight, though, he'd let the parasites feed. There would be enough to go around; Lara would look ravishing, and so would he (Jacks had never had a disagreement with a tux).

Two months after the official separation, so the timing would have been perfect. A formal event, Lara draped in something as expensive as it was fragile, wearing the new necklace he'd bought for her as a surprise, big and chunky, the diamonds and emeralds there for the spectator alone—it would be a bitch to wear—and if he was honest, it wasn't exactly Lara's speed, but he'd never known a woman to turn down over-the-top bling.

Besides, wouldn't this have been the perfect opportunity to cement her loyalty? To show her that he was standing by her? Suddenly the girl who didn't need anything needed him. They would take a turn on the dance floor, a prelude to their wedding night waltz, and they would be alone for an entire song, until Krach moved in, asked Lara for a turn. Jacks had seen it all in his head.

And in Liz Smith's column the next day.

Lara's meltdown had made the event more complicated. But if he went by himself, there would be talk. He'd feel the taps of the oh-so-sympathetic fingers along his shoulders . . .

"Where's Lara?"

"I hope she's all right."

"Give her my best . . ."

She should stay home, have a quiet night alone. Until he re-

turned. He looked up, all this thinking taking place right here between her thighs . . .

She was out. She was comatose after a few orgasms—like calming a lion by stroking it under the chin. *Sleep, go to sleep now, lion.
That's a good lion.*

Sometimes he wished she were different. Not her eyes or her
golden pussy or her funny, jagged voice or her hair that was always
in the way when they kissed on pillows because there was so so
much of it and it reminded him of how young she was and how
young she'd still be in ten years. (When did Cynthia's hair start staying put? When did she start wearing it back, even in bed?) Sometimes, he wished Lara were just . . . easier. Silent and unchallenging.

"So you don't want to come to that thing tonight?" Jacks asked.
"I'll have Harry swing back with some Chinese."

"Of course I want to come," Lara the Lion replied. "I wouldn't
miss it for anything."

ADRIAN was staring at his reflection in the restroom mirror after he'd
finished his business.

"What the fuck's going on here?" he pleaded.

The young man had no answers, just a sad, soft face with a little
too much of life lived in the eyes.

He took the note cards out of his pocket. His eyes ran over them,
a drunk driver picking up ephemeral signals—a flashing light, an
intermittent bass line, a wail of a siren—

Designer clothes
Ballet is her thing
Favorite movie: *The Red Shoes*
Tongue in her ear (long time ago, try it)
Yellow roses

Adrian put the cards on the sink, started washing his hands. He had one hundred thousand reasons to make this work. And only one reason not to. A passing fancy, a blip on the gray screen of his existence, a mere . . . kiss.

"Forget about her, you've got a job to do," he told his reflection, as his features wobbled, three martinis and a half bottle of good table wine later.

"Is there someone else in here?"

Adrian turned. Cynthia was standing inside the doorway. Adrian saw yellow tape tied across a crime scene, quicksand, marshes filled with snapping alligators, a four-alarm fire. Everything dangerous contained in her form.

Where did Vivienne come from? Adrian wondered, as he took in her mother's geometry. Where was Vivienne, sprung from the earth, voluptuous and unformed and ungainly, and he was sure those curls were full of tangles, just full of them, and if he could lose his fingers in there, he'd just cut them off and leave them.

A kiss changes everything. *She said it!* he wanted to scream and point, not him. "I didn't say it," Adrian said out loud. "I never said it."

Now Cynthia's lips were on his, she was eating him as though he were a piece of fruit, no, a piece of steak, something to chew, to consume and regret the next day.

It would be a battle of regrets, he thought, which amazed him, the way his mind was still working; this was Method, this was Character, this was a study of her Inner Life. Only the study had come up short. Who could've anticipated this move? Or that one, her hands on his shoulders, frantic, his arms, his waist, oh, his crotch, was the door locked? He was concerned, concerned for her well-being, her emotional stability; embarrassment would belong to this hedge fund master of nothingness, not him, he was just . . . a bartender.

She was Cynthia Power.

Her hands lurched at his belt—

He brought her up by her elbows then held her face and kissed her sweetly, the way he would want to kiss Vivienne.

A kiss changes everything.

He started nibbling her neck, up, up, his tongue reaching finally her ear, this was surefire, here was the Answer, now he'd be in control—

"Oh my God," she said, "Oh my God . . ."

"Mmmm," he said.

"Oh my God," she said.

Adrian was making a dessert out of that ear. The ear was strawberry shortcake, tiramisù, that Greek pastry at the bakery on Seventh Avenue—

"Stop that!"

"What?"

How fast can a man sober up? A man with three martinis and a half-bottle of good table wine in his system? Adrian clocked it at less than two seconds.

"Please!" Cynthia said. "I'm not an ice cream cone."

"But—" Who *was* this woman?

"Did you swallow my earring?" Cynthia pulled at her earlobe. "Still there, thank God. I'd hate to see one of those come out in the morning."

"I'm . . . confused," he said. To himself, more than to her. *Was this play going to close at intermission, too?*

"Let's finish up here," she said.

"By finish up, you mean . . . ?" There was nothing Adrian understood anymore. Nothing. Someone outside tried the handle, then knocked at the door.

Cynthia smiled. Despite the ear derailment, she was invigorated. She was an astronaut, on her mission to space—to pierce the stratosphere, and nothing tonight was going to stand between her and the moon.

"I have a few things to teach you before you go out in the world again," she told him. She replaced the lipstick that had been lost on his face and walked out, all dignity and ice and beauty. Indifferent to the base desires of the average human being.

Adrian almost fell to his knees. He held on to the sink to keep himself from folding. And saw the cards that he'd left on there.

Had she seen them? How could she not have? Adrian wondered. He threw them out. And bade good luck to his sorry reflection.

THE MOMENT he stepped into the Grand Ballroom at the Waldorf, a glittering Lara on his arm, Jacks's heart sank. Why did the first well-wisher have to be that old designer, the Brazilian, don't come over here, he had to, of course, I'm getting honored, don't come over here, here he comes, his Rio de Janeiro tan bouncing off the walls, all you can see is his teeth, giant bonded white teeth and those green eyes, can someone tell him we've seen it all before and this is not the eighties.

"Jacksssssss," the designer crooned, his arms out, as though flying off.

Jacks received the hug, then tried to move on. No such luck. The Latins stick around after the hug, holding on to both arms, an elbow at the very least, and since the guy's not only Latin, but gay, his eyes were holding on, too. *Tell me,* his eyes said, *tell me everything.*

A woman fluttered up, kissed Jacks, both cheeks, kissed the designer, rained flattery upon the designer, who turned the flattery hose full blast back on her—"I *love* this dress!"—and she turned not once but twice for them and Jacks caught that her ass was too big for the dress, probably was born too big for that dress, and at the very moment she walked away and the designer was blowing kisses, love love love, *bonita,* love—he was saying to Jacks, in precise, unaccented English: *What a fat pig.*

Then: *Tell me how much you're hurting,* the eyes implored—like two flashing neon orbs lined with spikes and suddenly Jacks wasn't talking to the world-famous designer—so famous he'd sold out not once, but twice to Wal-Mart—Jacks was now talking to the elusive and deadly vampire fish found only in the Amazon, the tiny fish with an entire head made of hooked teeth that would crawl up into your urethra if you dared wander into the river for a piss.

Jacks heard nothing the man was saying.

He was listening for a certain sound, a sound that is heard nowhere but in ballrooms. Voices that gathered and bounced off high, curved ceilings, the steady murmur of fabulosity escaping from the lips of women wrapped like Christmas gifts and the men using their "restaurant voices"—remember what Mother said when she dressed them for their first formal outing, to Grandma's house, to *La Bohème*, to cousin Lucille's wedding, what Mother said echoing through the years, reaching out as they dressed for the night in their tuxes. Then, the occasional booming laughter. Such fun. Pure encouragement and support, a bed of sound Jacks could rest his handsome head upon.

But tonight, the sound was different. *What was the sound of betrayal?*

Eyes on him, filled with ammunition. Eyes on Lara. He could hear the communal gasp: "What is she doing here?"

"He must be so embarrassed . . ."

"What goes around comes around—"

Was it his misperception or was the room more full than usual? Were spectators hanging from the rafters, soccer hooligans ready to riot? He was holding Lara's hand; was his sweaty or was hers? He turned to look at her, to reassure her; he would protect her, he was her knight in shining Armani.

But why had she come? Why had he let her?

Lara was all smiles, her chest thrust out, her shoulders back, every part of her giddy with life.

Flashbulbs popped in time. Dizzying, like a night spent on the dance floor at Studio 54. He could feel her loosening her grip on his arm. He could feel her taking the next step, her footing trusted. Or was she sprouting wings?

Lara didn't care about losing face after being booted from the morning news. *Embarrassment? Public humiliation? What was that to her? Who was she?* Jacks asked himself.

He would have to find a way to keep her on the ground. Next to him. Clip those wings, but do it with diamond-encrusted blades . . . Would Lara sense that he was keeping her earthbound if he dazzled her with a bloated yacht docked in Anguilla, fish captured before noon in clear Caribbean waters, roasted and drizzled with olive oil and lemon—a crisp rosé poured from quiet hands, sex with sun heating their skin and the smell of suntan oil completing the sensual brew—

She'll never leave you. Don't even think about it.

"What's your next move, Lara?" something from the press was asking her. And more questions: "How's your health?" "Do you have any comment about this morning?" And then: "Are you marrying Jackson Power?"

"Definitely," Lara said. She smiled up at her escort.

Jacks beamed. Beamed like concert lights were shooting out of his skull. That word "definitely" felt like Christmas morning, every good childhood memory (there were a few), his first major deal, his first million, Paul McCartney singing "Hey Jude," his first billion, his first jet, his first kiss, the first time he fucked, Penny Blansky's right breast, his first love, his children's births, all of them could be packaged and fit, snugly, inside that one word. *Definitely.*

Oohs and aahs from the press—and more questions—"Where?" "When?" "Will it be a big wedding?"

"But not right away," she added, cutting them off.

The concert lights cut out. Light and sound replaced by pitch-black, Dante-esque darkness.

"I have a feeling the next place you'll see me will be a surprise to everyone," Lara said.

Jacks had a hard time hearing her words over the din of his heart being ripped from his chest, stomped on by four hundred partygoers, thrown from an airplane, run over by a crosstown bus, tossed onto the third rail, squeezed into an electric juicer, and spread on someone's morning bagel.

"Are you looking forward to the mayor's speech, Jacks?" the press thing asked the six-foot-plus carcass who resembled Jack Powers. He looked good, the hair in place, always debonair in a tux.

The empty shell, drained of blood and matter, smiled and nodded.

JACKS tried to recover his equilibrium by counting tables. He'd been counting tables at his events since he could remember. If the number of tables hadn't gone up from one fancy dinner to the next, he was sorely disappointed. Disappointed? Not the word. Outraged. Occasionally, someone had lost his job over the diminishing store of tables—even if it was because the room was smaller. Say there were forty tables at one dinner, and the next had only thirty-eight. Someone was responsible for that. Someone was responsible for his humiliation. "No one else even noticed," Caprice would tell him. "No one else would know in a million years, Mr. Power. Why you bother with these things?"

But he knew. He knew.

But this night, he couldn't count. He would start and someone would talk to him, he would forget the number he left off at and start over, but the thing is, it never bothered him before, having people come up to him, it never bothered him, never would he forget, he could have a ten-minute conversation and he wouldn't forget.

His head wasn't in the game.

Did he not care anymore? What had he lost if he didn't care about the number of seats filled with shiny bottoms all there to honor him? Who was he if not the guy who *cared about the details*?

What next? Would he stop caring about the window on the twenty-third floor that's an infinitesimally different shade of glass from the rest (and only when the sun hits it just so at 4:21 in the afternoon)? The gutter that's a half-inch off? The plumbing contractor who's charging .05 percent more than a lesser competitor? What next?

He could see his entire kingdom crumbling, its foundation reduced to dust, the rest sliding into oblivion, and it all started here, with him not being able or willing or having lost his heart for counting tables.

A singer had sung. A group of underprivileged children had clambered onto the stage and testified to the generosity of one Jacks Power. He didn't recognize any of them. Had he spent the requisite fifteen minutes with them at their Bronx schoolyard?

Krach was about to take the stage. The MC, a late-night TV host, had introduced him. Something sortakinda funny about the mayor's lack of experience in government.

Funny, if you're not trying to build in the East Village.

The mayor began. "Tonight we're here to honor a man who . . ."

"I'm lost," Jacks whispered to Lara.

"What's that?" Lara whispered back.

"What did you mean, you're not sure what you'll be doing next?" he whispered.

"What?"

"We need to get married," Jacks said.

"We are going to get married," Lara replied, "I just don't know when."

The mayor was warming to his speech, a joke inserted about one of Jacks's legendary photo ops/press conferences: ". . . never met a historical landmark he didn't want to tear down ... never met a Miss USA he didn't want to ... give a lot of personal advice to ..." Then he launched into the capper: "The Top Ten List of things to do that day if you're Jacks Power."

10. *Fire me, the mayor. Talk about it at length on* Larry King Live.
 9. *Send muffin basket laced with Ex-lax to Bowery Preservation Group.*
 8. *Think up fun new names for tax loopholes, like "Sparky" and "Jurgen."*

"I need a date," Jacks was telling Lara. "June? July? When?"

 7. *Admire self in mirror. This may take some time. Decide on best side.*
 6. *Destroy historic neighborhood before brunch at the Four Seasons.*
 5. *Rename New York City "Power Town."*

"You're pressuring me," Lara said through clenched teeth. "I just lost my job today, I need to regroup."

 4. *Rewrite Page Six. Include adjectives like "dashing," "unstoppable," and phrases like "sex god" and "damn, he's good."*
 3. *Admire self in mirror. Decide on other best side.*
 2. *TP the* New York Post *offices. Same to the Zeckendorfs.*
 1. *Develop new pose and call it "The Jacks" or, better yet, "The Power Pose." Copyright immediately.*

Laughter and applause rumbled through the room. Jacks smiled and waved at the mayor—

"Keep it down. You hated that job," he reminded Lara. "You don't even care that you lost that job. You *wanted* to lose that job."

"That's crazy," Lara whispered back. "You don't even know me."

"Crazy? What's crazy is that you screwed it up on purpose. You knew they would fire you."

Though in his estimation, Jacks was speaking low, people were starting to capture the gist of their conversation. Not an eye wavered—

"Let's talk about this later." Lara beamed her smile, reassuring the multitudes.

"No," Jacks insisted. "I want to talk about this now. I'm giving you three dates. June fifteenth—"

"You're not even divorced yet!"

"It's taken care of. You're talking to Jacks Power—okay, we got June fifteenth, July tenth—"

Every head was turned their way. Lara wasn't backing down. "This is ridiculous, I'm not going to do this—"

Jacks couldn't stop himself. "August fourth the latest."

"I said—I'm not doing this."

"You would if you loved me. If you really loved me, I wouldn't be having this conversation."

The mayor's speech had come to an end.

"Of course I love you."

"No you don't! No, you don't love me!" His hand came down on the table. Silverware jumped. The waiters stopped serving. No one was moving a muscle—

"You're acting like a child!"

"You're acting like a bitch!"

Lara looked at him.

The last he saw of her was her smooth, golden back, those shoulders, oh, her calves emerging then disappearing under the sparkle of her evening dress, her famous mane bouncing happily, oblivious to the devastation as she ran out of the ballroom with the who-knows-how-many tables.

Wait. Wait. She was coming back—*look at that face, that beautiful face, she feels bad, I knew it,* Jacks told himself, *she's already picking the date—*

Ouch. Getting hit in the chest by seventy-two carats of diamonds and emeralds stings. The necklace dropped to the floor, winking up at him.

What had he done? What had he done?

Jacks Power would figure this all out. Jacks Power would solve everything.

Right after he picked up his trophy.

41

QUEEN TAKES PAWN

"THERE'S NO escape," Cynthia said, standing outside her car, looking up at the ominous blue towers Adrian called home. She laughed, one arm wrapped across her sliver of a waist, another over her mouth.

Adrian had come around to open her door. He'd been reduced to polite gestures, genteel mannerisms, everything he was, in fact; he was no longer pretending to be anyone else. "From what?" he asked.

"From Jacks Power!" she said, as the looming towers hovered like glass demons, the famous name stamped in heavy gold letters. "Is there anything he doesn't own?"

She walked past Adrian, as he still held the door open. He could feel the driver's smirk on his shoulders.

"No," Adrian said sullenly. He slammed the door.

"HOW LONG have you lived here?" Cynthia asked. They were inside the mirrored elevators, looking at themselves looking at each other pretending not to look. Well, Adrian was pretending not to look; Cynthia was studying him like something out of Animal Planet—a small furry mammal with underdeveloped defense mechanisms, short nails, blunt teeth good for chomping plants.

"Not long," he said, to the tiger. Tigress.

"Why did you choose this building?" she asked.

"Well, it's practically one of the eight wonders of the world—" he stammered. Oh, the stammering.

"Aren't there seven?"

"Well, then, because it's ... so ... modest—like me?" Perhaps humor would work with the tiger that was toying with him, tossing him back and forth between her paws.

"This building doesn't suit you," she mused. "It's like public housing for high society. I know a few people who live here. They're nothing like you."

"And who am I?" he asked.

They'd reached his floor.

"Not who I thought you were."

Oh, he hoped she didn't hear his heart beating through his cotton T, his silk shirt, his gray, slim-cut jacket. He dropped his keys, picked them up, opened the door. There was the view. He felt like running through the midnight-blue glass into the midnight-blue oblivion.

"Don't you want to know who I thought you were?" she asked. Cynthia was tipsy.

Adrian, ever the professional bartender, calculated body weight, divided it by alcohol and time, and decided he was dealing with full-on id.

"Would you like something to drink?" Adrian asked. "I have a very good Bordeaux, '86, reserve—"

Cynthia dropped her purse on the couch and flopped beside it. She'd put her boots up on the glass coffee table and draped her head back. Her eyes closed.

"I will have a glass, thanks," he said to himself. He went to open the bottle.

"Robert Jordan. I thought you were ... a dilettante. Undignified.

I thought you were . . . typical." She said the word "typical" as though it were laced with bad cologne.

"So you thought you'd ask me out." He brought her a glass. After all, her husband had paid for it. Along with everything else in the apartment, including him.

"So I thought I'd ask you out," she said, gracefully acknowledging the touché. "But now I see something . . . surprising. Like finding a perfectly formed shell on the beach after a storm."

"I'm a perfect shell," he said. She got it half right, he thought.

"Not exactly," she said, "but there may be hope for you yet, Mr. Robert Jordan."

"I appreciate the—"

"What are those?" she asked suddenly. She was jabbing her finger at the centerpiece on the coffee table.

"You don't like yellow roses?" he asked.

"Put them away," she said.

"But I thought—"

"I hate yellow roses," she said.

Adrian stood, staring at the arrangement. He'd called it in; he'd been specific. A dozen yellow roses, cut just so . . .

Cynthia Hunsaker Power was starting to scare him.

"Aren't they your favorite flower?" he asked. *Stupid!*

She looked at him. "What do you mean?"

"I mean," he said, "a lot of women seem to like them." *Oh, King of the Idiots, wear your crown with pride.*

"You bring a lot of women here and they all like them—"

"That's not what I meant—"

"Look, don't bother putting them away—I'm going—"

Adrian's phone started ringing. "No, don't—" he said.

"You should get that, it's probably one of those many, many other women who like yellow roses, maybe that's where my husband got the idea that I like yellow roses, because that's what all his other women liked—"

The phone stopped ringing. Then started again. "Don't move!" he said, "I'm going to take this in the other room, it's a work thing, a work thing, not a woman thing."

Cynthia was standing, her purse in the crook of her arm; she might as well have been in sprinter's position.

"Please wait?" he pleaded, over the incessant ringing.

She gave him a curt nod.

"Thank you, thank you," he said, closing the bedroom doors behind him.

"I can't talk," Adrian said, his back pressed against the door, the cell jammed in his ear. He feared Cynthia could hear Jacks's voice through the wall. Adrian was sweating. He unbuttoned his shirt. *Remember to button it,* he reminded himself, *before you walk back into the lion's den.*

"Why?" Jacks rumbled.

"Cynthia's here, of course," Adrian said, flopping onto the bed. He wished he could take his fancy shoes off. An old pair of Converse beckoned from inside the walk-in closet. His entire "real" life was beckoning him.

"Great. She's there," Jacks said.

"No thanks to you," Adrian said.

"Are you . . . did you . . . have you . . . ? "

"We haven't done anything—wait, we made out, a truncated version of making out—"

"Are you striking out already?" Jacks said. "She could be your mother, for crying out loud—how hard is this?"

Adrian heard something. He jumped up, opened the bedroom door a crack. Cynthia stood by the window, staring out at the water. *Good.*

"How hard is this?" Adrian asked in a tight whisper. "How about impossible? How about this—you're the one who's striking out with your wife!"

"What are you talking about?" Jacks said. "You're not making any sense."

"I've got to go," Adrian said. Cynthia's impatience was pulling at him. Jacks was right—how hard should this be? Cynthia hadn't slept with anyone in over six months, right? Unless . . . she was lying to her husband. (*Go, Cynthia.*)

"Not until you give me a time frame—"

"I'm working on it," Adrian said, "but can I tell you something? You know nothing about that woman who's pacing my living room like a tiger—a very annoyed tiger."

"*My* living room, junior. And I know everything about my wife," Jacks said. "Believe me, there's not much to know."

Adrian was insulted for Cynthia. There was nothing wrong with her; she was just an entirely different species from the one Jacks thought he'd captured.

"Man, you have no idea who you're divorcing," Adrian said. He hung up and stepped down the hall and into the living room—just in time; she'd grabbed her coat.

Suddenly, Adrian felt very tired. And remorseful.

"I'm sorry," Adrian said. "My boss, he's a real prick."

Cynthia hesitated. "Why don't you quit?" she asked, as Adrian maneuvered her toward the couch. "Life is too short to waste it on jerks. Trust me."

"Soon enough," Adrian said, his voice heavy. "The job's not over yet." He sat down next to her, and poured more Bordeaux into her glass.

"So tell me," he said, as he slid closer to Cynthia and handed her the wine. "What else don't you like?"

MARGOT was at the barre, performing deep jetés, beads of sweat glistening on her bony chest, when Cynthia scooted into class and squeezed in next to her. The Saturday 8:00 A.M. ballet series, overseen by the old ballet master, had been their weekly ritual for fifteen years.

"The fuck have you been?" Margot whispered. Her expression remained perfectly placid. The pianist, engaged in a Mozart sonata, was kind enough to cover her cursing.

"My date just ended," Cynthia replied. Together, they bent forward at the waist, then swayed back, their arms lingering overhead.

"That's my girl!" Margot said. "Good?"

"Good enough to awaken the beast," Cynthia said, smiling.

"Now no one is safe," Margot said.

"No one." Cynthia laughed.

"Cynthia! Margot! Enough!" The ancient ballet master yelled.

Margot turned her head toward Cynthia. "Coffee?"

"I'll be needing a triple shot."

"Girls!" The ballet master rapped his cane on the floor. Cynthia and Margot giggled.

AFTER CLASS, Cynthia and Margot walked around the corner to the funky yet pretentious coffee shop frequented by preppies. Smoking their French cigarettes, wearing black tights, their hair in buns, headbands keeping strays off their faces—they each looked fifteen years old.

"Very young," Cynthia was saying.

"How young?" Margot asked.

"I think he's still in his twenties."

Margot took a deep breath in. "Love that. Have yourself checked immediately. These young guys carry new diseases."

"I brought condoms."

"Oh, my little Girl Scout, of course you did. How many times?"

"Twice."

"Nicely done. Orgasms?"

"Yes."

"Number, please?"

"Hard to say."

Margot stopped and grabbed Cynthia's arm. "Over or under five?"

"Over," Cynthia squealed.

Margot screamed as they walked into the coffee shop.

Cynthia couldn't wait to tell Dr. Gold. In person. "There was a functional delay," she admitted.

"Alcohol?"

"No—nerves!"

"He was nervous?!"

"Yes! It took him forever just to get the first condom on. Margot, he was nervous—about sleeping with me!"

"How divine!" Margot clapped her hands to her chest.

Cynthia's old self, the one who lived in the Upper East Side terrarium world, would have taken her lover's soft-on personally. She would have attributed his lack of firmness to something lacking in her own outline. Was it only a short while ago that she'd placed a hand mirror on her pillow to see what her face looked like from a lover's perspective? All she could see were pleats! From that angle, her face looked like a cheerleading skirt. But last night, she didn't give a shit about her pleats. She was on a hormonal roller-coaster ride, anchored ever-so-briefly at the peak, hands waving in the air, screaming, exhilarated . . .

For a slim moment, Cynthia thought she should bring Robert to therapy to show off to Dr. Gold. *"See what I did? I had sex with this! Me! Cynthia Hunsaker Power!"*

Robert had led her into the bedroom, but Cynthia was the first one with her clothes off. She'd been ready since she'd made the call. Cynthia was going to make it to the moon if it killed her.

She'd stood naked, except for her pearls, against the window, a cape of stars resting on her shoulders. She thought of the man who'd brought that view to her. *"Watch me,"* she said, with Jacks in mind, *"I'm going to sleep with this hot young guy in your very own building!"*

Robert, meanwhile, was negotiating with his shirt buttons. Cynthia sat her naked bottom on his cool sheets and beckoned him over. She unbuttoned his shirt and slipped it off, then took his face in her hands and kissed him.

She moved quickly to unbuckle his belt. He gently pushed her back onto the bed and kissed the insides of her thighs before he sank his tongue between her legs and found her clitoris, balled up like a tiny fist.

Orgasm #1. Cynthia the Lamborghini came almost immediately. *Can a woman be a premature ejaculator?* Vivi claimed that oral sex was the only "real" sex, that a woman couldn't have an orgasm from straight intercourse. Cynthia would talk about oral sex only if they used a code word. Thus oral sex had become, appropriately, "French pastry."

Cynthia had several more French pastries—the last one in the morning before she ran off to 740 Park to pick up her ballet tights.

She would no longer argue over French pastry with Vivienne.

Cynthia doubted she would be calling Robert again. The night had been perfect, her entrée back into the unknown world. He had opened a door, with her frank encouragement, and she'd walked through, at one point on all fours. Robert was a booty call, not a budding relationship.

She bade Margot goodbye. She couldn't wait to tell Dr. Gold.

THE DRIVER stopped the car in front of Goldie's building and Cynthia dipped her legs into the cold air.

His office door was locked. There was a handwritten note on the door.

Dr. Gold's Patients:
Please call Miriam Ludwig. 917-555-0232. Sorry for the Inconve-
nience.

Inconvenience had been capitalized. As if knowing that not seeing
Dr. Gold for their scheduled appointment would be not only incon-
venient but tragic. Cynthia sighed. Goldie probably needed a few
extra days to recover from his procedure. She'd head back to 740
instead.

And stop at Paillard for some French pastry on the way.

ADRIAN struck his fist against the air as though shattering the cold, as
he began his inaugural run around the Central Park reservoir. *I've*
aced the final, he thought, *the rest of the semester will fly by!*

Sure, he'd had a few reservations. Cynthia was almost twenty
years older than he was. What would a forty-five-year-old woman
feel like? What would she taste like? What would she remember, not
remember, never have had?

Adrian needn't have worried. What was that David Lee Roth
Eddie Van Halen Old School Rock Your Socks Anthem? "Hot for
Teacher"? How about "Stacy's Mom"? *Oh man, Mrs. Robinson me up*
and down.

Adrian had awakened after Cynthia left and thought, *Oh, shit.* He
was not in fighting shape, given last night's sextravaganza. He couldn't
rely on youth. He'd have to rely on vitamin supplements and weight
training if last night's fuckarama was any indication of his future sex
life.

How could Jackson Lame Ass Power let her go? Adrian thought as he
jogged, one, two, one, two. *Cynthia was a beast. A beautiful, elegant . . .*
beast. But what about Vivienne, he thought, as his footfall slowed.
What about that kiss?

Well, last night's gymnastics weren't about love. Adrian couldn't fall in love with Cynthia. She was too mature for him. Cynthia topped him on every level: money, social standing, life experience. There was nothing he could succeed at with her, nothing he could teach her. And he wanted children. He definitely wanted kids.

Did he have to say goodbye to Vivienne? Their sweet hello had a stranglehold on his imagination. Dustin Hoffman screwed the mom, and he still got the girl. What happened after he and Katharine Ross got off the bus?

Adrian slowed. His legs suddenly felt like paint cans filled with cement. His lungs were seared.

He turned on his heel and headed home.

TWO NIGHTS. Jacks had called Lara over a dozen times. He'd called and he'd e-mailed and he'd even IM'd her. He'd gone by her apartment. The doorman said she'd be gone for a while, he didn't know how long. Lara was gone.

Jacks ached for her; his various body parts ached for her—his hard-on was waking him up in the morning, for crying out loud. He felt like he missed Lara more than he'd miss a limb.

Jacks Power couldn't get out of bed. He knew Lara wasn't coming back. The realization had come to him at 3:00 A.M., in one of those fucked-up Salvador Dalí dreams that make no sense when you're inside its walls, but suddenly hold every truth of every moment of your life when illuminated in the white morning.

That dream was the fucking Gettysburg Address of Jacks's life.

You are not going to be loved again in this lifetime. You do not deserve love.

(Intercom beeping. His butler: "Mr. Power, Petre is waiting for you in the gym.")

Wasn't self-pity, Jacks told himself, his eyes dodging blades of sunshine from his prone position. He wondered whether Cynthia was still sleeping in the master, whether she'd even made it home from

Adrian's apartment. From *his* apartment. Then he thought about the conquests he'd made there.

(Intercom beeping: "Mr. Power, are you there? You've missed several phone calls—")

Lara was gone. There was nothing to strive for anymore. Jacks didn't have to try. He didn't have to seek. He could just be. He was almost relieved.

Jacks knew a billionaire, a Manhattan Gargoyle. Traveled with a medical doctor. They'd all cheat death, all of them. Who among them had died? Death was a rarity in this group, as though they'd rewritten their DNA. Were they gods, these Gargoyles?

(Intercom beeping: "Mr. Power, Petre has to leave for his next client. Mr. Power?" Mumbling in the background. Hurried, muffled.)

Each Gargoyle had a phobia. Some were afraid of flying, some of heights, some of elevators, most were germaphobes and hypochondriacs. They were superstitious. They took special precautions. Don't step on a crack. Don't fly into this airport. Sleep with the lights on. Don't look down. No elevators! Take the stairs to the twentieth floor. Don't shake hands. Don't venture into a movie theater. Don't kiss your child when he's got the sniffles.

Their fears mirrored the size of their holdings. And suddenly, this morning, Jackson knew the truth: they were afraid because none of them were lovable. *Could they even say their own mothers should love them?*

So the Gargoyle who traveled with his doctor. He was short. Looked like a thumb. Married four times. Last wife lasted almost six years, he divorced her, catching her by surprise. He was engaged again within five months. Not unusual for this crowd. Jacks spent time with him between marriage and engagement. It was like watching a short, bald panther, pacing in a cage made of red leather booths with muted light. His eyes scattered wildly, throwing sparks over the new downtown watering hole they called their own. What girl could he find now? Who hadn't he found? Who? *Fix me up,* he implored

Jacks. *You've got women on the side, blondes, redheads, fix me up,* he said. *I'm a single man, isn't that great, fix me up with someone. I'm single. Living the dream, buddy, living the dream!*

(Knock at the door: "Mr. Power, we've talked among ourselves, Mr. Power, perhaps you should open the door—")

We are not lovable. So why do we try? What do we have to prove? What is the goddamned point?

("We are opening this door, Mr. Power! I'm putting the key in the lock!")

Then he thought of the one person who could help him, whose ancestors could raise the dead—

If he wasn't mistaken, Jacks thought, today was Sunday.

Gordo and a maid stood in the doorway of the sitting room in the guest wing, from where they could see a human blur hurtling toward the bathroom.

"Get me my secretary!" the blur shouted before slamming the door. "Get me Caprice!"

"WE ARE not goink to Bronx," Harry said.

Certain people you don't argue with: mothers-in-law, parking attendants, toddlers, Gargoyles, Harry.

"I have to go to church," Jacks said, "and we're late, come on." He was slouching like an angry child in the depths of the limo. Harry was staring at him, his layered face purple, his shave job ill-advised. Sunday mornings he usually had off.

"I not come here to go to Bronx!"

"If you don't start this car right now, you're fired—"

"Goot. I get day off." Harry opened the door.

"Wait—wait—shit, shit, I'll drive, fuck, I'll drive!"

Jacks got out, slammed the door, and started tugging on Harry's ridiculous coat, trying to pull him out of the car. Harry's pajamas peeked out.

"I'm no let you drive this car! You crazy!"

"Then you drive, you dumb Russki!" Jacks yelled.

Harry looked at him. Jacks felt five hundred years of bloody history bearing down on him. Then Harry's expression changed—his features fell into a relaxed position, and he started laughing—until tears formed in his big smoky eyes and grazed his grizzled cheeks.

"Get in back!" he said to Jacks, pushing the words out over guffaws. Jacks did as he was told.

"Ruuuu-ski!" Harry crowed as he threw the car into drive and peeled out.

HARRY lit a cigarette with one hand as he maneuvered the limo, drawing circles with the steering wheel with the butt of his other hand, into a red zone on the curb outside the church.

He got out and leaned his body against the car, welcoming the stares of passersby. *Yes, that's right, that's right. It's nice car, this car, he's rich man, but you have to go through me, the Russian, the Ruuusski (HA!) to get to him or car. And this Russian, he is aching for a fight, give him reason to go to jail. He needs a vacation from his family, from his wife, she is driving him mad, up the wall, her nephew, he's got baby on the way. No job. Wants to go on welfare. Bought car on credit. What credit? HA! His wife, she bought him car. Red sports car. Me? What do I got after years of this work. I got shit car. Anyway. Come through me to get to this beauty. You come through me, you over there. I see you looking.*

Harry chewed on his cigarette. The next hour would be fun. The stares would play out like a tennis match: *stare in your court, no, back to you—now take that stare, kid—I worked for years on that stare. That stare stood time in Siberian prison. It is professional. Many people said to me, Harry, you should act on one of those shows. You know. Big tough guy shows.*

Why? The stare.

A black lady stepped out of the crowd. She was beautiful and not deserving of this circus. Caprice.

She nodded hello to Harry. *A lady, this Caprice. Husband gone.*
Where was the crazy insane lunatic husband who leaves this lady?

Harry opened the door for Jacks, who popped a mint in his
mouth. His nervousness sent signals all over his body—forehead
sweat, slight tremor in the hands, and behind the sunglasses, eyes
blinking like a hummingbird's wings.

The church rose like a hooded angel with stained-glass eyes over
the depressed area it served. Jacks wondered if it would it be less
beautiful if it weren't escorted by liquor stores and graffiti-covered
bus stops, concrete slabs peppered with holes, brick apartments with
iron bars on the windows.

"I'll be damned," Jacks said, looking up at the church.

"That's not for us to decide, Mr. Power," Caprice said. "Come on,
then. The service is about to begin."

THE PLACE was standing room only. Caprice pushed her way through
the crowd, muscling over to two young men with shiny, shaved heads
like ebony icons, thick backs like the Jets' defensive line, and moved
them out of their seats.

Jacks amazed himself with his newfound capacity to change.
Here he was, in church. With lots and lots of black people. And he
was smiling. *Who said he wasn't flexible?*

"Take those things off, Mr. Power," Caprice said. "You don't need
no sunglasses. The Good Lord gonna find you anyway. No sense hiding in his own very house."

"Right," he said. Jacks handed them to her. He hated carrying
anything; he didn't like being weighed down. And he didn't like to
mar the line of his suit.

Caprice understood his quirks; he was worse than some, better
than many. Caprice was much more intimidated by the old lion than
by this cub. Mr. Artemus Power, now he was the one to look out for.
She'd made sure never to be alone with him in a room. Something

in his eyes—or the lack of something in his eyes—made her believe he'd died a long time ago. And the dead don't care who they take down.

A Haitian lady, a neighbor, had slipped a little juju into her hand one morning for protection. Caprice kept it in the drawer at her desk, reaching in and silently fingering it when Artemus Power walked by. She never looked that man in the eye, not if she could help it. She had two boys to feed, to clothe, to educate, to protect. Her baby birds weren't set to be pushed from the nest just yet. When that day happened, she would find herself back on the island. The house she was building, next to her mother's, it would be finished in a year or so. She'd rent it for ten more. And then, she'd live out her days there, days of color—deep, iridescent greens and blues, powerful reds and yellows, black skin and white teeth and pink lips, days of scent—ripe mangoes, the sea, the memory of her grandmother's roast goat. She would care for her mother until she died, then she would care for herself. Her children, New Yorkers, them, they wouldn't have to take care of their mother; she wouldn't be a burden to any but herself.

The Reverend Dr. Franklin Nash entered the room, his satin robe sending streaks of purple to warm Caprice's homesick heart. He was followed by members of the choir, mostly ladies, a few men, engulfed in red, red robes. Majesty was theirs.

Caprice knew that while God was everywhere, He penned in a special appointment in His daybook at the All-Saints Baptist Church every Sunday at 10:05 A.M.

The choir began to sing the spiritual "Lift Ev'ry Voice and Sing." Pride and love and solidarity and strength in note after note, layer upon layer, lashed the church, the believers, the disciples, wounding and healing at once. The song rained soul from the rafters.

Jacks's head started moving to the music as though the notes had reached out and were pushing him to and fro. His eyes were closed. *But did they see?* Caprice wondered. Perhaps a change was coming.

Anyone can change, her mother had told her. But only when their back is to the wall. Was Jacks's back to the wall? Caprice had her doubts; Caprice always had her doubts—they fed and comforted her, like family members you were glad to see and then wondered why.

The Reverend Dr. Franklin Nash raised his mighty arms, purple-and-white wings shimmering, then suddenly brought them down. The voices quieted to a hum, like bees in an enormous, splendorous hive.

Caprice felt a thrill run through her bones. She laid a hand upon her chest. The heart her ex accused her of not having echoed, a staccato beat. The good pastor, a slight man famous beyond these walls, began filling the great church with speech.

Jacks was taken aback by the Reverend Dr.'s booming voice; it belonged to a middle linebacker with a dash of Barry White thrown in. Jacks jumped in his seat as the audience hollered, sang out, and generally parroted the reverend's speech. Jacks saw women in tears, men wiping their eyes, children holding their hands in the air to better touch the words.

Jacks wondered why he didn't feel much of anything, except thirst and hunger. *White people are just different; maybe we've proven that we're heartless.* Could he leave? Could he just tell Caprice thank you, I'll see you tomorrow, we have an early meeting, remember?

Jacks rose two inches; Caprice turned toward him, and just as his voice was finding daylight—

"You there!" another voice called.

The booming voice had him by the throat.

"Did you not find what you were looking for here, my son?"

Jacks's eyes turned toward the billowing robes as he was pushed back down by that voice. The Reverend Dr. Franklin Nash looked like Shaquille O'Neal when looking down on you.

"I think I have a story to tell this man," the reverend said, looking around the church.

"Lay it on, doctor!" a woman screamed.

"Don't hold back, now!"

Did the voices seem eager? . . . bloodthirsty?

"You have lost your way, son!" the reverend bellowed. "You have lost your way, and you were hoping to find yourself in our little church, is that it, young man?"

Young man? Jacks opened his mouth to speak, then shut it.

"Give it to me!" a man yelled. "I need a piece of that!"

"I hear ya!"

"That's how I roll! I roll with Jesus!"

"This little sheep, people," the reverend said, "this little sheep has lost his way!"

"Sheep!"

"Baa. Yes, sir!"

"We gonna help him find his way home," the reverend said.

"But we all black sheep here!"

Laughter.

"But it ain't gonna be Park Avenue, and it ain't Fifth Avenue and it ain't Bergdorf's, people! That is not home!"

"Amen, brother!"

"Is home on a private jet?"

"No, SIR!"

"Is home on an island with bikini–clad harlots?"

"Uh-UH!"

"I roll with JESUS!"

"Is home committing adultery?"

"Is home drinking alcohol?"

"Is home eating fried food, destroying our bodies?"

"No!"

"Good Lord!"

"Is home living in sin?"

"Lord help us all!"

"Is home letting another man raise your children?"

"Lord help the sinner!"

"Is home living rich, eating cha-teau-bri-and and sipping cham-pagne while your brothers and sisters starve?"

"No, doctor sir!"

"Where is home, brothers and sisters?"

"Tell us, Brother Franklin!"

"We LISTENIN'!"

"Where is home? Where is home, I ask you!" The reverend was suddenly standing in front of Jacks. He placed a hand on Jacks's shoulders and held it there. Jacks couldn't have left if his feet were on fire.

"You don't know, do you, son? You don't know and that's why you came here, and we're going to show you right now, aren't we, brothers and sisters, aren't we, Lady Catherine and Brother Joseph? Aren't we, my children? We are all sheep, all sheep of His flock. Some sheep, they white, the sheep here, they black. Yes. But He is our shepherd, He is guiding us up that hill. And where is His home? Where does Jesus live? Where does His father, our Father want us to be? Where can He find us?"

"TELL IT, BROTHER FRANKLIN!"

"Home is here, my brothers and sisters. Home is where God lives. Home is in you!" The reverend poked a long finger in Jackson's chest. "Are you ready to go home? Are you?"

Jacks struggled to speak. "I think I am."

"I didn't hear you, son."

"Ah . . . I think so?"

"What's the holdup, son?"

Jackson hesitated. "Well, for one thing, I live on Park Avenue."

The reverend stopped. Then started laughing. He raised his arms and the singing began. "Son, it's okay with me and it's okay with the Lord—but someone like you, you gonna have to pay your way to heaven." He called over the tithing man. "Pass the hat!"

"I thought you couldn't pay your way to heaven."

"You can if it's your only choice."

Jacks handed him a fifty.

"Good gets good, son."

More.

More.

More.

More.

Jackson emptied out his wallet. A blizzard of bills spilled onto the tithing plate.

"You on your way, son!" The reverend turned toward his constituents: "He's on his way, my children!"

Caprice, her adrenaline pumping, was caught up in the human wave. She stood, clapping wildly. Jacks felt as though an electric shock had run through his body; his mouth was dry, his chest ached from the current. He knew the Reverend Dr. was speaking the truth. He knew it like he knew his own name.

Home, Jacks thought. *Home. I need to get home.*

42

RECESS

ADRIAN RAN around the reservoir. Checked his messages. Went for a bite to eat. Checked messages. Went to a French film. Checked messages. Went back to Central Park again, running some more.

It had been two days. Why hadn't she called him back? Oh God. Was he that bad? Was Jacks, in the end, right about him? He'd counted at least three orgasms. Was she faking? He knew actresses—this woman wasn't an actress—she was the real thing.

Adrian thought he should try her again. What if something had happened to her?

He wasn't going to call her again.

Fuck her. After all, it was just a job. He'd lived up to his end of the bargain. There was no fine print stating otherwise, nothing that said, "My wife must fall in love with you." Nothing that said, "You must have sex with her three times a week for the next six months." Nothing that said she should offer Adrian a country home in Roxbury where she could stable him.

This much he knew: Cynthia didn't seem like a woman who'd be holding off a divorce much longer.

Was she devastated? Adrian hadn't smelled devastation on her, the stench that hovers over the wreckage of a broken heart.

Jacks seemed to be wrong about everything concerning his wife. How could that be, to know someone for twenty-five years, to sit across from her at the breakfast table, to have seen her cry, laugh, to watch her skin change, her tastes change—in clothing, in food, in movies, books, politics—to sleep with her next to you night after night, to see her droopy eyes in the morning, her egg-beater hair, to have watched her brush her teeth over and over and over, to have seen her go to the bathroom. To have witnessed the birth of their child. Maybe he wasn't in the room. Nah. Jacks probably wasn't in the room.

Adrian would want to be in the room. Would want to cut that cord. Would want to be the first to hold that baby.

He wondered about Vivienne. A momentary flash. She liked his kiss.

Why wouldn't Cynthia return his calls? Well, Adrian thought, he still had his invite to the NYBT ball. He'd been fitted for a tux. They were seated at the same table. Cynthia couldn't escape him there. She'd have to face him then.

Adrian tossed his cell in the air, caught it behind his back, and ran full speed all the way to the scene of the crime—the apartment in the sky.

JACKS settled back into his seat as Harry nosed the car out of the church parking lot. Okay, so Lara was out of the picture. But Jacks Power could find his way home. He could turn this ship around. *Just watch.*

First, make a list. What are Lara's issues?

Drinking, lack of commitment, family (she barely talks to her mother, what's that about?). Okay, and she's way too opinionated.

They'd had an argument once regarding crushed versus chopped garlic. *Neither of them can cook.*

Last item on the She Did You a Favor by Dumping You List: Did Jacks really want to be known as Mr. Sizemore?

Jacks Power had to be the biggest star in the room.

Couldn't happen if Lara were in the picture.

And so the new strategy. Jacks could change on a dime. You bet.

Jacks convinced himself that Lara was "damaged goods." He'd drop those words into everyday conversations, a throwaway yet damning portrayal: *Damaged Goods. And that's a fact!*

Second: no listening to Sinatra, Céline Dion, or Bread for the next three weeks.

Third: No secret midnight viewings of The Way We Were.

Fourth: Go home. Win Cynthia back.

Face it; this whole divorce thing had been hasty. Kinda hard to be logical when you're thinking with your cock-brain. Did Jacks really need to flush millions of dollars down the toilet? (To be fished out by Ricardo Bloomenfeld!)

The king and queen could undergo relationship rehab: a romantic getaway, a sparkly necklace, a few turns in the sack—the famous Power mojo.

He could see the headlines now: THE PEOPLE'S BILLIONAIRE, BACK IN THE MARRIAGE BUSINESS; REUNITED AND IT FEELS SO PROFITABLE. (*Make a note: call Liz, call Cyndi, call Larry, call Imus . . . call Caprice!*)

He looked out the window of the car. A glorious fall day in New York. No time like the present.

OH *my God, this day,* Cynthia thought, *breathtaking!* Even the trees of Washington Square Park, skinny and bereft of visible life, struck modern dance poses. Today was the reason to move to New York. Tomorrow would be another story, another wind; a reason, perhaps, to move away.

Noon on Sunday. Cynthia discovered Vivienne still in bed, rolled up in her epic-thread-count sheets, head stuck in her laptop. Cynthia crawled in next to her and, squinting, read the screen.

"Climbing tours in Nepal," Cynthia commented.

"Change of scenery," Vivienne said. "I'm sick of this city."

"But trekking over a mountain range? Why not just fly to London, or Paris," Cynthia said, her regret almost as instant as the hurt on Vivienne's face.

"I'm sorry," Cynthia said quickly. "Let me check it out." She curled her legs under her while perusing ice cream cone mountaintops. Yaks. Buddhist monks. Crooked, blackened teeth. Temples. Lined, cheery faces. More yaks. Water. Poverty. Dirt. Beauty . . .

"Yaks," Cynthia said, pondering.

"It's stupid," Vivienne said, shutting the laptop. "You're right. I'm just looking for any escape. I'm a rich, spoiled brat. I don't care if I do wear cheap clothes—"

"Who are you talking to, Vivienne? I know your clothing allowance."

"Fine. I'll get a job."

"Such a beautiful day," Cynthia said. "Can we schedule an identity crisis later?"

"I'm serious, Mom. I need to get a life. That's what Aiko said."

"You have a life," Cynthia said, "but you'll get another one. After Nepal. Let's go together!" She grabbed Vivienne's hand.

"Mom, it's like camping. But with yaks," Vivienne said. "Yaks smell. They're dirty. Mom, they're . . . how do I say this . . . ? Animals."

"I grew up riding horses. How different can yaks be?" Cynthia said, as she flipped open the computer. "We'll go after the gala."

"You know I'm not—"

" 'Going to that awful thing with those awful people,' " they chorused. Cynthia put her arm around Vivienne and kissed the crown of her head, where her curls began, then gazed out the picture window overlooking the park, imagining the personal dramas being played out: NYU students debating, junkies scoring, toddlers walking on wobbly legs, mothers crying from newborn delirium, old men ambling along and remembering what it was to run after that girl, *the* girl. *Cynthia could happily die here, in this moment with her daughter.*

Instead, her phone trilled.

Cynthia had downloaded Teddy Pendergrass as her ringtone. *Too much wine, weak moment, don't ask.*

Vivienne looked at her, incredulous. "Love TKO?"

"Long story," Cynthia said, clapping the phone to her ear. "Hello?"

"Hold for Jacks Power, please." *Was that Caprice?*

"Wait a minute—" Cynthia said.

"Honey," Jacks said. "It's me. Jacks."

"Honey?" Cynthia said. "Jacks, what do you want?"

"Just sitting here wondering what you're up to," Jacks said. Cynthia could tell he was calling her from the guest wing bathroom. His voice echoed and ricocheted across all the marble. *Jackson Power Surround Sound.*

Why was he calling her? And why was he being so nice? Suspect phenomena—Cynthia was sure there'd be legal repercussions. "I'm with Vivienne," Cynthia said. "We're planning a trip to Nepal."

"Nepal?" Jacks asked.

"What's wrong with Nepal?" she snapped, although she'd had the same reaction. *Ah, the Divorce Games, some day to replace the Olympics.*

"I love Nepal!" Jacks said. "Hey, do you think I could go?"

Cynthia rubbed her forehead. "Jacks. This is Cynthia. The woman you're getting a divorce from."

Jacks glided past the remark. "I've always wanted to go to Nepal. What are those dumb animals called? The ones that Michael Jackson owns? I like those things."

"Yaks?"

"No, that's not it—hey, you and Vivienne want to go to Central Park today?"

"You want to go with us to the . . . park?" Cynthia asked. Vivienne pressed her head against Cynthia's to listen in.

"We haven't been in years," Jacks said. "Remember that time we went and Vivienne, she was two or three, insisted on not wearing diapers and she peed all over the merry-go-round?"

"Jacks, I told you that story. You weren't there."

"Okay, so I want to be there now."

"Vivienne is twenty-five years old."

"So let's not waste any more time. I'll meet you and Vivienne at the pond, we'll feed the ducks, we'll sail one of those motorized boats—"

"Dad, I don't want to go to the park." Vivienne finally spoke up.

"Vivi, hi, honey!" her dad said. "Okay, I'll meet you guys at the Museum of Natural History. Half an hour. Under the whale." Beat. "The whale's at the Natural History, right?"

"Yes, Daddy."

Cynthia looked at her, mouthing the word *"Daddy?"* Vivienne stuck out her tongue at her mom.

"Great. I'll meet you there," Jacks said. "We'll get a hot dog outside. This'll be fun!"

He hung up. But not before Cynthia and Vivi heard Caprice ask, "Do you need me to pick up the hot dogs, Mr. Power?"

Click.

Cynthia looked at Vivienne. They both started laughing. "We MUST go," Cynthia said.

"I'll get dressed," Vivienne said.

"I never even told you about my date!" Cynthia said.

"In the car," Vivienne called out, leaving a trail of clothes behind her as she walked toward the bathroom. An echo of a tan line taunted her mother.

Cynthia resisted the urge to encourage the new cayenne pepper diet. *Let sleeping clothes lie.* Then, she thought about Dr. Gold and imagined his big chest bursting with pride. "You've learned something," she imagined his voice saying. "Finally. My work is done here. Now go, spend the rest of your days enjoying. Breathe. Dance. Love. Share."

Cynthia smiled. *Oh, contentment.*

"And you were wrong about Zorba," Goldie said, in her mind, the mind that seemed crystal clear even though it still felt soaked in wine from Friday night.

Vivienne came out of the bathroom, dressed. Jeans. Old cowboy boots. Ski hat ambushing her curls. A ratty scarf. "Do you have to wear that?" Cynthia asked, frowning.

The Path to Enlightenment was strewn with mothering potholes.

THIRTY minutes later, the People's Billionaire stood beneath the ninety-four-foot whale, submerged in the ambient blue light of the Hall of Ocean Life, waving wildly at Cynthia and Vivienne.

"Honey!" he bellowed, kissing a stunned Vivienne on the cheek. *What was with that scarf?* he thought. *Why didn't she straighten her hair? And she could lose a couple pounds. Vivi was a smart girl. Good business sense, tough cookie. He'd seen her negotiate her grades at Spence. But God, where's her Power style sense?*

"Sweetheart," he said to Cynthia, nipping her on the cheek, failing to get a taste of lip. *Adrian couldn't even close the deal on a middle-aged (though spectacular-looking) broad. A kiss, yeah, whatever. Thank God they hadn't fucked. Jacks didn't know if he could take Cynthia back after that kind of betrayal.*

"Isn't this great?" Jacks said, oblivious that neither woman had uttered a word. "Look at that thing." He jabbed his thumb at the whale. "It's huge!"

Cynthia and Vivi just stared at him.

"This is going to be a great day, the greatest day ever," Jacks continued. "First, we got the Natural History. Next, we got lunch at Serendipity—frozen hot chocolate, your favorite, right, Vivi?"

Vivienne and Cynthia continued to look confused.

"And then, baby, Daddy has a surprise for you."

"Just add it to the list," Vivienne said.

Jacks laughed. "Don't even try to get it out of me!" After Serendipity, Jacks planned to head to American Princess, or American Kid or whatever it was, where his beloved daughter could pick out and dress her very own doll.

All right, he knew Vivienne wasn't six years old—he couldn't help that, even Jacks Power couldn't control Father Time! But Jacks needed to pick up all the memories he'd missed. Today he and Vivi would go to the museum, buy dolls, and eat sundaes. That would take care of ages three to eight. Tuesday or Wednesday they would take in a Broadway show (*Wicked*? *Hairspray*?) and buy horse gear. Boots, breeches, tack, maybe even a pony. Ages nine to fourteen: done.

Meanwhile, Caprice was making a list of places to go and things to do for the father of a teenager in Manhattan—shops, hangouts, nightclubs, concerts. Before he knew it, they'd be all caught up on Vivienne's formative years. Jacks figured it should take about a week.

Jacks put his arm around her shoulders. "I just want to spend time with my family. Is that too much to ask?"

"Jacks," Cynthia said. "You and I are getting divorced the good old-fashioned way. Remember? The nonamicable way—"

"Don't be a party-pooper," Jacks said, extending his other arm around Cynthia, squeezing the two women together against his chest. "Let's go check out the cavemen—"

"Dad, I don't want to look at the cavemen," said Vivienne evenly. "I'm not ready for all this paternal attention. It feels icky."

"You always were a tough kid," Jacks said, laughing and shrugging off the sudden drop in temperature. "I like that. Now, come on, let's go see the cavemen—"

"Daddy, seriously, should we call a mental health professional?" Vivienne asked as Jacks pulled his women tightly under his arms, dragging them off toward the Hall of Human Origins, where cavemen dwelled in their diorama on prime Manhattan real estate.

LARA hadn't driven in months; she'd forgotten how appealing it was to spend time alone in a car. She'd rented a burgundy luxury sedan, a car her grandmother would have favored. *Maroon,* Lara thought, as she signed the rental agreement. *How appropriate. Here I am, marooned on an island, the island. Without love and without work.*

That was over an hour ago. She'd been slinking north along a cold highway; she'd felt her breath return only when she saw the partially deformed isle of New York sinking in her rearview mirror.

Equipped with hastily written directions, a navigational device she had trouble taking seriously, and her own sense of Manifest Destiny, Lara was her own unsettled country. She needed focus. She needed an ally.

Lara was on her way to Sarah Kate's goat cheese farm. Her beloved producer had turned her back on a network career for a bucolic, bleating lifestyle. Lara had received e-mail bulletins from Sarah Kate on a weekly basis: "Good news. We've fixed the pens after last week's fiasco—who knew goats could chew through chicken wire?" or "Here's a JPEG of the bags draining whey into buckets" or "Sylvia just birthed a pair of kids at two o'clock this morning—first photo of the newborns (entitled 'Jus' Kiddin')."

Who is this person? Lara thought as she read the reports. *And what has she done with my producer?*

Two hours north, one hour east. Radio stations popped, fizzled, and twisted melodies into frayed rope, leaving only a country music station and a raging conservative in their wake.

Thoughts of Jacks stayed with her. *Would he ever try a road trip?* In her mind, he sat next to her, chattering, laughing, checking his Black-Berry. Wanting to stop somewhere to eat, have a drink, have sex. Wondering where all the people were to recognize him. Lara placed her hand on the curve of the passenger seat, sinking her fingertips into its maroon softness. *How could someone so impossible be so adorable?*

Lara shed a tear, then another. Then stopped by the side of the road, now slick with ice. She sat and cried it out. *Why was she so scared? Isn't this what she wanted? Was she wrong to jump off the party bus while it was still rolling?*

Lara wiped her hand across her eyes and maneuvered the car back onto the road.

"YOU LOOK . . ." Lara tilted her head as if a word was going to drop from the sky into her ear.

"Like a frikkin' nutjob," finished Sarah Kate, standing in front of her.

Lara took in her ex-producer's appearance. Black rubber boots swallowed the lower half of her bubble legs, baggy green pants tucked in, an oversize green khaki jacket. White apron peeking out underneath. Reading glasses on a chain around her neck. Hair wild, cheeks flushed. The whole ensemble coated with a deep, rich, pungent . . . mud.

Which made sense, as they were standing in a damp, grassy field surrounded by goats. Several were nipping at Lara's clothes; one tried to slip her purse from her shoulder. The goats were like unruly, hairy, long-faced, cud-chewing, clover-sniffing toddlers.

It wasn't just the switch from Anne Klein to Carhartt. Sarah Kate's whole demeanor had changed; her eyes had lost their executive "hood."

"It's the look on your face—" Lara told her, slapping a goat that was nibbling her on the butt. "Shoo! Go!"

"I look stupid, right?" Sarah Kate said, smiling. "I know I'm down about ten IQ points already."

"No. You look happy. Or deranged. I don't know how you do it. I've spent three seconds with these goats—they smell, they make strange noises, and they're trying to tear my clothes off. They're like a nightmare date."

"Do you have a cigarette on you?" Sarah Kate interjected. "My beau doesn't like me to smoke. He doesn't want me to die. Killjoy."

"Beau?" Lara's eyes widened.

"I got me a mister, sister," Sarah Kate replied. "And he's hotter than summertime in Dubai."

Lara's eyes teared up, and she gave Sarah Kate a huge hug. All evidence had pointed to Sarah Kate living her life out alone, surrounded by her cats.

"This calls for a celebration," Lara said, and pulled two cigarettes out of her jacket pocket. She lit them up and handed one to Sarah Kate.

Sarah Kate dragged on the cigarette, filling her large being. "Now," Sarah Kate exhaled, capturing Lara in her sights, "can I say what you look like?"

"What?"

"Scared shitless."

Lara flung her arm around Sarah Kate's shoulders, again. So solid. No equivocation. No ulterior motives. No looking over your shoulder for the more important profile. Was this what Truth looked like? A bountiful lady goat farmer? "Fair enough. I am scared shitless. Now get me away from these fucking goats?"

Lara could see the main house, a ranch-style structure, and a hundred yards away, a large barn where she presumed the goats were milked. There was another building where, as Sarah Kate described at length, the milk was turned into rounds of cheese, wrapped and stamped, and sent off to boutique groceries.

"Let's eat some cheese." Sarah Kate took her by the hand. They started walking toward the house.

"Not crazy about cheese, either."

"Too bad, I'm stacked to the gills. I got cheese for years—cheese pancakes, cheese waffles, cheese and eggs, cheese sandwiches, cheese salad, cheese toast, cheese and crackers, cheese bath oil . . ." Sarah Kate put her arm around Lara and guided her friend onto the least resistant path.

Inside, wrapped in the rough charm of the living room with wooden rafters, throw rugs under her feet, a soft chair to sink into, Lara accepted the mug of tea, wrapping both hands around the cup. "So, tell me about your man. Leave out nothing."

"He thinks I'm hot." Sarah Kate grinned.

"You *are* hot."

"Thank you. No, he really thinks I'm hot. They don't get V*ogue* around here. There's no *People* magazine. This man, he has no idea, no idea at all who Paris Hilton is, and I'm not kidding. If I told him I was a hundred fifteen pounds and five foot nine—"

"You *are* five foot nine."

"Yes, but I was one fifteen in second grade—I mean, this man would believe me. And I think he'll believe me the rest of my life."

"The rest of your life?"

Sarah Kate looked at her, her gaze clear. "Yes, I said it."

Lara breathed in that line. *Oh,* she thought, *how life does surprise us on occasion.* "One question," Lara said. "Does he think the goats are beautiful, too?"

Sarah Kate laughed. "That's just mean." And then they were both laughing. "But you know what? You know what? I think he does," she said. "But hell, I do, too."

They sat there for a moment. Teacups warming their hands. The waning light on their faces.

"Maybe I'll have a child," Sarah Kate said.

"Oh, shit," Lara replied. "Of course you will. And I'll be the god-mother. The seriously underqualified godmother."

They reached to each other at once and held hands and looked across at the pasture.

"But I miss it," Sarah Kate said. "Don't think I don't miss it."

"You do?"

"The thing is, Lara. There are no easy answers. You come to me, my child—you're looking for an answer here. You're looking for it in me. In my life. But this isn't your answer. This isn't even your question. There are choices, and then you live with the choices. Part of me wants the newsroom to call, to need me. I still leave my cell phone on my nightstand. I leave it there even though I know it'll never ring."

"Well, the service does suck up here."

"You make a choice and live with it. You've made one. Now you live with it. You've bitched and moaned since I've known you. Now be a grown-up. Don't use Jacks to save you. You're a big girl."

Lara looked at her.

"I know, you'll tell me you know that already. But what you don't know is that you're always going to disappoint someone in your life. Just don't disappoint yourself."

"I fucked everything up, didn't I," Lara said, her voice at a whis-per. Fear squeezing her throat.

"Well, did you shoot before you knew you were aiming at your-self? Or was that the point?"

Lara's eyes searched the beamed ceilings for an answer. She had to escape the cage; if she shed a little of her own blood in the mean-time, so be it.

"Did you want a proper drink, by the way?" Sarah Kate asked, peering at her. "I didn't even think to ask."

"No. I'm good."

"Mmmhmm. There's hope for you, yet," Sarah Kate said, and then, "Do you still love him?"

"Yes."

"Loser."

"Guilty."

A phone rang, echoing through the house. Sarah Kate rose to get it. "Could be important—got a mama goat at the vet—she's down with the blackleg."

Lara nodded and sat alone.

Sarah Kate came back, her face alert, eyes wide. "It's for you," she said.

"What?" Lara asked, blood rushing to her head as she stood up. "What is it?"

"You must shit diamonds, girl. Your dream just landed."

VIVIENNE accepted Serendipity. She accepted the charred veggie burger and frozen hot chocolate and watching her mother sneaking Gitanes on the curb, and filling up on Diet Coke (*how was it even possible they were related?*) and her father's eyes darting to the BlackBerry nestled on his lap. She accepted Dylan's Candy Bar for postlunch baggies of candy corn and Dad barking into a cell phone and Mom's pinched face as she looked at rows upon rows of sugary brightness. She even accepted her mother rushing off because of ballet gala crisis #738, stranding her alone with her father.

But now Vivienne had reached her limit.

"I am *not* going in there!"

Vivienne, fists rolled up and hissing through her teeth, was pitching a fit under a red awning; the massive American Girl Place on Fifth.

Jacks tugged her toward the doors—"Come on! We're going to miss the show." He was holding a brochure. "Look, you buy a doll and dress the doll and sit with the doll in your lap and watch the show. It's great, it's fantastic, it's very professional, by the way. You'll love it!"

"Dad, I swear to God, I'm going to scream—"

"What about Bitty Bear? He's in the show, too, it's going to start in a few minutes. C'mon, you love stuffed animals."

"You made me give my animals to poor kids!" Vivienne yelled. Like a sharp-eyed major-league batter, she caught something fast and fleeting in his eyes.

"Oh my God," Vivienne said. "You didn't give them away to poor kids! You threw them away!"

Jacks's face flushed with recognition. "You had allergies . . . ," he stumbled.

"I didn't have allergies—you have allergies!"

"You had a rash—"

"I had poison oak!" Vivienne said, her back sliding against the cool beige marble. "Oh my God. It's coming back to me—one night you walked into my room, tucked me in and sneezed, and the next day all of my animals were gone!"

"Did you want to be eaten alive by dust mites?" Jacks reasoned. "I cared about your well-being!"

Vivienne turned and pressed her forehead against the store window, where she was eye to eye with a doll with crisp black bangs, high cheekbones, and delicately slanted eyes. *Aiko.* The girl who had left her. The girl who was never happy. *Why?* Vivienne had given her everything. Sex, home-cooked meals, money, gifts. *Her pride.* The last was her pride. She had nothing left to give. Would you like one of my kidneys? How about a lung? Please, take the patch of skin tattooed with your name . . .

The tattoo keeps me lonely, Vivienne thought. A life sentence. But she was better off. Signs told her so—a change in the weather, a white dove (where did it come from?) cooing on a windowsill.

The kiss from that boy.

A sign.

A kiss changes everything. It told her she was better off. *Would someone please break that news to her heart?*

"I want to go home." Vivienne didn't want to fall apart here, in front of the convention center for eight-year-old girls.

"Please," Jacks said, "let's try. Buy one doll. Please. It's important to me. I need to do this for my little girl."

Her father's face suddenly appeared old. She'd read somewhere that narcissists escape the aging process, while their loved ones succumb to gray hair, wrinkles, ulcers, eating disorders (*hi, Mom!*), cancer. So maybe Jacks Power wasn't a true narcissist, maybe there was a piece of him snatched, safe and pure, from his wretched childhood, from those who molded this train wreck of a father.

"Please?"

Her father had kissed her mother on the cheek when she'd left. How old would Vivienne be when she stopped hoping they'd get back together?

"Fine," she said suddenly.

Jacks flashed his famous grin. "That's my girl!"

Vivienne pushed herself up, pulled her ski hat over her ears, and entered the store head down.

43

THE GOOD BISHOP'S FINAL MOVE

FINALLY. HOME. Cynthia had a moment to herself to wonder about the day's events: Jackson's abrupt turn-of-face, the bizarre impromptu family outing, the crisis at Brooke Astor Hall (Margot and Bruce Harold Raymond going head-to-head). Cynthia hadn't even had time to check in with Vivienne to see how the remainder of the Daddy-and-Me afternoon had gone. She'd returned none of her calls from the day—two alone from Robert Jordan.

Good God, she'd almost forgotten about her new friend, the Female Orgasm. *She must bring her around again!*

A knock came at the door. "Madame," the French butler said.

"Come in," Cynthia said.

"Sorry to disturb you, madame." This butler had been with them for years. Cynthia knew nothing of his personal life. Nothing of children, a wife, a lover, a fondness for dogs. Nothing. His one prominent streak of personality was the color of his hair. He dyed it, Cynthia surmised, every few weeks—a blinding platinum blond.

"Yes," Cynthia prompted. She suddenly felt certain she would sell 740. Why did she need such a big place? So many rooms? A French butler?

"A Miss Miriam Ludwig called. She wanted to know if you would be attending the memorial service."

"Memorial service?" Cynthia asked. "For whom?"

"For a Dr. Gold, madame," the butler said.

CYNTHIA didn't remember the sound she made through the fingers clasped over her mouth. She didn't remember sending the butler out or flopping onto her bed, holding a pillow to her face while she screamed. She didn't remember calling Jackson until he arrived at her bedside.

Goldie was dead.

How could she not have been concerned about him? Was she so self-involved that she couldn't have read the signs? Everyone knew his heart wasn't on speaking terms with the rest of his body—and yet, his heart had worked well enough to heal anyone who came into his office. Goldie was all heart. From the top of his bald head to the bottom of his Converse tennis shoes. His heart had finally let him down.

No more hugs.

Goldie. The one consistent person in her life was no more. She'd have to fight on alone.

"Cynthia," Jackson said. "Cynthia, I'm here."

She looked up. Jackson was standing over her. What was he doing here? What was he doing here and yet had he ever left their bedroom? Had he ever really left?

He bent down and kissed her face and ran his hand gently over her hair.

"I came here as soon as I could, left a meeting with some majors."

"Thank you," Cynthia managed.

And then he kissed her. And she let him. Why? She let him because that's what you do. That's how the story is supposed to end.

This is what everyone wants—politicians, nuns, schoolteachers, bus drivers, Page Six (well, maybe not Page Six), financiers, street musicians, waitresses, PTA moms, the FedEx guy; everyone wants the Happy Ending.

Cynthia had heard the admonishments, mostly from men: "You aren't who you think you are without your mate." "Do it for the children." "This is your marriage. You need to hold it together." "But he's a good guy, really, deep inside." "He loves you. He just doesn't know how to act accordingly."

And:

"Don't you want to dance together at your daughter's wedding?"

She'd given up on her daughter's wedding a long time ago. (Although, on Sunday mornings, she secretly took solace in perusing the *New York Times* weddings section. She loved the photographs of the gay and lesbian couples. The younger lesbians—the pretty girl and the potato-faced girl. The older lesbians with spiky hair, wire-rimmed glasses, PhDs, no makeup.)

Cynthia wished there were a nicer name for lesbians than ... lesbians. Something more civilized, like ... girlians. Femians. Fays? Female gays?

But the lesbians' proud, smiling faces had nothing on the photos of the male homosexuals, the ones who'd been together a lifetime before tying the knot. Oh, they were wonderful. Their heads touching, their jowly faces flush with love and pride. And the plethora of bow ties! It was all Cynthia could do not to kiss the page.

A kiss.

A kiss changes everything.

Moments later, Jacks and Cynthia were naked. Moments after that, they had performed the one act that seemed unbearable only that morning. *Sex with her husband? The man who had humiliated her? On a national scale?*

Never!

There's the old saw about sex bringing the living to life, in the face of death. Death makes us want to confirm our breath. We can fuck, therefore we exist.

"I still got it," Jacks said.

Cynthia's head was on his chest. Oh, the love of the familiar. Jackson was the serial killer of her emotional health, but Cynthia knew his body, his scent, his warped mind, and could still find comfort in his embrace.

"I'm amazed at how good that felt," he said.

Cynthia peered up into his nostrils. They flared as he spoke.

"So, we should call our lawyers," he said. "And then we should notify the press. No, no, let the lawyers do that. Let them do that, fuckers, they're getting paid, let them do something. Do you know how much this has cost me already? Fucking Penn and that creep Ricardo—putting their grandchildren's children through college. No, through law school, so they can screw our grandchildren's children!"

Cynthia waited, enjoying the entertainment value.

"We should go somewhere big, public, arrive together. As a family. We should take Vivienne. She's pretty. I hadn't really noticed before. Maybe she's lost a little weight. A few more pounds, she'll be in business."

Jacks was on a roll. He was on a roll in a speeding car on a smooth highway. Cynthia waited and wished she had had the foresight to sew her vagina shut. But then, she mused that she'd had a lot of sex in the past forty-eight hours. *A fine testament to the work of dear Dr. Gold.*

She stood and started picking her clothes off the floor.

"Wait," Jacks said, "wait wait wait. Oh, baby, this is good. When's your event? The ballet when dancing always goes on too long?"

"That would be my life's work. The New York Ballet Theater Fall Gala."

"Hey, oh yeah, I just heard something. Insider stuff. Fred Plotzicki might have to file for bankruptcy protection."

Cynthia spun around. "You're kidding."

"Nah. His company was leveraged out in the sub-prime mort-gage business. So much for Mr. Finance Genius. There's nothing like when an enemy gets his—except when a friend gets his, right?" Jacks laughed.

"Not enough that you should succeed, it's that your friends should fail," Cynthia said slowly.

"Yeah. So, we'll pop in together, to your show." Jacks sat up. "And then we'll make our announcement."

"What announcement?" Cynthia said coyly. She knew, but she had to make Jacks say the words. Was she cruel? A little. Could you blame her?

"That we're back together. The Power couple. We're back. What are you wearing? A little color would be nice. You look a little pale. I've been meaning to tell you. You should gain a few pounds. Not that you're not beautiful. You're stunning. For your age, especially."

"Jacks. Stop."

"Stop?" He looked confused.

"Yes," Cynthia said, "stop talking and don't talk again until you are outside on the sidewalk."

"You want me to leave?" Jacks asked.

"Now," Cynthia said.

"Oh, I see," Jacks said. "You're wondering about the other . . . well, she's gone. I'm completely done with all that. I lost my mind. It was nothing. A big nothing. You, you're the real deal. We are the real deal. The King and Queen!"

"Jacks. Now," Cynthia said, very deliberately. She gathered up his clothes and put them in his hands.

"Okay, still mad," he said. "Feeling feisty. That makes sense. That's fair. I can deal. This dog's got to earn his way out of the doghouse."

He turned to walk out of the room, then turned back, excited. "You know what I'm going to do? I'm going to woo you, Cynthia. You'll see. I'm going to woo my own wife!"

"Out!" Cynthia yelled, pointing at the door.

Jacks smiled and walked out. He couldn't wait to start his next big project—he'd made inroads with Vivienne today, Vivienne who was a mystery, so hard and so young. But by the end of the day, they'd exchanged, gingerly, tender jabs of the familiar. He was getting to Vivienne. And if he could get to his daughter, he could get to his wife. He could get his wife back, his life back.

The Reverend Dr. was right. There was no place like home.

Especially if home is on Seventy-first and Park.

44

OUTFLANKING

CYNTHIA WAS pacing in her office, pausing only to partake of the diet Red Bull on ice the maid had discreetly placed on the antique oak desk that once belonged to the baron of a Mayflower family. *At least, that was the designer's story,* Cynthia thought. Jacks had finally handed Cynthia a gift she could use: no, not his penis—*information.* If Fred were in financial straits, Cynthia could threaten to expose him to the board. How many members would remain in his camp if expensive favors started drying up and blowing away? How fast would Three-Named Bruce Harold Raymond change his tune?

Cynthia had appeased and accommodated, remained fair and reasonable—and had still been slapped down. *What did she have to lose by finally hitting back?*

How about her "Number One Good Girl" status?

Fuck that.

"Hello, Fred, how are you?" Cynthia said to herself. Caffeine on ice was helping her climb out of her sexual exhaustion and into a manic state.

"Fred, I'd like to fill you in on changes I want to make this season—if you're interested."

She paused. Gulped down more of the Bull. *And burped.*

"Fred, you are a fat man with an enormous appetite for everything, including destruction."

The maid, having heard her mistress's imaginary conversation, approached. "Another Red Bull, missus?" masked a maneuver to find out if Cynthia was losing her mind (and to report back to the rest of the staff, de rigueur). The penthouse at 740 was *Upstairs, Downstairs* but with a greater variety of accents; Brogue Irish, British, Uruguayan, French. They'd been on high alert for months, keeping two panthers apart; Cynthia in the master suite, Jacks in the guest quarters.

And now, the panthers had mated! What next??

The staff deserved to have their little fun, Cynthia thought, as she settled into her chair, and dialed.

Shoulders back, tummy tucked, sit bones steady.

Cynthia stood and sank into a plié when Fred's maid answered, then rolled back and forth on her toes, rehearsing in her mind words that would somehow navigate their way to her lips. *Mother?* she thought. *Zorba? Goldie? Help!*

"Mrs. Power," a voice grumbled. "Oh, I mean Cynthia."

Mount Plotzicki was going to be a rough climb, Cynthia thought. She would need all of her provisions.

"Fred," Cynthia said, fighting the urge to hang up, "you have to stop this shit." *What? What did she just say?* A smile started working its way to Cynthia's terrified surface.

"Now wait a minute, Cynthia." The voice deepened.

"No. You wait a minute, you overgrown toddler," Cynthia said. "You're destroying this company because of your petulance and I'm not going to let you do it. I'm giving you two options: you play in the sandbox, and you play nice, *or* you walk away—but you do *not* light the sandbox on fire, you big . . . baby!"

"Cynthia, I've never heard you talk like this—"

"*I've* never heard me talk like this—but Fred, so help me, I am done being made a mockery of by you or anyone else!" *WHERE*

THE HELL DID THAT COME FROM? Cynthia's inner voice screamed. *AND CAN I HAVE MORE, PLEASE?* the inner voice asked (but in a nice way).

"Now . . . just calm down," Fred said.

"I'm calm, Fred. I've never been more calm. Because you know what? You're talking to a woman who's got nothing to lose."

"You have a wonderful reputation—"

"Fuck my reputation."

"Cynthia. Do you really want to fight with me?"

"I'm not going to fight with you. I don't need to. Your world is on the verge of imploding, Fred, you know it and I know it. I make one phone call, and you lose the board. I make two phone calls, and guess what, you lose *your* reputation."

Cynthia heard a sound, like a slow leak from a hot air balloon.

"I'll call off the dogs," Fred finally said.

"Not good enough," Cynthia said. "First, you need to sit down with Margaret Lord Foster and tell that old bitch to reinstate her support of this company, or I will leak it to anyone who will listen that her husband buys fishnets at that lingerie store on Madison and they are not in her size."

Beat.

"Is that all?" Fred growled. More like a Chihuahua—less like the Doberman of Wall Street.

"No," Cynthia said. "You are going to keep your big mouth shut about me or this company, or so help me—"

"Will do, Cynthia," he said. "Can I make this up to you? Would you like to go out to dinner sometime?"

Cynthia was taken aback. "Of course not. You're married," she said.

"My wife left me. You only read your gossip, apparently."

"About time she left," Cynthia said. "Good for her."

"So that's a no?"

"Just . . . do what I asked," Cynthia said.

"Yes, ma'am," Fred replied.

Cynthia hung up and caught her reflection in the mirror above her desk.

She had color in her cheeks, and her eyes were sending off sparks. Sure, she was wearing the Balenciaga V-neck Vivi had made her purchase—but it was more than that. She'd traded in Polite Cynthia for Warrior Queen Cynthia; Polite Cynthia had given up her power for too long to men—Jacks, Artemus, the Freds—even the Bruces.

Think, Cynthia thought, *what else can the Warrior Queen change: What do you want to see? Where do you want to go? What do you want to learn?*

Whom do you want to fuck?

Or fire?

Cynthia picked up the phone to dial, then put it back down. This next conversation would take place in person. Time for the bitches to take over. Cynthia was ready to take the bull by the cojones.

Or maybe it was just a hot flash.

45

THE WOOING OF A QUEEN

GOOD NEWS, Harry. Good news," Jacks said, as the car rolled into traffic.

Harry grunted. *Always good news when you're rich.*

"Yes, I am getting back together with my wife, thanks for asking."

Harry shook his head. *Cynthia! She was almost over wall—what was she thinking?*

"And thanks for the vote of confidence."

Harry honked his horn; Jacks checked his BlackBerry.

Still no e-mails from Lara. Eh, he thought, it was for the better. He rubbed that empty spot in his chest. Still, there was disappointment. How could she just forget about him? Just like that. She should look at him now. He was back in the saddle. With his beautiful wife, his soon-to-be-beautiful daughter. Jacks Power was on top of the world.

And hoping that empty feeling would go away. Maybe he just needed a good meal. "How you know?" Harry asked. "You know what's in a woman's mind? In her heart?"

Jacks looked at the back of Harry's big head. Goddamn it if he didn't feel like punching it.

"How do I know? I just know. What the fuck?"

"My wife, I know her since we were *rebyata*—I know her braids, her dimples, I know the bottom of her baby shoes, her *tooflis*. But you know something? I don't know her at all."

Things had not settled down in the Harry the Russian household.

"Well, do what I do," Jacks said. "Learn from the master. You have to try to know her again, Harry. Maybe listen every once in a while. Maybe talk instead of yell. I don't know. Take her out to dinner. Buy her roses. It's easy!"

"I'll try," Harry said. "I think at certain point, what is determined is."

"That makes no sense. That's what you call 'fatalistic'—and I am many things, Harry, many things, but fatalistic is not one of them. The thing's not dead until it's buried. And even then, even then—"

He lost his train of thought. *Would Lara ever be just a memory? A flat-screen playing scenes in his head on occasion?*

Jacks dialed Caprice. If he was going to woo his wife, he could not be expected to do it alone. But first: "Harry, we need to make a quick stop." Jacks needed to tie up a loose end—one that he had loosened himself.

And now needed to get rid of.

MARGOT was in bed with a buzz-cut twenty-two-year-old dancer from Wisconsin when Cynthia let herself in. Her second bedmate, a dancer from a Philadelphia ghetto, older and more experienced at twenty-five, was showering off.

"Aren't you getting a little . . . mature for this?" Cynthia said, as she watched Margot get dressed. The twenty-five-year-old traipsed through, wrapping a towel around his waist at the last minute.

"Don't you mean 'old'?" Margot grinned. "Because 'mature' ain't gonna happen."

The two boys were now in the kitchen, where Cynthia could see them pouring themselves overflowing bowls of Froot Loops. Margot always kept the sugary stuff on hand for the younger merchandise.

"The little one was curious about my legendary flexibility," Margot said, as she lit up a cigarette and handed it to Cynthia.

"Hope you enjoyed it," Cynthia said, "because my new artistic director can't be screwing the dancers. I don't need the bad publicity."

Margot waved the smoke away from her face. "What are you talking about?"

"I'm talking about you," Cynthia said. "You're the new artistic director of the NYBT."

"Yeah, fuck you," Margot said. She slipped a sweater over her head without dropping the cigarette from her mouth.

"I'm dead serious," Cynthia said, images running through her head: Was this her twenty-seventh New York Ballet Theater Fall Gala? Her first year was indelible: she'd been a featured dancer in a pas de deux while dessert was being served—she could barely hear Brahms above silverware tinkling and murmurs of patrons anxious to dash to limos, which waited like prehistoric creatures exhaling exhaust into the clear night.

Few years later: a baby arrives. Then, another baby. Cynthia went from dancer to patron. "Patroness" had become attached to Cynthia's name—the caboose at the end of Power. Dancer. Former Dancer. Then, only: Patroness.

Twenty-seven years later: Cynthia was done busying herself with the usual set of horrors; mismanaged seating arrangements—ex-wives next to ex-husbands next to mistresses, business rivals seated across from each other—light skirmishes between pawns. All bullshit. It was time to move the major players around on the board. The NYBT was about to put on a performance that would be respectable. Again. And stun no one. Again. Cynthia could do better with this company. *Live dangerously, dance dangerously,* Cynthia thought. *Zorba.*

Goldie.

"I can't be an artistic director. I . . ." Margot stammered.

"I?" Cynthia prompted.

"I don't have the temperament for it."

"Margot Ashford afraid? I never thought I'd live to see the day."

"I'm too old to carry that kind of responsibility. I've never even had a husband! Cynthia, I've never had children! A dog, a goldfish— I've never owned a goddamned plant! I can't even keep milk without it going bad!"

"And yet, you've stayed with the same ballet company for over twenty-five years."

"I'm clinically unstable. I'm on meds. All sizes, shapes, and colors—"

"Enough with the bragging."

Beat.

"Okay. I'm scared," Margot confessed.

"You're also immensely talented. And inspirational. Most importantly, you're respected by the dancers. They are in awe of you."

"They won't listen. They're like puppies."

"They will when you have more power," Cynthia said. "Now, Margot, I took this position because of you. You owe me this."

"Low blow."

"We'll triumph together."

"Or we go down together, more like," Margot said.

"Either way, we live boldly."

"I feel nauseous."

"I know! Isn't it great?" Cynthia clapped her hands.

"The media will skewer you, the *Times* will lift its leg and pee all over you—" Margot said.

"Fine," Cynthia said, "I have a lunch meeting this week with Adeline Crisp, the *Times* critic. I'll tell her face-to-face. Then let the chips fall where they may!"

"Why you little Machiavellian—"

"Margot, you're a genius. I've always known it, since our first day of hating each other," Cynthia said. "Now others will know it, too. I love you, you know. That's why I'm doing this to you."

"I hate you, you're fucking up my life."

"You hate your life. You're bored and it shows. Look at those boys in the kitchen! It's time for you to be challenged. Now shut up and say yes. I have a firing to get to."

"Shut up and say yes?" Margot asked.

"Zorba!"

"Yes! Fuck! YES!"

The two dancers poked their heads in the bedroom door. "Everything okay?" the younger one asked.

"No!" Margot said, falling backward on the bed.

"SHIT," Adrian said to himself. He hid his face in his scarf and high-tailed it past the doormen, valet parkers, and security outside the blue glass building. *Something was up.* There was that one black Town Car in the sea of Town Cars parked in front of the building. That silly hat, fur poking out through a crack in the driver's side window. *Who could forget that hat?*

Elevator to the nosebleed floor. Hi to the nice neighbor lady with the mink-collared dachshund, Mr. Fibbs. Key in the door.

Jackson Power was lounging on the couch, feet up on the coffee table.

"You want the report?" Adrian said, trying to sound nonchalant. *Why so nervous, A?*

"I'm no longer in need of your services," Jacks said, standing up and brushing the front of his pants.

Adrian ran his hand through his newly cropped hair.

"Really," Adrian said.

"Hell of a job, you did," Jackson said. "Scared Cynthia right back into my arms."

Adrian looked at Jacks. "You're joking, right?"

"Hell no," Jacks said. "We've reunited. We're getting back together."

Adrian took a moment to let the information soak in. Then he started laughing.

Jackson appeared ruffled. "What's so funny?"

Adrian shook his head and went to the kitchen to pour himself some water. "Well, it's just that it's a surprise," Adrian said. "She didn't seem to miss you much, that's all."

"Oh really, Big Shot?" Jacks asked.

"Yes. Really."

"Listen, I don't like what you're insinuating."

"What I'm insinuating is what you paid me for."

Jackson suddenly rammed his hand into his jacket pocket, searching for something, as Adrian watched.

"You in a hurry?" Adrian asked. "To get back to the woman who doesn't want you?"

"Fuck you," Jacks replied. "You don't know shit."

"No. You're the one who doesn't know shit," Adrian said as he ambled into the living room. "Every answer to every fucking question I asked you about your wife was wrong. You don't know Cynthia any better today than you did the moment you met her."

"You're lucky I'm Jacks Power, kid, otherwise I'd throw you out that plate glass window," Jacks said. He finally produced his checkbook, scribbled on a check, ripped it out, and tossed it at Adrian's face. "For services rendered. You and I are through. This never happened. And stay away from my wife."

"How about we let the best man win?" Adrian said.

"Oh yeah?" Jacks asked. "How would she feel about the real you. Huh, barkeep?"

"How would she feel about the real *you,* scumbag?" Adrian said. "Hiring a lowly bartender to fuck her and get her off her husband's filthy hands?"

"You have ten minutes to clear out of here. Before I send Harry up. And I never want to see you again. You hear me?"

"I'll only take five. I don't need all your crap. And neither does Cynthia."

"Two minutes!" Jacks yelled, then rushed out, slamming the door behind him.

Thirty seconds later, beefy security officers were escorting Adrian from the premises, one giant mitt under each arm.

"Careful with that!" Adrian yelled, as they tossed his duffel bag to the ground in front of the big blue monster; he hoped a few of the Burgundies he'd stolen had survived the ride.

Adrian grabbed the duffel, vowing that Jackson Power would not toss him out of the picture that easily. *Rich people think they can buy their way out of everything,* Adrian thought as he fingered the check in his pants pocket. *Not this time. Not this guy.*

CYNTHIA took a deep breath, walked up the stairs to Bruce Harold Raymond's office, and then didn't remember how she had arrived there at all. She was that nervous.

She had never fired anyone before.

Three-Name Bruce barely looked up as Cynthia walked in the room.

"Bruce," Cynthia said, "we have to talk."

"A week and a half to performance, Cynthia. I'm sure whatever it is can wait."

"It can't. And the reason it can't is that much has to be changed in the next ten days. We can't waste a moment."

Bruce Harold looked up. Tall and cut and imposing, even while sitting. His long neck stretching like a sauropod, Adam's apple bobbing slightly as his chin tilted back. *All hail the Prince of Smugness.*

"Changed?" He leaned back in his chair.

"Yes."

"Change what? Napkins? Seating arrangements? What on earth do you propose to . . . change?"

"Two dance pieces, three leads, and one artistic director," Cynthia said. "You're fired, Bruce."

He looked at her. Her knees, which had been shaking, suddenly stilled. *Hey,* they seemed to be saying, *this isn't so bad, firing an asshole.*

"You can't," he said.

"I just did," Cynthia replied.

"You don't have the power," he said. "You're nowhere near a majority—"

"Oh, but I am," Cynthia said. "From my apartment to your office, I've made ten phone calls. It's done."

"I'm calling Mr. Plotzicki—we'll just see what he has to say—"

"I've already had that conversation. After hearing my concerns and suggestions, he threw his considerable weight behind me."

They stared at each other. Somewhere, a clock ticked. A piano wandered into its arpeggio.

"I'll sue."

"I'm certain of it. Pack your things," Cynthia said. "Goodbye, Bruce, and good luck." She turned on her heel and walked out, exhilarated and terrified.

What had she just done?

Ten days.

Five minutes later, she and Margot faced the corps.

"Why do we dance?" Cynthia began. "Who can understand our passion? We are artists. But more than that. We are warriors."

Cynthia noted the chests puffing out a bit.

"Each of you went into ballet because you want to create. To create beauty. You never feel more alive than when you're on that stage. I know that feeling. I used to live for that feeling."

Cynthia paused.

"But we must face the truth. We've gone numb. And safe. When did we stop taking chances? When did we stop testing our own lim-its?" *Was she talking about dance or her life?* "It's not too late for us to make a change. I want the NYBT to be a corps that people have to talk about. That they *have* to see. A company that makes the audience feel as alive as I want you to feel when you're dancing. We need to reinvent ourselves. That means enough with *The Nutcracker*. And screw *Don Quixote*. Ladies and gentlemen, we are going to dance without a safety net."

She told them of the new lineup. They were tossing some of the traditional offerings and adding a *pièce d'occasion* from Margot Ash-ford, NYBT's new artistic director and choreographer(!), interspersed with exciting palate cleansers by Tiffany Mills and Mark Morris. She expected the disappointment and fear she saw in some faces, the looks of surprise and excitement in others.

"Impossible. We only have ten days," the Russian lead ballerina spouted.

"A little less than that, actually."

"Can't be done," the veteran American dancer opined. His opin-ion was among the most revered in the corps.

"It can't be done, Joe, if we don't start," Cynthia said. "I'm going to need your leadership to make this happen."

He took a long look at her. Then, finally, gave her a nod. The dancers were all looking at them. Cynthia could hear tectonic plates shifting, energy rising.

"Let's get to work," Margot said, clapping her hands briskly. "We have a show to do."

And like that, they were up.

46

MARRIAGE REHAB: KING ROOKED

Jacks HAD a plan mapped out. He'd enlisted Caprice's help, who was eager to facilitate the Powers reconciliation. *Peace in Jackson Power's life?* Caprice thought, *peace in Caprice's life.*

Week One: Jackson choreographed a phalanx of romantic dinners, a trip to Harry Winston, a helicopter ride into Roxbury to Cynthia's favorite spa, hand-in-hand walks through Central Park, maybe even *Madama Butterfly*—if he could stand three hours at the opera (he'd take his BlackBerry).

And every night, every single night, Sunday through Saturday, Jacks would be at Cynthia's beck and call, to pleasure her in whatever way she desired.

Case in point: Jacks had Harry drop him off in front of a discreet West Village storefront to purchase a little something to get Cynthia's machinery geared up.

Let the wooing begin.

The problem was Cynthia hadn't received the memo.

"I can't go anywhere this week," Cynthia informed Jacks.

"But, I've made reservations, we're all set to go—"

"Jacks, I am spending every waking moment, and almost every

sleeping one, at Brooke Astor Hall until opening night—I've changed up the program, the dancers—Margot's actually choreographing—if I'm not there, there won't be a fall season—"

Cynthia sounded annoyed, but secretly, she was thrilled: she'd never felt so needed!

"But I've made all these plans! Can't you fit in one dinner this week? You have to eat—c'mon, Cynthia, I am your husband."

"My husband? My cheating husband who's trying to push me out of my home?"

"Well, you know ... the closest thing to a husband," Jacks said, then segued. "I think we should discuss Vivienne."

He knew that would get her.

Cynthia paused. Jacks counted the seconds on his fingers.

"I can do an hour on Wednesday," she said finally.

Jacks smiled, and said, "I'll pick you up at eight o'clock at 740—"

"That's not necessary—"

"I'll pick you up and drop you wherever you need to be afterward." *Never let 'em say no*—Jacks repeated one of his mantras—*a no is just a yes that hasn't been aged properly.*

CYNTHIA had never seen Margot so focused and intense—she hadn't even made a sarcastic remark in days.

And not one comment about all the sex she was missing.

Their vision was working. The troupe was coming together around Margot's piece and the other new interludes. Cynthia and Margot were exhausted, but exhilarated.

Cynthia was watching the married Ukrainians dancing a pas de deux onstage for the umpteenth time that evening when Teddy Pendergrass rang. "Where are you?" Jacks asked.

"I'm at the Hall."

"But I'm at 740." He sounded irritated.

"It's Wednesday, already?" Cynthia asked. "What time is it?"

"Eight o'clock. We have reservations at eight-fifteen."

"Oh, God. It's already eight o'clock?"

"I'll pick you up in ten minutes."

Cynthia was about to protest—but stopped herself. She hadn't eaten since lunch—something limp with dressing. She could order, find out what was on Jacks's mind regarding Vivienne (she never thought she'd hear those words), and be back at the Hall by 9:30. "Okay, fine," she said.

"Great, great. I made us a reservation at Aureole." He'd even had Caprice phone ahead for the special "aphrodisiac tasting menu." It was usually offered only on Valentine's Day, but if you're Jacks Power, you can declare any day Valentine's Day.

"No, no," Cynthia said. "Let's just grab a bite at Vince & Eddies."

Jacks hesitated. Lara had liked Vince & Eddies—it was a network hangout. "But—that's so noisy, so crowded—"

"Jacks, I don't have much time. It has good burgers and the service is fast. Pick me up in five." Cynthia hung up before Jacks could respond.

Cynthia waved goodbye to Margot, who was putting the dancers through yet another run-through, and hurried off.

JACKS was elbow-to-tweedy-elbow with the dinner crowd—and some of their kids! There were even a couple of dogs tied up outside. *Jesus Christ, what was the world coming to?*

He'd barely recognized Cynthia when she walked up to the car, with her hair loosened, strands settling along her face, her cheeks flushed. Not a lick of makeup. And wearing jeans! She looked like a twelve-year-old who'd just ridden in on horseback.

He watched her talk. *So animated! Where'd she get all these opinions?* he thought. *What's with all the energy, and she hadn't even ordered a diet Red Bull or espresso?*

She was going on about her week and the dancers and firing some guy (*Cynthia fired someone?!*) and how she could be in so much trouble if the company didn't pull this all off—(*"Oh, the press, Jacks, they're horrible!" She's having lunch tomorrow with the* Times *critic, Adeline somebody*) but how could they be expected to pull all this off? It's unheard of—using an unknown choreographer and changing the lineup and the dancers and the artistic director with a week and a half to go—

And if that wasn't enough, she couldn't keep her hands off his French fries.

"Anyway, enough about the gala," she said, exhaling. "What's this about Vivienne? What's your concern?"

"Vivienne?" Jacks asked.

"Yes, the reason we're having dinner, Jacks. Vivienne?"

"Ah. Yes. She seems . . ."

Jacks took a moment to think about this. Vivienne. *What did his daughter seem like? If he really thought about it* . . . "Sad." *Oh, Christ. That was painful.*

Cynthia nodded. "She is sad," she said. "She's getting over heartache."

"Oh," Jacks said. "I didn't know."

"She'll be okay," Cynthia said. "Vivienne is a very strong girl. She doesn't talk a lot about it . . . I wish she did"—*without the gory lesbian details, thank you,* Cynthia thought—"but she's a pretty private person. As you know."

"Yes," he said. *Private? Vivienne's private?* "But she'll be okay?" he asked. Suddenly, he couldn't bear the thought of anything happening to Vivienne.

"Oh, yes. In fact," Cynthia said, leaning in conspiratorially, "she may have already met someone new. A boy."

Jackson looked at her; he wasn't getting the true meaning of her statement.

"You didn't know," Cynthia said. "Vivienne's a lesbian."

Jackson pulled back, as though he'd been slapped. "What are you talking about? That's impossible!"

"Jackson." Cynthia put her hand over his. "She'd been living with a girl for a year. A beautiful girl."

"Living, yes . . . that's normal. Roommates! She called her her roommate."

"It's not the worst thing in the world, Jackson."

"Of course it's not," Jackson said. *Okay, think of what would be worse—drugs? Alcohol? One of those rich girls who party every night and put out sex tapes when the partying gets dull and doesn't pay?* Jacks thought about the press—how had the vultures not discovered his daughter's sexual preference? Maybe, he thought, *maybe that's why Vivienne is strictly under the radar.*

"So she met a guy?" Jackson asked, trying to temper the hope in his voice.

"Yes, she's kissed him. And *liked it!*" Cynthia said, not bothering to temper hers.

"Oh, thank God," Jackson said. He grabbed Cynthia's hand and squeezed. They sat, enjoying their moment of parental bullet-dodging, Cynthia thinking (*she couldn't help it*) once again of the *Times* wedding pages; Jackson wiping the image of Gertrude Stein (Billie Jean King?) with Vivienne's curls and cowboy boots out of his head.

"I have to get back," Cynthia said apologetically.

"Oh, already?" Jackson asked, then started patting his pockets. "I have a surprise for you."

Cynthia put her hand to her chest. "You do?"

"I picked it out myself," he said proudly, as he placed a small box with a white bow on the table. "I hope you like it."

"Oh, you shouldn't have, Jackson," Cynthia said as she slowly reached for the box.

"I wanted to show you how much I care," he said.

She sat, fingering the bow. Then, finally, opened it.

And stared. Then squinted. Then grimaced.

"Jackson, what is—I don't understand—"

"It's the latest innovation," Jackson said. "This stuff is selling like hotcakes."

"But, it's—" Cynthia faltered. "Jackson, it's wrinkle cream."

"The most expensive wrinkle cream," Jacks said. "You know what the secret ingredient is?"

Cynthia just stared at him.

"The leftover skin from circumsized penises, I kid you not!" Jacks said. "I've used it myself, I'd say it works."

"Do you know how insulting this is?" Cynthia asked.

"You don't like it?" Jacks asked, sounding crushed. "But the stuff's like five hundred bucks—"

"It's just so . . ." She shook her head. "You bought me wrinkle cream!"

"Oh! I get it," Jacks said. "Did you think it was jewelry? I'll get you jewelry—whatever you want—"

"No, no, no—" Cynthia put her face in her hands.

"I was trying to think of something practical, something you could really use," Jackson said.

Cynthia looked at him. "Take me back."

"Look," Jacks said, "I'll put it on myself—"

"Check, please!" Cynthia yelled to the waiter.

47

THE QUEEN EATS CAKE

LUNCH AT Per Se at the Time Warner Center should at the very least be pleasant, if not sublime. But not today.

Clues that Cynthia's noontime meal with the *Times* ballet critic, Adeline Crisp, would not go well:

1. The woman sported a lacquered helmet of black hair that Cynthia could not peel her eyes from. *Was it real? Was it a wig? Was she doing Kabuki in her off-critic hours?*
2. The critic pushed away the menu parading Thomas Keller's finest and pointedly ordered an espresso. *And only an espresso.*
3. Adeline, in her gravelly drone, informed Cynthia that one of her dearest friends was Bruce Harold Raymond. And smiled. *Like a crocodile.*

Cynthia bravely forged past the comment, and told Adeline of her bold plans for the NYBT.

"After next week's performance," Cynthia predicted, "we won't be seen as the 'other' ballet company. I guarantee you that."

"What about your financial situation?" Adeline asked, her signature fountain pen poised on her notepad. "Isn't it true that the NYBT is flirting with bankruptcy?"

"I've brought Margaret Lord Foster back into the fold. I have meetings lined up with the major communications and technology companies. I'm talking to the younger crowd, the new financiers. Even Fred Plotzicki has renewed his pledge."

"Interesting," Adeline replied as she scribbled, without sounding the least bit interested. "I'm afraid Bruce Harold Raymond has offered a very different view of your capabilities as head of the board, not to mention your tenuous fiscal responsibility. In fact, there are those who believe that you alone may well be guilty for the final death knell of the NYBT. Enjoy your meal. I have another engagement to get to."

Adeline stood up from her chair and gathered her notebook and purse. "I will be attending next week. I wish you the very best of luck."

Cynthia sat staring as Adeline scuttled away, in her black tights and oversize black sweater dress, looking like Cynthia's personal Grim Reaper.

48

TOURNAMENT PLAY

CYNTHIA AND Margot stood before their dancers, Cynthia the Queen in a floor-length Valentino, Margot her knight in a black viscose cocktail dress. They held hands, without actually realizing they were doing so, as naturally as children.

Margot spoke first.

"You had ten bloody days, and what happened? All the bitching and moaning, and guess what—you created perfection. You should all be so fucking proud, no matter what happens now. I love you all like I'd love my own children, even though you know I can't stand kids."

She was starting to cry.

"Screw it—Rudy, watch the turn on the first movement. Pilar, I need your height. You can do it. And Tanny—for God's sake, be yourself, but even more so. This is your moment. And that goes for each and every one of you. And Joe," Margot said, looking at the veteran, whose last season was upon him, "as much as this is my work, this is yours, too. You rock my world. If you weren't gay, I'd make you marry me. Thank you. Thank you all." She sniffled. "Now go out there and make me proud, and if you fuck up, don't come home."

She turned to Cynthia, who grabbed her waist and held her up. Cynthia turned to the dancers.

"Remember who you are, where you came from, and why you're here. You are the embodiment of not only your childhood dreams but the dreams of so many others, including people in the audience. Respect that. Respect yourselves, not just tonight, but for the rest of your lives." Cynthia paused. "And for God's sake, remember to have fun. Celebrate. It's all over before you know it. And this is your night. No one can take that from you."

Unless you let them, she thought. Cynthia turned to Margot, as the dancers dispersed. "I'll see you after the performance."

"I love you," Margot said.

"Beyond," Cynthia replied. She gave her one last kiss, and ran off in her Valentino.

TWO HOURS of ballet before dinner could try the most dedicated of balletomanes. Cynthia and Margot had worked the corps relentlessly; their dedication showed. All the parts fit together in a liquid jigsaw—edges blurred and fluid. The married Ukrainians, previously sidelined by a new baby, old injuries, and passionate temperaments, surpassed even their own expectations. The wife, a flaxen-haired vision with a hair-trigger temper, was having a torrid affair with a Russian oil billionaire that would soon hit the papers (she'd given him stitches with a target-sensitive flying ashtray). But tonight, as she pirouetted in the circle of her husband's arms, even the back rows could feel the steam coming off their bodies. *Perhaps tonight would be theirs to heal, to fall in love again, to make another baby,* Cynthia thought.

The tall, redheaded American with the porcelain skin reveled in her singular athleticism—and so did her audience. Cynthia watched in awe: *If only Bruce Harold Raymond could appreciate the genie finally being released from the bottle.*

The corps de ballet performed with more emotion than dutiful precision—their movements went beyond perfection; they were wonderfully, vulnerably human.

Had she and Margot pulled it off? Cynthia wondered. *Had they really pulled it all off?* Cynthia sat motionless for the entire performance. If someone said she hadn't blinked, she wouldn't be surprised.

She didn't think about Jacks, who had finagled his way into the seat next to hers, a seat put aside for luminaries and established patrons. The minute he'd sat down, he grabbed her hand, and he'd rubbed her fingers throughout the performance—until finally she'd placed his hand back in his lap, indicating in no uncertain terms that he was not to attempt to touch her for the rest of the night. There would be nothing to distract her. Not his sighs. Not him reaching inside his jacket pocket for his PowerBar. Not his dry cough. (Not the apoplectic calls from Ricardo Bloomenfeld demanding to know if she and Jacks were reuniting.) None of this would bother her.

Cynthia was no longer responsible for Jackson Power.

Her responsibility lay on that stage and in the hours ahead, at the dinner at the Pierre. As she watched, she felt herself dancing on the stage behind the Ukrainians. Muscle memory caused her feet to twitch, her calf muscles to bounce. She was airborne, legs scissoring, arms stretching out to touch the sides of the stage, feeling strong hands on her tiny waist lifting her, finding the sky and staying there—

Seating charts disappeared, dessert menus combusted, personality disorders vanished. The fog of the dance had rolled out row by row and had blanketed all distractions seen and unseen.

Cynthia unthinkingly grabbed Jacks's hand as she descended, in her imagination, the pads of her toe shoes finding the wooden floor. Jacks turned and smiled at her.

Her eyes remained on the stage.

BALLET? What fucking ballet? Adrian squirmed in his seat. He felt like a kindergartner whose mother was on a murderous cultural mission.

Had it even registered with Cynthia that he was there? He was five rows behind her, with a bird's-eye view of the back of her head.

She never turned her head. Not once. Adrian's stare reached right through to her brain. He'd kept his eyes on her throughout the performance. *Turn. Turn your fucking head. Turn. Turn. Turn.*

Cynthia never even flinched. *Impossible.* The weight of trying to make her head spin around exhausted Adrian's faculties. After the performance, he was barely able to stand. *Why hadn't she acknowledged his existence? How about a nod? A wink? I wasn't THAT bad, was I? And what the fuck was she doing sitting next to Jacks Power?*

He read their body language as though he were reading a haiku—a missed noun, a misunderstood verb would derail the meaning of the entire piece. And he saw what he needed to see: their shoulders never touched; her head never once leaned toward his big noggin.

Jacks's head, on the other hand, never stopped moving. His tics were out in full glory tonight. Looking around at who was watching him. Cracking his neck. Scratching his crown. At least, Adrian thought, someone else was feeling pain—as much as a sociopathic narcissist could feel.

And then he saw Jacks kiss her ear. *A wet kiss.* He could practically feel the spray from his seat. Cynthia tilted away from him.

Adrian stood on his wobbly legs to lead the ovation.

SILKS . . . silk satin, satin crepe de chine, China silks, crepe back satin, silk chiffon, charmeuse, shantung, iridescent taffeta, satin jacquard, silk velvet . . .

Cynthia stood outside the grand ballroom of the Pierre, having ordained the color of the season (to be featured in *Vogue* with ample pictures from tonight's festivities). Red—fire-engine red! Cynthia had been afraid to try the dress on—she'd already selected cream as her color, to match the décor and the centerpieces she'd chosen so carefully—callas, her favorite. However, Vivienne, of course, insisted.

Forget Muted Cynthia, Vivienne had told her, *we want the new Cynthia to come with a warning label.*

Reception line: Cynthia posed with the young, aggressively blond socialite who'd failed marvelously at law school and then a ballyhooed trip to L.A. to explore acting, before penning a children's book and finally slinking back to New York to remake herself as a fashionista. Always with a tossed-from-the-shoulder quote: "I wish there were train police here!" she'd cry to a mag staffer. "Everyone keeps stepping on my dress!"

Cynthia had the younger woman on posture; the socialite had her on height. Cynthia had her on name; the socialite had her on currency. *A draw.* The picture would look as if each would happily give the other a kidney.

Imagine, Cynthia thought, *if photographs really reflected what we're thinking?* Cynthia loved reading the society pages—*C'mon, fess up, who doesn't?*—sorrowfully average faces and manes wasting hundreds of dollars' worth of hair and makeup. Wrinkled elbows and flat backsides and fleshy spillage wrapped in organza. Priceless jewels adorning crepey necks and gnarled fingers. (Gorge on caviar, then tell the driver he can't get a raise.) We're all having the *best* time, the photographs lied. We have *perfect* lives. *Don't you wish you were one of us?*

The socialite flashed her a smile, then moved on. *Snap,* Cynthia thought, admonishing herself, *enough with the mean girl attitude. You've been in the city too long.*

Cynthia turned to see Adeline Crisp standing in front of her, wearing the same dress and the same expression she'd worn at their brief lunch. Cynthia stifled her gasp.

Adeline sniffed. "Do you know what Gandhi said, Cynthia?"

"I'm hungry?" Cynthia tried to joke.

"Full effort is full victory," she said. "Congratulations. I'll be wanting an exclusive with Margot Ashford. Everyone loves a comeback."

. . .

WHILE Jackson waited his turn before the cameras, he did what he always did on these nights—he stuck his head inside the ballroom and counted the tables. This was Cynthia's baby, but he wanted to know.

The number disappointed him. It was too high. He counted again as he walked through to the single-digit tables—clapping this guy on the back, shaking that one's hand—*just a wink for the one over there, don't even look at that creep, he doesn't deserve half an eyebrow lifted, ooh, look at that piece of shit, he got so old, crissakes, pull it together, man— hey, how you doin'?*

Christ, look at that one's tits. Are those new? (Jacks pulled at his jacket.) *Where's that power table? Right in the middle, right up front.*

And look at the flowers, look at those fucking flowers—if that didn't seal the deal with Cynthia, he didn't know what would. An island? Should he buy her an island?

Nah. All she needed was a little sensitivity—just what he was showing her tonight.

Jacks looked at the fruit of his labors. All seventy-six tables. Close to eight hundred people. And in the middle of each table, a beautiful, outstanding, ferociously expensive bouquet of yellow roses.

He did that. A million calls, a few bribes. Et voilà, *as the fucking French would say.* He found his table, but didn't sit. No one sat. *No one.* Everyone waited for everyone else to sit. Like a nursery school game. *Except it was the opposite of musical chairs—no one wanted to be the first to sit.*

That meant you had nothing left to brag about to the others who were standing.

But once a big name did park himself—then everyone else would sit immediately. If the mayor sat, if Jacks sat, if a few Gargoyles-in-training sat—then so would they. *Follow the money. Follow the Power.*

Jacks made his way back outside the ballroom to the phalanx of photographers, well-wishers parting like the Red Sea as he approached his beloved.

Cynthia was nearly blinded by the ensuing flashbulbs—nary a photographer paying attention to the dancers, the celebrities, the Oscar-winning actress, the Broadway producer, the famous novelist, chronicler extraordinaire of the city, and in his equally famous white pinstripe suit!

No. The cameras had but one focus: the King and Queen, Jacks and Cynthia Power—"Over here, over here, over here, please, good to see you back together, over here, can you give us one over here, could you look this way, I didn't get that, you look beautiful, Mrs. Power, love the color, who are you wearing . . ."

And Jacks. Jacks drinking it in as if the moment alone could slake his unquenchable thirst for publicity.

Cynthia got through the photographs as quickly as possible— easier to take the photographs than to explain that though she and Jacks had arrived at the gala together, they were not actually "together." Under cover of smile, she hiss/whispered (*hiss-pered*) to Jacks, "Get your hand off my back, please."

Jacks barely registered the rebuke. He was too busy imagining Page Six tomorrow. *This is great. Lara will see these pictures, serves her right. Who leaves me? I'm Jacks Power! This is great. Maybe this will work, this thing with Cynthia.*

Finally the moment was over. Most of the revelers had already made their way inside, to the post-performance dinner. As Jacks stayed on to take a few more photos, Cynthia turned toward the open doors of the Pierre Grand Ballroom.

CYNTHIA thought that her eyes were playing tricks on her. Practical jokes masquerading as flora springing up on table after table. Giant centerpieces displaying not her beloved, carefully chosen callas, but crass, overblown ornate bursts.

Yellow roses. Huge, spitting bouquets of bright yellow roses.

Everywhere her head turned, with every swivel, every uncompre-
hending blink, all she saw, in her mind's eye, were screeching
canaries.

She stifled a scream with the back of her hand as she floated,
seemingly held aloft by her supporters, to Table One.

ADRIAN had buffeted his way through the crowd, head down, arms
tight to his sides, searching for Table One. As he started to check the
name cards, Cynthia arrived, her face pale and taut.

"Are you okay?" he asked, reaching for her elbow.

Cynthia nodded, curtly, before being swallowed up by another
wave of dance patrons—"Brilliant!" Adrian heard. "Innovative!"
"Courageous!"

Adrian stood there, waited out the crowd.

Seconds later, a familiar voice reached out, strangling him with
its tone.

"What. The fuck. Are *you* doing here?" Jacks said, as he loomed
over him.

Adrian turned. "Good to see you, too, Jacks," he replied. "Robert
Jordan—you remember me? We shared a brief conversation not long
ago."

"I want my wine back," Jacks hissed. "I know every bottle in that
wine cellar—and five are missing. I want them back."

"I know. I'm sure you think it's odd that I'm here—we did just
talk about the fact that I was going away for a while—"

"Jacks!" Cynthia was momentarily alone, standing in front of the
two men—who seemed so close to be almost kissing. "You're unbelievable. I know this is your handiwork!"

"Darling!" Jacks said, grabbing Cynthia around the waist. "We
were just figuring out seating arrangements—"

"We're just having a little friendly reunion," Adrian said.

"Jacks, this is Robert—wait—you know each other?" Cynthia asked, momentarily thrown off the path of her rant.

"No—," Jacks began.

"Yes," Adrian said. "It's a funny story." *Oh, you're not getting rid of me that easy, Power.*

"Funny," Jacks said in a low, calm voice. "That's right. A funny story." *I'm going to kill you—no, no, I'm going to keep you barely alive and torture you for the rest of your small, small life, you mother—*

"You know what else is funny, Jacks?"

Adrian and Jacks looked at Cynthia; her face held no promise of amusement.

"No . . . ? " Jacks said.

"The fact that I could have been married for so long to someone as insensitive as you—"

Jacks started to laugh—*That's my wife, folks! Such a joker!* "Cynthia, darling, dove, what are you talking about?"

Cynthia pointed at the screaming yellow centerpiece in the middle of their table—"That!"

"The centerpiece? You like them? I knew you would. I—"

"Oh, man." Adrian shook his head. "How clueless can you be? She *hates* roses—"

"She does not! My Cynthia loves yellow roses! She's always—"

Cynthia cut in. "I hate them, Jacks," she hissed. "I hate everything about them—for the last twenty-five years, every time I saw a bouquet of yellow roses, I knew you had cheated on me!"

Adrian covered his face with his hands.

Jackson ducked his head closer, his voice low. "Cynthia, come on, now—let's not get hysterical—"

"How could you?" she said, starting to beat his chest with her little fists. "How could you?!"

"Now wait just a minute," Jacks said, grabbing her hands before she could attract more attention. "I worked hard for these roses—I scoured the entire country for these roses—some of them came from fucking Belgium or something—you know how much this cost me?"

"That's all you care about, isn't it?" Cynthia looked at him. Adrian's eyes flashed on the silverware. He knew he could grab Cynthia before she reached for a knife—but did he want to?

Yes. But only because Vivienne had just walked up. She wore an off-the-shoulder jersey dress and heels. Her hair was up, curls framing her cheekbones. *Manhattan, meet your Aphrodite.*

"Mom? What's going on?"

"Your mother's mad at me—about roses!" Jackson huffed.

"You ruined the night for me, Jacks," Cynthia said.

"Oh, now, wait a minute," Adrian said, interrupting. "Don't let this clown ruin your night—"

"You stay out of this!" Jackson roared.

"Wait," Vivienne said, now staring at Adrian. "What are you doing here?"

"I, ah," Adrian stammered. *Think fast, you idiot, think fast.* "I'm a dance patron—"

"You know each other?" Cynthia asked Vivienne.

"He's nothing, nobody," Jacks said. "And Mr. Nobody was just leaving—"

"This gentleman is a guest at my table, Jacks," Cynthia said, warning him.

"Him? Yeah, sure. Not going to happen—"

Adrian could see Vivienne's confusion. *Had they shared a moment, or hadn't they?*

"We do know each other," Adrian said. Vivienne smiled.

Oh, that smile.

"Mom, remember that . . . thing I told you about . . ." Vivienne said. She tilted her head playfully toward Adrian. She didn't notice her mother blanching.

"Oh. Oh, my gosh," Cynthia said. "Wow. Interesting. Really?"

"Your mother and I are getting back together, Vivienne,"

Jacks interrupted, as though making an announcement to the press.

"No, we're not," Cynthia said.

"But . . . we . . . you slept with me," Jacks said.

"You slept with him?" Adrian asked. "Recently?"

Cynthia shrugged. She was an adult—a full-fledged adult (finally!) at forty-five. She had no one to answer to (if her mother weren't asking).

"Oh, Jesus," Jacks said. "Cynthia, you slept with this idiot?" Heads swiveled toward the group.

"Mom?" Vivienne asked. "Did you sleep with Adrian?"

"I . . . um." Cynthia was about to answer. Then: "Who's Adrian?"

"I'm going to kill you!" Jacks said, lunging at Adrian.

"What is your problem?!" Adrian yelled, and dodged Jacks's grasp as he ran around the table—which had now become center stage for the second great performance of the evening, this one clearly in need of Margot's choreography skills.

"Stop it!" Cynthia yelled. "Stop it this instant!"

"You're dead!" Jacks screamed, as he leapt on top of the table, knocking the dreaded centerpiece to the ground and throwing his body on top of Adrian—

"You're crazy!" Adrian shouted.

They hit the floor with a thud.

Vivienne and Cynthia screamed and tried to pull Jacks off of Adrian. Patrons dodged the rolling explosion of fists and legs and elbows.

Security arrived, but not in time to save rows of tables, thousands of dollars' worth of silk draperies, platter after platter of *salade* and untold numbers of Belgian roses.

"I'm Jacks Power, goddamn it!" Jackson screamed as he was muscled outside. "Cynthia! Cynthia, darling, tell them!"

Adrian looked back at Vivienne, who was standing next to her mother, watching him as he was dragged from the ballroom on his heels. He had one thought as he tried to remember the feel of her lips on his, now bruised and battered.

Had he just ruined the rest of his life?

"OH MY GOD," Cynthia said, observing the wreckage, her hands in her hair. "All my hard work. Destroyed in seconds." Vivi put her arm around her mother's shoulders. "Come on, Mom. Cheer up—you hated the roses."

She looked at her daughter. "And Vivi, I feel terrible about this," Cynthia said, clasping her daughter's hand as she straightened what was left of her chignon. "I had no idea he was the boy you kissed."

Vivienne looked into her mother's eyes. "How could you know?" she asked. "Were you supposed to ask him if he'd made out with your daughter recently?"

Cynthia smiled.

"Do you love him?" Vivienne asked.

"God, no," Cynthia said.

"Good," Vivienne said.

"Vivi," Cynthia said, "are *you* in love with him?"

"Well, no," Vivienne said, shaking her mane. "I'm not. But that moment . . . our kiss. It was important. He made me feel attractive. Like I could go out and just be myself and somewhere, someone would love me again."

She turned to her mother. "How crazy is that?"

"Well," Cynthia said, "they'd be crazy not to love you. Shall we get a drink?"

"You beat me to it, Mom," Vivienne said, as she nodded and held out her elbow. Cynthia slipped her arm through, and the two of them, fresh as schoolgirls, stepped through the debris, strewn with yellow rose petals, oblivious to the onlookers.

49

THE CORNERED KING: CHECK

ADRIAN AND Jacks were tossed in a holding cell. "What are the charges?" Jacks demanded from the retreating police officer. "You're going to pay for this! What's your name, captain?! Do you know who I am? I'm Jackson Fucking Power!"

"Save your breath," Adrian muttered, looking for a comfortable spot to sit. "They're laughing at you."

"Fuck you. You are nothing, you understand me? Nothing. When I get out of here—"

"I'm just saying," Adrian said, "you landed in the one place where your name means shit."

"Fuck you, you know what?" Jackson said, pulling at his lapel. "If I've ever met something that was not worth one nickel—it's you."

"You paid me a bit more than that, my friend," Adrian pointed out.

"I can't believe Cynthia would lower herself—" Jacks said.

"What did you think would happen? You put the wheels in motion—I just went along for the ride!"

"Watch it, buddy," Jacks said. "You watch your mouth!"

"You know what? Let me give you some armchair therapy—

you're not even mad at me—you're mad at yourself!" Adrian said. "It's you who's the asshole. Well, that's not entirely true. I'm an asshole, too."

He fished something out of his pocket.

"I want to give this back to you," Adrian said. "I don't need it. I mean, I need it, but I can't accept it."

Jackson looked over his shoulder. Adrian was handing back his check.

"Don't be an idiot," Jacks grunted.

"Take it," Adrian said, and he shoved it into Jacks's pocket.

"You're never going to get anywhere in life, you know that?" Jacks said.

"That's fine," Adrian said. "Frankly, I've seen what getting somewhere gets you. And it fucking stinks. I hope to God I can get my job back. I would kill to just be a bartender again."

AN HOUR later, Jackson had his hands on the bars, staring down the empty hallway. Adrian was seated in a crouched position in the corner. Several more visitors had arrived, in varying stages of inebriation. All had recognized the People's Billionaire.

A group of Columbia students who'd been caught trying to pry a mailbox from its corner home immediately launched into a medley of Jacks's most famous quotes—

"No means later!"

"Later means now!"

"Never means I'm working on it!"

A lump in the corner added his own "Jacks-isms": "WRONG BE ELASTIC! AND THAT'S A FACT!"

At which point, the college students laughed so hard that two of the three threw up on their Pumas.

"Wrong *is* elastic," Jacks muttered to himself. Adrian cracked his knuckles against his head and laughed.

• • •

AT 6:00 IN the morning, Penn Stewart marched down the hallway, dressed in a mushroom-colored Burberry overcoat and carrying his briefcase. His spic was so span, he looked for all the world like noon in front of a judge, not early morning in front of a dreary holding tank smelling of vomit.

"About goddamned time, Miss America," Jackson grumbled. "What, did it take you that long to put on your makeup?"

"I came as soon as possible. There was another situation." Penn smoothed the front of his lapel. "I'll escort you home."

"Excuse me, Mr. Power," one of the college students asked. "Are you still giving your big speech this morning?"

Jacks shot him a confused look.

"At the Learning Annex," the boy said. "I bought two passes. They're having a buffet breakfast in an hour. My dad promised to get me out in time."

"Oh for fuck's sake!" Jacks said. "Penn, you have to cancel this."

"If you cancel," Penn droned, "you have to give back your fee, plus expenses."

"It's completely sold out, the entire auditorium," the boy said— "That's over two thousand people, right? I'll see you there. Can't wait to hear your pearls!"

Adrian chuckled and waved to Jackson as he growled and turned and pounded his way down the linoleum hallway.

Penn and Jacks made their way outside the police station, where a phalanx of reporters huddled behind a line of policemen.

"Of course, they're waiting for me. Fucking embarrassing," Jacks said to Penn. "How does my hair look?"

Penn took hold of Jacks's sleeve. "Before we head down the stairs, there's something I haven't told you," he said above the rush of sound. "I was late because I have some bad news. About your father."

• • •

HARRY was idling outside in the Town Car in front of 740, as usual, as Jacks raced downstairs after a quick shower and change. The *Post* was waiting for Jacks, as usual, in the backseat. *Open me,* it cooed. Jacks smoothed his hair, then reached over with tentative fingers, as though the paper were a used tissue.

Slowly, he thumbed through the pages, barely looking out of the corner of his eye. First, there was the inevitable: ARTEMUS POWER ARRESTED ON BRIBERY CHARGES screamed a headline. Then, the whopper: "Fight the Power" read the caption.

The first photo was taken right before he and Cynthia entered the ballroom. His arm circling Cynthia's waist, brilliant smiles (though Cynthia's eyes were trained off-camera). Typical red-carpet shot. The great news? They each looked like they'd been mainlining youth serum; *that's what was important.*

The second photo was taken as he and Mr. Shit-for-Brains were escorted from the premises—Jacks's hair askew, tuxedo ripped open, his tie nowhere to be seen—probably left on the ballroom floor.

"Get rid of this shit!" Jacks threw the *Post* at Harry's shoulder as they turned from the West Side Highway onto Twelfth, into the Jacob K. Javits Convention Center parking lot.

The huge electronic sign outside the center mocked Jacks: his giant head floated fifty feet above them in mega-wattage, his teeth lit up like planets:

JACKSON POWER—POWER UP YOUR WEALTH!
REAL ESTATE EXPO FINALE!
POWER BREAKFAST!

"You bring this shit into my car again, you're fired!" Jacks yelled. Harry ignored him and stopped the car in front of an attendant, who peered inside, then whisked them through to the underground parking lot.

THE PRESS swarm was waiting, along with the usual suspects—crazy fans who'd sneaked in past security.

Jackson headed to the green room behind a greeter with the Power YES!!! stretched across her white tank top; she'd be perfect parading around a boxing ring between rounds. Miss Seventh Round at his side, Jacks valiantly batted away the questions, shot at him like machine gun rounds—

"Mr. Power! Mr. Power! Did you see the *Post* this morning?"

"Mr. Power, I hear you're doing a talk show! I have a daughter who sings!"

"Mr. Power, can I have just five minutes of your time?"

"Mr. Power, my card—"

"Mr. Power, the *Daily News* would like to talk to you about your father's arrest on bribery charges—"

"Care to make a statement, Mr. Power?"

Jackson flashed his smile and waved. "The only statement I have to make is how terrifically happy I am to be here in the greatest city on earth, telling normal people how to make money and live like kings—"

It helped that the Learning Annex had recently bumped his fee to a cool million per appearance.

The green room door was five feet away—

"Think Artemus is gonna do prison time?"

"Is it true that kid kicked your ass?"

Two feet—

"That's a good one, my friend," Jacks couldn't help responding. "You live in a fantasy world."

The door opened, beckoning. Here was safety among the croissants and melon balls. And a tub full of iced Power Waters.

And there was Caprice, Jacks's Angel of Mercy, with her satchel over her shoulder.

"Nice of you to show up," Jacks said to her. He was gruff, but he actually meant it. Seeing Caprice was like eyeing a Coke dispenser in the Sahara. *Except she was the only thing about his life that wasn't a mirage.*

Could she and Harry be his only friends?

"You look terrible," Caprice clucked at him. "Prison life does not agree with you, Mr. Power."

"How's my lip?" he asked. He stuck out his lower lip, as self-conscious of the minor cut on it as a teenager with a pimple.

"Caprice'll take care of that, Mr. Power," Caprice said. A small jar of ointment emerged from her bag. She dabbed at his lip like a doting mother. *Oh, if only he'd had a mother like Caprice! How different would his life have been?*

"Thank you, Caprice," he managed.

"I have your talking points," Caprice said, pressing a crisp folder into his hand. "I was delayed momentarily. I was just with the elder Mr. Power—"

"You saw my father?" Jacks asked.

Caprice began tidying Jackson—patting down his suit, tucking his shirt in a little more. "Mr. Stewart wanted me to escort him home," she answered while straightening his tie.

"He's okay?"

"He offered Caprice twenty dollars for an indecent act, Mr. Jackson." She circled her hand in the air, as though driving the father's words away from her body.

"The man gets arrested, and he's out looking for more trouble," Jacks said.

Caprice raised her eyebrow while she took hold of his collar, pressing the stiff white triangles with the flat of her capable hand—

"He's unaffected, Mr. Jackson. Artemus Power has not changed a whit. And he never will," Caprice said, in her lilt. "But will the son?"

A low roar was building—it sounded as though the A/C/E train was making an unplanned stop in the auditorium of the convention center.

"Hear that, Mr. Power?" Miss Seventh Round squealed, her breasts appearing at his side. "It's the sound of thousands of your biggest fans! They're ready for you!"

"Showtime," Jacks said, as Caprice gave his arm a light squeeze. Miss Seventh Round escorted him out; when the door opened, Jacks was hit by the ocean of sound.

Seconds later, he was onstage, drowning in confetti and surrounded by dancing girls wearing tank tops with the word YES!!! screaming from their ample chests. Jacks held his hands aloft, pressed his face to the sky, and let himself be baptized by the paper deluge; he could have fallen forward and been caught by the roar of the crowd.

Jacks opened his mouth to speak. Words streamed out as though nothing at all unusual had happened to him in the last days. As though he hadn't lost his fiancée, then his wife (again). As though he hadn't been jailed. As though he hadn't finally grasped that his wife had slept with that *idiot* (though it was his own fault). His reputation had suffered and his business would suffer, especially in the wake of his father's arrest. His world, the world of New York real estate, had peaked. The housing market would plummet. *What happens in Vegas doesn't stay in Vegas.* Not with mortgages. Developers would go bankrupt. Good friends ("friends") would be out of the business forever. Jacks could hear the phone calls now, reaching through the din of the masses quivering before him—"Hey, pal," they'd say, "let's do lunch. I've got some new ideas, maybe I can help you out."

Jacks waved to the crowd. They rose in response. This was Mecca and he was Mohammed. He could have walked them all out of the auditorium and onto the West Side Highway in rush hour traffic and they would have followed.

Lara had left him; Cynthia had left him. But these people, with real problems and small hopes, they were his and they would never leave him, the People's Billionaire; they needed him exactly as much as he needed them. Jacks's relationship with his fans was equitable. He would never again make the same mistake with a woman—from now on, he would always pick the girl who needed him more than he needed her. *Look around,* Jacks thought, *start with the* YES!!! *dancers and work from there.*

"Do you want to know how to make money?!" Jacks screamed. All the colossal faces of Jackson Power on all the JumboTrons screamed in concert.

Jacks Power was in the building. *"My friends!"*

Jacks Power was back.

50

ENDGAME

THE INVITATION read:

"In Honor of Goldie, think Zorba, and dress accordingly. To Life!"

There was no name on the invite; just a phone number for the RSVP (*private address upon response*). Cynthia arrived at the town house, a few blocks east of 740, teetering like a newborn calf in red Louboutins. She looked up at the elegant, understated brownstone and wondered why the address felt familiar. Goldie had never discussed his other clients with her; she couldn't have known if they were Crowned Kings of Finance, Tweedy Intellectuals, or Junkie Artist types. *Whose place was this?*

Cynthia had spent an hour in her dressing room before settling on a full skirt and pirate-sleeved de la Renta blouse from three seasons past, her hair pulled back with an Hermès scarf, and those sexy shoes—it was the closest Cynthia would ever come to the Greek peasant girl look—if the girl could swing a hundred thousand drachmas, or euros, or whatever, for a pair of Louboutins. Cynthia felt like a fool, but was happy to play foolish for Goldie.

Cynthia ran her hand over her hair, straightened her skirt, took a deep breath, and rang the doorbell. A butler answered before the buzzer stopped. Cynthia stepped past him and was hit by a feeling of déjà vu. She looked around the entryway, at the familiar marble staircase, the carved oak paneling. Everywhere she looked were patterns, colors, shapes that were elegant yet warm. Everything she would have chosen for herself. Cynthia exhaled and turned to give her coat to the butler, and there *she* was, hanging on the wall—a Kahlo, peering at her as though annoyed Cynthia hadn't bought her twenty years ago, when she'd had the chance.

Is this home? Cynthia thought.

Cynthia followed the butler into the parlor, where cheery voices and laughs belied a memorial service.

The first person she saw, wearing a black gaucho hat, black cape, eye mask, and sword, was unmistakably Fred Plotzicki.

"Fred!" Cynthia gasped. "What are you doing here?"

"I live here." Fred grinned.

"But—you knew Goldie?" she asked.

"Sure. I was his patient. Twice a week, for the last ten years—one divorce, five mergers, twenty diets, and countless neuroses. I've got the hugging scars to prove it."

"I can't get over it," Cynthia said. "I never suspected—does this mean he wasn't such a great therapist after all?"

Fred laughed. "Well, don't blame Goldie! He tried his best—I mean, even Wall Street Kings, or should I say 'reformed' Wall Street Kings need love, too."

Cynthia stared at him, as though looking for the first time. "Fred. The theme is Zorba . . . why are you dressed like Zorro?"

Fred touched Cynthia's elbow as he guided her to the party. "My butler, the Brit, picked it up. It's the language barrier, I'm from the Bronx, he's from the Mother Country." He laughed, then stopped suddenly. "Cynthia, what are we going to do without him?"

Nat King Cole's "Mona Lisa" beckoned from the formal living room.

"Dance," Cynthia said as she took Fred's hand.

• • •

1. **THE INTRO** (ten minutes). Walk to center stage, perform a few high kicks with YES!!! Girls (*watch that groin muscle!*), toss out a few popular Power phrases (*"Power is Money!"*), wait for standing ovation(s) to subside; incorporate charming, self-deprecating mannerisms as cheers rage (palm to chest—*"Who, me?"*; hand to ear: *"I can't hear you!"*).

2. **THE MAKING OF THE POWER PERSONA** (twenty minutes). Jackson Power as child: the Creation of a Work Ethic. Jacks loved this topic. Loved it. The main obstacle to total success? The horrendous lack of work ethic! From day laborers to his coterie of executive VPs, hardly anyone felt the need to come in early or, God forbid, be the one turning out the lights. Jacks hadn't taken a day off (a lunch off!) since his honeymoon. When the children were born, he'd taken two hours off to welcome them into the world.

3. **THE POWER PRINCIPLE: THE ROAD TO HAPPINESS AND FORTUNE** (twenty minutes). People stood hours in line for this twenty minutes. This is what placed Jacks's books on the number one and two spots on the *New York Times* bestseller list twelve weeks in a row (*never done before—never!*). How could the huddled masses attain the Power Persona? How could they convert meager coffers into pyramids of gold? Trade peanut butter for Kobe steak? *The old wife for the trophy? The old husband for the trainer?*

   If Jackson Power *himself* was convinced they could do it— could they argue against him? They were mere mortals; Jacks Power was Ramses II, building temples to the gods.

   He felt like Jesus, Martin Luther King, and David Lee Roth in his prime wrapped up in one electric package. He would have paid the Learning Annex.

   Jacks could leave the auditorium and conquer the world— again! He didn't need anyone—Lara, Cynthia, his father, contractors, the blessings of tenant associations, Realtors, lawyers, presidents and senators, movie stars and golf heroes. Jacks Power could start all over, clean slate, and end up exactly where he wanted. He had reinvented himself before; he could reinvent himself again. Like the Madonna of real estate developers—but with *class.*

4. **THE FINALE: THE Q&A PERIOD.** Microphones were set up along the middle aisles of the auditorium. Lines formed immediately; men and women in their best suits, inevitably carrying a Power book to be signed. *Or waving one, dog-eared, that had already been signed.* (Caprice had ensured the Learning Annex security folks vet the questioners, so as not to let any nosy journalists roust the proceedings.)

It all came down to this: *What is the magic formula? What do we have to do to be our own Jackson Power?*

Jacks spun the usual responses as Miss Seventh Round discreetly tapped her wristwatch.

"We've got time for one last question." Jackson shielded his eyes from the spotlight and scanned the lines of eager Power wannabes. A woman in a floppy hat and dark glasses was waving her hand.

"You."

The woman stepped up to the microphone.

"Mr. Power, do you know what my favorite saying is of yours? My very favorite?"

Why, thought Jacks, *did that voice sound familiar?*

"See it, be it!" she said.

"I happen to like that one, too. See how simple that is?" Jacks pointed to his head, "See it, be it! Visualize the goal—we've talked about this, people—"

"I've recently been given the opportunity," the woman continued, "to live my dream."

"Congratulations," Jacks said. *That voice.*

"There's only one problem. My ex-fiancé."

"If he's your ex, where's the problem?" Jacks joked. He felt a slight tug in his chest. "Problems," he continued, pacing the stage, "are solutions in drag!"

The audience cheered.

"The problem is . . . I'm still in love with him," the woman said. "I want to be with him. But . . . my dream job involves a lot of travel, and he never liked me leaving—"

"How's the pay?" he asked.

"Enough," she said. "Mr. Power, do I have to give up love to live my dream?"

Jacks thought for a moment. "Simple decision based on one thing: Is his love for you big enough to carry your dream?"

The woman reached for her hat, then her glasses, and took them off. Lara.

Of course.

"I don't know, Jacks," she said, "is it?"

Jacks looked at her. He fought the urge to cover himself as the cape fell from Superman's shoulders.

"You got a new job?" he asked, croaking.

"Answer the question," Lara responded. "Is your love for me big enough to carry my dream?"

Jacks stared at her. The audience murmured, awaiting his answer.

"Hell, yes," he finally said.

The entire audience stood and cheered.

"Great," Lara said over the commotion, with tears in her eyes, "because I need a ride to the airport." The roar deepened, the crowd surging as Lara fought her way down the aisle.

Minutes later, Caprice, her face ashen, met Jacks and Lara backstage. "There's been an accident," Caprice said.

. . .

CAPRICE was already directing Harry to New York Pres. Jacks held on to Lara's hand like holding on to a life preserver.

"Your father."

"He fell." Jacks repeated the words in his head that Caprice had told him as they ran to get Harry.

What would be left of him? Anything? Besides bad memories?

"How is he?" Jackson croaked. Lara's hand squeezed harder. Stay with me, it said. *Here, I'm here.*

Caprice glanced back at Harry; Jacks caught it.

"How is he?" Jacks repeated. "He *is* my father, Caprice. I have to know."

"Mr. Power," said Caprice. "I am so very sorry. It was twenty stories. Your father fell twenty stories."

Jacks looked out the window. There was his city. His father's city. *Born, lived, died.*

Harry blazed through traffic, running red lights, horn blaring; Jacks was surprised the cops weren't on their tail. Caprice sketched the details. His father had fallen from the edge of a steel plank at the work site on Hudson. His father, with legs as steady as an oak, balance as masterful as a Flying Wallenda. *Was it an accident or something else? Was it,* Jacks thought, *an answer to a prayer? Now God chooses to listen?*

God has a pretty fucking morbid sense of humor.

"I will give him the best fucking send-off this town has ever seen," Jacks said. "Caprice—start making calls. Call the president. The vice president. I want Schumer, I want Cuomo, call the head of GE, Zucker, all the networks, I want Tom Hanks, Tom Cruise—no, not Tom Cruise, okay, maybe Tom Cruise—I want every movie star who's ever rented, leased, owned, spent a night, fucking walked by a Power Tower—I want everyone who's ever been anything at this thing, you got that?"

Caprice nodded. *If the old man couldn't love me in life,* Jacks thought, *he would totally love me in death.*

He put his head on Lara's shoulder and wrapped his arm around her as warm tears flowed down his face.

THE NURSES had been kind enough to escort Jacks and his party to a private room at New York Pres where the press couldn't reach him. Jackson held his head in his hands, rocking back and forth on a padded chair, Lara rubbing his shoulders, Caprice standing by with a cup of coffee, Harry, the redwood, his hat in his hands, head bowed.

Jackson was inconsolable. *"Why?"* he asked, looking up, his features twisted, the famous shit-eating grin dissolved by grief. "Why, why, why?"

The young doctor standing in front of Jackson, his white coat carrying an authority his features couldn't match, looked understandably befuddled. He tilted his head forward, his yarmulke drifting slightly. "Mr. Power," he said, slowly, deliberately, as though speaking to a patient who'd lost his sense of reason, "your father is alive. He escaped with barely a scratch. It's a miracle, what's happened here, nothing short of a *nes.*"

Jackson continued to sob. "I know!" he said, "I know!" He gestured wildly. Harry grunted and shook his head. Caprice looked away.

"He fell twenty stories," the doctor continued. "But thank God for the coat. Thank God. Because it caught on an I beam—Mr. Power, he doesn't even have a concussion."

"Don't you see?" Jackson yelled. "Don't you see? He's the devil! He's never going to die—who survives a twenty-story jump? WHO?!" Jackson turned and dug his nose into Lara's shoulder.

"Your father?" the doctor innocently suggested.

"I'm sorry," Lara said to the internist. "He's . . . in shock. A lot has happened in the last twenty-four hours."

"I understand," the doctor said. "Would you like to go see him? He's been asking about his son."

Jackson looked up at him. "He has?"

"Oh yes," the doctor said. "Quite adamantly."

"I don't want to see him," Jackson said. "I'm not ready."

"Mr. Power." Caprice knelt beside him. "Mr. Artemus, he is your father, the one and only forever. You got to talk to him. You got to listen to him. Perhaps he's found something, on the way down? Something he's been missing?"

Jackson looked at Lara.

"Maybe he *has* changed," Lara said, touching his cheek. "You don't look death squarely in the eye and remain the same person. It's impossible."

Jackson looked back into Caprice's eyes. And then up at Harry, who was leaning against the wall, his head down. *Perhaps thinking of his own father. The one he'd never known.*

Bastard didn't know how lucky he was.

51

A ROYAL REUNION

A<small>ND HERE</small> comes the ungrateful fruit of my loins now," his father was saying to the young Filipina nurse.

So much for change, Jackson thought. He thought back to a record mogul he knew, out of London. Cheap, mean, vicious gossip, hated everyone, even the sycophants who clamored for the annual boat trip into St. Bart's. This Gargoyle contracted cancer a few years back. A tumor shaped like an octopus, just inside his rib cage.

He was sure to die. Within weeks.

He didn't.

Two weeks after the doctors declared him cancer-free, the Gargoyle gave away money, houses, cars, compliments, tips—there was a medical center named after him, a children's theater that bore his name.

Three weeks cancer-free, he woke up with the question that had haunted him forever: *"Who can I destroy today?"*

Jacks wouldn't even be getting the two-week honeymoon period.

"Good to see you, Dad," Jacks said, bending over to kiss his father's speckled forehead.

"I need you to make some phone calls for me," Artemus barked. "Are you capable of that?"

"What do you need, Dad?" Jacks asked. "Are you feeling okay?"

"Sure, I'm okay. Call the mayor. This guy—this council-fuck—he doesn't know who he's messing with. Who the fuck does he think he is, getting me arrested for bribery!"

"Dad, you just had a big scare, don't you think you want to take it easy? Maybe forget about work for a while—"

"I'm fine. May, here, she thinks I look fifty-nine!" Artemus nodded toward the nurse, who gave him a coy half smile while she checked his blood pressure. "Will you give us a moment, dear?" he asked, winking. He watched hungrily as she closed the door behind her.

"Dad."

"Just call the mayor," Artemus said, and then, "Fuck it, I'll do it myself."

"I'll call him," Jackson said.

The truth was, Jackson already had a call in to the mayor—to help make the arrangements for his father's funeral.

"Forget it. I'm going to clear this up the old-fashioned way," Artemus said.

"Buy your way out of it? That's how you got arrested in the first place."

"These pencil dicks don't appreciate how it's done. A prostitute and a Nikon. Problem solved."

"Will that be all, Dad?" Jacks asked, standing to leave. "Oh, and tell me, am I supposed to ban you from the work sites? I mean, now that we almost lost you."

"Nah," his father said. "Looks like I'm never going to die."

"No," Jacks said. "No, you're not."

"You know," his father said, "that hair of yours looks ridiculous."

"Dad."

"I've just always wanted to tell you that."

"Dad."

"When I was up there, hanging by my collar, staring into the abyss, hearing the yells, the honking, thinking that I had just missed taking one of those motherfucker towelhead cabbies with me and saving this city from terrorism—I was thinking, I never told you that you should get yourself a decent haircut."

"Let's do dinner next week," Jackson said, "when you're feeling up to it. We'll go somewhere nice—Elio's, something like that. We'll walk in together. Triumphant. Nothing keeps the Powers down."

Jacks was back to producing the circus of his life. And his father's death. And rebirth. *Make a call, make sure it shows up in Page Six.*

"Well, you've royally screwed up your marriage." His father looked up at him. "At least you hung on to 740. You took my advice, there."

Jacks looked at him. *Should he just go ahead and tell him? Or should he pretend that he didn't hear him? Go with sudden deafness.*

"Can I get you anything else, Dad?" he asked.

"The Powers never sell, number one rule of real estate!"

Oh, what the hell, Jacks thought, staring at his diminished father—*it's not like the old man can leap up from his hospital bed and start pelting me.*

"I signed 740 over to Cynthia."

His father lowered his eyes at him. "You did *what?*"

"We were—I thought we were getting back together. It was a total win-win," Jacks said.

"Get it back. Call Penn right now. Get it back."

"Can't," Jacks said, almost enjoying this. "It's done."

His father stared at him. Ice floes traversing his gaze.

"Get out."

"Dad, this is ridiculous—"

"Get out!"

"Dad, come on, I'm the biggest landlord in all of New York. I own thirty-five thousand units in Manhattan alone—"

"May!" His father was pounding the buzzer next to his bed. "May!"

"What difference does it make?" Jacks asked him.

"Get out! Get out! Get out!" Artemus yelled. May rushed in, shooting Jacks a look before she put her hands on his father.

"Goodbye, Dad," Jacks said. He turned, a million pounds lighter, serenaded by the beeping and whooshing of the machines attached to his father. He turned as though spinning on the dance floor with his wife at the Plaza, all eyes on them, the perfect couple. *Another mirage.*

He turned and was gone.

52

QUEEN TAKES KING

Cnn has you flying out of Kennedy," Jacks said. He hadn't flown out of Kennedy in years. Private jets flew out of Teterboro or White Plains.

Lara was already tapping away on her laptop, oblivious. The limo was filled with everything she'd need for her trip to the Middle East—tripod, camera, lights, videocam, bag filled with notebooks, tapes, recorders.

"Air Force C-17 usually flies out of there. We'll be in Jordan in . . ." Lara checked her watch. "It'll be five in the morning your time." She looked up, trying to appear cool, but Jacks could feel the excitement jumping off her skin.

Harry parked outside the departure gate. Waiting at the curb was a familiar figure—Sarah Kate, waving and holding a large round of cheese.

"She going with you?" Jacks asked, as Lara squealed, then jumped out of the car, big black sack over one shoulder, camera and equipment over the other one.

Sarah Kate hugged her, holding tight.

"What are you doing here?" Lara asked.

"You didn't think I'd send you off without upstate's finest?" Sarah Kate said, holding out the cheese.

Lara put down her satchel, and Jacks got out of the car.

"Had to see the dream happen in person," Sarah Kate said.

"I'm so glad you did," Lara said. "You remember Jacks, right?"

Sarah Kate looked him up and down and then offered her hand. "I think we've met." Jacks took her hand. Lara watched them, beaming.

"Are you sure about this?" Jacks asked Lara, then turned back to Sarah Kate. "Tell her, tell your friend not to do this."

"I think you know Chicken better than that," Sarah Kate said, then looked at Lara. "This is where I say my goodbyes." She handed Lara the cheese round.

"You shouldn't have," Lara said.

"I know, but I couldn't resist," Sarah Kate replied. "Now, I'm goin', so you don't catch me blubberin'." She gave Lara a hug, pulled her billowing coat around her, and walked away. Lara turned to Jacks.

"Honey, I'll call you as soon as I land. I'll e-mail you from the plane—you know, it's got broadband—"

"Just . . . please stay safe. Please. I can't . . . I don't want to do anything anymore without you."

Lara looked at him. She put down the bag, then the camera equipment. She took his face in her hands. "I'm with you, Jacks. We're together in this. For better or worse."

"Don't say richer or poorer," he said. "Bad luck."

"While I'm gone, organize the wedding," Lara said. "You're better at that kind of thing than I am."

"Really?"

"Sure—the guest lists, the florists, all that crap."

"A big wedding?" Jacks asked, hope against hope.

"Whatever your heart desires," Lara said, smiling.

"You make me so happy," Jacks said. "I'll call the mayor. I'll get them to loosen up St. Patrick's—"

"I'll be back in a week," Lara said. "You'd better carbo-load and get plenty of rest, because when I come back, you are in trouble."

"I love you," he said.

"I love you, too," she said. "I really do."

Jacks kissed Lara's cheeks, her lips, the top of her head. And then watched as she gathered her things and walked away, into her new life.

Jacks could feel good; he was a part of that dream, too. He turned toward the limo. Harry was staring at him.

Oh, that dumb fucking hat.

"What?" Jacks said.

"You drop off your woman at airport. You finally done something right in your sorry life," Harry replied.

Jacks turned back and watched Lara disappear into the crowd.

"I think you're right," Jacks said.

"Don't get carried away," Harry said. "You have lot to learn." He opened the door and waved him in.

Jacks phoned Caprice the second his butt hit the seat. "What do I have this morning?" He listened as she went over the litany of meetings.

"Let's see what Vivi's doing," Jacks said. "I'd like to have breakfast with my daughter."

Harry smiled. "That's two things you do right today!" he said. "What you do wit' Jackson Power?"

"Shut up, Harry," Jacks said.

And then Harry laughed, and sped away.

ADRIAN didn't realize he'd fallen asleep outside the service entrance until someone wearing a doorman's hat and epaulets kicked him in the shoulder.

"Hey!" the doorman said. "Wake up, you can't sleep here— whaddaya think this is, the Chelsea?"

Adrian opened his eyes. He hadn't gotten a lot of sleep in the last couple of days—truth is, he hadn't had a full night's sleep since he'd taken that lousy job.

"I work here," he croaked.

"You work here." The doorman looked at him. "Right. Come on, get up, get the fuck outta here before I call the cops."

Adrian found his feet, roped his duffel around his shoulder.

"Hey, kid," a voice said.

Adrian looked up.

"You know this guy, Lionel?" the doorman asked.

Lionel assessed the situation. Adrian could see the wheels turn behind that big, mopey façade.

"Yeah. He works here."

"Well—tell him this ain't no fleabag motel. He ain't supposed to be sleeping here. He does it again, I'm reporting him."

"Thanks for your understanding," Adrian said.

The doorman looked at him, disgusted, and walked away.

Adrian eyed Lionel, squinting in the light. "I've done some bad things, Lionel," Adrian said. "I'm ready to come back. I missed the hell out of this place. I missed the hell out of you."

"It ain't what it was, kid," Lionel said, and beckoned for him to come in from the cold.

"That makes no sense, Lionel."

"Don't you think I know that, kid?" Lionel asked. "Look," he said, putting his big hand on Adrian's shoulder, "you're gonna be a real bartender, you have to have your line ready. The one line that sums everything up. Find your line, you'll have work for the rest of your life."

"What's my line?" Adrian asked.

"I can't find it for you, kid." He walked Adrian inside. "You have to find it yourself."

Adrian thought about this. He thought about it for the next ten hours—all of them on his feet, pouring drinks, the usual and not-so-usual, for the old, the young, the rich, the desperate, the tired, the energetic, the happy and unhappy.

And finally, it came to him.

"The slower you go, the faster you get there." *That's fuckin' beautiful,* he thought, as he watched a head nod in response. *That works. That'll work for the rest of my life.*

VIVI burrowed inside her coat as she studied the board, oblivious to the sea of strollers, pot dealers, and NYU students rushing past the chess tables.

Her opponent, a regular, gave her an appraising look, then grinned as he deftly captured her knight with his bishop. He peered at her through his steel-rimmed sunglasses as he slapped the button on top of the timing clock. "Your move."

He'd fallen for it. He'd actually fallen for it. Vivi made her move, no hesitation. "Queen takes king," she said.

The grin melted off the opponent's face. "Good game," he said thinly, folding his arms across his chest.

"Congratulations." A woman's voice came from behind Vivi. She turned. Wavy black cap of hair. Pale skin. Blue, blue eyes.

Vivi felt the color rush to her cheeks. "I've never beaten him before. Never."

"Maybe I'm your good luck charm," the woman said, her smile large and bright.

"Oh, you think so?" Vivi teased.

"In which case, you can at least buy me a green tea before my next class."

"Green tea," Vivi said, "the drink of choice for the downtown lesbian."

"It's too early for a Lone Star." The woman smiled.

Vivi smiled back and rose from her seat. The woman was just as tall as she. "Are you a student?" Vivi asked.

"Professor. Greek mythology. My name's Zoe," she said. "Have you heard of Caïssa?" Zoe gestured toward the chessboard.

"The goddess of chess," Vivi said. "She's hot."

"Read the Jones poem," Zoe said. "She's even hotter than you think. You'll never play chess the same way."

"You'll have to read it to me," Vivi said, smiling. Together, they turned to walk down Sullivan.

53

SOME TIME LATER

W HAT DO you mean, you can't make the press conference, of course you can make the conference." Jacks barked into the phone, then paused. "Harry, take a right here, a right, a right . . ."

Harry ignored him.

"Goddamn it, I've gotta fire my driver. Russian diphead. I swear to God . . ."

Harry turned up the next street. "Is faster, idiot."

Jacks waved him off. "So listen, listen, I've got to get the mayor on the line, he'll deal with this—I want the groundbreaking to be . . . world class . . . something this town has never seen before. I want it to be like a movie premiere. I want every movie star in town. You got that? Good."

Jacks hung up, grabbed the newspapers. The *Journal*, check, *Times*, fucking rag, check, the *Post*. He quickly flipped to Page Six; *maybe there was something new on him? On his upcoming nuptials? Who'd been invited, who was rejected*—Jacks loved this stuff. *Hold on. What the hell?*

"Stop!" Jacks yelled at Harry.

"I am stopped," Harry yelled back.

"Did you know about this?" Jacks yelled, waving the paper in Harry's face.

"What? What I know? I am only Russian diphead."

"You know I didn't mean that. I love you, you're my best friend. You're my best man, for God's sake. Look—did you see this? I know you read this before I do—did you see this?!"

Harry looked over his shoulder at the offending item. And shrugged. *Maybe he did, maybe he didn't.*

Jacks was already dialing. "Penn! I don't care if you're dropping off your kid—you have a kid?—did you see the *Post*—you don't read the *Post*—well fuck you, you do now—Cynthia—Cynthia is selling 740—she's selling it!" Beat. "I know she's allowed to sell it—I mean . . . is she allowed to sell it?" Beat. "Well, I want it. I don't care what you have to do—I want it, I don't want to pay full asking— Jesus, she's selling the furniture, too—and artwork! Holy Christ! What, is she out of her mind? Has she finally lost her mind?! Penn, get me 740 back!"

Jacks threw the phone. Then looked out the window.

"I can't believe she's selling," he said. "I can't believe she has the nerve . . ." His eye went up, catching the spire at the top of St. Patrick's Cathedral, piercing the morning sky.

"Oh, I got to give you this," Harry said, handing him a small box.

Jacks took it. "What is it?" he asked, sourly.

"How do I know? I open your gifts?" Harry said. "It's from ex-wife. Miss Cynthia. She asked I should give to you, other morning."

Jacks looked at the box, then shook it by his ear. "It's not ticking," he said.

He opened it, and took out a small item and held it. First, Jackson Power looked baffled.

Then, he smiled.

"Good for her," he said, looking back up at the spire.

Harry honked a few times, and the limo was moving again. "Why you think she give you old chess piece, boss?" Harry asked.

"Harry, you didn't—" Jacks said.

"The queen," Harry continued. "What is significance?"

"Harry!"

THE ORANGE sun was climbing out from behind jagged, snowcapped mountains.

"So, what do you think?" Vivienne asked. "Is it everything you've ever dreamed of?"

Kathmandu, Nepal.

Gazing at terrain treacherous enough to fend off invaders for five hundred years were two privileged women and one ragged yak.

"Ah, Vivi. I never really dreamed of Nepal," Cynthia said, holding on to the yak's mangy hair. Vivienne was seated behind her, arms around Cynthia's waist, cheek against her back, eyes on those perilous mountains.

Six more days, Cynthia thought, *six more days of interesting culture, amazing views, mountain air . . . and Max the Yak. She'd never make it.*

"I know what you're thinking," Vivienne said. "I know you, Mom."

"I wasn't thinking about him," Cynthia lied.

"You can't just jump into another serious relationship," Vivienne said.

"I know, I know," Cynthia said.

"Fred Plotzicki was your archenemy just a few months ago, if I may be so bold to remind you," Vivienne said.

"I know," Cynthia responded dreamily.

"You'll never learn," Vivienne said.

The yak stopped in its tracks. Cynthia looked out at the mountains. And wondered which she would climb next. And had no doubt she could.

"I know," Cynthia replied.

ACKNOWLEDGMENTS

I'LL TRY not to turn this into a bad Oscar speech, but there are a lot of people I wish to thank: my invaluable team, Jennifer Rudolph Walsh, David Rosenthal, Marysue Rucci, Stephanie Davis, Sylvie Rabineau, Jason Sloane, Elizabeth Rapoport, and Sophie Epstein. I am grateful to Mark Kriegel for his love and sage advice, and to Brian Grazer, for his friendship and our beautiful boys.

A heartfelt thank-you to my family: my parents, Phillipa Costa Brown and Frank Levangie; my sisters, Suzanne Levangie Kurtz, Mimi Levangie, and Julie Levangie Purcell; my brothers-in-law, Ron Kurtz and Mark Purcell; my nephews, Frankie Levangie, Jonathan Sanchez, and John Henry Kurtz; my niece, Angelina Garcia; and my extended family—Brad Golden, Gladys Perdomo, and Ana and Wilson Ramirez. I have the deepest appreciation for Dr. David Hoffman and all the nurses at Tower Oncology. Thank you to Jessie, Sierra, Seza, and Karen at the George Michael Salon. I am indebted to Wade Gasque and Aleks Horvat at the Office in Santa Monica and the staff at the Writers Room in Manhattan.

Finally, I thank Mimi James, Julie Jaffe, Suzanne Todd, Jennifer Todd, Helen Fielding, Josh Gilbert, Robin Ruzan, Michael Smith, James Costos, Stacy Title, Laura Day, and The Tomb, for their support, encouragement and inspiration.

And Goldie, I miss you.

ABOUT THE AUTHOR

GIGI LEVANGIE GRAZER is the author of three prior novels: *Rescue Me* (2000), *Maneater* (2003), and *The Starter Wife* (2006). *The Starter Wife* was adapted for an Emmy Award–winning USA Network miniseries starring Debra Messing, and later for a television series; *Maneater* was adapted for a *Lifetime* miniseries starring Sarah Chalke in May 2009. In addition, Gigi wrote the screenplay for *Stepmom*, starring Julia Roberts and Susan Sarandon. Gigi's articles have appeared in *Vogue, Harper's Bazaar,* and *Glamour.* She lives in L.A. with her two children and three miniature dachshunds.